D1510958

BASE HIT

BASE HIT
A Novel

Alan Posner

VANTAGE PRESS
New York

This is a work of fiction. Any similarity between
the characters appearing herein and any real persons,
living or dead, is purely coincidental.

To Dawn, my loving partner in life, and to my father, whose greatness lies in his unsurpassed goodness

Acknowledgments

I consulted a number of publications on the scientific aspects of the book, including: 1) *Baseball bat collisions and the resulting trajectories of spinning balls* (Watts & Baroni); 2) *Batting the Ball* (Kirkpatrick); 3) Aerodynamic drag crisis and its possible effect on the flight of baseballs (Frolich); 4) *Sportscience*; 5) *The Physics of Baseball*; 6) *Discover Graphology* (Gullan-Whur).

In addition, my partner, Barbara Grossman, read my manuscript and offered valuable encouragement.

BASE HIT

1

This would be the moment, he thought. As he stepped into the batter's box in the first inning of the first game of the new season with two outs and nobody on, this moment would be, not like spring's first breath but the climactic moment, as autumn's final glory. He wouldn't wait for a sultry midsummer night, nor even the final inning of the season's opener. *No, this was the moment.*

As he ground his spikes into the left-hander's batters' box, its dirt still virgin-groundskept—his two right-handed-hitting teammates having preceded him—the echo of the public-address announcer's booming voice still resonated: "Now batting for the Yankees, number fourteen, the left fielder, Chris Donovan." Veteran fans always complained that April 1 was too early to be playing baseball in the Midwest, but this day had blossomed bright and sunny like the daffodils emerging from winter's hidebound earth. Now, as the temperature rose to seventy degrees and the center field flag hung limp, Chicago's bleacher fans were in shirtsleeves. Forty-four thousand filled the stadium, and now they rose as one to give Donovan a raucous standing reception of boos. Howling boos. From the gut. For they remembered.

Last fall, in the play-offs, Chicago was leading the Yankees 3 games to 1. In the eighth inning of game 5, Chicago was up 2–1, playing at home, and their can't-miss rookie pitcher, Don McGinniss, was cruising. The gangly 24-year-old fireballer sometimes controlled his fastball and sometimes it controlled him. On bad days, it would send him to the showers, pushing him beyond self-doubt into a sense of worthlessness, unable to tame either his talent or his emotions. Yet at other times that fastball would purr and hum for him as though he were guiding it all the way to the plate. But in the eighth inning of game 5, the curse returned. With two outs and no one on, with two strikes on Donovan, a McGinniss fastball unaccountably sailed straight at Donovan's right ear. The pitch had been clocked, on the slow radar gun, at 98 mph.

That untamed pitch had crashed into Donovan's hard plastic earflap—the flap that saved his life, doctors would later say—and shattered the protective helmet so forcefully that several box seat customers sitting nearly 100 feet away caught tiny royal blue shards in their clothing. One struck a 10-year-old boy, one of those quintessential young fans wearing a baseball glove who thinks every popup is going to be a home run because he hasn't yet learned to watch the fielder's reaction to the batted ball, and drew blood from his forearm. "Awesome!" he said and repeated, gaping first at his arm and then back toward home plate, where the larger pieces of the helmet lay scattered as after a battle, and then checking his arm again, as if his eyes had deceived him the first time.

Donovan was out for only two or three minutes, but the dizziness he suffered as a result of what the doctors called a moderate concussion kept him out of the remainder of postseason play, let alone the pennant play-off. And what a turn that play-off had taken. Chicago fans didn't know McGinniss was too shaken by beaning Donovan to throw another strike or whether the cursed fastball was simply reasserting its independence, but it didn't really matter. After Donovan's replacement went to first base and the grounds crew had retrieved what was left of the helmet, McGinniss had promptly walked the bases loaded without coming close to throwing a strike.

Having grown up on a ranch in Nevada, McGinniss's crusty old manager, Vern Simmons, well knew the difference between a mustang and a saddled equine. He pulled McGinniss, brought in his set-up man, and promptly watched the Yankees score six runs before a mop-up reliever stemmed the tide. From there, the rejuvenated Yankees, with the series now in their backyard for the duration, continued to pound Chicago pitching, winning easily the last two games to get into the World Series. And that was the end of the season for Chicago's long-suffering fans.

Or so it seemed. After the play-offs, after the Series—which the Yankees won, 4 games to 2, no thanks to Donovan, who awoke each morning railing at the vertigo that tormented him like demons—after even the year's MVPs were chosen, after all that, when the ferocity of autumn's competition had been cooled by November's rains, Donovan said the words that

Chicago's partisans would never forget.

By this time, the Yankee's dizzy spells had improved considerably. The doctors offered a hopeful prognosis for the next season. As Donovan, who had flown back to the Windy City from his home in upstate New York for medical follow-up, left Chicago's top neurology clinic one morning, a local TV news crew, there to do a story on a sick child's "miracle" recovery, recognized him and thrust a microphone in his face, demanding, "How do you feel about having missed the Series on account of McGinniss beaning you?"

"TV whores," muttered Donovan under his breath. He wouldn't dignify their work by even thinking of them as reporters. Having taken a single journalism course at NYU while majoring in engineering, Donovan had learned enough to know that *broadcast journalism* was an oxymoron. To him, these people who always seemed to have a microphone appended to their hands and Cam-corders attached to their skulls were like puppets: cute, brainless, and manipulated by a higher power for profit. At worst, they were shameful self-promoting rumormongers. At best, you might get out of them the shocking news that much of the nation was frigid in January.

He would not be kind to the intrusion. Spitting out the words with all the contempt he had for the holder of the recording device that was only inches from his chin, combined with all his lingering frustration at missing the Series, Donovan—and soon the country—heard himself saying, "McGinniss will get his. I'll get even with him if it's the last goddamned thing I ever do."

So on this April day, the Chicago fans, who had reacted in a collective horrified gasp when the pride of the Yankees was beaned in their ballpark some six months earlier and who had politely applauded with relief when he regained consciousness and was helped off the field, finally had their chance to answer Donovan's vow of vengeance. They howled the boos of betrayal, where no good deed goes unpunished. And then they booed some more. All of them, and they sustained it for more than a minute, as long as Donovan took to set himself in the batters' box.

First, he erased the rear chalk line. He would need every inch of reaction time against McGinniss. Then, Donovan dug in with each spike, methodically moving away the dirt, some to the left, some to the right. Once his feet were planted, he gripped the bat and waved it slowly and straight ahead several times so that its barrel end targeted the hurler who was glaring back. The whole routine played itself out like two generals surveying the battle-field-to-be at dawn's first light.

Of course, McGinniss didn't idle away this interlude. He pawed at the rubber with his spikes or more precisely, the dirt just in front of it. He continued staring in at Donovan until they met each other's gaze, then spit down at the green, green grass in front of the mound. It wasn't a natural green, of course, not at this time of year. Sure, the baseball mavens of the Windy City had insisted on real grass for their new ballpark. But early spring is fickle in the Midwest, so one couldn't count on the frost completing its escape from the ground, let alone those tender blades regaining their chlorophylled glory. No, this grass was summer's green thanks to USDA Certified Green dye #2.

McGinniss had just begun to wonder how many gallons of the stuff it took to cover the field when he saw the home plate umpire motion him—a hot dog wrapper had escaped the stands, landed on spring's most sacred surface, and ambled its way behind the mound, where it halted, as if to take a ringside seat at the bud-ding confrontation. McGinniss wheeled around in response to the gesture from the man in blue, spotted the intruder, and scooped it up with his pitching hand just as a ground crew mem-ber came out to get it. The pros don't do maintenance. McGinniss handed him the balled-up waxed paper, and as their eyes met, the crew member mouthed *Go get, 'im.*

McGinniss turned back to the mound—to the task at hand—and began staring in at his catcher, Matt Mullens, for the sign. He had to respect Donovan's hitting talents. Donovan, after all, was the game's premier player, on his way to the Hall. At 34, he led the league the previous year with a .347 average, with 36 homers to go with it. Adding his walks and runners advanced to his totals, Donovan had failed fewer than six times for every ten at-bats, statistical proof positive of his elite status. Now, Matt was signaling for a high hard one—up and in. Donovan could take all the time he wanted to plant himself. McGinniss would uproot him if, in his interminable struggle with his stubborn fastball, he had anything to say about it.

4

Now, a fan in the third row, a twenty-something who had taken the afternoon off from his spot on the commodities floor—it was a slow day for pork bellies, he rationalized—to attend his twelfth consecutive opening day, cupped his hands and prepared to holler. He was, of course, more cynical now than the first time his father had taken him to a ballgame. In that one, played in the old ballpark, a foul ball had been hit into the stands three sections away from him. But that was on a Saturday in mid-April, a week after the opener, on a day when the wind off the lake whipped at the stadium flags. And those three sections were completely empty. On that day, this future pit trader would race to the spot where the ball landed, but an usher arrived just before he did and retrieved it like picking up a stray cat by Animal Control. When he had seen this, Ray—he liked his single-syllable name; it was as efficient as any to use in the pit, where split seconds counted—meekly stretched out his small hand toward the usher and, with the voice of the child whose fright is outweighed only by his naïveté, asked, "Can I have it?" The craggy-faced usher replied by raising his hand as if to strike the youngster. And when the boy flinched, his tormentor just laughed and walked away, spheroid treasure in hand.

Wiser, Ray now understood the mimed language of the game. As he watched the pitcher and hitter in their silent, separate dances of preparation, Ray counted the number of trades he could have made in the pit during this interlude and shouted, "C'mon, play the game, you millionaires!" Several nearby fans who, as the privileged box seat patrons, were worthy of the label themselves chuckled their agreement with the rejoinder. The fans' sentiment, after all, wasn't oft heard in the modern version of the game.

Most hitters are never quite the same after a beaning. It's said that the better a batter, the more he loses after a 90 mph fastball pounds the soft scalp, crashing headlong into the skull, forcing the brain back and forth like jelly while the hitter is struck senseless. Donovan had been wearing a helmet with an earflap only because his ear had been grazed once in the minors by a wild speedballer. Once was enough to convince him to take cover under that protective shell each time he stepped to the plate.

5

Now, Donovan would be tested by his first live-game pitch six months after this same flamethrower had knocked him cold. Oh sure, he had reacquainted his reflexes with the round white bullets in the spring grapefruit league, but that was like riding a bicycle with training wheels. In the relaxed sunshine of spring training, even the veterans were giving him the inside half of the plate, partly out of respect but mostly because the pitchers didn't want to give him the advantage of getting used to the inside pitch all over again before the bell rang on a new season.

Donovan knew the history of beaned ballplayers. He'd heard about their fears, their nightmares of blinding white cowhide—horsehide had been phased out in the seventies—targeted right between their eyes, of jumping right out of their sleep just before impact, of the warmth of the dreamy ballpark blown away by the shock of cold sweat. And then, back on the field, of bailing out on a curve before it breaks, of stepping into the bucket instead of into the pitch. Unlike those guys, Donovan would not play defense. No, he had spent his winter thinking offense, working offense, living offense. He was dug in and he was ready. Oh, was he ready. This was the moment.

McGinniss had a windup like no other pitcher in the game. First, he would rock to and fro not once, but twice. Then, he would lean back, way back on his planted right foot, so far that you thought surely he would fall right over backward. But then suddenly he would thrust his left foot into the air higher and higher until it was above the bill of his cap. Next, as he brought his pitching arm forward, his left foot would come crashing to the ground and he would have to catch himself in order to stop his momentum from tossing him right onto the grass. The windup never varied. That was the funny thing about his fastball—his mechanics were so consistent, so precise, it must have had a mind of its own. He would deliver it the same way every time—and for that matter his change-up as well. But the same methodical windup that made his change-up so effective could not retain dominion over his heater. Like the one-armed bandits in Simmons's native state, its players could deliver the same coinage in the same fashion every time, but the result was always unpredictable.

Now, in that familiar windup, McGinniss delivered his first

pitch. On this day, he was master of his gift. The ball sped up and in—not too far inside, just enough to drive Donovan off the plate, more than enough to let him know that, beaning victim or not, the inside half of the strike zone belonged to McGinniss. Donovan, expecting as much, easily backed off. Ninety-eight mph of rock-hard sphere coming right at you? *No problem*, Donovan thought. "Ball one," said Howard Rome, the umpire.

To Donovan, the pitch produced no déjà vu or any of the fear his own fans back on the East Coast felt for him. Still, he was surprised at how serene he felt at this instant. He exhaled along with his followers watching at home, a breath of relief borne of the knowledge that the anticipation of this moment was over. In a game with no clock, Donovan was reveling in the full measure of each sweep of the second hand.

After the Yankee took a moment to reset himself in the box, Mullens signaled another fastball, this time lower and toward the outside. Donovan, betting on this as well, was ready. He swung and, remarkably, was in front of this pitch, which was clocked at 95 mph. The ball was lashed foul past first. One and one, Donovan knew. Just one more fastball he figured should do it. You could count on McGinniss to throw at least 80 percent heat. Most of his change-ups—his only other pitch—were delivered once he got two strikes on the batter. Donovan wanted no part of the change. He needed to hit the hummer.

A foul ball, even more than the inside opening delivery, called for another interlude of repreparation between hitter and pitcher amid rising tension in their audience. Donovan, following the flight of the line foul, now stepping out, now looking at the white line he had missed, tugging at his shirt, resetting his hands, looking out at the mound. The pitcher, obtaining a new ball from the umpire, rubbing it up and rejecting it like a gambler who discovers the dice are loaded, now getting a new ball, rubbing it up, stepping back behind the mound to finger the resin bag. As though McGinniss needed a better grip. Hell, he practically made the stitching bulge when he grasped that ball. Now back to the mound, looking in for the sign, and almost before you knew it, the millionaires were ready to play ball again.

Donovan, counting on one more fastball before he would have

to look at the change-up, calculated—he was no guess hitter—
that it would be a strike, toward the inside part of the plate, just
above knee-high. If McGinniss continued to control the heat. He
did and it was. Donovan knew immediately. This was indeed the
moment after all. Donovan swung viciously. He laced a line shot,
straight up the middle, a rocket head-high.

To its followers, the American pastime is the best of all games
not only because it is so intricate in its strategy, so rich in its statistics, so steeped in its traditions, but also because so much
about the game is so precisely in balance. The shortstop knowing
just how deep he can play so that when he dives into the hole to
snag a hard two-hopper he can still nip the runner by a half-step.
The curveball that somehow knows it must wait 59 feet along its
journey to the plate before breaking in order to accomplish its
mission of fooling the opponent who battles to reverse thunder-
ously its course. In this game within the game, the hitter's vulnerability to the pitched ball is also in equipoise with his
opponent. For there is a moment in every pitcher's delivery when
he is defenseless to the returned serve that is lined his way. As
he storms down from the rubber in his follow-through, his glove
momentarily is a useless appendage: his reaction time is simply
not up to the task even of merely deflecting a shot whose speed
may exceed 150 mph, a projectile returned through the middle in
the blink of an eye. With each pitch he throws, the hurler gam-
bles—like the apprehensive airline passenger who takes comfort
in the industry's minuscule death statistics—that the batter
won't hit the ball directly at the one small spot in the universe
where the deepest fears of both reside.

Before Donovan could get out of the batter's box, his wicked
shot found its mark. As McGinniss completes his follow-through,
his head instinctively turns to the right, about forty-five degrees.
Every time. Every student of the game knew that. Less than one-
quarter of a second after striking his bat, this ball, now this
deadly weapon, slammed into McGinniss's right temple just in
front of and above his right ear. In the box seats, some would
later swear they could hear the bone shatter. McGinniss fell
instantly, his legs kicking violently in spasm as his doomed brain
sent out its final distress signals. The glove hand, which had only
begun its journey to meet the missile, wavered at first and then

joined its other limbs in a helpless final protest Several bone fragments penetrated the scalp, whose rich capillaries now splayed forth bright red blood all over the right side of his twitching face until rivulets began running down his neck, staining crimson the new season's uniform. The ball, by now harmlessly motionless in the green, green grass between home and the mound, betrayed no evidence of its deed. Donovan, fulfilling the hitter's first rule of fundamental baseball when he makes contact, raced to first without looking to see if a fielder gloved it. He knew he didn't need to.

The scene at the mound sent out a shock wave that momentarily paralyzed the game's participants, followed by a collective gasp of recognition. High above the stadium, the lone cry of a wayward seagull dispelled the sudden hush and sprang to life a burst of activity. McGinniss's teammates rushed in, then both benches, with the umpires, not even thinking to call time, right behind. The Chicago trainer, who later would have no memory of doing so, seized the stretcher like a prayerbook and raced out to carry McGinniss off, shouting at everyone and no one to make room. Several players assisted, but the last life had drained out of McGinniss before he could be placed in an ambulance.

2

In a bar near the old ballpark, the one they tore down a few years ago, and across from the prosecutor's office, the eyes of an assistant DA, Robert Kasoff, caught the TV screen. He froze, transfixed at the images being transmitted. Kasoff, 37, had not missed attending an Opening Day in over twenty years. He was not one of those fans who would shamefacedly slink out of the office and off to the ballpark. No, each spring he would proudly tell anyone at work who would listen: "I only observe two holidays. Thanksgiving and Opening Day." Then, he would smartly remove two tickets from his wallet and wave 'em at whoever was within earshot. "Who wants to go? Who wants to go?" he'd ask, but it sounded more like a taunt, so no one ever took him up on it, figuring he was just teasing, as he did so often.

But last year, he had decided to boycott the game he had so loved as a boy. It wasn't just that the owners had ruined any semblance of a pennant race by going to the wild card play-off format. And it wasn't just that the millionaire players employed by the billionaire owners had made such a fuss over all the money that they had managed to do what Hitler and the Great Depression couldn't—cancel the World Series. To Kasoff, for this alone everyone connected with the professional game deserved permanent banishment, preferably to an Arctic island where playing the game was impossible. But that would mean that Hell really would have to freeze over. And it wasn't only that the players always seemed to be making new demands that amounted to having their cake and eating it too. The security of the long-term contract was always soon followed by the demand to renegotiate the dollars. Or that the players were always moving to other teams—it wasn't merely the grass that was greener—where new owners were all too willing to accommodate them, leaving the loyal fans to root only for the uniforms. And it wasn't just the artificial turf, which forced even the most graceful gazelle prowling the outfield to pull up short so the base hit wouldn't bounce over his head, instead of trying the daring dive to snare it. Nor was it merely the domed stadia with their sterile atmospheres and fly balls lost in the ceiling—in the ceiling! No. It was all of these things. Enough already.

As a kid, Kasoff used to wake up early on Opening Day like it was Christmas morning, all juiced up and not even hungry for breakfast, and he couldn't wait, couldn't wait for game time, all the while thinking up imaginary lineups and the trades he'd make to put his team over the top if he were GM. He usually ended up in the distant seats of the old ballpark, the ones where two or three support poles obstructed parts of the field, even—horrors—home plate from view. But this was a minor inconvenience in the days when the game was grand, and besides, he could certainly dream, as the upwardly mobile always did, of one day being well connected enough to obtain a coveted field box.

Even into adulthood and, yes, beyond that solemn ceremony where he took his oath to become a member of the bar, he'd awaken that morning each April with the excitement of the kid within, lingering at breakfast over the sports page with its special baseball season premiere section. Each year a week or two before the big day he'd had the same recurring nightmare. He was at the ballpark in a seat so obstructed and far away that he could see only a portion of the outfield. Now, with the new stadium engineered to eliminate all obstructed-view seats, the dream had disappeared. But so had its reason for recurring: the ghost of the game that remained no longer had the soul to invade his sleep. Now, the daily beat of a watered-down gonfalon race was but a distant drum.

This morning, Kasoff had risen at his usual hour, knowing he would be absent when the umpire hollered, "Play ball!" just a few blocks from his office. As he rode the L train to work, he found he was too restless to concentrate on the *Tribune*'s front page coverage of the latest Middle Eastern crisis. Instead, he found himself humming that old baseball anthem, while his mind updated the lyrics:

Take me out to the skybox
in the tax-deductible dome

The train stopped to discharge passengers, and the next couplet came out:

Buy me a shortstop for twenty mil,
I don't care if he's over the hill.

Another stop. This time, a heavyset older man, obviously running late, dropped his briefcase on the way out; as he tried to retrieve it before the train doors closed, it spilled open, scattering the contents—some papers, a glasses case, and two files. And more spilled out of Kasoff:

Oh, it's pay me, play me, or trade me,
That's every player's refrain . . .

As the train approached downtown, Kasoff was heading for home with the final verse that was now bringing a broad smile to his face in the midst of these expressionless commuters:

It's a lockout, a strike, to Hell with the fans, they've betrayed the game!

As he entered his office, he couldn't stop grinning. Monday or not, this was going to be a good day. As Kasoff walked down the hall toward the corner office where Al Green, assistant to the chief deputy DA, worked, he stopped to watch his secretary, Sharon Torres, as she admired the new season's swimsuit collection from one of the innumerable catalogs she always seemed to be flipping through. Sharon was thirty-five and a wonderful person. Her tired eyes betrayed her lifetime of men—the verbally abusive father, her first serious boyfriend, the one who taught her how to bring the swelling down from a shiner, never mind that he had inflicted it; her first husband, the one lucky enough to marry her, who while living the best possible reality did drugs to escape it; her second husband. . . . She should have known, she would later admit, that trouble was brewing when he suggested they set up a joint bank account before the engagement. His financial schemes had driven them to bankruptcy. It was the old story: behind every unsuccessful woman, there's a man.

12

As Sharon eyed the bathing suits, she shared the catalog with Carol Randall, a coworker and 38-year-old single mother of a precocious teenager. Carol had put on a number of pounds over the winter in her never-ending battle with a bathroom scale that never said the same thing twice. Kasoff couldn't resist. As Carol wistfully checked out a bright two-piece, calculating, you could tell, the weeks available 'til summer multiplied by the number of pounds she would have to lose per week, Kasoff hit her with another of his finely honed barbs: "Why bother, Carol? It used to be that when you would sunbathe on the beach you'd attract guys. These days, only Greenpeace shows up!" Sharon broke out laughing—she was an easy audience for his jokes and knew that Kasoff really enjoyed that. Carol, who was frequently Kasoff's target, was half-amused but frustrated because, as always, she had no quick clever comeback.

Carol, who had little use for men—and would use Sharon as her Exhibit A—was baffled by her cohort's unflappable reaction to what she viewed as the typical male inclination to belittle anything not measured on a scoreboard and asked her why she encouraged him. But Carol herself was resigned to it. After all, she long ago had checked the employee manual. Race. Age. Sex. Handicap. National origin. Religion. Whistleblowing. All were prohibited categories for harassment. It was silent on weight.

Green wasn't going to the game, either, so he and Kasoff had gone to Ed's Bar & Grill for lunch and to catch the new season's first inning on the tube. Kasoff was willing to concede that much to what had been the grand old game. On the way, Green couldn't resist renewing the old game of their own with baseball names. "All right, the all-time Presidents team," he had announced to Kasoff as the two set off. The rules always varied slightly. For this one, "no repeats, unless there are two Presidents of the same name, like Harrison."

"OK," Kasoff responded. Thanks to his childhood collection of baseball cards and his fascination with baseball records, no one knew as many ballplayers, both the great and obscure, as Kasoff. "Here goes. I put Otis Nixon in centerfield, Walter Johnson on the mound, and Gary Carter behind the plate."

"Great strength up the middle for starters," Green marveled.

"John Kennedy at short—"

"Ooh, that's a good one. First and last name both."

"At second, Tony Taylor."

"Taylor?"

"Sure. Zachary Taylor."

"Oh, right."

"Hack Wilson in left. Shoeless Joe or Reggie in right. First and third base are tough. Hmm. Chuck Harrison at first."

"Who the hell is he?"

"Played for the Astros in the late sixties. And Bobby Adams at third."

"Another no-name."

"No way. He played more than a dozen years in the forties and fifties."

"OK. I'll give it to you."

Kasoff was always able to field a full team, and he had managed it during the short walk to lunch.

Now, as Green was politicking in some remote corner of the bar, Kasoff saw the pitcher go down and dropped his jaw when he saw the close-up of the dying man. But the next camera angle brought Kasoff to his feet in utter disbelief; he slowly stepped toward the screen as though getting closer to the image could somehow make his brain comprehend what his eyes were telling him.

In the trade, it's called a reaction shot. The cameraman uses it when he wants to show a player's, a coach's, or a fan's response to a play on the field. It's a shot that requires the cameraman to be the detached professional he's hired to be. It's hard, after all, to ignore the excitement of the play on the field in order to search out that one face lit up in glory or ashen in defeat that will round out the story. Here the reaction shot was focused on the first base area. As the umpire and the Chicago first baseman, looking stricken, began to run toward the mound, the camera's eye closed in on Donovan. He had crossed the bag, looked back toward the pitcher, and thrown his hands heavenward while gazing nearly straight up into the bright sunshine. And a broad grin betrayed his emotions. It was the triumphant smile that a world-class pro allows himself only when he's reached the pinnacle.

Kasoff's own reaction would have been worth recording. He

staggered on his feet, put his right hand to his forehead as if to block the realization that this evil deed was entering his brain, and immediately flashed back to Donovan's November words of vengeance: Donovan was nothing but a perp, and Kasoff had just witnessed murder in the first degree. It was the basest of all hits. And for Kasoff, a crimson pennant.

In that instant of realization, Kasoff pushed through the crowd to retrieve Green, tugging him by the shirt as Kasoff wheedled him away from a local alderman. Green, unaware that the low buzz of the crowd at the bar watching the tube had abruptly changed to hushed murmuring, exclaimed only "Wha-wha!" It wasn't every day that the unflappable Kasoff was in such a state of high excitement, so Green allowed himself to be pulled along like a raft upstream against the crowd.

Green knew, too, that Kasoff's brain often seemed a step ahead of everyone else. Thanks to his quick thinking, Kasoff had made the greatest play in the history of the sport of football before age twelve, even if it was only a schoolyard game of touch. The opposing team was aligned in punt formation. Kasoff was planning to try to block it and was sure he could anticipate the precise timing of the hike. He would get a running start and would burst through the line at the instant of the snap, barely avoiding the off-side call. And he was quick. He timed his bolt perfectly. The hike was a bit high and wobbly. And Kasoff raced through. And intercepted the hike! He was gone for a touchdown before the punter knew what blew by him. No one at any level of the game had ever attempted the feat, much less succeeded. Yes, Kasoff had always been quick off the mark. And now, he was resolving to try what had never been attempted before in yet another sport.

"You gotta see this! You gotta see this!" was all Kasoff could sputter, knowing that there would be at least a dozen instant replays, slow-mos, stop action, the works. Kasoff pointed at the box suspended above the bar. Sure enough, the fatal line shot was on its way again, this time in motion so slow there was time to yell at McGinniss to get the hell out of the way, and then—crack—the bat's bullet finding its target, the right temporal area of the skull. And Donovan's hideous moment of ecstasy. "Jesus," said Green, "Jee—sus!"

15

"C'mon, we've got work to do," and now Kasoff was tugging Green toward the door. "We've got a murder case to prove."

"You're kidding, right?" Green, who had grown up in Oklahoma and moved to Chicago after law school, was a baseball fan all right, but he had long forgotten Donovan's vow.

Kasoff, who couldn't get the five-month-old threat out of his mind, could only sputter, "It was premeditated. It was premeditated." And as if suddenly realizing that he was proposing to charge a man with murder for getting a base hit—even if it was against the home team in a hometown courtroom—Kasoff perseverated, "We've gotta clear this with B.D. We've gotta clear this with B.D."

B.D., aka Dan Gorski, was the chief deputy DA and, at six feet, five inches, 265 pounds, an imposing figure. He hadn't put on a pound since his playing days as an All-Conference lineman at the University of Illinois. Gorski had risen through the ranks of the Prosecutor's Office by nearly always winning convictions as well as the loyalty of his fellow assistant DAs. A few would occasionally grumble that his victories proved nothing more than that he never took chances bringing a close case to trial— those would be plea-bargained. But everyone in the office knew that line was always drawn somewhere, and the fact was, Gorski obtained far more convictions than he surrendered. Fundamentally as conservative in his appearance and tastes as he was in arguing the law, he was not the sort to tilt at windmills.

Kasoff had an abiding admiration for Gorski, and not just because B.D. had hired him a decade earlier. Gorski's office was where the real decisions, the tough strategic trial work of the busy office, got done. His bosses, the prosecutors, were elected pols who would come and go with the ebb and tide of each Chicago-style election. These showhorses would take a varying degree of interest in the work done by Gorski and his staff of assistants, but one thing was constant. Whenever the cameraman stopped by for a video blurb on the latest crime story that would help TV5 or its competition sell next week's soap, Gorski would brief his boss, who would then go into makeup so the camera would be kind to his politically scarred face. Gorski's contributions were only rarely acknowledged. That was fine with him. The workhorse had no time to waste on sketching out silly sound bites.

By the time Kasoff and Green, breathless from the three-block run, if not the excitement, got into the office, someone had plugged in a portable TV. A dozen or more staff, including several attorneys, were transfixed at its images—shaking their heads at each replay, the game having been postponed by that time and muttering barely discernible whispers of horror. One of the lawyers was explaining to two of the secretaries who had never followed the game Donovan's prediction of last fall. Standing behind the others so as not to block their view—he was always considerate that way; he would take the last row in the movie house—was B.D.

"C'mon, we need to talk, B.D."

"What's on your mind, Bob?" And they headed back toward B.D.'s office in the corner opposite that of Green.

Before he even closed the door, Kasoff was chanting, "This was murder; this was murder."

"What are you talking about?" And B.D., normally a patient man, began to furrow his brow.

Kasoff remained standing, airborne almost, as B.D. calmly took his seat behind his desk. Green sat opposite B.D. This, Green decided, was Kasoff's battle alone.

"He planned this. He vowed to do it. This was premeditated." Kasoff barked out the short declarative sentences that he had learned were so effective with juries in rapid-fire fashion as though that would be more persuasive.

"What, what, and what?" B.D. stared blankly. All he had seen was a wicked liner that had struck home with tragic consequences.

"Last fall, in the play-offs, remember? McGinniss beaned Donovan, kept him on the disabled list through the Series. Weeks later, Donovan is interviewed. He vows to take his revenge if it's the last thing he ever does."

B.D., who had been out of town the week of Chicago's media storm over the comments, now vaguely recalled hearing about some such brouhaha around that time. "So. Since when do we prosecute idle macho talk?"

"You don't understand. Donovan is the game's best hitter. And not just for average or power. He's the game's best place hitter. You want a guy to hit to the opposite field, he's your man. First baseman guarding the line against him? He'll hit it in the hole. Need a fly ball to score a run? He's led the league in scoring runners from third base with less than two outs every year. The whole idea is to hit it where they ain't. He hits it where he wants."

"And what's his lifetime batting average?"

"It's three sixty-two, second highest in history. Only the late Ty Cobb did better."

"So much for your expert witness." And Green laughed. "Seriously," B.D. continued, "you mean to tell me that nearly sixty-three percent of the time he wants to hit it where it'll take him right back to his seat in the dugout?"

Now Green chuckled to himself. It was a brutal way to die, but Kasoff was really off on a tangent if he actually believed he could prosecute it.

"Look," Kasoff continued. "I've read about this guy. Donovan is known as the most dedicated student of the game. He studies videos of all the pitchers and his own swing all winter long and during the year as well. He's at the ballpark by nine A.M. for a nightgame, a damn night game, for Chrissakes, and by five A.M. for a day game. I guarantee you he's spent the last six months watching tapes of every pitch McGinniss has ever thrown, analyzing where his ball goes so he can meet and place it where he wants."

"You really ought to think about getting some of your money out of the bank and into the stock market. If you had ever seen a prospectus, you'd know that past performance is no guarantee of future results. Those tapes can't tell him where the next pitch is coming. All he can do is make an educated guess. That's why he fails a majority of the time. And we're talking about a McGinniss fastball no less. No one, least of all McGinniss himself, can figure out where in blazes that damn thing is going."

Kasoff wasn't giving up. "He's vulnerable in his follow-through; all pitchers are, you know. And Donovan planned that perfectly placed hit. I'm sure of it. This was no accident. Donovan had the means, the motive, and the opportunity. This was murder, pure and simple."

"Now let me get this straight. This guy Donovan puts on his

18

baseball uniform, joins his team in a game of baseball, steps into the batters' box, swings the bat, hits the ball—which incidentally is the whole idea—doesn't break a single rule of the game, let alone of society's conventions, and you want to charge him with murder? Suppose the official scorer had charged McGinniss with an error on the play. Would you call it suicide?"

Even Kasoff had to chuckle. He had real affection for his boss, enjoyed his wit, appreciated his ability to boil down complex legal issues to their essentials. But this was different. "Goddamn it, if this doesn't amount to a crime, it sure as hell oughtta."

B.D., whose forehead lines deepened each time he reconsidered the TV image he'd seen—the thought that this was so obviously a deliberate act certainly got his prosecutor's juices flowing—and who saw the value in time as an opportunity to placate an able assistant, counseled patience.

"Let's give this a few days. Maybe Donovan will grab all the rope he needs to hang himself. After all, he blew up once on camera; maybe he'll reprise that role. Baseball is bound to make a big deal out of this. He's going to have to explain himself. Who knows what evidence may fall into our laps off the living room screen?" B.D. looked out the window toward the high-rises obstructing his view of the lake. "We're in the business of punishing illegal deeds, not thoughts. Can a monstrous thought brought to fruition by legal means be prosecuted? You're going to have to hit a home run to convince me."

Kasoff smiled, thinking how far he had come in winning B.D.'s trust over the years. Nearly a decade ago, Kasoff had been granted a job interview with this rock of a man. Kasoff was then fresh from clerking for a state appellate judge, but the robe hadn't rubbed off. In the opening moments of their meeting, he had sat there before Gorski, who, glowering, towered over him as he paced behind his desk, firing questions. Kasoff had been interrogated pointedly before—that was the stock-in-trade of his judge upon reading Kasoff's draft opinions—but not where his future livelihood was at stake. Finally, after what seemed an hour of feeling like a grand jury target—Gorski's grand jury—B.D.'s hardened jaw slackened as he suddenly asked, "So, what's your personal philosophy?" Kasoff was baffled but, having sized up Gorski as a tough realist, was certain he did not want to hear a zen reply. Utterly disarmed, Kasoff went with self-deprecation—it had gotten him out of close calls before; it was worth a try here. "If I can accomplish it, it's not much of an accomplishment," he heard himself blurting. He believed it, too, though he certainly hadn't meant to spill the beans now. To his astonishment, B.D. replied without missing a beat and with a hearty laugh, "You're hired. I like a guy who knows his limitations and is willing to admit them. Even one prima donna around here is one too many." And Kasoff thought he saw B.D. tip his head ever so slightly in the direction of the recently elected prosecutor. Kasoff himself recovered quickly. "Thanks. You know, normally my self-deprecating humor isn't funny!" After that, B.D. and Kasoff had quickly become close colleagues and friends.

Now, Kasoff was smiling, too, because he was thrilled to have his work cut out for him. He knew just where to start. He would ring up his old friend Greg Townsend, down at TV11. They'd known each other since elementary school. It figured, Kasoff thought, that Greg had gone into broadcast news. Back when they were high school freshmen, Greg had run down the hall screaming into every room, "The president's been shot! The president's been shot!" Some woman had taken a shot at the president that day—and missed—but this detail had been lost on Greg. Not one to confuse the facts with the excitement of a good story, Greg reveled in the thrill of self-importance as his broadcast exclusive disrupted the day's lessons. The principal had chosen not to punish Greg that day—extenuating circumstances, he reasoned—which Kasoff was convinced only reinforced Greg's sense of special privilege. If you were reporting something important, you earned an immunity from the humdrum rules everyday mortals were expected to observe. Maybe if Greg had been made to face the music that day, Kasoff thought, for the disruption as well as the error, Greg's excitability at the mere thought of being the one to break news would have been harnessed.

As it was, Greg had gone on to become one of TV11's most popular reporters. Recently he had done a five-part series on a local toxic dump that was fouling a downwind neighborhood. It was hardly news. The EPA had declared it a Region 5 top-priority site three years earlier and the painstaking process of cleanup had been under way for several months, but the station's teasers and promos for the story had garnered big ratings for Greg and the station. Oh, those teasers. Greg staring intently into the camera, video stills staring out menacingly from behind him, Greg using all the right code words approved by the ratings mavens—*toxic, deadly, sludge*, mixed in with *your kids*. It turned out that Greg, in his series, had done nothing more than paraphrase a two-year-old government report and drawn several unwarranted conclusions at that. No matter, Greg couldn't be expected to understand all those polysyllabic chemical names. Hell, TV11 didn't even require he have a journalism degree. And, anyway, didn't he receive a Peabody Award among the local broadcast media for the series? And didn't management reward him with a nice bonus when the first Arbitron survey after the series showed his favorability ratings up 10 points? Kasoff shuddered not so much at the thought that Greg was vested with the responsibility of informing—ugh—the populace, but at the realization that Greg was considered by his peers as one of the better ones at it. Were America at century's end not quite so banal, a guy like Greg would have peaked in high school.

Still, Greg had his sweet side, thought Kasoff. Even though Kasoff never called Greg unless he wanted a professional favor, it didn't seem to bother Greg, who always greeted Kasoff enthusiastically and seemed honored to be his friend. When they would meet for lunch, Greg, the local celebrity, would introduce Kasoff to persons known and unknown around the restaurant as "my friend Bob Kasoff, the prosecutor," as though Kasoff was running for office and Greg was his proud campaign manager selling him to the electorate. Kasoff never seriously entertained the possibility that Greg might have an ulterior motive—could Greg, in the ultimate scoop, know that Kasoff would be running for office before he himself knew it? Nah. Somehow, thought Kasoff, Greg had managed to grow up without acquiring any of the cynicism so common—no, universal—among their generation.

And, Kasoff knew, Greg was scrupulous when it came to keeping a confidence. More than that, like it or not, the fact that Greg performed his job in front of a camera gave him access to people and places off limits to ordinary folk. I am seen, therefore I am.

"Hey, Castoff," cried Greg when he realized who was calling. The nickname, of course, dated back to eighth grade when Kasoff, who was bound and determined to play in the junior varsity league championship football game in spite of a hairline fracture of his right wrist sustained five weeks earlier, sawed off his cast the morning of the game—one week before it was due to be removed. He had scored the touchdown that had sent the game into overtime but had caught hell for it, first from his parents, who forbade him to play baseball that season, and then from the principal, who suspended him for the first three games the next year.

Kasoff smiled. "Howya doin', Greg?"

"What's up?"

"Were you at the game today?"

"Couldn't make it, I'm working on a big story—" any story was big to Greg—"on student drinking during spring break." Bursting with his own self-importance, Greg seemed to Kasoff utterly unaware of the day's most tragic event in the annals of baseball history. Greg wasn't the station's sports guy, so sports weren't important. Even with his innocent ever-youthful exuberance, he knew that his own story was the sort about which Kasoff just loved to needle him. Still, Greg didn't mind—he enjoyed Kasoff's barbs. But all Kasoff could do was shake his head and smile at this embryonic investigative reporting that was bound to belabor the ever so obvious.

"Hey, we need to talk," said Kasoff, impatient to get to the point.

"What's on your mind?"

"No, we should meet." Kasoff knew that Greg enjoyed this game—if the subject was too sensitive to discuss over the phone, Greg's excitement impulse would instantly rise.

"How 'bout tonight?" said Greg half-breathlessly.

"Now, don't get your scoop juices flowing. Let's meet outside Ed's for lunch tomorrow. Is noon all right?"

"I'll be there."

3

A pall of subdued frustration hung over the Yankee locker room. The Opening Day butterflies had barely abated when the game was suddenly halted. Only once before had a game—and a season opener—been postponed on account of death, and that was the heart attack of an umpire. Like so many of the statistics that ruled the rhythms of the game, this record would be shared. As the players changed, several walked by Donovan's locker. "Not your fault, Chris." "Nothing you could do about it, babe."

Their eyes having been transfixed by the tragedy on the mound, his teammates hadn't noticed Donovan's heavenward glance of triumph. And Donovan had quickly caught himself and his emotions. Though he couldn't bring himself to become part of the crowd that had gathered around the mound, he had remained beyond first base, bent over with one hand on each knee, head down and shaking it back and forth as if to show the world that he shared the horror while secretly savoring each second.

Now, in that most intimate of ballplayer hangouts, the postgame locker room, only the eyes of Dutch, the hitting instructor, penetrated Donovan's facade of the consoled but tormented victim of happenstance. Dutch, after all, remembered the films. The films and Donovan's bat speed.

It's on every scouting report form completed by every baseball scout in the country and beyond. Bat speed. It stands out among the other talents—strong arm, steady glove, foot speed—as the make-or-break quality for every kid who dreams of hitting in the big leagues. True, foot speed, like bat speed, is God-given. But the game has always had its share of lumbering giants, those slow-footed power hitters who invariably seem to come up with two men on. Every fan in the park knows they won't be bunting. So what? They all root for the big tater anyway. Weak arm? He can play left field. Poor glove? First base or DH. But the hitter who lacks bat speed is doomed to be labeled "no hit," because that's exactly what he'll do. If he can't get that bat around in the .46 seconds it takes a 90 mph fastball to reach home plate and can't do it quick enough to drive the ball hard, he'd better go back to school and learn something else, because—aside from a drill or two to refine the gift—no one can teach him bat speed, nor can he acquire it through practice, exercise, or nutritional supplements.

Sixteen years earlier, when Donovan was eighteen, baseball had already been Dutch's life for more than forty years. He'd seen it all by then—he thought. The World Series perfect game. The home run and stolen base records broken, both single-season and career. The hot-shot rookies who faded and the ones who stayed on to eclipse still more records. But Dutch had never seen a scouting report on a teenager that bore a perfect grade—an 8 for outstanding on a scale of 1–8 on bat speed. Not until he saw the scouting report on Donovan.

At that age, talent is raw. For all the quickness of his stroke, Donovan, as ever with youth, lacked discipline. He'd chase wild pitches. He'd change his stance with the breeze. He'd fidget—setting and re-setting himself as he awaited the pitcher's delivery, even during the windup. As a result, his batting average as a high school senior had been rather ordinary, at .336. But the scouts are grading their subjects at that age, qualitatively. If the talent is there, honing it should eventually produce the quantitative results that grace the back of every baseball trading card.

The Yankee scouts had long been the best in the business at grading the raw talent and drafting accordingly. Paul Graham, the Yankee GM for more than two decades, liked to explain that the draft was like playing blackjack against the house: you were bound to lose a lot of hands, but if you knew how to count the cards, in the long run you'd come out ahead. The Yankees knew how to count. Bat speed was the sine qua non in drafting these teenagers. Most, like the pebbles that hide the gold nugget, would wash out long before reaching the show.

Once the Yankees selected Donovan as their number-one draft choice, he came under the tutelage of baseball's most brilliant batting instructors. After two and a half years in the minors, Donovan had been sufficiently seasoned to be promoted to the parent club one August night, just before his twenty-first birthday. Dutch would now be his teacher. In the 13 years since, he had combined his historic lifetime hitting percentage with great power, having swatted 529 homers, at a rate of more than 40 per year, the best pace ever. And Dutch, convinced the moment he saw Donovan's scouting report that he was bound for greatness, had taken a father's pride in Donovan's success. Oh, what that bat speed could do, Dutch would marvel. Donovan could be fooled on a pitch, a fastball no less when he was expecting a change-up, and still manage to pull it foul. Hit-and-run? No one placed the ball better. Centerfielder overplaying him to pull? There goes a gapper to left-center for extra bases. It was the bat speed, Donovan knew, that gave him the gift of being able to spray the ball all over the field. This game worshipped at the temple of Wee Willie Keeler: He hit it where they ain't. And where he wanted.

And the tape. Dutch had loaned it out to Donovan over the winter. Dutch well knew what was on it. Hell, he'd reviewed it several times himself. Now, he wanted to see it for the first time through Donovan's eyes. But that would have to wait. Manager Steve Trasker had a few words for his players in light of the day's extraordinary tragedy, and Dutch had other work to do. As for Donovan, he remained silent, impassive through whatever the hell Trasker had said—he wasn't really listening. Behind the poker face he'd been displaying, Donovan's emotions continued to revel in his base hit. He even hoped that the lords of baseball would pick up the game where it left off instead of washing it out and starting anew tomorrow—just so he could save the box score, even if it would merely look like any line drive single in that summary of the game's statistics. Donovan smiled to himself at the thought.

That night, Donovan returned to his hotel room and searched out the public television channel. He had no desire to hear the news he had made, no need to see the replays, again and again, in excruciatingly slow motion, the hit that was the topic in every tavern. And so he didn't see the TV11 exclusive interview. No, Donovan knew nothing of the typical "how do you feel" fare, much less that McGinniss had left a widow.

Dawn brought a cold rain, a reminder that early spring in the Midwest is like an old car—racing forward one minute with a burst of warmth, only to sputter and stall with the next Arctic wave as the jet stream battles with the continent for the sun. The storm's patter on his window woke Kasoff out of another one of his trial dreams. But this wasn't the recurring one of standing up in court naked or, worse, unprepared. In this vision, Kasoff was trying a homicide case and, with great excitement and ceremony, had removed the murder weapon from a diamond-studded chest in front of the jury box as the finders of the facts craned their necks forward for a better view like the rubberneckers who crawl past a highway accident. Kasoff revealed the deadly instrument—a baseball—and was confronted with a chorus of guffaws. Worse, the ball resisted the efforts of the court reporter to affix an exhibit sticker to it. Why, this ball still had its shine, rendering it impervious to the glue on the back of the label that read: PEOPLE'S EXHIBIT 1. And, its virgin horsehide could only mean that the pitcher hadn't rubbed it up, which meant that it hadn't even been used—it was the wrong weapon, er, ball! "Your Honor!" cried out Kasoff, and then the rain, the merciful rain, adjourned the proceedings.

Kasoff ran through his morning routine, which he no longer took for granted. If certain unwanted traits had grown on him with the job—like a magnified fear of crime and an inclination to be suspicious of the motives of people—it was also true that his line of work had given him an appreciation for the simplest things in life, even the basic activities of daily living that the victims of the crimes he prosecuted could no longer manage. As Kasoff ate breakfast, he reviewed what he'd say to Greg. He couldn't be too careful. In spite of their friendship, station policy would control any request he might make. TV11 could piss away press freedom with its incessant knack for broadcasting the banal, but it would be awfully high-minded when it preached the First Amendment—stressing to its staff that it must never become a tool of inquisitive government investigators.

It's a different L train ride in the rain. As one looks skyward, the skyscrapers fade like treetops in the gloom, instead of reach-

26

ing with their fingers out toward the distant blue. But Kasoff was preoccupied with matters more mundane. As he waited for the train, briefcase in one hand and umbrella in the other, he struggled to negotiate the newspaper he'd just bought so as to reach the jump page on the headline story everyone was already talking about.

"Can you believe what happened yesterday? Never seen that happen in baseball."

"Wasn't there a guy who got killed years ago after being hit by a pitch?"

"Why do you think they called it the 'dead ball' era?"

The wiseacres were already having a field day. But before Kasoff could manage to finish the page, the inside section fell onto the puddled pavement. "Damn," he muttered. He could be as much a prisoner of the mundane as anybody on days like this. But not today. Everyone talked about yesterday's game. Unlike the weather, Kasoff would do something about it.

"Good morning," chirped Carol as Kasoff entered, shaking off the chill and dampness.

"How 'bout if we just call it morning and skip the editorial?" Kasoff scowled, but it was more feigned than real. Delivering an effective rejoinder was the quickest way to restore a little sunshine to his mood.

The morning was strictly routine: The daily schedule briefing from his secretary. Three calls from defense attorneys puffing their cases for possible pleas. Reviewing a dozen police reports to recommend or deny the issuance of an arrest warrant. Kasoff was all for the mandatory arrest policy in cases of domestic violence, but not only had it doubled caseloads; it also sure made for a lot of sorry reading on the state of affairs domestic. It was as though a lone gunman had holed himself up in the Sears Tower, firing randomly in all directions near and far, and each home he hit started another battle in the war—between the sexes? Hardly—this was a war of men against women, if the hundreds of domestic violence reports Kasoff had scanned were any indication. This morning, however, his mind uncharacteristically wandered as he read these sad tales.

At last, high noon at Ed's Bar & Grill. Getting a table without a wait was a good prospect today. The rain would keep many of

27

the office minions within their own towers. Greg spotted Kasoff first. "How you doing, Castoff?" Kasoff smiled. He hadn't seen Greg since his three-part "up-front" series on credit card scams, the chief revelation of which was, guess what—the thief tricks the victim into giving out his or her card number over the phone. Greg's hair was a bit shorter and his lapel a little wider. Kasoff could always track the latest fashions with a glance at Greg.

"Good to see you, Greg. How are things at TV Eleven?"

"Great! We're about to start a project on—"

"No. Don't tell me." Kasoff had no time for the latest on liposuction or whatever the hell their buffoon of a producer was hot and bothered over this week. Greg looked hurt—the ebullience drained out of his face. Kasoff surveyed the damage and quickly retreated. "You don't want to blow a scoop by having someone overhear you."

It was true—simply because he performed his work in front of a camera, Greg couldn't walk into a restaurant without drawing not only stares but also the uninvited ear as those nearby paused in their own conversation in the hope of hearing his. Self-importance restored, Greg asked Kasoff what was up. Kasoff replied, "See the game yesterday?" Kasoff knew that Greg wouldn't realize Kasoff was no longer making small talk, that he had just introduced the topic for discussion. So he patiently awaited the inevitable inane return banter.

"Couldn't be there, but I saw the replays in the studio. Man, what a horrific sight."

"In the studio, in the studio," repeated Kasoff to himself. *Why does he always have to describe any event in his life as occurring "in the studio"? You'd think it was Stonehenge, for Christ's sakes, where all the TV Druids must gather to chant before they hop in their vans to chase fires. "Hey, Greg. I tried a criminal conspiracy last week. In the courtroom. In the courtroom."* Christ, it wasn't going to be easy to kiss-up to get what he needed. What the hell did they have in common anyway except spending adolescence in the same classroom? At last, Kasoff replied.

"I watched you guys last night. And I knew you'd replay Donovan's threat from last fall. I'll bet you were the only guys that ran it as a voice-over on the replay of the hit."

"You're right," Greg beamed. "Did you see the super slow-mo

of the ball striking Mc- McGinty—"

"McGinniss."

"McGinniss, right. And the reaction shot of Donovan? It was only a second or two, but man, I could swear that guy looked like he was in ecstasy."

Kasoff nodded, then cleared his throat. From here on, he would have to choose his words carefully. "Tell me, that interview with Donovan from last fall. Will you be playing more of it?" Kasoff could reasonably assume parts had been cut to fit the broadcast time limits for snappy sound bites. He knew he was broaching the subject that always made the media so touchy. Editing was the key ingredient of editorial control, which TV11 guarded as jealously as an absolute monarch regarded the crown itself.

"Hell no. Evans told me it happened just like that. They were at a hospital, doing a story on some burn victim or something—"

"No, that was the miracle recovery." This was not promising. Kasoff was seeking background information in the highest-profile homicide case of the century from rumormonger Greg, the guy who couldn't get a story straight if he read it off a TelePrompTer.

"Right. Anyway, Donovan said what he said. Evans got it all, and Denise, our program director, decided to play it as it was, last night as well as last fall."

"From whom do I order a copy of the tape?" This was safe. All the stations in town would supply, for a nominal charge, any tape they had broadcast. It was the cutting room floor stuff that was highly classified. Heaven forbid someone should see video of a shooting scene before the reporter had all her hair in place.

"Just call our production department. Ask for Jim Sullivan. It may take a few weeks, though, because every affiliate from here to both coasts has ordered a copy, and so have all the other locals. Course, we'll get 'em to our affiliates first. Why do you want it?"

Kasoff paused. This wasn't the courtroom, where the witness he was cross-examining couldn't turn the tables and ask him a question. "I've got a nephew in Jersey who loves Donovan." This was true. It wasn't an answer to the question, but it was an accurate response, and Kasoff could simply leave it to Greg to draw the inference with which Kasoff's statement was pregnant—that his nephew had asked for a copy of the tape—even though this inference was decidedly untrue. It was at times like this that Kasoff was grateful for law school having taught him how to think.

"Oh. No problem."

"So, I imagine you guys'll be following up big-time on this story." Kasoff dropped his voice when he said this, as though not to reveal a scoop when he knew he was stating the obvious.

"You bet. Of course, I can't give details, but we'll be giving it five-alarm treatment and then some."

"You guys have such an advantage over us. If we try to talk to a suspect, all we get is the Fifth Amendment shoved up our ass. You guys can stick a camera in someone's face, by appointment or by ambush, and every Tom, Dick, and con man is so thunderstruck at the thought of getting his mug on TV that he'll say just about anything."

"No way. Half the time all we get is a guy covering his face with his lawyer in ours."

"Yeah, but that doesn't happen until after we charge 'em." Now Kasoff decided to make his point. "Well, I never went to journalism school, but if I wanted to get the story of this case, and I mean the real story—" Greg was now leaning forward, and not just because Kasoff had again lowered his voice—"I'd want to find out just exactly how Donovan did it."

"What do you mean? He hit a line shot up the middle. Not the first time a pitcher's been hit. No story there. Now, how Donovan felt when he saw it happen, there's your story."

"Look. We know who did it, what was done, when it was done, where it was done, and, as of last fall thanks to your station, why it was done. You've got the who, what, when, where, and why of mundane journalism. But we don't really know how. Oh sure, he swung the bat and made contact with the ball. But did he know where it was going? Did he wait for a certain pitch? Did he change his stance to do this? His hitting stroke? Did he study McGinniss's delivery? Did he know what the pitch would be? Where it would be? You could get the story that no one else will." Now Kasoff headed for home. "The story that will really lock up your future."

Kasoff knew from Greg that the network types liked what he referred to as his telegenic qualities and what Kasoff called his superficial ones. Good face man, good voice man, they said. But they felt—what a shock—he was too shallow, needed more seasoning. If Greg, by delving deeper into this story than anyone else, could present a unique in-depth perspective on the case, he could be on his way. And if, incidentally, he turned up something that could be useful to Kasoff, so much the better. Something useful—like a statement or even a slip—that would furnish probable cause.

Greg didn't have to say a word in reply. His face told Kasoff he'd made the sale. Greg knew that everyone wanted an interview with Donovan. But he had to admit to himself that Kasoff's ideas could bring a whole new spin to the story.

* * *

That same morning, the speaker approached the podium, tapped the mike with a tentative gesture that betrayed his own hesitation, and called the gathering to order, as if a mob of press, many bleary-eyed after flying into the city overnight, could be termed *orderly*. The game's commissioner, on the job just three months after an interregnum of more than five years, knew he was facing his first trial by media. Based in New York, he had been watching the game when, seeing the shot, he grabbed the first available flight out of La Guardia, arriving before rush hour had wound down. Though convinced that he couldn't be expected to put out every fire, when the mayor's house is burning the fire chief races to the scene. Opening Day, play-off teams, bad blood. This was a major blaze.

That evening, the commissioner had managed to speak to the American League president, who had been at the game, as well as both managers and the Chicago catcher. Yes, Mullens had called for a fastball, but on the inside corner. Instead, McGinniss had delivered it out over the plate. No, Donovan hadn't said anything before the swing. He had seemed locked into his usual competitive concentration, those steely eyes that seemingly could bring down a game bird if Donovan had chosen to pursue hunting instead of striking a ball with a stick. The Yankee manager

31

was equally clueless. Donovan seemed his typical pregame self: no one could talk to him, at least not if they expected an answer, civil or otherwise.

The commissioner knew, of course, about Donovan's threatening words uttered what now seemed ages ago, B.C. as one writer put it, "Before Commissioner." Hell, he had 'em memorized, they'd been replayed and printed so often in the previous 18 hours. But without more, the commissioner viewed this as mere "be careful what you wish for." Donovan, regardless of his mind-set last autumn, hadn't done anything but what every hitter tries his darnedest to do—hit the ball hard somewhere. And now the owner's hand-picked leader spoke:

"The family of baseball extends its deepest sympathy and condolences to the family and friends of Don McGinniss. Yesterday's event—a tragic, tragic accident—has shocked not only the baseball world, but the entire nation."

There was more about a memorial tribute and the game going on, including that day's makeup game, weather permitting. If he spoke more than three minutes, it hardly seemed so. As it became apparent he was wrapping up, the press hounds began shouting questions in a din of babble. The commissioner raised his hand in a silent stop sign.

"There will be no questions," he harrumphed. As he turned to take his first steps on the return journey that would take him back to the comfort of his new office in New York—he had yet to try the ice machine in his minibar—several reporters, almost in harmony, shouted one final inquiry: "What about the threat?" But the commissioner was gone, in mind if not fully in body. Later he would tell a *New York Times* reporter, on the record, that "we'll certainly be taking a good look at trash talk, threatening language, and any other inappropriate conduct on the field." And that was it. Game 1 would be played one day after the first hit of the season by the game's number-one hitter had seen the game's first death by batted ball. If every statistic should tell a story, this one spoke volumes. As one sports wag would write in his daily column, it took baseball, a game of colorful characters who spawned wonderfully descriptive nicknames, a full century to see Happy, Dizzy, Daffy, and Doc come along. Now the new mouthpiece for the owners was, all at once, grumpy, dopey, and bashful.

*   *   *

The national anthem, to be followed by a moment of silence, was just beginning when Greg's cab dropped him off at the station. He met Denise, program director, in the lobby as they headed for the elevator. "Listen, there's a story behind this—" there was no need to specify the subject matter. "We have to find out what he did, why he did—I mean how he did it."

"What are you talking about? He did it with a bat because he hated the guy for plunking him out of the play-offs. End of story. Unless, of course, you can get an exclusive with him." Both were convinced, of course, that they'd get more sound holding a mike to the Sphinx.

"Look, just lemme nose around a bit, talk to a few people. Maybe travel to New York." Denise, of course, not only had to OK all out-of-town travel and expense reports submitted by local beat reporters but also had to justify them to the accounting department of the media conglomerate that had purchased the station in a leveraged buyout nine months earlier. Incurring more than $1 billion in debt while swallowing up assorted communications media, the titan pretended to make it up by squeezing nickels out of its locals. Still, thought Denise, Greg was a real comer, one whose numbers were steadily rising in terms of both recognition and favorability, and his contract was up next year. Though convinced he wasn't network material, Denise wouldn't want to find herself in the awkward position of explaining to management how she had managed to let a rising star walk because she had nixed his initiative.

"OK, let's talk about it," she replied, and Greg beamed as they headed to her office, confident that he had already won this battle.

*   *   *

"Mahogany or walnut?"

"Sure." Mary, who hadn't yet contemplated the label of "widow," was numbly indifferent to her elder sister's inquiry on coffin details. Like the fog of anxiety that intrudes following a bad dream, Mary's mind couldn't fully grasp the thoughts and events that now engulfed her. She hadn't yet even realized that to cope she would have to return to a career she had placed on hold much sooner than she had planned. Of course, she wouldn't need to do it for the pocket money. Though only beginning his second year in the big leagues—and his first full year at that—McGinniss had been a big bonus baby. But financial security paled when she considered the new life within—and her decision to wait until after Opening Day to break the news to Don made the pain so much more excruciating. It had seemed like the right thing to do at the time. After all, he had needed to stay focused on the game. McGinniss had been so honored and excited to have been chosen by the manager to pitch the opener, even if his opportunity came about because the veteran ace of the staff had pulled a hamstring the last week of spring training. She was determined not to do anything that would distract him, even if it meant postponing the day they would share the most exciting news of their own lives. Now, the thought that he would never know that he had fathered a child, combined with the fact that this budding life would replace him instead of joining him, was a blow so crushing that Mary couldn't get a deep breath, couldn't stop the pounding between her temples, couldn't dislodge the lump in her throat. How, she wondered, would she manage even to sit through the funeral service?

And a sense of guilt welled up within her, the misplaced guilt of those who bear no responsibility. Why hadn't she told him to take Donovan's threat seriously? At the time, she was the only person she knew who viewed his words as something less than a deadly warning. *Empty trash talk*, she thought. And the reporter had probably baited Donovan before pressing the "play" button on the video camera. Weren't they famous for that, in order to provoke the hot quote they could lead with? The TV cameras had cried wolf once too often. She had told McGinniss, in response to his angry reaction when they watched the clip that November night, that it was nothing to take seriously. Mary could always find a benign motive in the other guy. Her sister called her naive for it, but McGinniss preferred to think of her as innocent, as he defined the distinction: Mary was certainly aware of man's baser instincts. It was simply that, in her view of the world, she chose to reject the malign for the benign. It just came naturally to her.

And Mary momentarily found comfort in knowing that McGinniss would declare her utterly innocent of responsibility. But, emerging from the daydream, she was struck with the realization that she would never hear his comforting voice again, except as she would replay it in her mind's ear. And the sound of it was now drowned out in her sobs.

4

The visitors were restless. Two days in Chicago. Two games. Less than four innings played. All for naught. The day before, the morning's rains had let up just long enough to allow play for less than 90 minutes before returning with redoubled intensity. Only three innings, played as sloppily as the weather, had been completed, and so no box score would preserve the 4—4 tie. Like a court hearing without a record, if there was no box score, it never happened. Dutch had watched Donovan double and single, but on this day he was looking behind the hitter at the man, and what he saw now was a cipher. Not a sign, not a trace, that Monday's tragedy had affected Donovan the slightest. He was his usual picture of competitive concentration, silent, probing, and glaring at the opposition for any advantage. Now, as the players dressed and blew off their stored-up energy and emotions in horseplay and hijinks, Dutch felt like he was on an ice floe that had broken loose from the fishing party. His mind kept returning to those tapes.

For several years now, the Yankees, with a program for winning as rich as their tradition, were the only team that employed a video department whose job it was to record in action every pitcher and hitter in the league. From a whole series of vantage points in different game situations, with wide-angle and zoom lenses. A staff of full-time scouts employed solely for this purpose would then review the recordings, direct the editing, and preserve the key moments captured: the pitcher who ever so subtly tips his fastball, the hitter who fouls off the curve at his knees but misses badly when it comes in a few inches lower. Those distilled moments were indexed and cataloged for review by the coaching staff before each new series. Every team did some videotaping of its opponents. Hunch had surrendered to high tech years ago. But no one was as thorough, some would say obsessive, as the Yankees. Their competitors had mere snapshots by comparison.

Players who had trouble with a given member of the opposition were expected to watch and learn from the videos of their nemeses, in the off-season if necessary. And Dutch remembered.

A few days before last Thanksgiving, Donovan had called him at his winter home in Scottsdale. Dutch had just walked in the door after a week-long camping trip in the red rock country near Sedona. Donovan had gone to the team video library, he explained to Dutch, only to discover that the two hours of distilled video on McGinniss had been checked out. Who had them? Donovan assumed it was either Yankee first baseman Jaime Rodriguez or Bill Hines, a spare outfielder. McGinniss owned both of them, and they were free agents after next season. Time to do their homework if they were going to have a big year and get the big contract, Donovan calculated. He had guessed right. Rodriguez, who spent his winters in San Juan, had checked the video out two weeks earlier, Dutch explained, and was expected to ship them back after the holiday. Dutch remembered thinking at the time how curious it was that Donovan didn't want to wait—there was plenty of time before spring training, and Donovan usually picked a number of pitchers to study each winter— but wanted Rodriguez's number in Puerto Rico.

But what really got Dutch wondering was Donovan's next question: "Do you guys keep the out-takes?" *My God*, Dutch thought, *there's thousands of hours of film.* No player had ever asked to see the out-takes. And, anyway, Donovan had hit McGinniss hard in their two encounters before the beaning. Dutch had even joked just before the play-offs that plunking Donovan might be McGinniss's only way to keep the Yankee star off the bases. Having just returned from a vacation free of all modern communications devices, Dutch was ignorant of Donovan's intent toward McGinniss, which had gotten brief play on nearly every local TV sports show in the country that week.

Dutch told Donovan to check with Wayne Cartwright, director of video scouting, for the edited film. "Why do you want it anyway?" Dutch, who knew that Donovan generally kept his own counsel, didn't really expect a revealing reply, and he wasn't disappointed.

"Never know what I might be missing," was all Donovan would say.

37

It was several days later before Dutch had heard, in a telephone conversation with the front office, of Donovan's televised threat. Donovan had never been known for his hyperbole. Dutch was concerned. Still, he assumed that if all Donovan wanted to do was study McGinniss's moves on the mound, his revenge would be measured merely in a box score, not a body count. But a small part of Dutch wondered, Why did the game's greatest place hitter want to study these tapes? Had he picked up a flaw in McGinniss's delivery that made him vulnerable not merely to the base hit but also to baser instincts?

*　　*　　*

The sun was back out, along with the summer fashion catalogs in the employee lounge; it was moments before start time. Kasoff, pouring himself a coffee, saw Sharon and Carol wander in and begin perusing their glossy pages. He gave Carol a smiling, "Hello, sunshine." She radiated one in return. "You know, your nickname ought to be Sunshine; because when you walk into a room, your smile lights it up." Just when she was expecting another brickbat, she thought, he'd toss her a bouquet. But he was only setting her up. "And once you're there, like an eclipse, you cast a big, round shadow." Kasoff didn't stick around to watch the storm clouds roll in. With a hardy laugh that told all that he was the best audience for his own jokes, he turned and left. A full plate awaited.

Kasoff soon found, however, that the telephone banter he normally enjoyed with his opponents begging for a deal was today nothing more than a tedious distraction. His first call that morning had been to another friend old enough to know him by his nickname. Pete Churikian had saved Kasoff from failing high school physics. Churikian had gone on to teach the dreaded subject at a local university, and now Kasoff would actually need to learn and understand something of bodies in motion. This time, there'd be no filching an advance copy of the test and supplying it to Pete to get the answers. Kasoff had left a message—Churikian was in the lab, he was told—and now eagerly awaited the return call as he half-listened to the annoying voice of Alicia on the other end of the line as she sought mercy for a local robber.

38

Drugs, she explained, and therapy was what he needed, she declared, sounding more hopeful than certain. Kasoff, unpersuaded, was fiddling with his pen when a second line lit up—Sharon knew not to put another call through unless she was certain Kasoff wanted it. Kasoff immediately nixed Alicia's career criminal, as he put it, cutting off his last few words as he simultaneously pressed the blinking button.

"Hey, Bob, what's up?" Kasoff instantly recognized the voice he hadn't heard in nearly a decade.

"Pete, howya doing?"

"Great. I see you're still putting the bad guys away."

"Trying to. Hey, listen, Pete, I need your help."

"If you're looking for an expert to testify that a bullet took a ninety-degree turn on its way to a victim, I can't help you there."

Still Pete, Kasoff thought, *still suspicious of authority, as antiestablishment as when he was an adolescent.* "Ironic, isn't it Pete, how you chose a field where there's no arguing with the rules?" Pete's rejoinder, of course, was effusive praise for the laws of nature, perfect and paradoxical in their simple complexity, while dismissing the imperfect, inconsistent laws and ways of man. But Kasoff had no time to reopen the debates they had enjoyed on starry summer nights two decades earlier.

"Pete, if you don't mind, I'd like to visit you at the lab; it's easier than trying to discuss what I want to talk about over the phone."

"Sounds serious."

"It might be."

"Well, why don't you stop by around three? My class will let out at two-thirty and I can give you some time then."

"Great. Thanks a lot. See you then."

The crocuses were in bloom as Kasoff strode across the campus to the physics lab. Entering the building, he noted the peeling paint. Compared with the law school, the science department had gone to seed. When the hell would the legislature wake up and give universities carrots to increase their science programs combined with sticks if they didn't reduce their law school admissions proportionately? If Kasoff, through the bias of his own profession, could see that lawyers had been transformed from a force for social justice three decades ago to a drag on a high-tech society today, why couldn't the representatives see it and reappropriate funding accordingly? Kasoff had mentally begun to compose a letter on this subject to his state senator when he saw the room number that the directory had told him belonged to Pete's office.

As Kasoff reached the door, it was just being opened by a student who was on her way out. Pete, still behind his desk, looked up, stood, and smiled broadly. There were gray flecks in his beard, but he otherwise looked pretty much as he had all those years ago, slim, with the long brown hair whose curls seemed to spiral wildly, as if exempt from the rules of his chosen discipline. "Great to see you, Cast-off." And the two shook hands enthusiastically, observing this social nicety that had never been necessary between them back in the days when they had hung out practically every night together.

"Listen, I know you're busy." Pete was well known as a guy who got by on four hours of sleep and seemed to spend the rest of his time in the lab. "I'll get right to the point. Did you see McGinniss get killed the other day?"

"I caught a replay of it. Sure, who hasn't?"

"Well, you're the one who proved even to a scientific illiterate like me that a hot grounder can't speed up after its first hop and that a fastball doesn't really rise. Now, I've got some questions for you."

Pete, intrigued, eased back down into his chair without taking his eyes off Kasoff.

"You're going to call it murder by horsehide bullet, aren't you?"

Kasoff smiled. One thing still stood out from all their debates during those far-off nights, Pete was always a step ahead of him. And that was saying something.

"So what do we know so far?" Pete inquired.

"All I know is what I saw on TV. I've ordered the video but don't have it yet. Donovan lines the ball, and the camera captures him a moment later thanking God."

"Maybe he was cursing Heaven instead of embracing it," replied Pete, always the skeptic.

"Look, I know this. Donovan is baseball's best place hitter and he vowed revenge against McGinniss last fall."

40

"Sounds like you've got your case made. What do you need me for?"

"Donovan's no dummy. I'm willing to bet he studied this thing long and hard. If he did learn something about the mechanics of whacking a pitcher upside the head with a batted ball, do the physical forces involved clearly show that the force would be deadly?"

"You want to know what he knew—or presumably learned?"

"Precisely. Without that, I don't have the sine qua non of a murder case."

"Which is?"

"Malice. I need to prove that he acted with knowledge that his deed was one of deadly force. If all he expected was a line drive that would merely cause a concussion, no judge in the county would let a murder charge—first- or second-degree—survive a preliminary. So, let's assume for the moment that Donovan is studying the problem of whether or not he could kill a pitcher with a batted ball. What would he have found?"

"Well, this presents a very complex problem involving aerodynamics, collision geometry, trajectory calculations, and stereomechanics."

"What the hell is that?"

"The classic theory of collision. It's based primarily on the laws of momentum. And there are so many variables. As many as there are ways for the batter to fail. Now, in general, there are some things we do know. For example, the collision between the ball and the bat lasts approximately one one-thousandth of a second. In that time, the ball is compressed to half its normal size and then manages to resume its shape before the human eye can even perceive it. Even the bat compresses slightly before springing back. This is known as elasticity or resilience. Stereomechanics doesn't take into account these deformations at the point of contact, not to mention variation in the values for the coefficients of friction and restitution."

"Of course not. Who could think otherwise? Listen, I need to make this understandable to a judge for heaven's sakes. Is there any way to simplify this?"

"Sorry. I don't make the rules. I just explain them. But there are some things that the average layman can follow, so there

41

might even be some hope for your judge. The average hitter takes about one-fifth of a second to swing the bat, so he has to start his swing when the ball is just halfway to the plate. When he is one-tenth of a second into his swing, the ball is still about 15 feet away. It's in that last fifteen feet that half of the ball's movement—curve or drop—will occur. It's a wonder that anyone is able to make contact at all with a stick that is less than three inches in diameter. Ted Williams didn't call it the hardest thing in sports for nothing."

"You're not helping me, Pete. I need to show that Donovan was so skilled at place hitting, let alone making contact, that he could have planned this."

"Well, here are just some of the variables that occur to me right off the bat, if you'll pardon the pun."

"Let's hear 'em."

"By watching the video in slow motion, we should be able to determine the speed of the batted ball. And it will be easy to establish the weight of the ball—I believe they're five or six ounces. We'll need to know the force of the blow in pounds per square inch. In order to determine that, we need to know the size of the surface areas of the contact point between the ball and McGinniss's head. We'll need to determine the resilience factor of the soft tissue that covers the skull. Was McGinniss's head moving forward or backward at the instant of impact? We need to know the thickness and density of the skull. If I'm Donovan, I want to know the answers to all of these questions."

"Look, we can assume Donovan knew the standard ball weight and that McGinniss had normal anatomy. For God's sakes, we're not talking about aiming a laser beam at an incoming ICBM here. We don't need the numbers down to a billionth of a decimal point." It was all coming back to Kasoff—Pete had always been maddening in his quest for precision. To Kasoff, for whom good and evil were easily discernible, it was OK to round the world off a bit. Witness memories, coroners' opinions, re-creations of crimes—they were all estimates, good enough in his domain, where juries never returned a verdict of approximately guilty. And beyond a reasonable doubt was never defined as the equivalent of 100 percent scientific certainty.

Pete gave Kasoff an exasperated look that told his friend,

How can you expect me to get to first base on this without some numbers?

"Look," Kasoff said. "I'll check into these questions. We should be able to come up with some pretty decent numbers."

"'Pretty decent' does not describe a number. Even a damn batting average is calculated with precision; it's just that sports editors round 'em off. Exactness explains the universe. Your world's numbers are abused for political purposes. Don't mess with my numbers."

Kasoff explained with more patience than usual the difference between legal and scientific certainty, that even within a range of values it might become clear as a matter of law that Donovan's state of mind involved malice even if there was room for scientific doubt. "If the facts demonstrate a solid likelihood of malice, will you help me?"

"Sure. I'll do what I can."

"Great. And remember. Simplify. It's a judge you got to persuade and, with a little luck, perhaps a jury one day."

"The persuasion part is your role. I just explain the numbers." But the old friend said it with a smile and a thumbs-up.

"OK, OK. Say, what time you got?" asked Kasoff, seeing that he was due for a new watch battery.

"It's *around* four." Pete smiled, emphasizing the estimation. "Let me know what you find out. I'd like to see the numbers nail that bastard."

"I'll be in touch—count on it," Kasoff replied.

Kasoff was getting back to his office just as the game was ending, though the small midweek day-game crowd was hardly noticeable as it dispersed in all directions among the city's streets. On the cab's radio, the team's new play-by-play announcer—the old one, beloved by the fans, had been fired by the team's new ownership after more than three decades at the mike because the owners desired a "new direction"—was telling the listeners that the Yankees' 14–3 victory over the hometown favorites wouldn't have been so lopsided "if only" the Chicago starter hadn't walked four straight hitters to start the second inning, followed by reliever Dan "Whiplash" Andrews's "mistake" pitch that landed in the upper deck. *Good old Whiplash,* thought Kasoff. *He'd whip 'em in and they'd lash 'em out.* Apparently, the home team's new voice didn't yet realize what a bum this guy was. Kasoff wanted to know how Donovan's day had gone, but he'd have to wait for the next morning's box score to see that he was 3 for 5 with a home run, a double, and a single. The paper's game photo showed the ring of police around the front row seats, with an extra concentration in left field, all to protect Donovan from vengeful fans. The show of force had been effective. There had been no incidents.

Now the Yankees were enjoying the fruits of the victorious locker room and packing up to leave for their next series, in Kansas City. The batboy was dutifully carrying out his strict instructions: all shards from broken bats, after being retrieved, were to be turned in to Dutch. It wasn't like the old days when the spent lumber, having served its purpose, was thrown out. These days, the bat's pieces were reapproximated and placed in clear plastic after being autographed, to be sold as souvenirs at the trade shows, the proceeds being split by the team and the player whose bat had broken. After each road series, Dutch would package up the shattered lumber for later reassembly once the team returned home. This time, he also boxed up one club that was intact. In Monday's panic and confusion that followed the McGinniss tragedy, Dutch had watched the batboy retrieve Donovan's bat from the home plate area, unsure at that time whether it belonged in Cooperstown or an evidence locker but well aware that someone might come looking for the weapon. And so Dutch, in turn, had obtained the bat from the young man.

Donovan had just left the locker room and was walking down the runway to the player's parking lot to meet the team bus when Greg trotted up, meeting his eyes.

"Where's Chris Donovan?" panted Greg.

Donovan instantly spotted the TV11 patch on Greg's blazer and scowled, "Who the hell wants to know?" Forty-eight hours earlier, Donovan had caught himself gazing skyward in glory as McGinniss's brain tissue felt the shock of air as its protective bony shell broke away. Since that instant, he had assumed—correctly—that all eyes were on him at all times. When the spotlight's glare is unrelenting, even the acclimated eye yearns for the shadows. And so Donovan had said nothing publicly, except to release a prepared statement expressing deep regret for the

44

"unbelievable and unavoidable" tragedy. Even that comment had seemed as canned as the clichés the reporters would parrot each time they sought adequate words to express the situation.

Greg, guessing he had met his target, decided to take an almost obsequious tack.

"Look, the media in this town have been all over Donovan the last two days, demonizing him." He would refer to Donovan in the third person just in case his instincts were wrong. "I'm not interested in a 'how do you feel' sound bite. Giving Donovan an opportunity to explain in detail his side of the story is only fair. He's human, too."

Donovan, for a moment, stood motionless, staring back at Greg. It was clear that Donovan was calculating the odds here. *Is honesty possible from the press, or has he already got one finger on the 'edit' button, ready to cut me to ribbons with cheap shots no matter what I say?* "I'll think about it," he finally barked, and then resumed walking.

"Oh, Mr. Donovan, thank you," and Greg pushed his business card on him. "Just call me anytime. I'll fly to wherever you're at and we'll do it any way you want." Even Donovan, no student of TV journalism, knew that Greg was merely referring to format. The questions and the power to edit, splice, and dice his remarks would be totally controlled by the media monster.

"I said I'd think about it." Donovan, as much as he detested these clowns, knew he had to do something, not because the hated media were pounding the drums, but because the firestorm might influence the new, untested commissioner to overreact by suspending him or even banning him from the game he still loved to play. He shoved the card in his breast pocket and continued down the runway, leaving Greg to pump, ever so subtly, his fist in partial triumph, like the rocket engineer who watches lift-off knowing that the booster rocket is yet to fall away. But Greg's private celebration was cut short when Donovan, now several steps away, turned back and added, "I meant it: The next time you contact me will be the last time I consider it. If I decide to do it, I'll call you. Don't call me."

"Sure thing," Greg smiled, because now he was convinced it was. And just a matter of time.

5

Thursday. An off-day for Chicago's team, with travel plans hastily rearranged. McGinniss's funeral was set for 11:00 A.M. Baseball's dignitaries had been arriving overnight; even the vice president would be sweeping in on *Air Force 2*, as though the funeral motorcade alone wouldn't tie up traffic enough. Mary, staying with her sister, Melanie, awoke at 7:00, after getting several hours of drug-induced sleep following an injection administered by her brother-in-law. For an instant, it felt like just another morning, until she was fully oriented, when the crushing weight of her husband's death hit home again. As she lay on her back, her head, which she had just started to raise, crashed back onto the pillow and she began to sob, the tears running what would become two well-worn paths down her cheeks until, as she tilted her head a bit to the right, one little rivulet met the left corner of her mouth, and she tasted it with her tongue, almost relieved to sense something through the shroud of sedative and grief.

Her sister, her sweet, protective—most would say overprotective—older sister, entered. "Are you OK? I heard you sigh—" a sound that, to Mary, had been imperceptible, or perhaps Melanie just made it up as a pretext to breach gloom's curtain. Melanie helped her sister out of bed and walked her to the bathroom. Now, Mary realized, a second sense had survived. She could smell the aroma of her favorite tomato-garlic bread. Melanie must have gone out and bought it fresh for her from the only bakery in town that carried it. And she began to cry again, but this time her sadness mixed with a sweet seven-year-old memory evoked by the fragrance.

Division Street was aptly named. On one side was the southern border of the gentrified classic homes, some dating back to the Gilded Age. On the other, just south of a gritty warehouse and light industrial district, were the projects that stood as monuments to a nation's inability—or unwillingness, depending on which side of the street you came from—to embrace all its citizens in its grandest dreams. There, just across the street from a graffiti-strewn storage building, was D'Amico's, a fourth-generation Italian family bakery. On weekends, the lines formed early. By 6:00 A.M., the smell of garlic and baking bread was beckoning all. Vince D'Amico, the current owner, carried the full line of Italian baked goods of course, from bread to cannolis, but his specialty was the family recipe for the garlic-tomato bread that Mary now longed for as she got ready to go down to the kitchen. Each piece of the baked treasure was round, like a pizza pie about six inches in diameter and two inches thick, topped off with a generous layer of sun-dried tomatoes and sliced fresh garlic bulbs along with the usual mix of spices. Bite into it while it was still warm, and you'd savor every morsel.

She had found herself at D'Amico's the first time all those years ago after spending a Friday night at the home of her sister, in one of the stately houses about a mile north. Mary was divorced at the time, having problems with a boyfriend, and Melanie had insisted she stay. In the morning, Melanie told her about this great Italian bakery with the wonderful bread, and Mary—grateful for the night's refuge—left Melanie's that Saturday morning with the intention of bringing some back as a surprise. She had hopped in her car—was it whining a little funny this morning?—and found the place OK, but she hadn't counted on the line. *Still,* she thought, *am I going to rush home for my boyfriend's sake?* So she took her place amid the orderly throng that snaked its way back to the door.

And then a big young guy took up the spot in line just behind her. "How ya doing?" he said, as though they were both regulars and, having in common the knowledge of this jewel in its nondescript surroundings, it was only natural they commiserate while awaiting their culinary reward.

"Hi." She didn't smile, didn't make eye contact—she'd grown up with Melanie's regular drumbeat that most guys mistook friendliness for sexual interest—but she noticed he was at least several inches over six feet, well built, and a friendly sort, with some of the awkwardness that betrayed his teenage years.

"Man, these lines get longer every week. I hope they don't run out." So, Mary thought, the bread Melanie had raved about did have a reputation. She nodded in reply as the most minimal socially acceptable acknowledgment of the stranger's comment. *Still no smile*, he thought. *Well*, he continued to himself, like the poster in coach's office, *you've got no chance of making the shot you don't take, so here goes.* "I'm Don McGinniss," he said with a smile, and extended his right hand to shake hers.

"Nice to meet you," and she tentatively took his hand and shook it for only the briefest moment.

Seven years later, and now groggy in a fog of sedatives, Mary couldn't remember the details of the small talk they had made as they wended their way through the line until it was their turn to place their orders. The conversation was the usual fare. Where she worked, what he did, and so on. But she did remember this. Mary had said good-bye to McGinniss and had walked out of that bakery alone, with no thought of ever seeing him again. As she reached her car, he was still awaiting his order. And then whatever mystery under her car's hood that had only hinted its presence earlier now took center stage. The vehicle wouldn't start. Two, three, four times she tried turning it over, but nothing. She sat there a moment trying to figure out what to do. She had no mobile phone, and there were no pay phones on the block. D'Amico's seemed to be the only business around that was open. She was about to exit her car to return to the bakery when a shadow suddenly appeared at her driver's side and, turning to it, she heard the now-familiar voice say, "What'sa matter? Car won't start?"

"No, it's OK. I can call—"

"Look, I don't know much about cars, but let me give you a ride to get help."

"No, that's OK—really. I can walk. I'm not far."

McGinniss could sense that her hesitation was genuine only because of the ingrained fear of strange men every wise woman acquires—but there was no doubt she wanted help. The skies were beginning to threaten pedestrian travel. "Look. I don't think this bakery has a public phone. I'd go make a call for you if you wanted to sit in your car in the meantime, but I'm not so sure that's such a good idea." And he turned his head, his eyes leading her to look across the street where four teenagers were smoking and kicking old beverage cans as they walked. "It just makes sense to let me give you a ride."

"No. My sister would kill me if she knew I took a chance getting into a car with a strange man." She felt more comfortable blaming her sister for her own discomfiture. But McGinniss was pleased that at least the unspoken was now out in the open. He could deal with that.

"Here, tell you what," and he started placing his hands or, more precisely, all his fingers all over her car's hood. Before she could ask what the devil he was doing, he explained. "Look, if I was a serial killer, would I leave my prints all over your car? And here, you can hold my driver's license in your purse," as he removed it from his wallet and tossed it into her bag.

"A lot of good having your license will do me. You'll just take it back after you slit my throat." But she said it with a sheepish smile, feeling foolish to think that this amusing, if a bit gawky teenager would harm her.

McGinniss didn't see a woman feeling silly. It was the first time he had seen her smile, and he liked the fact that he had had to earn it. There was nothing phony or frivolous about her, he thought, and though he was only seventeen, and soon to learn that he was seven years younger than Mary, his insight was right on target.

So he would drive her to Melanie's, which took all of two minutes—though it had started raining and that made him feel his offer was doubly worthwhile—after which they had said their good-byes, and that was that, Mary thought. Until later that day when she discovered, just before Melanie was going to drive her home, that his driver's license was still in her purse. It revealed that he lived several miles north, and she would have no car of her own at least until Monday, according to the mechanic to whom Melanie had gotten her. Mary thought of mailing the license, but that wouldn't be fair. What if he got pulled over in the meantime? And besides, he'd done her a favor and would surely be knocking on Melanie's door as soon as he discovered it missing—if he remembered the house. No, she would drop it off at his home. Could this have been a gambit on his part in the hope of seeing her again? No, she immediately dismissed that thought. He was simply trying to ease her mind at the time.

So she asked Melanie to drive her to McGinniss's address,

explaining only that she had found a driver's license and wanted to return it. Melanie was suspicious—figuring there was more to it than that—but with her kid sister's lovelorn problems these days, this was no time to sweat the small stuff. Still, when they pulled up, Melanie accompanied her to the door. McGinniss answered, pleased but surprised to see her, not yet having discovered his loss. He greeted her with a broad smile and a, "Hello again."

The jig was up. "You forgot your license. What kind of Jack the Ripper does that?"

It was McGinniss's turn to smile sheepishly. "Thanks a lot. By the way, that Audio Tronics place where you work—"

"Auto Tronics," she corrected him.

"Do they need any help this summer?"

"I don't know. You might check there on Monday."

"Where they located?"

"On Ogden. Ogden at Seventeenth."

"OK. Thanks a lot."

She said good-bye and they exchanged thank-yous. With her sister as chaperone, Mary did not return his smile.

"*OK*," he thought to himself. *Monday. Monday it will be.*

McGinniss didn't realize, of course, that he had blown her cover. The ride home with Melanie included a lecture followed by the third degree, and then another lecture.

*   *   *

Mary had not been to St. Michael's Cathedral with Don since they had taken their vows there. Now the church was jammed with friends, acquaintances, and fans. It was nothing like their wedding. As Melanie helped her sister into the front-row pew, she couldn't help noticing that most of the folks in the first two rows were strangers, people the press would call the lords and dignitaries of the national pastime, representatives of all the teams, league officials, and so on and so what. The commissioner was present. He had decreed a moment of silence in ballparks across the land, with flags to be flown at half-mast for a month. A few miles away, the black patches that would be sewn on the home team's uniforms were already being manufactured. *Silence and darkness*, Melanie thought. *What an awful way to honor such a young and vibrant individual.* She placed her right arm around her sister and gently eased Mary's head into Melanie's shoulder. She would be there for Mary whatever it took, she vowed to herself. She knew, she was sure, how to help her sister get through it, even if she saw Mary's life exclusively through her own eyes.

But the grief in that church was much deeper than what Melanie could get an arm around. Don McGinniss Sr., a gentle bear of a man, bawled uncontrollably, his massive chest heaving and bouncing like jelly with each wail. The deceased's mother, slim and looking more frail than ever, held her husband's arm and dabbed at her eyes with a small white lace handkerchief that she placed carefully beneath her glasses, as though methodically controlling her movements could keep her emotions contained as well. Father O'Rourke's eulogy was standard fare, but even the hardiest of the throng were brought to tears by the speaker who followed.

Ten-year-old Timothy Trainor explained that, three years earlier, two eight-year-old bullies had just stolen his mitt when McGinniss had happened by. The decedent had retrieved it and befriended Tim, whose father he'd never known, stopping by to play catch or just see how he was doing. But more than that, somehow McGinniss had managed to persuade the two young thieves to apologize to Tim, after which the three young boys had become fast friends. "He turned bad guys into good guys and nobody even had to get punished. I'll always remember that—" he paused as his voice cracked and quivered, and his rapturous audience held its collective breath, hoping for him that he would be able to regain his composure—"as long as I live." And he ran to the priest, burying his head in the Father's chest. Not a dry eye in the sacred house, not even of the two boys standing just behind the back row of seats—it was a standing-room-only crowd—now both eleven, who knew the story best. Standing next to those redeemed adolescents was the man who intended to prove that this gathering was a testament to more than the Father's description of it as an unspeakable, unavoidable tragedy. Kasoff felt he had to be here: it was so important, he knew, to meet the victim's family. Seeing their unbridled suffer-

51

ing energized him for the fight that at this point he could only hope, and even then only with a lot of luck, lay ahead.

For Mary, it was a day she would remember only as a snapshot out of focus. She had approached Don's open coffin, touched his cheek with her palm, and then recoiled at the strange cold hard feel of dead flesh. At the cemetery, had she really collapsed as his casket was lowered into the ground, or had she managed to fight off the urge to do so? It would be weeks before her brain could process what felt like a continual information overload of the present. The only focus she could sustain was the past.

And the irony of it was more bitter than her tears. How she wanted so badly now to remember every detail of the first weeks, months, and even years she had known Don. She realized that people remember what's important to them at the time, and for a long time—more than five years—he had not been terribly important to her. During that period, she had been his friend. Nothing more. Oh, if only she had loved him at first sight, she would be able to replay forever in her mind all those earliest conversations, the first time their eyes met when they shared a spontaneous mutual smile. She would, she decided, use this awful grieving time constructively. She would try to recall and reconstruct as much of their friendship years as she could. At least McGinniss had often filled her in, during the brief year of their marriage, on the details he recalled with breathtaking clarity of those early days. His memories, combined with her efforts, she knew instinctively, would get her through these next dreaded months.

*   *   *

"The left temporal bone at the squamosal suture sustained a severely depressed fracture. . . . Hematomas are present both subdurally and epidurally." Kasoff pretty much knew what the dry medical terminology of the autopsy report would show, but it was nonetheless a necessary piece of stitching in the fabric of criminal responsibility he hoped to weave. No question about the cause of death here. The coroner's report was mere formality. And here it was in the his concluding paragraph: "Death was virtually instantaneous due to moderate velocity impact of blunt object, i.e., batted major-league baseball." But then the final offending words leaped off the page at Kasoff. "Death was accidental."

But Kasoff's eye had been caught by an entry in the opening paragraph, not its closing: "Instrumentality which projected the baseball was a 34 oz., 33 inch long thick-handled wood bat."

How did the coroner learn that? "Hello, Dr. Patel. Kasoff here. I'm looking at your report on McGinniss."

"What's your interest in that?" Jagdesh Patel, the county's chief pathologist, knew that Kasoff must have sent a clerk to pick it up, hardly standard operating procedure in an accidental death.

"I'm a fan. Listen, how'd you find out the specs on the bat?" The report was silent on its current whereabouts, contrary to the SOP to list a weapon's current location if known—chain of custody concerns of course.

"I called up the Yankee manager and asked him if he had the bat. Said he had no idea what had happened to it in all the confusion, but that he always used a thirty-four-ounce."

"Did he use it this time?"

"Well . . . " The pause told Kasoff the answer.

"How do you know he used it this time?"

"Look, you and I both know that evidence of habit or routine practice is admissible in court—as if this were anything other than an accidental death."

"Then the report should say the bat was unavailable but that thirty-four-ounce was habit. And how can you possibly conclude this was an accident? Were you on Mars last fall when Donovan issued his threat?"

"Tell you what. If you won't tell me how to write an autopsy report after twenty-five years of doing them, I won't tell you which rainbows not to chase."

Kasoff was in no position to escalate this debate. He might need Patel later, if additional evidence turned up. A supplemental report, hell, even a coroner's inquest could overturn the original opinion. Besides, at least Kasoff now had a lead on one of Dr. Physics's elusive numbers. Still, if he was going to follow up, he would not only have to be discreet; he'd also have to rely on a world over which he had no influence—the baseball fraternity, with its players, coaches, and even umpires mingling all over the country. It was simply too soon to let it out of the bag that the law was looking into this. Still, he wanted badly to get his hands on that bat, if it could still be found. He would have to limit his strategizing on this to his sparest of spare time. For now, the South Side carjacking gang case was up for trial.

But the very next day brought another diversion from the routine work of the office. It came in a plain brown envelope, and for once, Kasoff was pleased to see the call letters of TV11, prominent as they were in the upper left corner. The video! Kasoff ripped it open with the glee of a kid at Christmas. There it was! Of course, banded to it was a slick four-page brochure featuring the pretty faces of the TV11 news team. They just couldn't help themselves.

Kasoff immediately walked the tape over to the police lab two blocks away. He wanted personally to place it in the hands of Dr. Chin—he was known for his discretion—in order to get the answers to two questions. Less than three hours later, Chin had what Kasoff wanted. The ball took .23 second to go from Donovan's bat to McGinniss's skull. And the two were 56 feet apart—Donovan had met the ball squarely over the plate as McGinniss was storming toward it in his follow-through—when the ball began its journey. Kasoff had more numbers for Dr. Science.

*   *   *

The Yankees started the season strong, winning 13 of their first 17. If there was guilt, it was not to be found in Donovan's batting stroke. He was leading the league, hitting .412. To head off any possible action by the new Milquetoast commissioner, Donovan's agent drafted a press release for his signature:

> Along with all of baseball, I, too, wish to express my shock and sadness over the tragedy that occurred on Opening Day. My heartfelt condolences go out to the family of Don McGinniss. I've played baseball all my life and love the game as much as anyone. All of us in the game recognize it can be hazardous, but no one dreamed anything like this could ever occur. Last fall, in anger and frustration over missing my first chance to play in a World Series, and after being badgered by a TV reporter, I made some

54

foolish statements which I now deeply regret. I never meant anything by them—they just came out at a bad time for me. I apologize to all for any pain I've caused due to the misconstruing of those unfortunate remarks.

"No, you didn't dream it, you fervently wished for it," muttered Kasoff to himself as he watched the spectacle. To Kasoff, it was obvious that Donovan was speaking straight from the TelePrompTer, not the heart. But Kasoff did appreciate the nugget of new information: it was a momentary lapse of judgment, according to Donovan. And this gave Kasoff a standard by which to measure Donovan's conduct against those words. Perhaps Kasoff could show that Donovan had spent the previous five months preparing or, in the language of his trade, premeditating and deliberating. A defendant's out-of-court mendacity wouldn't prove a crime, Kasoff knew, but it would keep him off the witness stand, lest he open the door to impeachment.

Kasoff's own deliberations, conducted as the South Side gang case was going to the jury, led him to conclude that his next step would be to reconstruct how Donovan had spent his winter and compare it to previous off-seasons. Was he a creature of different habits during the most recent one? Kasoff was still reluctant to start talking to the baseball types, assuming their tightly knit clique would quickly get the word passed to Donovan. Better a trail gone cold than one covered. So he decided to start by researching the local papers in Donovan's hometown. Perhaps they would tell him something about Donovan's winter activities. He had a week of vacation coming. Mid-May would be a good time to go.

Obtaining a Yankee media guide was easy enough, and it showed Kasoff that Donovan resided in the off-season in a little town in upstate New York named Richmondville, population 1,000. This was promising, Kasoff thought. One doesn't just blow into a town that small on a lark in midcareer. In all likelihood, Donovan had called it home for a long time; perhaps he had grown up there. And a town that size would no doubt have a small local paper that would cover nearly everything Donovan did, and it would probably be a weekly, which would speed up the research. Kasoff also noted when he checked the map, that Rich-

55

mondville was not far from Cooperstown; if Kasoff had his way, Donovan would never get there. And it was located in the middle of several "villes": Warner, Hynds, Charlotte, Portland, Gallys. All were villes. There was even a Lawyersville nearby. Kasoff would stay there.

Before booking his flight, Kasoff checked on the library facilities. "Good morning. Richmondville Public Library. May I help you?" The female voice was sweet, elderly, and Kasoff could just picture her with her bifocals and gray hair tied in a bun, no doubt finishing out her productive years as the town's local historian. *Perfect*, he thought, *a quintessential small-town librarian.*

"Hi. My name's Bob and I'll be in town next week as part of a research project on small-town papers. How far back do you maintain issues of your local newspaper?"

"Richmondville has had a weekly for more than a century, and we have every issue dating back to the twenties, though anything more than five years old is on microfiche." Better than perfect.

"And what days and hours are you open?"

"Tuesday through Saturday. We open at ten each day. We're open 'til six Tuesday through Thursday, and 'til five on the weekend. We used to be open six days, four of them until nine, but the governor cut our share of local funds and we couldn't make up the difference."

"I understand. Thank you very much, ma'am."

"Well, I'll be looking forward to meeting you, Bob. I'm Dorothy, and I've been here nearly as long as the paper."

Next, he put in a call to Greg. "Do me a favor, would you? Ask your sports guy how long Donovan's lived in Richmondville."

An hour later, the answer came back: "We've got every media guide back to his rookie year, and he lists it every time."

For the lords of baseball Donovan's contrite, if quietly contrived, statement closed the book on this tragic chapter. No action would be taken against him. All he had done was play the game, for Chrissakes. The stadium flags would be flown at half-mast, the commissioner oh so boldly ruling that this would apply to the National League as well. The Chicago players would wear their memorial patches. And the team's life insurance carrier

56

would pay McGinniss's widow a $100,000 death benefit in installments over five years. And that was it. The game goes on, after all; no one is bigger than the game. To which Kasoff would have replied, "And no one is above the law."

As April waned, the Yankees, and Donovan with them, stayed hot, winning 8 of 10 to end the month. At 20-7, they were already 5 games up in the Eastern Division—subdivision to those baseball purists who detested the Balkanization of the leagues. The Midwest was warming up, too, as the tulips bloomed and the buds of the trees began to show promise of the summer shade they would soon provide. But this was no succor to the widow McGinniss. Family and friends by now, of course, had resumed their regular routines. Though they would still call to see how she was doing, she could sense the discomfiture in the disconnected voice at the other end of the line as it struggled to change the subject when she tried to discuss what she was still going through, as if a new topic would be for her a new day.

Mary spent long hours on her couch—not reading or watching the tube but simply ruminating. The trick, she gradually realized, was to transport herself into the past long enough to summon her favorite memories but not so long that her stomach would begin to churn as she would start to long for Don. On this last day of April, as the sun shone warm into her living room, she remembered the story of his hiring at Auto Tronics.

McGinniss had shown up there right after school on the Monday following his chance meeting with Mary, his coach having excused him from practice to make the application. Sure enough, there was an opening in the shipping and receiving department. The supervisor, Jim Nagy, liked McGinniss's size—no problem for him lifting the heavier deliveries—even if he wasn't crazy about the diamond chip earring, but that was typical teenage fashion he understood. Besides, management had recently issued a directive: it was against the law—sex discrimination, apparently—to deny a job to a man with an ear adornment but not to a woman. Equal rights for women had come full circle, he concluded. Nagy also brightened when McGinniss told him he'd be playing sandlot ball that summer several nights a week. McGinniss needed to work the day shift on account of this, he pointed out. But until school was out he could only work part-time in the evenings, plus weekends, because his high school played weekday games. In spite of the schedule limitations, Nagy knew he would hire McGinniss on the spot. This earnest, innocent youth would be an asset, he was confident.

"Let me tell you a little more about our product and what your job will involve. We manufacture and sell accessories for the automotive after-market."

"After-market?"

"Yes. After you've bought your car and you want to upgrade your speakers, add a CD, cruise control, whatever, you go to an auto parts store and buy our product to install. This is our number one production facility and we ship out of here over two hundred and fifty thousand units per year. We also get returns on defective merchandise which we break down, analyze, and either repair or replace for the customer. Right now, we've got a backlog in our returns. Your job would be to open the boxes, read the customer complaints, tag the merchandise accordingly, and send it to our repairs department. You'll be working alone much of the time. The starting pay is eight dollars per hour plus medical insurance sixty days after you start full-time. What's your last day of school?"

"June third."

"Fine. You can work seven to ten P.M. week nights and eight to five Saturday until then. Are you interested?"

"Sure," replied McGinniss, betraying no hint that he was a bit unsure now that it sounded like he would have little or no contact with the employee whose beguiling manner had brought him here.

"Great. Can you start today?"

"Sure," was again the reply.

Nagy led McGinniss on a brief tour of the front offices, making the usual introductions. At one empty desk, he spotted Mary's nameplate. He didn't even know her last name but concluded this desk must be hers. *Great*, he thought, *strategically located closest to the shipping door and on the way to the men's room. Time to start drinking more coffee*, he decided. "OK, let's head through the production facility back to the shipping and receiving warehouse." Heading through the door, McGinniss was hit with an odor that seemed to be a combination of an electric motor overheating and plastic as it began to burn. It was not overpowering, but, even as a mere high school science student, he sensed it was nothing to be breathing day after day. His father, who had worked in the slaughterhouses, had always complained of the stench, which permeated his clothing so that the son never had to take the father's word for it. Success, to Don, would be working where the nose welcomed the aroma of the task. And he remembered his first trip as a kid to the ballpark, with its pleasant whiff of spring in the air, the garlic smell of the hot dogs, even the fragrant leather of his new glove. The ballpark, he knew, would be the best of all places to toil.

"Now we're heading toward our shipping area." Another door. Two truck bays, which provided better lighting than existed on the shop floor, and a work area virtually odor-free. A sign: RECEIVING. And a mountain of boxes, each no bigger than a breadbasket. UPS, FedEx, parcel post. From all over the country. And all awaiting a reply. "We had a production flaw with one of our model cruise controls. Thousands were shipped before we caught the problem. They came trickling back to us until we ordered a recall, and now you can see that a flood washed in. Hell, I'll bet some of 'em weren't even made by us.

"You'll need to break down this heap, open 'em up and sort 'em by product and by problem, and I want 'em done FIFO."

"FIFO?" Blank stare.

"First In, First Out. What else don't they teach you in high school these days?" The question being purely rhetorical, Nagy ignored McGinniss's stammering attempt to answer it. "Anyway, do it by postmark date. Unless it was shipped bulk mail. Those folks are sure to blame the government for the delay. You can use the floor space available up to the yellow lines." He pointed, and McGinniss saw he had an area of about two hundred square feet in which to sort through this pile that was twice his size and several times that distance around.

McGinniss began to attack the mountain, slowly at first, then building speed as he developed a knack for spotting the crux of the problem amid the customer's letter of complaint. A cruise control never simply failed. It gave out at a crucial moment around a bend while passing a truck. The occasional CD player mixed in didn't merely break; its sudden stoppage invariably broke up a romantic interlude.

McGinniss, anxious to get rid of this backlog, didn't check the clock until it was nearly five. Time to use the rest room. Maybe Mary was at her desk. He walked up front and spotted her, but she was engrossed in what appeared to be her own tale of woe. The pained expression on her face revealed, like a spark neglected to smolder before it bursts into flame, but a fraction of the acrimony passing over the phone wires as she strained to keep reason's tone in her voice. McGinniss gave her a sympathetic wave but kept walking, and he was careful to notice that her furrowed brow softened a bit as she recognized him. She was still on the phone when he returned from the rest room, so it was "back to the rock pile," he figured.

By 9:00 P.M.—dinner was a couple of candy bars—McGinniss had read so many letters that the complaints were old hat. The cruise controls either would not disengage or failed to engage. From Jason in Denver: ". . . cruise control would not disengage as I was descending a curve on the interstate. The extra speed could have killed me." From Juan in El Paso: ". . . would not engage as I approached hill." *Maybe*, thought McGinniss, *we should trade Juan's cruise control for Jason's, plus a CD player to be named later.*

And that was it for day one, as Mary remembered McGinniss describing it years later. Of course, she had no recollection of her distracted acknowledgment of his presence that day, though she remembered all too well the source of the conflict.

Mary was 24 at the time and had been dating Bill Emery, twenty-five, for nearly a year. He was pressuring her to move in with him, but there was no talk of marriage. He had made three false starts at college in three unrelated fields in the previous five years. Now he wanted to be a chiropractor. It was good money, he had heard, and the science wasn't that difficult. He had had a string of jobs. The common thread in leaving them, some voluntarily, others not, was his problem with authority. Friday nights he enjoyed several beers, to relax, he insisted, but they seemed to make him surly. It was her big sister, of course— Mary still referred to Melanie that way—who had pointed all this out. "Look," Melanie had said when Mary first broached the subject of moving in with Bill. "All men are either beasts or children. At all costs, stay away from the beasts."

"How can you tell the difference?"

"If you don't know by now, he's a beast. The children reveal themselves for what they are before you know it. The beasts take longer to show their true nature—sometimes not until after the honeymoon. Drop this guy. He's trouble. You're too good for him."

Mary had decided to break it off at that point, but not because of Melanie's male gender theories. Melanie could use her head when it came to Mary's love life. Mary was ruled by her heart. But this just didn't feel like true love. The phone call that McGinniss had briefly witnessed had been Bill's attempt—with all the usual emotional blackmail as Mary endured listening to the desperate gasps straight from the belly of the beast—to try to talk her out of the Dear John note she had dropped off at his home that morning. To no avail. She would never be Ms. Emery.

6

"You ever been to Detroit?" The caller hadn't introduced himself, but the voice was vaguely familiar. As Greg went through his mental Rolodex, he suddenly hit on the name.

"Donovan!" And then, to answer his question, "Not except on a layover. And, even then, I fired my travel agent. Why?"

"We'll be there for a series this weekend. Thursday is an off-day and I can meet you for lunch at noon at the Magnum One Restaurant downtown. Show the maître d' your press credentials, let him know you're on business meeting a ballplayer, and they'll set us up in a private room. No video. No recorder. No notes. And it's off the record, not for attribution, the whole shot, until I give the OK? Got it?"

"Well, I'll have to talk to my editor to clear that."

"Look, you can talk to your editor or you can talk to me. Now which is it? Time is something I don't have to waste."

"It's a deal. I'll be there."

Donovan hung up and Greg instantly circled May 2 on his calendar. Checking the flight schedule, he saw several airlines would get him to Wayne County's Metro Airport by 10:30, which would be ample time for a cab ride to the meeting that was just four days away.

"Hey, Cast-off. I bagged him. Just between you and me of course."

"Donovan sung?"

"No, but I'm meeting him Thursday in Detroit."

"That's too soon," Kasoff countered, wincing as he said it, knowing the inevitable reply.

"No such thing in my business. Why, anyway?"

"Never mind."

"But he's off-the-record, no attribution for now, so you can't say anything."

"Nothing to say. There's a world of difference between meeting and saying something. You want to get together Wednesday

62

to brainstorm this thing?"

"Lemme check. Sure. I'm doing a six P.M. story that will run taped at eleven. How about seven-thirty at your place?"

"Terrific." Kasoff knew this would require some careful planning. How to get a simp local reporter to ask some intelligent questions while appearing to be utterly incapable of trapping Donovan? Maybe it was best to just let Donovan ramble. Ask some open-ended softball questions. He might spill a few more nuggets. In any event, it would have to wait. Sharon had just handed him a note that said the South Side gang defendants were appealing their convictions.

This would usually be left to the appellate section, but the trial court had decided first to conduct an evidentiary hearing on Kasoff's use of peremptory challenges—the ones without cause, or at least where any cause was permitted except for race or gender. Of 12 such challenges, Kasoff had used 9 against black females, leaving 10 white males out of 12 to convict four of the five young African-Americans on trial. Now, as part of a motion for new trial, their defense attorneys had persuaded the chief judge to require Judge Richard Taft to do what he had refused to do during jury selection: force Kasoff to testify as to his state of mind and the real reasons that he had chosen each of the prospective jurors for exclusion.

Hell, Kasoff had tried so many cases and met so many people that this group of jurors, particularly the ones excused, were already fading memories in spite of the recency of the verdicts. He would have to check and rely upon his notes, and of course they would be scrutinized by the defense attorneys, all paid by the hour, if inadequately, Kasoff had to concede, with his tax dollars. The subpoena commanded his appearance on May 2 at 9:00 A.M.. His Wednesday night meeting with Greg would have to be brief in deference to this diversion.

*   *   *

7:30 P.M. Wednesday. Kasoff felt nearly ready for his next day's testimony. Where was Greg? Whatever his faults, tardiness wasn't one of them, not in his trade, where the talent damn well better be ready when the final countdown to air time begins. At

63

last, 20 minutes late, Greg knocked on the door, his hands cradling his explanation. "I decided to pull all the Yankee media guides and get faxes of all the past year's press clippings on him from the *New York Post*."

Kasoff, grateful, nevertheless had to chuckle—one of Greg's journalism school buddies had obviously stuck it out at least half a semester longer than Greg and made it to tabloid heaven: the biggest-circulation rag in the country. "Terrific. How long 'til you need this back?"

"Coupla weeks."

"Great."

"So, Castoff, whattaya got on Donovan? I'd sure like to catch him with his pants down."

"Nothing yet. I've been tied up—" and he motioned to the file folders that filled his kitchen table. "I'll be taking a week off later this month—if this judge doesn't keep me tied up in his court-room 'til then—and I should know more at that point. If Donovan seems willing to talk, and I know this goes against your grain, see if you can cut the conversation short as an excuse to meet again in June. By then you'll have the benefit of what I've learned."

Greg looked crestfallen, like a wounded puppy, at the delay. Kasoff quickly added, "But, hell, it oughta be safe to ask him how he managed to come back so strong this year with the bat after a beaning like that. He'll probably be happy to describe it. Beyond that, just see where he decides to take you, listen well, and see if a second meeting is possible."

Greg, consoled now, agreed. "Yeah, what the hell, he's off the record anyway. Ain't no story I can tell yet even if it's a damn con-fession."

"So, how are you going to approach him?" This was a switch: Kasoff asking Greg for his thoughts on interrogation.

"Well, I want to ask him first why he decided to talk and why now. I figured I'd just let him go on awhile, telling me what he wants to get off his chest. I don't think he'll sit there very long if I start getting accusatory, but I intend to point out to him that some people think he did it on purpose, and I'll ask him what he would say to those people."

"Find out what he did over the winter. Ask what he usually

does in the off-season. Ask this early in the interview; make it like small talk before you get to work. He's so intense a player, I hear, that he'll probably give you a blow-by-blow account of his regimen. If he tells you what happened to the bat, great, but don't ask him."

"Why not?"

"Just a hunch it will tick him off. We want him for a repeat performance. Maybe then. Find out why he won't talk for the record."

"I think he just doesn't trust reporters—"

"Good God, the man should be shot!"

"—and wants to control the process. He gave me more ground rules for this than a pregame meeting at home plate. I think— I'm sure he wants his story out there. He just wants to play editor."

"I can live with that, as long as we get his story."

"My boss can't."

"Your boss can't live with anybody," replied Kasoff, alluding to her recent third divorce, which, of course, his station never reported.

"I tell you too much."

"And too little worth knowing," teased Kasoff.

The old friends went over a few more details, and Greg mentioned that the high school reunion committee had just contacted him to request that his station announce the twentieth reunion next year. They had begun to reminisce when Kasoff pointed out it was after 9:00 P.M. Judge Taft beckoned in the morning, and Kasoff still had some work to do. Truth did not come unvarnished. Even without sanding, it required meticulous preparation. He begged off their meeting and buried himself in the file until nearly midnight.

*　　*　　*

Eight A.M. in the basement restaurant of the courthouse and Judge Taft was in his element. Opened thirty years ago along with the building the same year that His Honor was sworn in, the place hadn't changed in all that time, and neither had the judge. Now age 70, he had twice the energy of the law clerks who

65

sat with him, on half the coffee. As the best entertainment in the judicial branch, Taft always had his share of the other judges' clerks as his breakfast companions along with his sole assistant, Albert Larabie. Thumbing through the morning paper to call out 10-second editorials on headlines that caught his eye, he suddenly let out a joyful, "Hooey! Bring me some more eggs, Edna." The napkin he had carelessly placed on his lap shuddered and fell to the floor, helpless to catch the jam running through the hole in the toast he had begun wolfing down. His shirts, unlike his reputation and family background, had several generations of stains. The judge was a practical man. No need for presoaks when you've got a black robe to cover it all. And soon the crackling of sunny sides up in the making could be heard. Taft had just spotted another article on the heart hazards associated with egg consumption. At three score and ten, Taft was, like the president to whom he bore no relation, well over 300 pounds, with a cholesterol level barely more than half that.

Some lawyers swore that Taft was a judicial activist—and a liberal one. Other members of the bar were sure he was a conservative. In truth he was a virtue-crat who refused to accord due process its due when it got in the way. And a contrarian. The attorneys who knew him best would walk out of his courtroom only half-joking that His Honor was about to rule against them until their client confessed. They would raise the weakest point in their own case, the one their opponent couldn't wait to pounce on, and let Taft take the opposite position. The man just didn't have it in his constitution—including the one emblazoned on his courtroom wall—to agree with anybody. A bar journal article on trial judge affirmance statistics seemed, at first blush, to justify this bent, its table showing that his rulings were affirmed 91 percent of the time, second-highest in the state. But a closer study in a follow-up law review article revealed that he led the judicial league in being right for the wrong reason. Appellate courts were often finding fault with his reasoning but endorsing the final result on different grounds.

Once, a religious fundamentalist group financed litigation to enjoin distribution of obscene materials, claiming, as one element of the law required, that the materials violated contemporary community standards. Taft, who sat down to craft the opinion after visiting a supermarket and glancing at the check-out tabloids, thundered on his page: "Contemporary community standards? There are no standards! Anything goes! The materials plaintiffs seek to ban are no worse than the trash available to all—even the eyes of babes—to see when they buy their groceries." The fundamentalists were apoplectic. They couldn't agree with him more but were livid that he used such reasoning to deny their injunction. Taft had a good laugh with his clerk and then explained his conviction that the fundamentalists simply could not appreciate that "while we are a nation of mostly Christians, we are not a Christian nation." Taft loved confounding his enemies, and anyone who sought a favorable ruling was the enemy of the moment. And he had the last laugh. The Court of Appeals, while criticizing his reasoning as usual, ruled that the materials at issue did not meet other requisite elements of the test for obscenity, and so it affirmed His Honor.

Perhaps the answer lay in the fact that though not descended from presidential stock, he looked to the virtues of Adams and Jefferson as his touchstones. His ancestors had been Brahmins in Boston long before there was a Yankee team to hate, but his father had struck out on his own, moving to Chicago at the age of 21, back in 1898 when the Windy City was predicted by some to be the next century's New York. Taft loved to amaze his law clerks with the historical nugget that when his father was a boy in Boston there were elderly people who could remember when those two founding fathers were still alive. By his reckoning, Taft was only two degrees of separation from rubbing elbows with Washington's vice president. To Taft, technology aside, most of the country's values had gone downhill ever since. His living icon had been his father, who had remarried following his first wife's death in the Swine Flu epidemic of 1919 and had been 50 when Taft was born. And so, in his courtroom, he would rail against anything that smacked of civilization's decline, and these days, that seemed to him to be just about everything. But in his quest to uphold virtue, Taft's reach exceeded his grasp, for he often bent the rules so meticulously constructed by the founders in order to accomplish the result he wanted to reach.

At 9:00 A.M. sharp—Judge Taft was always punctual—the clerk intoned a ceremonial, "All rise." Struggling to their feet in the audience were three mothers of the boys, along with four siblings of the convicted youths, plus one grandmother of the fourth boy. The convictees sat in their prison grays at counsel table, two extra bailiffs having been brought in for the occasion. Judge Taft began: "All right, now this is a Battson hearing. In the Battson case, as I am sure counsel are aware, the Supreme Court of the United States ruled that a prosecutor cannot exercise his peremptory challenges to exclude a racial minority from the jury panel. Based on the answers of the prospective jurors in this case and the challenges made by the Prosecutor's Office, I did not believe that was occurring, and so I did not require, over the objection of the defendants, the prosecutor to state a nonracial reason for any such challenge. However, pursuant to the recently enacted statute passed by the legislature in an effort to take some of the burden off of our appellate courts, the chief judge of this court has been vested with the authority to review the trial court record for certain procedural errors and, if deemed warranted, grant a new trial or other appropriate relief. Therefore, pursuant to the order of the chief judge, an evidentiary hearing is required to explore the reasons for the People's exercise of their peremptory challenges in this case."

Fiddling with a paper clip, Kasoff was growing nervous. Taft wasn't just shooting from the hip today. He was reading his words, a measure of the care and seriousness with which he would apparently treat this matter. Who knew? Taft might even take over the cross-examination of Kasoff himself. He had been known to do that if he perceived a witness as recalcitrant against an overmatched attorney. And the lawyers in the Public Defender's Office just didn't have the funds to hire or train the top legal puppies churned out of the state's law schools each year. But Kasoff exhaled as Taft continued.

"Now, in Battson, the Court made it clear that the reason articulated by the advocate in question need not, I repeat, not be a convincing reason. It must simply be a nonracial reason."

Talk about a free pass! Kasoff, his recollection refreshed by his review of his jury selection notes, could easily explain the first seven of the nine challenges, though the last two were much more, to put it mildly, problematic. And even the plausible seven were identified in his notes—each a name inside a box with occupation and marital status—with simple abbreviations: "WM," "BM," "WF," "BF." Defense counsel would be seeing these notes for the first time, and for the first time in his career Kasoff would have to defend his right to record the race and gender composition of his jury. For the peremptory challenge had stood, until the Supreme Court's intervention, as the last sanctuary of arbitrary advocacy. In the exercise of such challenges, counsel ruled the court. The judge was not even allowed to ask the lawyer why a given juror was struck from the panel. Finally, the high court had decided that the inmates had ruled this wing of the asylum long enough. Henceforth, there would be limits on using the peremptory, and this gave judges, or so they thought, entrée into the secrets of the advocate's bias. In reality, counsel in courtrooms all across the country quickly learned, like the urban cops who stop every young black male driver after midnight, to articulate a plausible pretext for their action. It was tougher for the lawyers, of course. They had no busted taillight to point out.

"Mr. Kasoff," began Sandra Reese, "have you brought with you today all of the items covered by my subpoena?" Reese and Kasoff had opposed each other for years. Outside the courtroom doors, they were on a first-name basis. Kasoff knew that in all their battles, this would likely be the only time that one would get the chance to cross-examine the other, and damned if it wasn't his opposition that would now rev up the engine of truth.

"Yes."

"May I see it please?"

"Certainly." Kasoff sat straight and his body language spoke openness, just as he had long instructed his witnesses, as he gave his interrogator a look of angelic cooperation he did not feel. Then, with a slightly exaggerated motion of his left arm, he handed it over. He was sending the judge a signal, of course, that he had nothing to hide.

Only two documents were inside. One was the Court's computer sheet on the prospective jurors with sketchy information consisting of their names, marital status, and occupation. This record was devoid of Kasoff's markings except for a circle drawn around the number of each juror chosen to be seated in the jury box. The other consisted of Kasoff's handwritten notes.

"This is everything?"

"Yes, Ms. Reese," responded Kasoff, and to himself he added, *You know damn well that's all there is. If we had the resources for jury research or consultants in every routine gang action case in this city, there would be nothing left over for the rest of law enforcement.*

Reese didn't even bat an eye when she saw the abbreviations. She had expected as much. Lawyers on both sides did, after all, make such notes. Still, to any attorney participating in such a hearing, this information could be pivotal. "Before we get into specific questions concerning individual challenges, I would like to ask you a few general questions about your notes."

"Counsel," Judge Taft interjected.

"Just a very few," Reese tried to plead, but she was overridden as Taft continued.

"We are here to get those specific answers—to which you just alluded—to the individual challenges. Aren't you putting the cart before the horse?"

"Your Honor—" when challenged by the court always acknowledge its office before making your point—"I believe, based on a review of the document, that a general question," which concerned the abbreviations of course—"may save us some time in getting answers to the specific questions."

Well put, Kasoff had to concede to himself. *Always make the court believe that you're willing to rush through the matter even faster than the judge hopes you will, without, if possible, tipping your hand to your opponent concerning what you really want to do next.* Of course, Kasoff knew the question dealt with the race and gender notations. And Reese knew he knew but, competitor that she was, didn't want to give Kasoff any more time than absolutely necessary to ponder the precise question.

"Proceed," said the judge, still wary.

"Mr. Kasoff. Can you and I agree that this is your handwriting?"

"Of course." Only the requirement of making a proper record necessitated asking the obvious.

"Can we agree that you do not record everything said during jury selection?"

"Yes." Of course that was true. Any attorney picking a jury has to study the faces of the panel as they answer the questions,

70

has to watch with whom they make eye contact and what they say with their body language.

"Can we agree that you make it a habit as a top-notch prosecutor to record the observations that are important to you?"

Oh, that's sweet. So I'm unworthy of the compliment if I deny it, thought Kasoff. But this, too, had an easy answer. "Only to the extent it doesn't interfere with my focus at the moment. It's more important to me, to the People—" always remind the judge of the real party in interest—"to make the right decision than to record it. I rely on the trial transcript to record everything that is important." But this took things a bit too far, and Kasoff immediately realized the trap into which he had fallen.

"Oh, so you only record the most important things about your state of mind that won't be reflected in the record?" Having cast the net wide, Reese was now beginning to haul it in.

"Not necess—"

Taft interrupted. "All right, counsel. We all take notes. Sometimes we record what's important, sometimes what only seems important at the time, and sometimes we don't record what's most important because it stands out so clearly in our minds. Let's move on."

Kasoff breathed easier. He knew he had made the right decision when he chose not to have a fellow assistant DA accompany him to this hearing. Contrarian Taft would protect him as long as he did not protest too much himself.

"Can we agree that 'WF,' 'WM,' 'BF,' and 'BM' stand for 'white female,' 'white male,' 'black female,' and 'black male,' respectively?"

"Yes."

"Can we agree that you made such an entry next to each and every juror's name at or about the time each such juror was summoned into the jury box?"

"Yes."

"And that you used that information to assist you in deciding who to keep and who to kick?" You could tell that Reese was enjoying this by the fact that she had deserted the stilted legal terminology of peremptory challenges for the vernacular.

Kasoff was ready for this one. "Yes. But that doesn't mean I use the information to exclude a race or gender. The People

71

believe in diversity, and a fair balance from a cross-section of the community is an important goal of this office in maintaining respect among the public for the judicial branch in general and the DA's office in particular." Suddenly Kasoff realized that he sounded more like the DA at one of his curbside press conferences. The answer was pure PR, but it contained a kernel of truth. In some types of criminal cases, especially where both defendant and victim were black, their own racial compatriots could come down the hardest on the accused.

"Impressive. Does the DA have any statistics to support that bald assertion?"

"Hold on!" thundered Taft. "This is not an inquisition into the data at the DA's office. If your next question doesn't relate directly to this witness's race-neutral reasons, if any, for the nine challenges in issue, I'll conclude the interrogation on my own."

Reese knew that she would never get that question past Taft, but she wanted to make a record for appeal. And so she meant it when she said, "Thank you, Your Honor." And now she preserved her objection: "I'd like to request, just for the record, that any such statistics, data, or analysis be produced to us within seven—"

"Denied."

"Thank you, Your Honor."

"All right, Mr. Kasoff. Juror Number One. Why did you challenge her?"

"Her nephew had been a criminal defendant once."

"Why challenge Number Two?"

"She was a single parent with several children, as I recall. It would be too hard for her to send another single mother's kids to jail."

"There but for the grace of God . . ." replied Reese. She could concede these two herself. "Why challenge No. 3?"

"Pulled over by the police twice in the last year for no reason. It's right in my notes: 'Cops, two; x 0.'"

"Why challenge Number Four?"

"Landlord evicted her. School expelled her kid. She's not going to like any authority figure, let alone the police."

"Why Number Five?"

"Sweetest old grandmother you ever saw. Too much compassion." Kasoff was proud of this answer. Who could suspect him of a prejudicial exclusion—such an ugly phrase—if all he did was love her to death?

"How about Number Six?"

"Two younger brothers had been in a gang."

"What of Number Seven?"

"Has a grandson in prison, and she bakes him cookies." Seven down, easier than blowing out birthday candles. The preliminaries were over. Judge Taft's face told Reese she was getting nowhere. But Reese wasn't through yet, and Kasoff knew it. Two innings to go.

"And Number Eight?"

"I didn't like the way she looked at me."

"What didn't you like about her looks?"

"Not her looks. The look she gave me. It was stone-cold hostility I sensed. I never saw her look that way when you were questioning her." Kasoff knew that this was the sort of answer that a judge suspicious of his motives would look askance at, based as it was on someone's mere appearance. Still, hostility alone has nothing to do with race.

"Did you assume her hostility was based on the fact that a white male like yourself was trying to put in jail youths of her own race?"

Clever parry, thought Kasoff. *Reese is trying to tie the hostility to race while simultaneously attempting to get me to admit that I was racially biased against Number Eight because I assumed she was racially biased against me.* But before Kasoff could even begin to articulate the "C" in, "Certainly not," Taft was after Reese again. "Look, he has stated a reason. It's a race neutral reason. It doesn't have to be a convincing reason. It's enough. Move on to Number Nine."

Last inning. Toughest one coming, Kasoff knew. "And No. 9?"

Kasoff managed to inhale and then exhale slowly, so his increased tension wouldn't be evident. "As I recall, she was a heavyset woman and her breathing appeared to be that of a person suffering from early congestive heart failure. I thought she would have trouble, because of her health, sustaining herself through a potentially lengthy deliberation."

This was true. Kasoff remembered the way she had labored

73

in the courtroom. But, he had not noticed this until after he had stood up to challenge her. Too busy making the notes that had just saved him on jurors one through eight. The whole truth was, he had no clue as to a nonracial reason. His only note on her was a downward-pointing arrow. But Reese had gotten sloppy after asking the question several times. The inquiry was merely, "And Number Nine?" Now, everyone in the courtroom knew what the question meant, but it was worded so that it did not expressly ask what his reason was for challenging her. Kasoff had convinced himself in a heartbeat that the query was broad enough to encompass any observation he had made about her at any time. If Reese wished to persist, she could re-frame the question properly, in which case she would get a different answer. But that was her job. Kasoff wasn't here to volunteer his help. And hadn't he always instructed his witnesses that the number-one rule in submitting to cross-examination is to listen to the question? Answer only that question. Don't volunteer anything. Should he demand less of himself than of his witnesses? These juveniles were clearly guilty, after all.

"And when—"

Uh-oh, thought Kasoff to himself. *Here it comes.*

"Hold on, Ms. Reese," interjected the judge. "I've told you repeatedly that the Supreme Court requires only that the attorney state a race-neutral reason. He's done that. Now cease." Taft, of course, had failed to realize that Kasoff had scratched out the rear chalk line of truth while seated in the witness box. Kasoff knew how to play the game. And that was it. Reese had struck out.

"This Court," continued Taft, "finds no evidentiary basis to believe, no reasonable cause to believe, that the People exercised any peremptory challenge with intent to exclude a member of a racial minority, of either gender, in this case black females, on the basis of that race or gender. This Court therefore denies the motion of the defense for new trial on that ground. So ordered."

"Your Honor, we had wished to file a supplemental brief with this Court prior to its decision." Reese, of course, knew the effort would be futile.

"You can file whatever you want within seven days, and it will be made part of the record."

74

"Thank you, Your Honor."

It was over in barely more than an hour. Kasoff stepped down from the stand, thanked the Court, and walked out to enjoy the spring day and thoughts of vacation. As he walked briskly back to the office, the breeze told him there was much more dampness under his arms than usual after a mere hour's work.

Kasoff immediately ducked into Gorski's office and, seeing him on the phone, gave him a quick thumbs-up. B.D. nodded an "I-knew-you'd-be-OK" smile. As Kasoff was reaching his office, the cubicle nearby was abuzz with discussion of this year's office picnic, the memo having just come out informing the staff of the June 30 date. "Hey, Carol," Kasoff brightened even more than his legal victory warranted. "You remember the photos from last year's picnic?"

"Yeah?" Her tone indicated she hadn't yet sensed what he was up to, but when he turned the corner and she saw the devilish smile forming on his face, she had an idea what was coming.

"Well, I've got some bad news."

"Let's have it," she sighed, resigned to whatever punch line he was about to send her way.

"I picked out the one of you and mailed it off with an application, but I'm sorry to say you've been rejected. You will not be next year's poster child for world hunger relief."

"All right. Is that it?"

"No, you don't understand. I suggested they use your picture as the 'After' photo with a caption that would say: 'Send us your dollars and the natives can look like this again.' But they tried it out on a couple of focus groups and the response was usually something like, 'I'll be damned if I'm paying for twelve thousand calories a day!'" Zing! And Kasoff laughed that infectious laugh that even got Carol going right along with his audience. This time, his self-induced hilarity was especially satisfying, tinged as it was with relief.

"One of these days, Kasoff. One of these days."

Kasoff was still beaming as he got into his office, thinking of his imminent week off. But as his mind turned to the matter that would occupy much of his time away, he knew it wasn't yet ripe for fist-pumping.

Green heard the good news and gave Kasoff a new challenge

on the way to lunch.

"How about the all-time wildlife team? No repeats."

"OK. Jimmy Foxx at first. You sure no repeats? I'd like to put Nellie on second. There ought to be an exception for Hall of Famers."

"Fair enough for members of the Hall."

"Billy Martin at short, Kevin Bass at third. OK, let's see. Tim Salmon, Lyman Lamb, and Pete Fox in the outfield."

"That's three foxes and a nobody."

"I know; I know. Otherwise, I get rid of Billy Martin, but then I have to put Jay Partridge at short, and he was a second baseman. Catcher. How about Yogi Berra?"

"I'll give it to you."

"Ted Lyons on the mound over Bob Moose or Craig Swan."

"Not bad for a tough category. Not bad at all."

7

McGinniss's next few weeks at Auto Tronics passed without much incident. Working the rest of that spring part-time after school and on Saturdays, he made steady headway against the tide of cruise control returns, the days highlighted by his occasional opportunities to see Mary up in the front office. But he wasn't much at small talk, and he preferred brevity to awkwardness. He needed to think of something to earn this woman's smile, and she didn't seem to be smiling much these days. Her birthday! He had overheard Jean, the secretary, ask Mary when it was. "June twelfth," came the reply. A Saturday, realized McGinniss. Perfect.

That morning, McGinniss was early in line at D'Amico's. "Two garlic tomato breads, please." The plan was to get in at least ten minutes before 8:00, Mary's starting time, and place the Italian delight on her desk with a candle lit before she entered. A simple Post-it note would serve as the card. *Let's not overdo this*, he thought.

As usual, Mary was right on time. And the scheme was executed perfectly. Only the garlic aroma gave away part of the surprise as it wafted through the office upon Mary's arrival. She had just begun to ask, "Who got the garlic tomato—" when she saw the flame-topped confection. Now she broke into a smile—a broad smile as if to say, "How sweet," but then her face flickered in puzzlement at . . . who? McGinniss, who had been watching from behind a cabinet and lit up when she did, now emerged. "Happy Birthday," and he returned her smile more broadly as their eyes met and he saw her brighten.

"How did you know?"

"I heard. Hey, did you read the card?" He pointed to the note, and she read to herself. "This ticket entitles the bearer, on her birthday, to one free car wash (you know, to remove the fingerprints)."

Mary laughed, tickled at the way he chose to poke fun at her initial reticence in accepting his help.

"Thank you. You're sweet. It's my sister—she's always told me not to trust men," Mary replied, feeling the need to close out that initial chapter by letting him know it wasn't really her talking that day.

"Well, I don't know if I've done anything to earn your trust, let alone hers, but if you don't have lunch plans today, why don't we head over to Lukens'?" Suddenly insecure for having made the offer, he hastened to add "This ain't a date or nothin'. I just forgot to bring my lunch and I thought we could talk. Say, how old are you anyway?"

"Twenty-five. And you?"

"Eighteen. Today."

"You're kidding. You don't give me much time to reciprocate, do you?"

"Come to lunch and we'll call it even."

"OK. I'll see you at noon." And she smiled again.

There was plenty of work to do in the warehouse on Saturdays, but the time dragged for McGinniss all that morning, except when he went up front for a moment and saw Mary, however briefly. Her smile told him she would keep their lunch date.

The booth at Lukens' in which they were seated was in the back, and the conversation with Mary came surprisingly easy to McGinniss, even if his prospects, which he had not even begun to contemplate, weren't promising. As they talked, McGinniss learned something of the reasons for her sister's wariness. Mary had been briefly married a few years back to a guy who, from day one, her sister had been convinced was a disaster, rightly, as it turned out. On McGinniss's first day at work, Mary had just broken up with her boyfriend of more than a year. McGinniss had glimpsed her end of the "I'm not changing my mind" phone call. Her sister had nixed that guy, too.

"What was wrong with these guys—I mean, from your sister's point of view?" he asked, anxious to show that he wasn't the one jumping to the conclusion.

"My husband had a problem with commitment." This was a polite way of saying he hit on every woman he met, as Melanie would one day tell McGinniss. "Ken, my first boyfriend after my divorce, was committed all right—to cocaine. I kept trying to get him help, but my sister kept insisting that he would just pull me down the drain with him."

"And you trust your sister's instincts about men more than your own?"

"Well, her track record is better than mine. She's twenty-eight and happily married for the past five years to a guy who seems to treat her terrifically."

"And now?"

"I just started dating an engineer named Mitch. He's twenty-six. He seems nice enough. I don't know. My sister has this theory about men."

And she explained it to this young man, who now asked, "And how are you supposed to tell the difference?"

"She says the children reveal themselves for what they are long before the beasts ever show their true selves. So I guess if Mitch doesn't show up on my doorstep soon with cotton candy and a yoyo, Melanie will be banging the drums for me to leave him."

"Well, it sounds to me like your sister will take good care of you. And I hope you end up as happy as she is, because it seems to me like you deserve it."

"Thank you." And she realized, this was the first time she could remember when she had talked to a guy who seemed like he didn't have his own agenda for her. And that earned him another smile.

"You know what I find interesting about you?" he continued. *Uh-oh*, she thought to herself. *Here it comes.*

He saw the wave of concern crease her forehead. "No, no. You have no pretenses. You're just you and you're nice to people, but you don't give them a phony smile or special attention just because of who they are and—oh, I don't know; I'm babbling. But I've watched you—well, just happened to notice is all—and whether it's the boss or the janitor or the biggest customer, you're just yourself. You're so . . . so damn real."

"Thanks. No one's ever told me that except Melanie." And if Mary hadn't been so used to taking for granted what she was without seeing it in herself, she would have marveled at this teenager's insight. And they returned to the office, both silently looking forward to their next conversation.

Word traveled fast back at the warehouse. The dozen or so guys, mostly in their twenties, couldn't believe Mary had gone to lunch with this big, gangly kid. "Hey, are you hittin' on her?" teased Juan.

"Yeah, you two going out?" added Mike.

The ribbing was pretty tame—they didn't know McGinniss well yet, and they hadn't really tested him, and after all, he was a big guy, so there was none of the obscene razzing that so often went on.

"Whattaya talking about? We just went to lunch. It was our birthdays."

This only multiplied the rejoinders. "Oh, your birthdays. You gonna make more birthdays together now?" And so on with the mindless drivel that passes for wit in testosterone packs when one makes a move at a dominant female.

McGinniss simply rolled his eyes their way, though his face now did betray just a hint of enjoyment of their envy. His gesture of denial was met with disbelief. "Come on; with her body, who you kidding?"

"Hey, it ain't like that," though he had to admit to himself that she had the best one he'd never seen. But this only made him reflect that, sure, guys must hit on her all the time if she was friendly to them. That's why her smile was held in reserve, to be taken out and displayed only on deserving occasions. Her sister had probably taught her that, he figured. He would be different. He liked this woman. He would be her friend. She would never be able to say about him that he had misconstrued her smile as sexual interest when it was meant to signal nothing more than friendship.

Once school was out and McGinniss was working full-time, he began lunching with Mary on a regular basis. The guys in the warehouse were mystified. Mary had never shown any interest in getting to know any of them, but the teasing pretty much ended, and so did the offhand comments they'd make from time to time about her body, at least when McGinniss was around, for they knew where his loyalty lay.

As summer waned, the young ballplayer and the clerk-typist found themselves talking about everything under the sun, silly stuff mostly, but about their dreams, too. Though seven years older, she still thought as he did, with romantic visions of falling in love and living in a big home with fruit trees and two or three kids. One Saturday in August, a morning thunderstorm knocked out the power at Auto Tronics before 10:00 A.M. Work was canceled and McGinniss went up to the semidarkened office and suggested to Mary that they visit the Lincoln Park Zoo. Mary had seemed a bit subdued lately. He suspected that problems with the engineer might be the reason, but when he had attempted to broach the subject one recent day at lunch, she had insisted that everything was fine. McGinniss was convinced otherwise and knew the animals would be therapeutic for whatever ailed her.

She agreed, and as he drove, his eyes took in the brightening skies but failed to notice that her sunglasses were darker than usual. She didn't talk much as they stood outside the gorilla cages. The skies began to darken again, and now her eye protection seemed notably out of place. "What's with the shades?" he inquired, bringing his hand up toward them. When she flinched, he knew there was trouble. McGinniss placed his right hand gently on her shoulder and said, "Please, let me help." Then he reached with his left hand upward, slowly, slowly, as if this invasion of her privacy would be less jarring in slow motion. Removing them revealed the nasty shiner, and he immediately knew the engineer was a beast. Now McGinniss placed his right arm around her shoulders—he had never held her before—and he drew her toward him.

"Oh, Mary, no. I'm so sorry." And she buried her head in his shoulder, sobbing softly. "I'm so sorry," he repeated, "but you know you can't see him anymore."

"It's the only time he's hit me."

"And you know what that means. Like they all say, it's only the first time."

She attempted a diversion. "Come on, let's go to the Penguinarium. I really love the penguins."

"Why? Because they're content to live in a brutal environment?" And he immediately drew back from hearing his own words, knowing their sting was too strong. Before she could react, he drew her near again. "I'm sorry; I'm sorry." And she accepted his apology by nodding into his muscular chest.

Now he gently disengaged. "You want I should beat him up?" And he smiled just a little.

She returned it. "No, you're right. It's over. If I let him hit me again, I'd have to take a bigger beating from my sister."

Thank God, he said to himself. "You deserve so much better." She knew that, too, and so she would continue to search far beyond the arms of this dear friend for the right man with whom to share her life.

Now McGinniss had a problem. Mary had begun to dance about in his mind in the preceding weeks, and he didn't want her to keep looking. But he would never betray their friendship. It simply meant too much to him. And he was certain, absolutely certain, that she would never want anything more. If he told her how he felt or even asked her out, he was sure she would instinctively withdraw from him, give him the brush-off, say no to lunch. He had reached the point where his time spent with her, every moment of it, was the time to which he most looked forward. He had noticed that he would be on an adrenaline high at work and knew she was the one producing it. Now that she was sans beast, perhaps he could spend more time with her—but only as her friend. He would cherish every moment he was with her.

And so a couple of weeks later, as they were walking back to his car after lunch, he asked her, trying to be casual about it, if she minded if he stopped by for a while Friday night. Mary froze and looked at him, and in spite of his best effort at nonchalance, he could feel his teenage face warming with embarrassment, knowing he had been caught crossing the line. And what followed became the defining moment in their relationship for the next six years. She said yes—caught unawares and too nice to decline, but her face said, *Uh-oh, I think this kid's getting attracted to me, I better be careful here,* and McGinniss knew at once he had made a mistake. There was no erasing the line. He wanted to retract his words, but there was no jumping back and, anyway, the offer having been formally accepted, there was no graceful way to withdraw. Besides, this would give him the opportunity to prove to her that he could be content with nothing more than her companionship. He had to go through with it. "OK. How about seven-thirty?" he said, trying to resurrect the casual tone. She assented.

He needn't have worried. Mary arranged to have Melanie chaperone, and she was only too happy to do so. Increasingly wary of her kid sister's abysmal taste in men, Melanie concluded, in spite of Mary's protestations to the contrary, that she was interested in McGinniss and simply wanted Melanie's impression, if not her approval.

The three of them enjoyed a couple of hours of old stories, mostly about the sisters' childhoods. Family lore had it that Melanie was dominant and protective of Mary from the day she was brought home from the hospital. By the time Mary was a preschooler, Melanie was speaking for her so frequently that the younger sibling had developed a stutter.

McGinniss described his father as a physical giant of a man who went out of his way never to frighten him. It wasn't just that the senior McGinniss never hollered or froze the child out emotionally. His nurturing was much more than avoiding these twin terrors of childhood that from time immemorial have produced poison between father and son. Mr. McGinniss had been gentle when there was reason to be stern and always praised what was good instead of criticizing what wasn't. As a result, McGinniss had grown into a praiseworthy young man, secure inside himself.

McGinniss was relieved at evening's end. Mary appeared to accept that this was just a friendly get-together. She had seemed amused by his jokes, even the corny ones.

Even Melanie, always on her guard on Mary's behalf, did not dissent when, after McGinniss left, Mary assured her that she enjoyed his company because he was a nice guy, but there was nothing more to it than that. And McGinniss resolved, he would never, ever ask her out or invite himself over again. He would enjoy her friendship for what it was and accept that that was all it would ever be and, most important, embrace all that was positive about it.

One positive that was nearly as important for him that summer was his pitching. The lifting in the warehouse no doubt helped build his arm strength, but there was something more. He found a new durability in the late innings, and he had Mary to thank for it. He would find himself in a tight spot late in a game, getting two quick strikes on a hitter only to have him foul off the next several pitches and then work the count to 3-2. On a steamy night after throwing 130 pitches, mostly heat, McGinniss would be gasping for air, so dog-tired that with each step when he would finally leave the mound his lower lip would bounce up and down and he lacked the strength to hold it up. Now, on such occasions, he would walk behind the mound and summon a thought of her, and the adrenaline shot he sought would immediately kick in. He would return to the rubber and blaze a fastball for strike three. And purse his lips as he strode back to the dugout.

McGinniss needed the extra store of stamina, because he would walk more than he would strike out. So he was grateful to her, all the more so because he knew he couldn't thank her. One night, she decided, with Melanie, to attend one of his games. He spotted Mary in the stands as he took the mound and threw harder than ever that first inning. And it just happened to be the night when two radar guns were watching. The major-leagues, after years of expansion, were short on pitching, and scouts were beating the bushes for prospects with live arms. And this 18-year-old was 98 mph live that night.

At the McGinniss kitchen table two nights later, there was no dissent. Father and son were agreed that McGinniss would attend college at Northwestern as planned. He would participate in their baseball program and consider a career—whatever career—from there. The dinner guests, the two men from Kansas City who had double-checked the calibrations on their radar devices after McGinniss's recent performance, left empty-handed, ruefully aware that those guns, while precise at taking the measure of their target, were powerless to bring it down.

In the next game, the left fielder on McGinniss's team tore up his ankle sliding into home. McGinniss went to visit him in the hospital the following evening. On his way to the room, he passed the pediatric ward and heard a familiar voice reading to a child. McGinniss couldn't resist ducking his head in the room. "Mary!"

Startled, she instinctively snapped shut the book, as though she had been caught in class reading a trashy novel, and now it was her turn to try to play it casual. "Hi."

"What are you doing here?"

"Just reading to my pal Bobby." And the boy looked at her with guileless eyes, so happy to hear that the stranger of an hour ago now considered him a friend.

It didn't take long for McGinniss to size up the situation. She was a volunteer. And now he was convinced. "You're the crown jewel of the earth," he said, and there were smiles all around. But he was putting it mildly. She was too good for this planet, in his eyes.

When McGinniss returned to school in the fall, he would be working part-time in the warehouse—and no Saturdays. No more daily lunches with Mary. Their conversations would be brief. But he would get to see her smile, and that would be more than enough to sustain him.

8

"Good afternoon." And Greg introduced himself to the taut-faced, well-built man who extended his hand out of respect for social graces, a respect that did not extend to this representative of the broadcast media world.

"I'm Donovan." Greg had expected the powerful handshake from the crew-cut, unsmiling stranger. He had reserved a table back out of the way of the advertising executives and business people chatting up the latest auto sales figures and forecasts. Donovan had no inclination for small talk. "You remember my terms?"

"Sure do. I'm clean. It's your meeting, your agenda."

As soon as they sat down, Donovan began. "I don't have much time, but I don't need much to say what needs to be said, what hasn't been said."

"Shoot."

"No one, and I mean no one, has worked harder at this game the last fourteen years than I have. I've studied films of every inch of my swing, of every pitcher from every angle. I have an off-season regimen that would exhaust any other player. And I've played this game the way it was meant to be played. I wasn't handed anything. When I was coming up, you didn't get into a major-league game until you demonstrated major-league skills, aside from a September call-up for a few meaningless games when your team was out of the race. So-called natural talent didn't get you there. It had to be honed, tamed, and disciplined by so much practice that you could execute the fundamentals in your sleep.

"These days, with expansion gobbling up more and more players and all the owners spending their money on the stars, signing each other's free agents, there's no incentive to invest in a decent minor-league program. No effort to develop and retain the top coaches down there. So you get guys with talent so raw they don't know what to do with it playing the game at this level.

They can't bunt. Hell, they don't even know that on the hit-and-run the runner is supposed to look to see where the batter hits it instead of racing head-down toward second." And he slapped his weathered right palm on the edge of the table as though describing this bit of baseball arcana were a declaration of war.

"And so you end up with a kid like McGinniss, goddamned diamond chip in his ear and all, throwing fastballs all over the place like a kid shooting off an AK-forty-seven, never knowing where they'll land. I heard there would be days when he'd get pulled early after being wild and go into the clubhouse and cry. Cry to Momma for God sakes. They let a baby whiz bullets at the guys who earned their way to stand there.

"But the owners are so greedy they don't want to spend the money on the coaching expertise you need to develop a pitcher's mechanics. Hell, Chicago's own pitching coach knows less about pitching than I do. What the hell did they ever do to teach this kid control over that fastball? They could never find the flaw in his delivery, let alone tame it. So I figured it was my job. If I was going to be the one to stand in and face this guy and his wild missiles, dammit, I'd study him until I knew when the one with my name on it was coming. And by last year's play-offs, I thought I was getting damn close."

Donovan, with cool efficiency, had managed to place his order merely by pointing to the menu when the waiter approached. Now Greg followed up on the star's last comment. "How'd you do that? What's your secret?"

"You people and your damn secrets. The only secret is hard work. But that doesn't qualify as news, so you all pretend it doesn't exist. We're the only team willing to invest the R and D money necessary to compile a complete video library covering all major-league ballplayers, with a coaching staff dedicated to painstaking review and analysis of every frame. We've got zoom, stop-action, slow mo, you name it. And I study it all myself.

"Anyway, by game five of the play-offs, I stood in against McGinniss convinced that I had almost cracked the code, but aware that what I was missing could still kill me. And then, bam! He plunks me and I'm stuck on the DL during my first chance to play in the World Series. The game's most deserving player—that's just a fact—deprived of what may be my only opportunity ever to play in the Fall Classic by a kid thrower pushed by greedy owners onto a field he had no business being on.

"Now, it's a team game and so I'm supposed to be thrilled that we won the Series and all, but any pro athlete will tell you that winning doesn't mean a damn thing if he didn't participate. I may never get that close again, goddammit! Of course, none of us will admit that to all you pretty people in the so-called press holding your damn cameras in our faces all the time.

"When those dizzy spells continued after the Series, I couldn't concentrate on completing the remainder of the jigsaw puzzle that was McGinniss. I had already determined, after I awoke from the beaning, that I would figure out when the high hard one inside was coming. Hell, at least I would have some fresh video that would help, even if it was at my expense. And if I could learn enough to send him a message back, so much the better. But then, here it was mid-November and I'm wasting time shuttling back and forth to some inner ear clinic in Chicago. Then, one of you clowns, without any warning or even the courtesy of a 'hello' or 'may I?,' shoves this damn mike and camera in my face. It may have sounded like a threat against McGinniss, but it was just a tongue-lashing at all this shit. But you can't use any of this. Fans don't understand when a guy like me, making millions, complains about the game they'd all love to be playing."

"How'd you manage to come back so strong this year? Most guys who got beaned like that would hang it up, or play like they should've."

"Like they say, and like I told you. The same way you get to Carnegie Hall. There are no shortcuts in this game. Not for me, not for McGinniss, not for the owners, not for anybody."

"You know, of course, what people are saying about your reaction that was caught on tape right after the shot hit him?"

"Hell, I wasn't reacting to that." Greg just stared in bewilderment. "I was just celebrating my own return to action, to the thrill of feeling the ball meet the bat solidly, to produce that sweet sound of perfect contact. I didn't even realize how serious it was until I looked back and saw everyone running. As far as what people make of it now, they have no cause to speak. They know nothing about me. They have no idea how hard I've worked to get here and stay here, let alone stay on top of my game." And he slammed his fist on the table with all the finality he was bringing to the conversation, except, for just a moment, he softened a bit and added, "Besides, I never meant to kill him." Then, it was back to business. "Listen, I've got to run," concluded Donovan as he wolfed down the last of his spartan meal.

"But . . . why are you telling me all this if I can't use it?"

"You can't use it now. I might need you later. I'll let you know."

Remembering Kasoff's admonition to try to arrange a second meeting, Greg quickly added, "Listen. I'd like to hear more about this. You know, how the greed of the owners has caused the level of play to fall and all."

"Hell, you don't need me for that. Just watch your own sports broadcasts or pick up a newspaper sometime and check the walk–strikeout ratios, to choose just one example." And Donovan got up from the table without another word, heading off past the patrons waiting in the lobby. But Greg didn't notice. He was already scribbling in his pad. Just what had Donovan said about sending McGinniss a message?

Two nights later, Kasoff listened impassively as Greg, flipping through his hastily made notes, repeated the conversation. The seasoned prosecutor sprang to excitement only when told of Donovan's peculiar form of special delivery. The Yankee star had obviously spent all winter preparing it. "Good work. I knew that SOB was lying when he claimed he never dreamed this could happen. He planned this nightmare every step of the way."

"Slow down, Bob. The guy has a point. He says he just lost it when he spouted all that crazy talk last fall. He had a whole winter to cool off."

"He had a whole winter to prepare."

"He didn't seem very angry to me, except at the business of baseball for letting the game go downhill."

"Sure, and to him, McGinniss came to personify what was wrong with the game."

"You've been working too hard, Bob. You're seeing murder weapons where the rest of us see bats and balls."

"It's not the cards that do the cheating. It's how you use 'em."

"You're still the old Castoff, aren't you?" Greg finally conceded.

"Well, I'm off to New York. Albany to Lake Champlain and points in between."

"You ought to stop at Cooperstown."

"I went there as a kid."

"I hear they've got a prison and crime museum. Or is that a ballfield and Hall of Fame?" Greg teased.

Kasoff wasn't buying any of it. For he knew the power of the excited utterance, the expression one makes while under the stress of a sudden exciting event or immediately after. Before there has been time to fabricate or rationalize. And Donovan's excited utterance, though silent, had spoken volumes. Transmitted for all the world to see, that glow of triumph, arms uplifted immediately after McGinniss fell, mortally wounded, was burned into Kasoff's brain. Only a successful prosecution could put this fire out.

*   *   *

The nearly two-hour flight to Albany gave Kasoff precious time to reflect. There were too few opportunities to do so in spite of his daily routine of being the first one in the office each morning, for the quiet time was usually occupied by playing catch-up. Now, he considered the principals in the game's only danse macabre with bat accompaniment. The Yankee superstar, the guardian of the game and its standards, using its tools to lash out at the symbol of those who would defile it, yet betraying everything the game is supposed to stand for in the process. It was simple, too. This was just another case where the end justifies the means. If he could keep the focus there and prove malice, he just might be able to prosecute. Proof of malice would require knowing and showing what his adversary knew. Kasoff was counting on Richmondville to help point the way.

The two-lane country highway linking the Empire State's capital and the bucolic village of Donovan's home was a tourist's delight in mid-May, with colorful blossoms of every variety bursting forth along both sides of the asphalt path. But as the road meandered, Kasoff's focus remained straight ahead.

The town library was easy to find, located at the blinking light intersection that passed for downtown. It was housed in a

90

red brick building that also contained the village museum. At first glance, it appeared the structure had been nicely restored, but a closer look revealed that no such facelift had been necessary. This town treasure had been lovingly kept up year after year, decade upon decade, for well over a century as immaculately as the Victorian era homes that dotted the surrounding hillsides as if standing sentinel against the encroachment of homogenized suburbia. The marble steps just inside the door had been worn down following the pattern of generations of foot traffic. The silence inside that greeted Kasoff was not the still of the cemetery he had passed on the way in, for this repository of the town's past was a vibrant link to the descendants of that burial ground who dwelled here.

On the wall behind the temporarily vacant desk of the librarian was a plaque: TO DOROTHY OTT, RICHMONDVILLE LIBRARIAN/HISTORIAN, IN RECOGNITION AND APPRECIATION OF 50 YEARS OF DEDICATED SERVICE. It was signed by the town council and mayor and dated March 1, 1995.

"May I help you, young man?" Kasoff turned to face the elderly woman, barely five feet tall, who nonetheless somehow managed to appear to be looking down at him over her reading glasses. He instantly made a wry mental note that in recent years the folks who referred to his youthfulness were looking much older. Her smile and sincere tone told him that he was a welcome stranger.

"Yes. I called a few days ago. I was interested in looking through the back issues of your local paper."

"The *Gazette*?"

"Yes," he agreed, unfamiliar until that moment with its name.

"Well, come along. The *Gazette* serves western Schoharie County. We've got each week's issue dating back five years in these stacks here. If you want to go back further, we have microfiche in the basement." And she took his elbow and walked him along past the bust of the town's highest-ranking Civil War soldier, Col. Joseph Jackson, toward the newspaper and periodical section. Old Joe, it was said, had been up for promotion to general when a scandal had broken that involved the organizing of a futures market in Union scrip. Jackson was said to have been only tangentially involved in the wagering, if at all, but that had been enough to deny him a star.

Though Dorothy's back was bent a bit, she led Kasoff at a good pace, and he noticed she maintained a firm grip with her bony, wrinkled fingers.

The *Gazette*, Kasoff soon found, had been published each Wednesday since the 1890s. It generally ran 24 pages, half of which was advertising. There were the usual milestone announcements of births, deaths, weddings, and so forth, as well as the typical local fare that fell under the general headings of pothole repair and fish stories. Absent were any columns that debated the merits of development over preservation. That was easy even for an outsider like Kasoff to understand. There were no signs of new construction anywhere in or near the village. Absent, too, was any detailed account of the hamlet's baseball hero. Each autumn, there would be a brief mention near the bottom of the milestones column announcing that Donovan had returned home for the off-season. And that was it. No interviews with him, no keeping tabs of his progress during the season, not even his final statistical totals each year. There were a few group pictures that included him as a participant in local charitable efforts. But even in these, nowhere in the caption did his name stand out. It was simply listed along with the others. It was clear that Donovan received no special dispensation in his hometown. Perhaps a deeper look into the microfiche files would record Donovan's ascent to the majors, but whatever the record showed of events of a decade and a half ago, Kasoff figured it wouldn't do him much good.

The prosecutor didn't even realize his sigh had been audible until Dorothy reappeared. "Is there something else I can help you with?"

"I'm doing some research on Chris Donovan, the ballplayer," said Kasoff, certain she knew who he was.

"Well, what is it you're looking for?"

Even though the local paper showed no favoritism, Kasoff had to assume this charming woman, no doubt the town's number-two icon, would be protective of this hamlet's heroes as well as its heritage. At last, he answered. "How he manages to achieve his level of success year in and year out. I've read that he has a back-breaking regimen in the off-season, and I thought that since this is where he spends it, I might learn something."

Dorothy's face bespoke her curiosity for only an instant. This nice-looking stranger didn't exactly seem like a writer or journalist, but she was a firm believer in the librarian's creed that one does not inquire why another seeks to drink from any particular font of knowledge. "Well," she replied, "Mr. Donovan is a very busy man all winter and we leave him alone to his own business, but if you talk to Jake Crawford, he ought to be able to tell you something. I believe he's about the only one in town who visits with him in his off-season. And if you have any more questions after talking to Jake, feel free to come back here. I close out at five P.M., it being Saturday."

"Why, thank you, ma'am. And where would I find Jake?"

"Oh, he owns the barbershop just up the street."

"Thanks again." *Time for a haircut,* Kasoff realized as he spotted the barber pole the minute he left the library.

The shop itself was tiny. Only one barber chair but after all, there was only one barber. The shop was attached to Jake's home, and it wasn't only the barn on the home's opposite side that told Kasoff that Crawford did not do this full-time. Playing the role of his friend Pete for a moment, Kasoff ran the numbers: *If there are five hundred males in town who get their hair cut an average of ten times a year, that's five thousand haircuts, and Jake charges only five dollars per cut. Subtract his overhead, whatever it is, and he must do his share of milking cows to maintain a homestead this size.*

They exchanged greetings—no one else was in the shop—and Kasoff asked for just a trim. As he hoped, Jake was a talkative sort, and Kasoff was soon explaining that he was here doing some research on Donovan, quickly adding that Dorothy—he used her first name to buttress the impression of familiarity he wanted to make—had sent him over.

"Well, what sort of research?"

Kasoff was relying on the stranger to infer for himself that Kasoff must be a writer.

"How does he excel so year after year? How did he manage to come back so strong after the beaning?" Kasoff was counting on the fact that flattery of the local hero would open the door to the

93

secrets held by Donovan's local compatriots.

"The man's a machine, pure and simple. I've never seen anyone like him."

Kasoff smiled to himself, knowing that Jake was about to tell him everything he had never seen.

"Each fall, ever since his rookie year, he comes back after the season and buries himself on his farm. No one sees him all winter. And I mean nobody. He even has his groceries delivered and left on the front porch. Even gives himself a buzz cut, if I can permit self-interest to intrude just a moment. Hell, I'd never even see him myself once he became a big leaguer. And I've lived in this town all my life, all seventy-six years of it."

And Kasoff noticed with some dismay that Jake's scissors hand quivered just a bit. "Just a little off the top," he now interjected, with more hope than conviction, and he chuckled to himself that he now sounded like the defense attorneys pleading with him for a shorter sentence for their clients.

Jake continued. "Until one winter night about half a dozen years ago. I had to go out to the pharmacy about nine P.M. because Ma was sick, and on my way I noticed a light was on in Donovan's barn. I couldn't figure out why, so I wasn't just playing dumb when I decided to stop and walk up there. From outside all I could hear was this steady *thump, thump, thump* every five seconds. Now my curiosity was really up, so I stiffened myself and knocked, timing it so he would hear it in between those steady thumps. After a few seconds, the thumping stopped and he came to the door with a bat in his hand.

"'Excuse me, Chris'—I knew his daddy, so I figure he's still just Chris to me—'are you all right in there?' His face softened to a sheepish grin and he said, 'Sure, I'll show you.' And he opened the door for me to enter. There, inside this old barn, he had set up a high-tech batting cage. The thumping was the baseball hitting the padding. He had two video screens, one that displayed his swing from all different angles and one that showed which opposing pitcher he wanted to study. I told him I didn't realize he was so busy and was about to be on my way—after all, my wife wanted her pills—but he just felt like talking that night, I guess. He would swing that bat for hours at a time, he explained, interrupted only by viewing and reviewing the videos.

94

"Each fall, UPS would bring him a big box full of the tapes from the Yankee offices, forty in all. Each one containing two hours of tape on one opposing pitcher. He would have twenty off-season weeks to work, two tapes a week. Anyway, he must have enjoyed the company, because he invited me back to see his routine. I'd go, too, two or three times a year. After a couple of hours, I'd get weary just watching. He'd play a small section of the pitcher's tape, then watch the tape of his own swing, and then fire up his pitching machine. He even had it rigged up to throw curves and split-fingers. And he'd swing that bat until his calluses came off.

"It got to where I knew what day each year the UPS truck was coming, and, sure enough, I'd see it pull up to Donovan's home every October fourth—the Yankees never made the play-offs in those years. Last winter, of course, was different. The Yankees got into postseason play, and then Donovan got beaned. The UPS man didn't show until the first of December. I didn't see him, but I received a delivery myself two weeks later—home-made Christmas fruitcake from my daughter in Buffalo—and I talked to the driver, Joe Young. His father used to teach at the area high school. I mentioned to him that that Chicago fellow, McGinniss—boy, wasn't that a tragedy—had thrown off Joe's schedule. He laughed and said, 'Yeah, and that's not all.' I asked him what he was talking about, and Joe just said, 'This year, I delivered to Donovan only one tape.'"

Kasoff's head suddenly bolted upright, and the scissors grazed his scalp. "Whoa, young man. Hold still now."

After they reset themselves, Jake continued. "Anyway, I came around to Donovan's barn just like I'd done in past winters to watch him, but this time when I knocked, he told me that he was sorry but that he wouldn't have time for any distractions this winter. I just figured he needed to make up for the lost time, so I apologized and excused myself.

"Now, I'm an early riser and a sound sleeper. You could parade elephants down Main Street after ten P.M. and I'd never know it but for the peanut shells. But Bob, my neighbor, is a night owl, and he tells me that the light in Donovan's barn burned each night all last winter 'til well after midnight, a good two or three hours later than ever before. So I figure that's the answer to your questions."

"What questions?" replied Kasoff, so caught up in the revealing pictures he imagined on the single videotape that he had forgotten just what he had inquired.

"That's how he's so successful and how he came back so strong. He just outworks everyone."

"I don't suppose you know what was on that video?"

"No, but it sure must have helped."

More than you know, thought Kasoff, certain now just what and who Donovan had been studying all winter.

"Funny thing, though."

"What's that?"

"When I looked in on him that time he told me he was too busy for me, he hadn't been working on any of his usual drills."

"What do you mean?"

"Well, he was just standing there with a bat in his hands, like in midswing. And then he would roll the bat forward and backward touching each shoulder as it would complete the arc. But fast. He must have done it a dozen times in the five seconds or so that I watched before knocking."

"Hmm." Kasoff would make a mental note to find out the purpose of this drill.

Jake dusted off his customer, removed the sheet, and asked where the stranger was headed.

"I thought I'd see Dorothy one more time before I leave." Perhaps the town historian could reveal something about the invention of this machine. "'Crawford.' Is that spelled the way it usually is?"

Jake smiled, assuming this young man felt that to call someone a friend, you first had to have his name right. "Sure is." But Kasoff just wanted to be certain that he would have the spelling correct on the trial subpoena.

Upon Kasoff's leaving the barber, the sign that said: LINDSTROM'S LUNCHEONETTE beckoned. For all his hopes of an eventual prosecution, the protests of his stomach told him he was far from trial. Battling in the courtroom had a way of keeping sanguine the beast of hunger. The organs of digestion were content at such times to limit their gnawing to his insides. Now, having consumed nothing more than a package of airline peanuts—even if they were fresher than the ballpark variety—since a 6:00 A.M. bowl of cereal, Kasoff picked up his pace as he made a beeline for the door of this oasis.

Once inside, Kasoff took a stool at the counter. The diner had only nine tables, most of them occupied in spite of the midafternoon hour—a good sign, Kasoff thought. Overhead, two ceiling fans whirred lazily, helpless to fend off either the growing warmth of the afternoon or the home-cooked aromas escaping the kitchen.

As Kasoff reached for a menu that was stashed between the napkin holder and the sugar bowl, one of the town's older residents entered and sat down beside him. Short and slim, dressed in blue jeans with red suspenders clinging to his white cotton pullover shirt, the stranger removed his cap—was that a Boston Braves insignia on the front?—turned to the lawyer, and smiled.

"Howdy. Name's Robert. Robert Maranville. Where you from?" The welcoming voice was both gentle and humble.

Kasoff, who had already adjusted to small town mores—these people actually appreciated strangers!—smiled, and the two exchanged pleasantries.

"What can I get you two?" Kasoff immediately sensed a dissonance between the sweet, mellow voice of the waitress and her dyed blond hair, coupled with a bit too much makeup applied in a vain attempt to conceal the pockmarks of an adolescence that, aside from its pain, seemed too long ago.

"What's good here, Robert?" Kasoff inquired.

"It's all good. All homemade. Right, Martha?"

Martha Gehrig, a hometown product herself and who hadn't missed a day's work in her 10 years at this lunch counter, beamed. "The best."

"Too bad you didn't get here while they were serving breakfast. The buttermilk pancakes are made from scratch—none of them mixes—they're just unbeatable. Right, Martha?" as though he needed any confirmation. Kasoff ordered a tuna—hold the mayo—on whole wheat and a baked potato dry "and a piece of that apple pie," as he pointed to the scrumptious-looking item that had first caught his eye upon entry.

The stranger asked the usual questions that Kasoff anticipated. Upon hearing that Kasoff was researching Donovan's life,

97

Maranville uttered a low whistle. "Only one thing you need to know."

"What's that?" Kasoff brightened with interest.

"The most singleminded individual I've ever encountered. Not that I've known him particularly well. But if he determines to do something—"

"Watch out," Kasoff interjected, expecting this warning.

"His will be done," rejoined the stranger.

"So I've gathered. But how do you know?"

"I don't, but that's his reputation around these parts. And I imagine with the Yankees as well."

Kasoff, disappointed that the stranger harbored no special secrets on his quarry, was now distractable and couldn't help but notice the sullenness of a second waitress, young and otherwise attractive, as she left the check at a nearby table. *She must really be nasty*, he thought to himself, *if she behaves like that at tip time*. Kasoff's disdain for her must have been ill-concealed, because Maranville suddenly said to him, "That's Lois. Lois Kiner. Four months ago, her sister's three-year-old boy fell through the ice and drowned in Hornsby Creek. Hasn't been the same since."

"An explanation is not an excuse. Her customers didn't drown him."

"You're a hard man, Mr. Kasoff. Big city do that to you?"

"People aren't shaped like clay by their environment. They have the free will to form and re-form themselves, and all the excuses in the world are just cop-outs."

"I disagree with you." The stranger's eyes now seemed saddened. "You'll never understand people if you refuse to see the crosses they bear."

Kasoff made no reply and the stranger didn't press the point. They each ate their meals in silence. Kasoff had to admit that the meal was terrific, though it never occurred to him that the stranger could be right about more than just the fare.

"I don't know Mr. Donovan very well, but of course I was well acquainted with his parents, more so his mother." Dorothy's voice wanted to help, but her body language told Kasoff that she had plenty to keep her occupied in the hour before closing. "Say, young man—"

"Bob, Bob Kasoff," he replied, providing her the name she could place on the invitation he anticipated she was about to extend.

"Bob, are you going to be in town tomorrow?"

"Sure." Kasoff had no plans to be anywhere tomorrow.

"Well, Velma Sisler had planned to come over and help me plant the spring flowers, but she threw her back out pruning her evergreens the other day. If you'll take her place, I'll answer your questions as best I can. How's that sound?"

Kasoff pictured himself following around a sweet old lady pointing to every vacant spot on her property for him to dig. From his Chicago apartment the only flowers he saw grew in pots in the windows of the building across the street. Still, it was a fair price to pay, even if the town was too small to support the chiropractor his back would be aching for just 24 hours from now. "Great," he replied in a tone that suggested he had just agreed to let her order his favorite deep-dish pizza with the one topping he could not abide. "We won't be planting any green peppers now, will we?" Kasoff smiled, revealing the detested item.

"Just begonias," and she allowed herself a smile that presaged her pleasure at the company as well as the task. "Ten o'clock OK?"

"Sure," he concurred.

*   *   *

Dorothy organized her garden no less meticulously than the town's literary treasures over which she was guardian. "OK, I've got twelve dozen to plant. Two of them red, ten white, and we'll put them on that mound over there." Kasoff surveyed the hill that sloped down toward the road's oncoming traffic. Nearly fifty yards from the house, it seemed an odd location in which to place these smiles of summer, but sure enough, the center of this spot, a round area 20 feet in diameter, had been cleared of weeds and stones, its dark earth beckoning.

"You start with these and I'll handle the white ones. Plant them in two separate rows, semicircles, turning away from each other, like a smile and a frown, about four feet apart at their closest points." As Kasoff began digging, the historian started to reveal what lay underneath Donovan's character.

"Chris's father, Roy, was a military man. Landed in Normandy on D day. Must have seen a lot of men die. He didn't smile much before he went off to war, never saw him smile after. But his father, Chris's grandfather, was like that, too. He'd made the army a career. Both were silent, stoic men—or emotional cripples depending on your point of view. Roy raised Donovan military-style. Everything was order and efficiency. He lived the proverb that lost time is never found again, and drilled it into his son. Once, when Chris was four years old, Roy found him playing with matches behind the barn. Instead of scolding him about the dangers of fire, he punished him for idling away his time.

"Donovan, the typical firstborn dutiful son, learned his father's lessons well. By the time he was in high school, he had his own disciplined routines to maximize his efficiency. He was doing well in all his classes, working after school, and devoting every spare minute to hitting baseballs. His father thought that was really a waste of time—he wanted Chris to be an engineer, as you might expect—until his coach came over to talk to Roy one night. Told him Chris had the most efficient swing he'd ever seen and he could do great things with it. *Efficiency.* That was the word Roy needed to hear.

"Chris's mother, Sally, was another story entirely. The only way to explain it was the cliché that opposites attract. She was light and lively, and laughed all the time. She had been raised to believe that the man was the boss, but after Chris was born in '63, why, he seemed like such a serious little boy, she couldn't help but assert herself with him in little ways. So by the late sixties, when Roy was starting to tell Chris tales of military duty and derring-do, Sally had already been singing Chris to sleep with songs like 'Where Have All the Flowers Gone' and 'Blowin' in the Wind.' She never directly challenged her husband on his way of raising Chris, but she was determined to show her boy another way. She knew, though, by the time Chris was five years old, that he was his father's child.

"And then she got sick. Mercy, she was only forty-two. It was that awful year, 1968, when you never knew what you'd see when you turned on the TV, what with the assassinations and riots, and everything just seemed to be going to hell, pardon my language. And Sally was going to Sloan-Kettering in New York three times a week for radiation. She knew then that she would never see her boy grow up. And she feared, Lord how she feared, what her son would miss out on if she wasn't there to show him the laughter, the gentle side of life. And she was also terrified of what the world was becoming—all the violence and all—and so she resolved to leave him a legacy.

"With each trip to the cancer center, she would first direct whoever was with her, often it was Roy, but he couldn't always make it, and I'm not sure he could always take it, either, to stop at one of the networks in Manhattan where an old friend of hers had gone to work. And piece by piece, with her friend's help, she made a home movie—this was before there were VCRs, remember—to leave to Chris. One day near the end she told me about it. The movie was nearly three hours long. One section of it was simply herself on film talking to her son as if on each birthday until he was eighteen. 'OK, now that you're turning twelve...' And so on each year, each one a few minutes that she had thought about for days, rehearsed, and tried to make every bit as precious as her own days were numbered. And spliced in between her messages of advice were recent news events—I guess that's why she needed the help of her network friend—but not just any events. She had become a great believer in the teachings of Martin Luther King: turning the other cheek, the nonviolent response to violence, professing love for one's adversary. She had tried once to explain to her husband how much white folks owed Dr. King, but he didn't seem to understand. And so she knew that she would have to find a way to reach her son herself if he was ever going to learn that lesson. And after King's death when all the violence multiplied, she was afraid no one would even remember his philosophy. So she had her network friend splice in snippets of his speeches, and the demonstrations, the passive resistance where his followers would be hosed and clubbed and attacked by dogs but refused to fight back. And she finished it just a week before she died in 1970. On Chris' seventh birthday. Talk about a child feeling abandoned. But I was at her funeral and he never cried. He stood and looked up at his father, who maintained that stony bearing, and did just what his father did.

"But, so far as I know, Chris never saw his father the way I saw him one night."

"What'd you see?" Kasoff was about to plant his last red begonia.

"My dog got loose one evening. I went to look for him, having no idea where he was. And here, it's so quiet late at night that all I have do is step outside and listen. So he must have been contentedly lying somewhere. It was cold, the middle of November as I recall, and several months after Sally's funeral. I walked past the cemetery—she's buried near the road—and everything is so silent that I'm trying my best to walk softly because each crunching sound of the gravel underfoot seems so magnified, like a trespass on the tranquillity. Anyway, then I abruptly hear a low wailing sound—like an injured puppy. Well, I knew it wasn't my dog. But of course I looked around. At first it was too dark to see, but the clouds that were obscuring the moon parted for only a moment, just as I happened to glance in the direction of her grave. It was an old habit with me, unconscious, really, still is, like you simply can't believe it's true until you see her tombstone, and then you believe it all over again, until the next time.

"Anyway, what I saw sent shivers down my spine. There, in the moonlight, not fifteen yards from me but a world away, was Roy, on his hands and knees on her grave and crying his eyes out. No one had ever seen that man show any emotion. I felt—no, I knew—I was invading his privacy, so I just started slowly backing up right in my tracks, the way you would if you saw a bear with cubs. And I cried myself that night, for him, for her, for their child, it was just so awful. But by the next morning, I was angry. Here was Roy, sneaking out of the house late at night, as though he was ashamed of himself, just to do what he should have done out in the open with his son, for his son, so Chris could cry, too. God knows he needed to. They both should have cried to high heaven, and proudly, too. You take a look at Chris's school pictures. Kindergarten and first grade, he shows that wide smile of innocence. Then look at his photos from later years. You never see a smile after that." The small pond is helpless against the winter that overwhelms too soon. Frozen over prematurely, its teeming life is trapped below. "And for what?" she continued. "Because his father was too proud to cry in front of his child as his wife is being buried. Let me tell you something, young man. Ninety-five percent of all pride is foolish. It keeps people apart. It keeps nations divided."

"And the other five percent?"

"Dangerous. Scratch at that last fraction and God knows what kind of an explosion will result." And Kasoff nodded, knowing that Donovan's elite status placed him in that top percentile.

Kasoff took a deep breath. He had begun helping Dorothy with the white flowers.

"And the movie she made. What happened to it?"

"She made two copies. One she gave to Roy, of course, for Chris. The other she left with me in case something happened to the original. When Chris was seventeen and at the library for a school project, I asked him if he had watched it, after I gently told him how much I had liked his mother and how she had told me about making it. He showed no emotion and just said he couldn't understand why his mother left him a film about old riot scenes. That's what he called it, riot scenes. He just didn't understand. Yes, he was his father's child. All order and discipline and stoicism. And one more soul who never learned to turn the other cheek. It's just so sad." And now this repository of town memory took a tissue from her pocket and dabbed her eyes.

"Yes, it is, ma'am." And after a respectful pause, Kasoff continued. "By the way, that school project Donovan was working on in high school, what was it?"

"I don't remember exactly, something to do with physics, though. It was his best subject."

Physics! So Donovan did understand something about force and mass and acceleration and bodies in motion. And enough to render one motionless, no doubt.

And Kasoff realized something more important as well. Donovan had not been some abused or neglected child, impervious to empathy and decency from lack of love. No, he had been shown the nurturing so necessary to give him the ability to choose good over evil. He had won the parental as well as the biological lottery yet had chosen to exercise his free will in a vile pursuit.

Now the roots of the final begonia were firmly grounded. "All right, now let's see what we've planted, young man." And

Dorothy took him by the arm, leading him to a nearby hill a bit closer to the road to look down on their work. Immediately, Kasoff was struck by the familiar pattern. The circle of white begonias was split by his two red semi-circles. They were the stitching. She had sculpted a giant baseball. Now she removed winter's cover from the sign nearby, and it read: WELCOME TO RICHMONDVILLE. GATEWAY TO COOPERSTOWN.

"Why so surprised?" Dorothy smiled sweetly at Kasoff, who appeared dumbfounded by the garden variety welcome mat.

"It's just—" He shook his head in wonder. "It's just that you seemed so unaffected by it all. You know, Donovan's celebrity as a star right in the Hall of Fame's backyard. Not only you, but the whole town. Your newspaper studiously ignores his fame. You don't see—"

"What, a statue in the town square, for heaven's sakes?" she replied, laughing.

Kasoff chuckled to himself. "It's just that, frankly, these days it's refreshing to see a place where the people haven't been initiated into the cult of celebrity. Of course, I'm sure that, this being a small town, with everyone knowing him all his life, he's just one of you and you let him keep his privacy here."

Dorothy paused a moment, looked up, seemingly beyond Kasoff, and began a deliberate reply. "That's part of it, but only a part. For us, it's not the individual players we honor; it's not even just the game itself, though it is a great game—greatest one ever invented. No, what we revere are the character traits exemplified by excellence at the game. Humility, for example. The very best fail six or seven times out of ten. To come back and succeed after all those failures requires a certain serenity in battle. Perseverance—you see it every time a pitcher and a base stealer duel over one pickoff attempt after another. Teamwork—as when you see the hit-and-run perfectly executed. Practice making perfect. Determination. The game is like magic. Between the white lines, it has the power to transform even the nastiest characters into practitioners of these virtues, or they'll fail at the game. It's like the ballpark is a church. As long as the people are inside participating, the sinners are cleansed by the virtues that surround. The problems occur when mass is over. So the same pitcher who wins thirty games is guilty of stealing from his business associ-

104

ates. And that's why we consider the game holy, but not the people who play it. As we look at it, the Hall of Fame is really about the game, commemorating its greatest triumphs. The names attached to those performances don't really matter. Too many of them didn't amount to much after their bodies betrayed them and they retired. So while we respect Donovan's records, we don't consider him any more worthy of attention than the local postmaster. Does that make any sense to you?"

"It sure does. It sure does. By the way, do you still have your copy of the film?"

"I'm sure I have it stored somewhere in my attic."

Kasoff noticed that Dorothy's tone had changed, as if suddenly she's grown protective. Still, he couldn't resist asking. "I don't suppose I might have an opportunity to take a look at it?"

The veil had descended. "Well, I don't know. I feel like the film was entrusted to me as a Donovan family matter. Where'd you say you were from?"

Kasoff hadn't, and he didn't have the heart to mislead any longer this dear woman who had been so open with him, though he couldn't bring himself to reveal his interest.

"That's OK. I understand completely. You've been most kind."

*   *   *

From Richmondville, it was time to head north past Fort Ticonderoga to the eastern shore of Lake Champlain. Here, in Burlington, Vermont, Kasoff would visit an old college friend, Lisa Ottinger, and her husband, Richard. Lisa had received an MBA from NYU and had gone on to become an investment banker in New York. But after her first million-dollar bonus earned before her thirtieth birthday to close out the go-go eighties, she perceived an emptiness in her spiritual coffers, and so she had junked the baser confines of the material world for the green of this portion of New England. It wasn't Kasoff's cup of tea, but he admired her for it.

Lisa had met an artist at Stowe a few years back—no starving one, he—and they now shared a comfortable life in a chalet on the lake. Lisa's entrepreneurial instincts hadn't deserted her entirely. She had opened up a combination flower shop and used bookstore. "That's right," she explained to Kasoff, "a sort of 'gather ye rosebuds while ye browse.'" In any event, with her marketing and managerial skills, it had found a solid niche in this college and artists' community, which had no shortage of still-lifes, romance, and required reading. Lisa's husband, meanwhile, spent his days sketching his beloved lake from every conceivable angle. Champlain was a landscape for all seasons.

"Anyway, it was great to get the call you'd be coming, Bob. Thanks to a good manager, I can even take a couple of days off."

"You? Hell, you were the only person I knew who worked harder than I did."

"I still do. But the most rewarding work needn't always be measured in dollars."

The first evening of their reunion would end early. Richard wanted to be up well before sunrise to drive to the northeast corner of the lake. "Sometimes at that hour," Lisa explained, "if we're lucky, we'll see a moose wading just offshore. The trick is to get our rowboat into the water just after first light, but before the sun is high enough to start casting shadows. Richard is hoping to spot and sketch both a bull and a cow this summer."

"What are the chances you'll see one or the other?"

"Oh, about one in a hundred when you consider how few moose are left around these parts. Most of 'em are up in Maine. They do like the freshwater lakes and ponds, though, as long as there's no development around. Are you game for getting up at three-thirty A.M.?"

"Three-thirty?"

"Sun rises early here this time of year. What do you say?"

"I'm game for seeing a moose. It's worth a shot."

"Great. There's an alarm in the spare bedroom. We'll be leaving around four-fifteen. Good night."

The forty minute drive to Saint Alban's Bay had them out on the water by 5:00 A.M. The eastern sky was just coming alive with what promised to be a brilliant sunrise. Lisa and Kasoff took turns rowing—slowly—as Richard began work. They maintained a path parallel to the meandering shore, about thirty to forty yards away, close enough to permit a good view of any creature spotted at shoreline yet sufficiently distant to avoid spooking the animal. Conversation was sparse and kept at barely above a whisper as the search party strained to scan the shore in the emerging light. This particular stretch of land was state park, and forested nearly to the water, separated from it only by a slim stony beach.

Suddenly Kasoff pointed and cried, in a voice whose volume he struggled to stifle, "Look, there's one!"

"Where?" "Where?" were the excited replies in unison.

And then, from Lisa, "Oh, that's just a tree stump." And she giggled softly.

"No. Are you sure?" And then, as the vessel drew a bit closer, "I guess you're right."

Not five minutes later, Richard's setting-up work was interrupted again: "There's one. I'm sure of it." This time, it was only the rocking of the boat that restrained Kasoff from standing straight up.

"There you go again, Bob, always jumping to delusions. Those antlers are branches."

Twice more in dawn's fleeting hour Kasoff insisted he had seen the elusive ungulate, only to be proven wrong by more objective eyes. Richard just shook his head. He'd seen it all before in visitors who viewed this country through city-slicked glasses. It took patience to enjoy an encounter with one of these beasts, a trait that had long since been bred out of America's urban dwellers. But even granting this, Kasoff was exceptional. For a bright guy, he seemed to revel in his ignorance, persistent in his refusal to learn this lesson out here, in spite of nature's cooperation in furnishing such a picturesque setting for a class-room. Or was he just a stubborn SOB? Richard knew he might navigate this stretch of the lake for months before catching a glimpse of a bull moose. For him, that would be time enough. Meanwhile, today he would create yet another sketch of this fabled body of water.

Kasoff spent another night and day with Lisa and Richard. He enjoyed the reminiscing but said his good-byes with a tinge of regret—not for what he had missed but for what he hadn't. He had realized that he now had little in common with Lisa except the past—and evoking the memories of those days did not reinvigorate the feelings of their old friendship. Fifteen years ago, they had been close enough that several of their mutual friends were convinced it was only a matter of time before the relationship became romantic. Both knew that wouldn't happen of course, but back then they couldn't wait to share with each other the day's news, personal or otherwise.

"Let's do this again sometime," she said to him just as he turned to leave.

"OK," he replied, doubting he ever would.

Now it was Wednesday afternoon and time for the five-hour drive south to New York. As he scanned the radio dial, a Yankee game suddenly came in, straight from the Bronx. Must be a getaway day for the visiting Texas ballclub. Otherwise, it'd be a night game. Kasoff was unacquainted with the play-by-play announcer, but his descriptions of the contest were as familiar as the billboards he was passing with their overbearing presence dotting the highway landscapes all across the country.

The count was 2-2 on the Yankee's number-nine batter, their light-hitting second baseman, and he had now fouled off three consecutive pitches. *Don't say it,* Kasoff thought, though he knew what was coming. "Ball three," intoned the announcer, with a gravity out of sync with the early inning being played.

"Oh, no, I know he's gonna say it now. Please don't," Kasoff pleaded out loud.

"And another foul ball."

"Oh, for sure it's coming. I just know it. Go ahead; get it over with."

"And what a great at-bat this has been for the Yankee's second sacker."

"He said it. I knew it. He just had to say it." Kasoff marveled with disdain at this recent spin on the game's Achilles' heel. The absurdity of the great at-bat. The action took too long to develop, especially for the attention span of the younger generation. Now, in a PR ploy that Barnum would have loved, a hitter who spends, not to say squanders, several minutes wasting good pitches while going deep in the count has had a great at-bat, no matter if he pops up after all that. Apparently the game was now placing a premium on futility deferred. *Funny,* thought Kasoff, *there's no shrine to such plate appearances in Cooperstown. Yet the way these new-style play-by-play guys get excited over 'em, you'd think they were planning a new wing at the Hall.*

108

Kasoff would spend Thursday afternoon at the Museum of Modern Art—and conclude that the twentieth-century world of painting, like the game he grew up loving that had since betrayed him, couldn't compare with the departed masters of the past. Who would trade DaVinci and Rembrandt for Pollock and Warhol? Even the second tier of Renaissance stars shone brighter than modern artists. Where have you gone, Caravaggio? Except Mondrian. There was something about those taut black lines and bright colors. The reds and greens all knew their places, never spilling over those solid borders. You knew exactly where you stood with Mondrian.

On Thursday night, he would take in a Yankee game, to see the target of his wrath perform within the storied confines. Minnesota furnished the opposition, and their weak pitching staff—the typical by-product of today's small-market team—was no match for the Bronx bombers this evening. Before the fifth inning was history, Donovan had batted four times and scored on each occasion via two home runs, a double, and an intentional walk that backfired when the cleanup hitter lived up to his label. The Yankees led 12–2 in a game that was averaging nearly half an hour per inning. With an early flight back home in the morning, it was time for Kasoff to get back to his hotel. Donovan had taken his turn at impressing the prosecutor with the skills of his craft. Eventually, Kasoff promised, he would reciprocate.

9

McGinniss broadened his horizons in his first semester at North-western, but not as he had planned. Meeting new people had convinced him: Mary wasn't just one in a million. She was the one and only. He couldn't exactly point to a specific moment when he realized it, but by that Christmas he knew he was hope-lessly in love with her. And the operative word, he knew, was *hopeless*. At first, he cursed his fate. This wasn't a 13-year-old's puppy love that fades as surely as the hound grows up. This was overwhelming; this was forever. Eventually, Don would come to appreciate that if this was to be a lifetime curse, he could imag-ine far worse afflictions than to be saddled with utterly raptur-ous feelings for another human being. But at the age of 18 he was too much of a prisoner of his newly overpowering emotions to tame them with sweet reason.

And he found himself full of adrenaline whenever he knew he would be seeing her at Auto Tronics. The weather turned cold, but he didn't even wear a jacket to work, he was so hyped. Though he had less time to spend with her now, their conversa-tions came easier than ever. McGinniss had feared the zoo inci-dent would put her off, but the moment seemed to have brought them closer; she seemed more willing to confide in him than ever before. Wasn't he always underestimating just how extraordi-nary she was?

Over Christmas break, he would work full-time and thereby get more opportunities with her to catch up. On his first full day at work after exams, McGinniss spotted Mary at her desk and noticed she seemed to be humming a merry tune to herself. "You're chipper this morning," and he gave her a broad smile, which she returned.

"Yeah."

"Lunch, later?"

"Sure."

And when it came time to eat, she revealed the reason for her happy glow. She had finally met the right guy, she confided. He was sweet and he was good to her, and she was not even dimly aware as she went on that McGinniss had fallen so hard that now his heart was on the floor as he fought to maintain the frozen smile on his face, nodding and repeating like a mantra, "I'm happy for you; you deserve it; great."

And wasn't it true? If he couldn't be happy for her and want for her what she wanted, he wasn't even worthy of her friendship. That wasn't love, of course, just selfishness. And so he resolved that the big part of him that treasured her companionship was happy for her, even if his roaring emotions cried out in anguish.

Mary allowed that her sister wasn't yet convinced that Victor was deserving of her, but Melanie was always overprotective. "I'm her kid sister and all, you know." Still, up until this point, Don had occasionally allowed himself to entertain the slightest hope, fantasy really, that maybe, if she didn't find the right guy in the next ten years or so, she would be willing to settle. He had figured all along, of course, that the odds of this were astronomical—she was too nice and attractive for no one else to notice. But now he would have to learn firsthand that false hope is indeed more painful than despair, that only the former is hope's true opposite.

McGinniss wouldn't ask too much about him. If Mary wanted to tell him, fine. No point being too inquisitive and risk having her think he was jealous.

And so he willed himself to enjoy these two holiday weeks off school when he would get to spend each lunch hour with her, discussing things large and small while saying silly things to keep her smiling as he gazed into those gorgeous green windows to her soul. And if inner beauty was possessed of speed, light itself would lag behind her.

And she rewarded him. On his last day before returning to school, as they waited for the check to arrive, she reached across the table, put her hand on his forearm, and said, "You've always been able to make me laugh. And from the start, I've always felt very comfortable with you. I'll never forget our friendship." He was touched, of course, but concerned, too. Was she quitting Auto Tronics or, worse, moving away? Was this a requiem or just an expression of appreciation?

"Sounds like a eulogy. I'm only departing for school. Are you going anywhere I should know about?" He tried to convey his concern without betraying it, but he could feel his facial expression revealing more than his lighthearted tone.

"No. Of course not. I just don't believe we should wait until the funeral to tell people how we feel about them." Once again, he had underestimated her. And he knew he would never forget her.

Back at school, McGinniss plunged into a rigorous routine. Calesthenics and a four-mile run each morning. A full schedule of classes followed by indoor baseball practice.

Evenings were studying and pick-up basketball. He enjoyed hoops, but each night as he walked off the court toward the locker room and the adrenaline drained away, the vacuum would be filled by an overwhelming longing to be with Mary, to hear her voice and see her smile, or even just watch her roll her eyes if his attempt at humor was hopeless. And the dejection followed him on his ride home, lodging in the pit of his stomach as he would crawl into bed. On those nights, he would lie on his back staring straight up into the blackness, careful not to blink or tilt his head. For at such times, if he could prevent the tears that welled up from spilling out over the borders of his eyelids, he could pretend to himself that he never cried over her. Survival on the salt of self-delusion.

Sleep usually brought relief, except when he would awaken in the middle of the night with the recurring dream—nightmare really—that he would have about her. Once or twice a month, she would appear in his sleep, desperately trying to verbalize an excuse to leave his company, and she would have a discomfited look on her face, as though she couldn't wait to escape. On those nights, he would toss and turn until dawn, and only his morning run would bring him out of the doldrums. Only later would he come to appreciate that the one thing missing from those dreams of her would, after all, render him worthy of her friendship.

*   *   *

No malice, no murder. The words his esteemed criminal law

professor had pounded into his brain now reasserted themselves, as if to taunt Kasoff with the enormity of his task. Malice: knowledge on the part of the actor that he or she is committing an act so reckless that it carries with it a high degree of the risk of death to another. Kasoff knew now that Donovan had studied McGinniss's delivery, that Donovan knew how to calculate the speed of the ball off his bat and the force with which it would collide with McGinniss's temple. He knew that Donovan had taken dead aim at that spot. Would these calculations clearly demonstrate that such a line shot would indeed deliver a deadly punch? If so, Donovan would have known just as surely as a triggerman that the projectile carried with it a high risk of death. Time to return to his friend the physicist.

"All right. Here's what we know. A ninety-eight-miles per hour fastball. A thirty-four ounce bat. The ball takes point twenty-three seconds from the instant it's hit to the point of impact. Distance to target is fifty-six feet. The ball's circumference is between nine and nine and one-quarter inches with weight of five to five and one-quarter ounces. What's the likelihood that the ball will cause a depressed fracture severe enough to penetrate brain matter?"

Pete did the calculations in just a few moments. The ball would reach McGinniss's head at about 170 mph. Then Pete looked up and said, "I've done a bit of research on this. A baseball will fracture a skull if its force is anywhere from four hundred twenty-five to nine hundred psi, depending on the location of the blow. Apparently, there's quite a bit of individual variation in the thickness and density of the skull. I'll need some additional information on that. But given what we do know, the psi at impact should be sufficient to fracture bone. Whether that fracture is sufficiently severe to cause death is up to your coroner."

"What if McGinniss was on the high end of the bone thickness variation?" Kasoff was placing himself in the devil's shoes. Suppose, for example, Donovan had actually run a series of numbers. At best, he could only assume a set of variables concerning the victim's skull. Had Donovan sown nothing more than his own doubts if he had gone to the trouble of performing a series of equations?

Pete gave Kasoff a look that both understood and added, "It's

113

an iffy proposition. A close call. You may still see a fracture, but enough energy may be dissipated at the impact site to avoid serious brain involvement. It could conceivably be no more serious than an extended trip to the disabled list." And then he gave vent to what they both knew he was thinking: "Just how mushy are your numbers?"

"Mine are solid. It's Donovan's working assumptions I'm concerned about."

"Well, you don't have a recipe without knowing the amount of each ingredient, that is, unless you're looking to cook the numbers."

"Don't worry. This case will be fully baked without cooking anything."

It was time to get back in touch with Patel. This time with newfound humility.

"Hello, Dr. Patel. Sorry to bother you again on that McGinniss autopsy, but if you don't mind, I have just one more question."

"What is it?" The edge wasn't off the coroner's voice.

"If you have an opportunity, could you tell me the thickness of the section of bone that was fractured?" The information was absent from the final report, but it was the sort of measurement concerning which a note typically would have been made on the handwritten draft.

"Hang on a minute."

Kasoff waited with growing anticipation.

At last, the pathologist returned to the phone. "Two millimeters—on either side of the suture. Of course, the impact point bisected the gap. The poor bastard was struck in the worst possible location."

"Two millimeters. Is that normal?"

"Three is about average at this spot. It's the thinnest area of the entire skull. Elsewhere, it ranges up to six millimeters or more."

"Thank you very much." The news could hardly have been better.

"B.D., how 'bout we meet for lunch?"

"I thought you were on vacation 'til Monday."

"I am. I just miss you is all, you big lug."

"Oh, cut the crap. You must really want a big favor this time," B.D. teased back.

"Just the pleasure of your company. And bring Al along, too."

"And here I thought it would be just the two of us. You really know how to hurt a guy. Where at?"

"How about McDonough's?"

"The one with those romantic out-of-the-way booths?"

"I told you I missed you. Twelve-thirty OK?"

"Sure. See you then."

McDonough's was one of those restaurants that was past its heyday. It served a full course lunch with a steak or seafood entrée, and these days people just didn't have that kind of time to while away their workday. Over the previous decade, the median age of its average customer had increased by at least ten years, and the number of native Chicagoans who thought of it as a landmark had noticeably declined. The owner, John McDonough, still active in the business, was 83. Two of his sons helped run the place, but they lacked the dedication of the old man—who for years was at the farmer's market daily at 3:00 A.M. to select personally the finest and freshest fish and produce. And you had the feeling that when the patriarch gave up the ghost—everyone knew that he would have to be carried out—his kids would surrender the business, by either running it into the ground or selling out to take the money and run. With its tinted windows and soft—some would say dim—lighting, the place was not one in which to read a newspaper, even on the sunniest of days. Toward the rear were several high-backed booths where a couple could enjoy a private conversation. Kasoff called ahead to reserve the booth at the back. He knew, with its slow business, that he could count on privacy there. He knew, too, that B.D. would not want to take up office time with the subject Kasoff wished to discuss.

"Greetings. And to what do I owe this interruption in your vacation?"

"How you doing, B.D.? Where's Al?"

"Fine. He'll be along in a minute; he was just one elevator behind me. How was your vacation?"

"Interesting." The maître d' intervened, acknowledging Kasoff's reservation, and led the two men past several vacant

115

booths to the back and the one Kasoff had requested.

"I've got forty-five minutes," said B.D. as they sat down, pointedly letting his subordinate know that he was not in vacation mode. Green now approached the table, complaining that this was no place in which to be cooped up on such a nice day.

Taking the cue, Kasoff got right to the point: "Did you know that Donovan was a physics student?"

Kasoff may have been the one on vacation, but now it took B.D. a moment to reorient himself and place the name. "Donovan? Oh, you mean Donovan."

"Sure, who else?" replied Kasoff, temporarily forgetting the solo nature of his quest.

"So?"

"So we're well on the way to having malice nailed down." Kasoff decided that he would take the silence with which he was met as a green light to continue. "Donovan would have known how much force was necessary to fracture McGinniss's skull and kill him. And you know what else? Instead of studying videos of dozens of pitchers in the off-season as he usually did, Donovan last winter reviewed films of just one. And guess who that was?" Now the silence of his colleagues bespoke intrigue more than incredulity. "He was obviously looking for the vulnerable spot in his delivery in order to target the location of his head at that point so he could place his drive right there. And guess what? He found it. The coroner says he nailed it. No doubt he was examining his mechanics as well so he'd know where a given pitch was likely to be. I'm telling you this guy, with premeditation and deliberation and with malice, set out to kill McGinniss, and then he accomplished it."

"Tell me something," began B.D. "How many times in the history of the game has a pitcher been killed by a line drive during actual play?"

"Never."

"Never. Well, that sure helps. How the hell do you prove that a man set out to kill another man in a way that's never been done before?"

"Wait, don't you see? That's the beauty of it. It proves that you've got to try awful damn hard to do it!"

B.D. was unmoved. "Legal impossibility," he said flatly.

Green piped in. "Look, suppose I want you to die. I get myself a voodoo doll. I say the doll is you. I stick pins in it with the intent to kill you. Two days later, you drop dead. Am I guilty of murder?"

"Wrong analogy," replied Kasoff. "In your example, there is no reasonable connection between the means used and the result. Everyone knows, or at least everyone who doesn't claim to have been abducted by aliens knows—and these days I'll concede that that's a dwindling minority—that you can't kill someone by sticking pins in a doll. But you can most certainly blow someone away by lining a baseball at his head at a hundred and seventy miles per hour from a distance of less than sixty feet."

Even B.D. was nodding in agreement. But now he had his own case with which to challenge Kasoff: "Remember the English case everyone studies in law school where the British dame travels to France? She buys some lace which she is convinced requires a customs declaration and duty payment. She doesn't want to pay, so she hides it in her baggage or wherever in order to smuggle it in. Customs finds it and has her arrested. When she goes to court, it's discovered that this wasn't really French lace she purchased. It was a cheap British knockoff sold in France for which no custom declaration or duty payment was required. Case dismissed: it was legally impossible for her to commit a crime with that lace, even though she had the motive, the opportunity, and the means by which to smuggle it. That's your case against Donovan. His act was lawful even if his mind was guilty."

"Not exactly. The British smuggler knew, or at least thought she knew, that smuggling the lace was a crime. She tried to conceal her act. Here, Donovan was willing to commit his act for all the world to see because he was convinced it was perfectly legal."

"Whose side are you on? If Donovan thinks he's committing a legal act, how is he any more morally blameworthy than a smuggler who's convinced she's committing a crime?"

"First of all, lace won't fracture a skull. This was a brutal act, not merely a sneaky one. More important, it's Donovan's willingness to carry out his murderous intent in public that makes his act so reprehensible. At least the smuggler recognizes her own guilt. Donovan's convinced he got away with murder."

"I still think he did. I hate to admit it, but I think he did.

117

Show me a case like this one anywhere in the Western world that was prosecuted successfully and I'll turn you loose on him." B.D. had thrown down the gauntlet. Kasoff needed to convince him to give him more time.

"I can't do that. At least not now. But maybe this is the case to try. I want to do some more checking. I'd like to see if I can get my hands on the McGinniss video. And get the bat if it still exists. It'd be nice to have the murder weapon."

"How you fixin' to do that?" With no prosecution pending and lacking probable cause to believe that a crime had been committed, a subpoena or search warrant was, in B.D.'s mind, out of the question.

"I'm working on it. I'm working on it."

"Well, don't work so hard. You're still on vacation."

Green then intervened, ready to challenge Kasoff again on his knowledge of the game's players. "All right. How about the all-time occupations team? No repeats."

"OK. Let's see here. OK. In the outfield. Home Run Baker, Tris Speaker, and Brett Butler."

"Speaker an occupation?"

"Why not? Otherwise, I go with Bing Miller or Chuck Tanner and you'll just tell me that they're a couple of guys named Joe."

"OK, OK. I'll bend the rules again for a Hall of Famer."

"Darrell Porter at catcher over Andy Merchant. Billy Gardner at second. Jim Mason at short. Pie Traynor at third."

"Another Hall of Famer. But the spelling's off."

"I thought homonyms were OK unless you said otherwise, remember?"

"Fair enough."

"Pitching. Mike Marshall over Bill Singer and Steve Barber."

"You're still missing a first baseman."

"I'm thinking. I've got it. Dots Miller."

"Dots, schmots. Get outta town."

"Are you kidding? He played all through the teens. Lifetime average two-sixty-three. That was good enough to get Joe Tinker into the Hall."

"OK. OK. Dots Miller. Whatever you say. You've done it again, Bob."

As the group got up from the table, several gray-haired businessmen entered the restaurant, but the sunbeam that broke through the open doorway didn't penetrate to the farthest reaches of the establishment. Upon opening the door for himself, Kasoff had to squint until he reached his vehicle.

*　　*　　*

That same afternoon, a time zone away.

It was one of those old-style phone booths. The boxy stand-up rectangle where the door closes like an accordion and you can make a call in conversational if not visual privacy. And even on a busy street, the caller will manage to hear the other party most of the time, unlike with the newer open-air telephones affixed to a stand, hapless as they are to compete with the decibel level of the central city. Of course, the old boxy booths brought out the territorial instinct in people along with the privacy they afforded. Nestled inside, callers would thoughtlessly toss litter on its four-foot-square floor or scratch graffiti on its plexiglass. In recent years, the language preserved on these transparent walls, like the vernacular on the streets, had gotten increasingly coarse and intractable to clean-up. The maintenance costs combined with deregulation of the industry had led the phone companies to conclude that the expense of these enclosures should no longer be borne. And so most of these old booths had been removed, only occasionally replaced. This being the age of cellular phones and pagers, there just wasn't as much demand for the old public telephone.

This one, however, had so far escaped the scrap heap. Standing in the shadow of Yankee Stadium, a weary victim of unsolicited urban art, it nevertheless continued to beckon callers with the option of a private cubicle. That and anonymity. And the finger that now turned its old rotary dial belonged to a man for whom the two dollars in change required for the long-distance call was a cheap price to pay to assure that his identity would remain concealed. As his fingertip summoned each number, the hand trembled, not from an accumulation of too many years, though there were plenty of those.

"Chicago PD First precinct," answered the voice.

"Uh, could I speak to a detective, please?"

"Please hold."

And a moment later, "Detective Spinelli here."

"Um, yeah. I'd um—"

The detective was patient with the caller's hemming and hawing. Often the tip that broke a case came from the most fearful, reluctant, or troubled informants. And this male voice sounded elderly. Whatever the situation, it seemed to Spinelli, old folks didn't call a police detective to tell them anything other than what they believed to be true. Of course, there were times when what the caller thought was accurate and what really happened were planets apart. "How can I help you, sir?" Spinelli replied in as friendly and deliberate a tone of voice as the mound of paperwork on his desk yellowing for his attention would allow.

"That ballplayer who got killed on Opening Day, that was no accident."

"May I have your name please?" The impassive bureaucrat took over. He knew that the best way to prevent crank calls was to demand identification. Caller ID wasn't effective against the pay phone crackpots.

"No names. At least for now. I could lose my job for this." And the voice got edgier.

The reply told Spinelli the caller was at least sincere. "Sir, you can't be fired for talking to me. There are whistleblower laws to protect you. Besides, we protect the identity of our informants."

For the caller, this came as a great relief. He had grown up at a time when "I know my rights" just wasn't part of the lexicon. He hadn't even had any contact with the police since some six decades earlier when, when he was a boy, an officer came to the door to thank his father for helping out the local factory when some rabble-rousers, as the patrolman put it, tried to force a union on the company by blocking a street with a sit-down strike. The boy had swelled with pride as that man in blue had patted his father on the back. And so the caller had always had faith in the police to maintain order and do the right thing.

"How do you know it was no accident?"

"Because I know how he did it."

"Donovan?"

"Yes, sir."

Spinelli continued to debate with himself as to whether or not the caller was a nut. Of course he knew what had happened. Donovan had hit a line shot through the middle for a base hit with tragic consequences. As he was paid to be suspicious, Spinelli's radar concluded he was picking up "crazy" signals on this line. He was about to hang up when the caller continued.

"And I've got the evidence to prove it."

"What evidence?"

"I'd rather not say right now. But I can be in Chicago the week after next to show you."

Spinelli was still dubious, but by now his tracer was telling him that this call was coming from the South Bronx. Why would a nut want to turn in Donovan if he was a Yankees fan? Hell, all those Yankee fans were nuts, but not one would betray his team. Spinelli put his hand over the mouthpiece. "Hey, Mac, you got the sports page there. Where are the Yankees playing today?"

"Hold on a minute. Let's see here. They're at home."

"Home," repeated Spinelli, and it occurred to him that perhaps this New Yorker was no mere fan. Now, he returned to his caller. "What day that week?"

"Monday. I'm off. How's four P.M.? That should give me time to get there."

"You know where the precinct is?"

"I'll find you."

"Say, you mind if I have someone else sit in on this?"

"Who?"

"Someone from the Prosecutor's Office. Whenever there's a question about whether a crime has been committed, we like to have a legal adviser to assist. After all, they're the ones who ultimately decide whether to prosecute."

"Sure, I'll talk to the prosecutor. And don't worry. A crime's been committed, all right."

"Be sure and bring that evidence you say you've got."

"Oh, I can't forget that."

The caller hung up the receiver and opened the door to the outside world. And then Dutch walked quickly back into the ballpark, leaving the old booth alone to await the next user who needed refuge.

The Yankees had cooled off along with Donovan's bat. By the

121

end of May, his average was down to .326 and he had hit only one home run in his last 14 games. Still, heading into June, the Yankees remained in first place by 3 full games with a record of 36-19. No one noticed that Donovan's locker now contained on its top shelf a bottle of aspirin. To this premier player, who had missed only half a dozen games in 13 years and who never took painkillers, the container sat there like an intruder reminding him that all was not tranquil. Still, he was visiting this interloper almost daily, though its tablets didn't seem to have much effect on his headaches.

"Dan Gorski, please," Spinelli inquired, and a moment later heard the familiar voice.

"Gorski here."

"Dan, how are you? Spinelli here at First Precinct."

"Tom. How you been? Haven't seen you since we put away the czar and czarina." The Romanovs had been Russian emigrés whose Soviet education had convinced them that Chicago was the Wild West—which of course dated their schoolbooks to the decade of Stalin's purges. To them, the Windy City was a free market where anything went. Their financial scams, however, had been as sophisticated as their education had left them anachronistic, and it had taken a whole battery of accountants to untangle the mess and nail these two. Spinelli had interviewed the first group of victims, and Gorski himself had prosecuted the case. They had worked well together but hadn't spoken in nearly a year.

"Listen, Dan. I got a really weird call today."

B.D. sat up straight. For a big-city detective only a few years from retirement who had seen it all, *weird* wasn't in the vocabulary.

"Some old guy," Spinelli continued, "says McGinniss—the ballplayer—his death was no accident. Says he has evidence to prove it."

"You didn't trace the call to Kasoff's home, did you?"

Distracted for only an instant by the reply that seemed to him a non sequitur, Spinelli continued. "This call came from the Bronx. Says he's flying here next week to meet with me and show me what he's got. My instinct tells me this guy's legit or at least believes he's legit."

122

B.D. rolled back in his chair and stroked his forehead. *Wait'll Kasoff hears this,* he thought.

"Anyway, we'd like to have someone from your office sit in on this. I don't know what the hell this guy's referring to. All I saw that day was a liner up the middle. It was a helluva tragedy, but if that's not an accidental death, I better get out of this business." Short pause. "What was that you said about Kasoff again?"

"He's your man. You know him?"

"Vaguely."

"He's got the same bug up his ass, and when he sinks his teeth into something he's a bulldog. I mean he just won't let go. Maybe your visitor will throw him some raw meat."

"Has he got anything on this?"

"Nothing discernible. On the one hand, I can hardly wait to tell him, but I'm not sure I want to encourage him. I'll have him get in touch with you. Good to hear from you. Let's keep in touch."

"I'll expect his call. Good talking to you, too."

And so, on Monday, June 3, after spending nearly two months trying to reconstruct Donovan's thinking process, Kasoff would, if the caller delivered as promised, see some tangible fruit of Donovan's poisonous labor.

10

The blooms were off the rhododendrons by the time Mary was able to bring herself to visit McGinniss's grave site. She approached the stone warily, apprehensive that the presence of its closing date had not lost its ability to shock. DON MCGINNISS. 6/12/72–4/1/97. DEVOTED AND BELOVED SON, HUSBAND, FRIEND, read the unadorned inscription.

"And father-to-be," she whispered to herself as a teardrop silently emerged from her left eye and streaked down to her chin, hanging there until she sank to her knees—the ground was still wet from a recent storm, but she didn't notice. And her sobs flowed freely for several moments. Only then did she remember to place the small bouquet of white roses entwined with baby's breath up against the cold slab that marked her as a widow. And then she let her mind wander from this field of finality back to the field he had loved.

He had called her after his first freshman game that spring—was it really six years ago?—to tell her he had pitched a no-hitter. Of course, he had walked 11 and, no small detail, lost 2–1, but the school had decided to promote him immediately to the varsity.

More important, he was hopeful that he would now get better coaching, he explained, to help him with his mechanics and control. Mary was thrilled for him and said so, though she tried to temper her enthusiasm when Victor, seated on the sofa with her, began tapping impatient fingers. McGinniss sensed she was preoccupied and, always one to put her first, let her know he had to get going, after thanking her for letting him share this victory in defeat with her.

When she hung up, Victor wanted to know who the caller was. Mary tried to explain that McGinniss was a friend from work, but he wasn't buying it. "He wants you," Victor said bluntly, as if to toss cold water on this platonic relationship.

"He's not like that; we're just good friends."

"Don't be naive. He wants you."

Mary, though she had once suspected as much, had—in the year she had gotten to know Don—long since become convinced that even if he did, he would never seek more than her friendship. She could afford to let her boyfriend have the last word. She knew better.

McGinniss had taken that spring off work in order to play ball. His season had unfolded pretty much as his opening game went. Not many college players could touch his now 95-plus mph fastball. But, too often, no one could reach it, either. He walked nearly as many as he struck out, and he averaged two Ks per inning. The pitching coach worked long hours with McGinniss and succeeded in getting his mechanics down right; his delivery was now refined to a consistent fluid overhand motion, but the ball still seemed to have a mind of its own. And McGinniss, usually a mild-mannered guy, became increasingly frustrated when his pitches failed to follow the plan. He'd swear a blue streak at himself. Out loud. On the mound between pitches, off the mound on the way back to the dugout. Following a particularly wild outing, not even the locker room was spared. He would slam the first thing in sight—anything but that precious fist—against a wall. He never took it out on his teammates, though. The anger was purely inner-directed. And it was good cover for the self-doubt within.

In June following his freshman year, McGinniss returned to Auto Tronics full-time, while playing sandlot ball at night. At his first lunch with Mary, during a pause in the conversation, she suddenly looked down, back at McGinniss, and then said, "Victor and I are getting married," with a tone that seemed almost as if to beg for reassurance that she wasn't hurting him, Victor having resurrected doubts in her mind as to McGinniss's true feelings for her.

"I'm happy for you," he replied as he willed his jaw not to drop and maintained the frozen tundra of a smile—barren of the emotion that lay below. And he repeated it, told her that she deserved happiness, while silently trying to reassure himself that his face did not betray his true sentiment.

"The wedding itself will be just family, but I would like it if you could come to the reception. I'll have just a few close friends there myself. Mostly, it'll be family and Victor's friends."

Victor, he thought. *He's certainly earned that name now.* But it was consoling and flattering that Mary counted McGinniss as among this select group. "I wouldn't miss it for the world." And he meant it. *After all*, he thought, *you can't really believe a loved one is dead until you see her in the coffin.*

And that night, despair overwhelmed him. He took his powerful right fist and had to force himself to restrain it with his left arm so as not to punch every wall in sight. But he played it out in his mind. Again and again he would pound it as he imagined himself beating that precious hand into a bleeding pulp while crying out from the pain. And for days each time he summoned the memory of this terrible fantasy he would wince.

But in the weeks that followed, he resolved that he would channel his powerful emotions into positive endeavors. He would squeeze a measure of his frustration into every pitch he threw and get an extra two or three mph on his fastball. He would summon the anger over his predicament to run faster with each morning jog, to lift that much more weight. And eventually, he hoped, even if it took decades, the volcanic feelings of his youth would cool to a warm memory in middle age. But he would not allow such positive feelings to drive him into negative behavior. Resorting to booze or falling into depression would be a betrayal of those wonderful feelings. No, he would embrace what was positive about the immutable and use it to keep himself on track in all his future ventures.

*　　*　　*

Monday morning and Kasoff was back at work. B.D. was about to open his morning can of one-calorie cola when he hailed Kasoff just as he happened by. "Have you seen Carol? Is she looking really attractive or what?" Carol, who had shed winter's extra pounds, smiled proudly. Unfortunately, the government-issue refrigerator from which B.D. had obtained his drink had a finicky thermostat. Unknown to him, the soda pop was half frozen. As he pulled back the tab immediately after giving Carol the compliment, icy cola suddenly shot out, turning B.D. into an instant and sopping juggler. "Whoa, whoa," he cried as he

126

attempted to lasso the wayward can.

Without missing a beat, Kasoff replied, "She's not that attractive." And instantly, it was as though Kasoff had never left. But only for a moment. The trial lawyer's reward for a week's vacation is a stack of mail and messages as well as a cabinet full of files that are seven days closer to their court dates. Sharon had gotten good at prioritizing for him, separating the urgent from the merely important, while turning over the emergencies to B.D. in his absence. Kasoff plunged right in, only to be surprised within a few minutes by his superior standing in his doorway. This was uncharacteristic. B.D. always knew when Kasoff needed to be left undisturbed.

"Looks like you've got an informant."

His train of thought interrupted, Kasoff had no time for games. "What are you talking about?"

"You know, the People v. The Pride of the Yankees." Kasoff knew B.D. well enough to know that the smile on his face was communicating good news and not a practical joke. B.D. continued. "I got a call from the First Precinct last Friday, right after our lunch. There's a guy coming in from New York today—insists McGinniss's death was no accident. Claims he's bringing evidence to prove it. He'll be there at 4:00 o'clock. I told Spinelli—you remember him?—you'd be there. I know you're backed up and all but I figured—"

"You figured right. Damn! What else did he tell you about this guy?"

"Not much. He's an older guy, didn't want to give a name, and was calling from the Bronx. That's all I know."

"Damn!" was all this wordsmith could say. "Thanks, B.D."

"Don't mention it."

And Kasoff returned to his work with renewed vigor, knowing it was the only way to make time fly until the meeting.

The Yankees were in Milwaukee, having flown in late the night before from La Guardia. This being an off-day, the players had a brief workout—about an hour—at noon. Dutch would have the rest of the day to himself. He was on the road before 2:30 and arrived at the police station right on time. Traffic hadn't been heavy and the rental car was comfortable, but the 90-minute drive had been draining. The three packages he carried, each one neatly wrapped in brown paper, held their secrets, including some that might not be evident to the casual observer. Should he point out all he knew about their contents or leave it up to the authorities to find the key to unlock their full significance? If he followed the latter course, would he be shirking his responsibilities as a citizen?

Dutch had never been faced with this sort of dilemma. The closest he had even come to a spirited ethics debate was the time, more than thirty years ago, when he and his manager disagreed over whether one of the team's pitchers should be ordered to stop throwing spitballs. Dutch wanted him to cease: it was a clear violation of the game he revered, a game whose rules needed no revision in his eyes, and therefore breaking those rules cheapened the game. The other members of the coaching staff all opposed Dutch. One of them, a clubhouse lawyer in his playing days, pointed out that there was no duty of full disclosure according to the rules of the game. If an outfielder dived for a ball and caught it on a short hop, he had no duty to admit it if the umpire missed the call and ruled the batter out. No, went this line of argument, it was up to the umpire or the opposing team to discover the infraction and deal with it. In vain, Dutch had responded that there was a world of difference between playing the game by the rules and benefiting from bad calls—which, he pointed out, tended to balance themselves out—and cheating those rules while hoping not to get caught.

Nevertheless, Dutch found that he could live with being on the short end of this argument. After all, he concluded, the umps probably condoned the spitter anyway. How else could they miss the gobs of saliva that would sometimes fly free of the ball on its way to the plate? Anything that fooled hitters and kept the game moving was fine with the umpires, Dutch had decided. Especially in a game with no clock, where they're not paid by the hour. But this was no spitball, whose only consequence was a foolish-looking hitter. This was a death-dealing blow at the game itself. Ultimately, Dutch decided, as he drove down the interstate toward the Midwest's largest city, telling all he knew would not betray the game or his employer. He would be fulfilling a responsibility he felt to return something—yes, something as precious as honor—to the game that had given him a lifetime of joy.

At 4:00 P.M. sharp, Dutch entered the First Precinct. In his civilian clothes, he looked older than his seventy-two years, his knees arthritic from his playing days—surgery to remodel the joints wasn't far off, his orthopedist had explained. The nape of Dutch's neck was wrinkled from a thousand distant days of sunshine warming him when he patrolled the outfield back when night games were a novelty. Still uncertain of revealing his identity when the desk clerk inquired, Dutch had said only that Spinelli was expecting him. Tipped off by the detective, the clerk promptly buzzed Spinelli to announce the arrival. Kasoff, who had come early and was already in the detective's office, bolted out of his chair. This was one visitor Kasoff would walk up to the lobby to greet.

"Welcome. I'm Bob Kasoff." Kasoff extended his hand and offered his most earnest forthright smile as Spinelli trailed behind.

"Nice to meet you. Listen, I'm still a little leery of—"

"Losing anonymity?"

"Right."

"Relax. This conversation won't leave this office."

"OK. Thanks," replied Dutch, feeling a bit better.

Spinelli escorted Kasoff and Dutch to a conference room. Spartan quarters. A simple four-by-eight hardwood table and four chairs. Nothing on the walls but a bit of peeling paint near one corner of the ceiling. A single overhead light. No windows. Tile floor. Dutch understood. The atmosphere was "just the facts." No embellishment. No rambling.

"So McGinniss's death was no accident," Kasoff began. Neither he nor Spinelli had with them a recording device. Not even a pen. First, they had planned, let's get this guy comfortable enough to tell his story without fear that he was speaking for the record. After a witness tells his story once, the catharsis makes it easier to repeat—and, they hoped, on-the-record.

"Boy, you guys don't waste any time, do you?"

"Sure looked accidental to me," countered Spinelli, using the old technique of challenging the witness with doubt, so he'd be motivated to prove the cop wrong.

"Look. I told you guys I don't want to lose my job, and so I need you to protect my identity. But what I saw on Opening

Day—and I had a bird's-eye view—was planned." And then, looking into the eyes of these enforcers of the law, Dutch decided to take the leap of faith. "Here, open this." And Dutch handed Kasoff the first of three packages the prosecutor had not taken his eyes off since Dutch's entry.

Inside was the videotape. Kasoff opened it and immediately noticed the label: CHICAGO WHITE SOX, 1996. MCGINNISS, DON.

"Now let me explain. The Yankees videotape or obtain copies of video of every pitcher in the league from various games. Then we edit it and place the key moments on alphabetized videotapes for the hitting instructor—that's me—and the players to review. For years, no one studied those tapes like Donovan." And Dutch proceeded to tell the story Kasoff had heard from Donovan's hometown folk, right down to the detail that this was the only tape the slugger had sought the previous winter.

"This video shows all of the pitching moves and mechanics of McGinniss from when he was still in triple-A—we knew he was a comer—as well as when he was called up to the parent club in September. Study it long enough, and you'll be surprised at what a great hitter can learn. They've got amazing vision, you know." Kasoff knew. He had heard the stories, that eagle-eyed Ted Williams, for example, could spot the rotation of the stitching as a pitch made its way to the plate, cluing him in to the direction of the break the ball was about to take.

Dutch continued. "Twenty-ten eyesight! That's twice as good as the average human being. Imagine a wolf whose sense of smell is twice as good as the rest of the pack. He's gonna get the sheep every time. Well, Donovan has that refined sense. He can spot things on those videos the rest of us can't. And I believe that he figured out the flaw in McGinniss's delivery that caused his fastball to go every which way from time to time. So that Donovan could predict where his next fastball was going. And not only that. You got a VCR here?"

"Sure. Let's go down the hall."

The group entered a conference room, newer, almost plush by comparison, carpeted, with a TV that contained a built-in VCR.

"I'm sorry," said Dutch. "We actually need two VCRs for you to see this right. Is there another one that could be set up next to this one?" Dutch had a second gift-wrapped video package he was about to turn over.

"Uh, yeah, hang on a minute."

Spinelli scurried down the hall to the employee lounge, to which Sandra Burke, a dispatcher, had recently donated a TV with VCR after she had won a newer model as a second prize winner in the police league raffle. He unplugged and carried the contraption to the conference room. Now the two chroniclers of the wasteland sat side by side. Dutch inserted the two tapes.

"This one on the left is McGinniss last September in a game against Cleveland. I've got it cued up to show him just as he completed his windup." The tape rolled. "OK, there he is." And the paused still frame showed McGinniss in midroar down off the mound.

"Now here's the tape of Opening Day showing him at the instant he's hit." And the frozen image revealed a tiny white object at McGinniss's temple area, milliseconds from striking its target, having reached its destination so swiftly that McGinniss's face betrayed not a trace of horror. If the hand is quicker than the eye, so are the wrists that turn on a ball with such ferocity.

"Now, it's not easy to do, but if we rewind this tape exactly two-tenths of a second—" and Dutch himself, having warmed to his subject, began rewinding and fast-forwarding several times in order to capture the moment—"there, look at that."

Spinelli and Kasoff gazed at the two TV pictures and then at each other. There, locked in time, were two views of McGinniss, his follow-through having been captured at precisely the same instant. And the images on the two screens could not have been more identical. It was as though Donovan knew precisely where lightning would next strike.

"The one from last year—I told you Donovan had all winter to study it. Now, I'm sure you guys know more about this than I do. But I've got a nephew in the FBI who says you can look at a videotape microscopically and tell from subtle wear patterns how much it's been played—and if certain portions have been played more than others. You look at this tape. I guarantee you you'll see that this part of McGinniss's follow-through"—and Dutch pointed to last year's image—"was played over and over and over again."

131

Dutch wasn't telling Kasoff anything he didn't already know about videotape analysis. In fact, before Dutch even mentioned the FBI, Kasoff had in mind the agent at its Chicago office to whom he planned to take the film.

"We'll certainly look into that. Thank you," was the reply of Spinelli, who was dubious about what all this would prove.

Kasoff saw this as one more piece of the puzzle but was anxious to have Dutch's hypothesis tested before he got too excited about this information.

"And finally, here—" and Dutch now unwrapped the third package—"I kept the bat Donovan used when he hit McGinniss." And out came—at first glance—a nearly pristine product of Louisville. Just a bit of pine tar on the handle and a single scuff mark on the finish up at the sweet spot, 180 degrees around from the trademark. Now, Dutch hesitated. He drew a breath and continued. "You guys have a scale?"

Spinelli buzzed the officer at the desk to have one retrieved, "You know, the ones we use to measure the bricks of pot."

Dutch explained. "See, Donovan always used a thirty-four-ounce bat." Kasoff knew that. "It says so right here on the handle's bottom." Dutch displayed the small "4." "But it never felt like a thirty-four to me."

The scale was brought in.

"Measure it."

Spinelli placed the bat on the scale that was used to handling kilos. "Thirty ounces," he read, a bit puzzled. "Does the factory sometimes miss the mark?" he inquired.

Kasoff, a step ahead, smiled.

"No," said Dutch. "But I'll tell you what makes a thirty-four-ounce bat a thirty-ounce bat."

"Cork it!" cried Kasoff, his voice rising with the excitement he felt as Dutch nodded.

And now Dutch's face seemed to drop a bit, as though the secret inside this weapon had ruined the game itself for him. "Cork, you're right," he sighed. "I didn't see Donovan actually do it, but let's just say I put two and two together. If you open the top of this barrel, I'm certain you'll find it."

And now, the three of them took a closer look at the barrel end. Dutch ran his fingers around its circumference less than an inch from its top. "There!" he exclaimed. He was sure he had detected the seam where the cross section had been cut and reglued. Kasoff felt for himself, but his untrained hand had come up empty. *Not a problem*, he thought to himself. *The lab boys will have plenty to say about this.*

But Kasoff's fingers did pick up on something else, something Dutch had not yet had a chance to point out. For this veteran of the game did not appreciate its significance. Now, running his hands along the barrel of the bat, Kasoff wondered aloud, "What's with the dimples?" One had to look close to spot the dozens of tiny indentations, each less than a millimeter, in the wood.

"I don't know. I noticed that myself."

"Are all his bats like that?"

"No sir. Not a one."

"Did he do this to it?" Kasoff knew the answer before he asked the question.

"Can't think of anyone else who would've."

"Any idea why?"

"Nothing specific. But he must have thought it would help him hit the ball better."

Perhaps, thought Kasoff, the scientist would know those specifics.

The corking alone, Kasoff would argue, established an overt act. No longer could he be tagged with the moniker of the thought police.

Believing for the first time that he would have a clear shot at his quarry, Kasoff now adopted the cool contemplation of the professional assassin. "Look, Mr.—" and Kasoff realized he hadn't even learned the man's name.

"Dutch, Jan actually, Vandiver."

"Mr. Vandiver, I can't tell you what we'll do about this yet, but we're obviously going to take a close look at all of the evidence here. And if we take action, we may need you to testify. We'll naturally subpoena you as well as other members of the Yankee organization, so it won't appear, at least initially, like you're the informant. But if this case does go forward, it'll all come out in the wash eventually. Can we count on you to tell us on the record what you've already told us today? Remember, you'll be under *oath.*" And Kasoff stressed that last word, to impress on Dutch

133

that his obligation here wasn't merely moral.

"Of course I'll tell the truth," Dutch sighed wearily, having reconciled himself to his involvement. "I'm too close to retirement not to. If I had kept quiet about this, I'd never have the time to redeem myself."

The two talked awhile longer. Kasoff needed to satisfy himself that Dutch would be able to answer the inevitable technical questions that would be raised about chain of custody. Kasoff had to be certain, of course, that no one else had had access to the bat. Then, the hitting instructor stood up to leave.

"Just one more thing," Kasoff interrupted. And he asked Dutch if he was familiar with the drill the barber had described for him, the one Jake Crawford had witnessed the previous winter when he had called on Donovan.

"Oh, sure. That's a very common practice drill we teach our rookies right after we draft 'em. Course, the veterans don't bother with it. Why do you ask?"

"What's it supposed to improve?"

"Bat speed."

"Of course." Kasoff managed to contain his excitement. "Thanks for all your help. We'll be in touch." Kasoff shook Dutch's hand and smiled. Spinelli just shook his head.

Dutch was still awaiting the elevator in the lobby when Kasoff was already doing a jig and high-fiving Spinelli, who wasn't sure he'd seen anything worth celebrating. "We're gonna nail that SOB!" cried Kasoff, whose exuberance wasn't dampened by Spinelli's reply.

"For as high as you're aiming, you better have more firepower than this," as he gestured toward the innocent-looking fruits of what Kasoff saw as contraband. But dutiful detective that he was, Spinelli methodically tagged the evidence for identification even as he said it.

Time for another talk with B.D., Kasoff knew as he left police headquarters. As he entered, Sharon was complimenting Carol on her outfit, noting how she appeared so slim in it. Kasoff couldn't believe the luck of his timing. "It sure beats the one she had on last week when her pockets were in different time zones." And the trail of his own laughter could be heard all the way to B.D.'s office as he left Carol in his wake pretending to be offended while she silently enjoyed, just a little, the attention.

"Big news, B.D. We've got a big fish in our sights."

Gorski looked up from the pile on his desk. "Could you stop mixing metaphors just long enough to tell me what the hell you're talking about?"

"We've got Donovan. And I mean we've got him."

"You're still fixated on that ballplayer." It was an observation, not a question. B.D. had been far less excited about the emergence of an informant than his subordinate.

"Just listen to this. The Yankee hitting instructor—and he wants strict confidentiality for now—is the guy who called Spinelli. And guess what he brings us?"

"Donovan's dart board with McGinniss's picture on it?" Kasoff was too focused for this barb to deflate.

"A video of McGinniss that Donovan studied all winter. Plus the bat he hit him with. And not just any bat. This bat was corked—you know—to make the ball go faster. We've got an overt act now. We can nail him."

"Cork? That's your case? Cork?"

"That's a piece of it."

"That's the only piece of this case that won't sink. Corking a bat may break a rule of the game, but it doesn't violate a law of society. Look, if a base runner goes outside the base path and knocks a fielder flying to escape a rundown, he'll be out for breaking a base-running rule, but no one's gonna charge him with battery just because he ran outside the line to knock a player on his ass. If that's what you've got, you've got nothing."

Kasoff was neither ignorant nor naive. He knew this would be the defense argument and had wrestled with it all the way back from Spinelli's office. Kasoff had already visualized himself in court, articulating his response to this proposition before a skeptical judge. As he began his reply, Kasoff adopted a detached professorial tone to show B.D. he wasn't emotionally involved in the case, the worst thing for a trial lawyer, who needs to remain sufficiently detached to argue both sides equally well in his mind in order to develop the winning response. "The base runner in your hypothetical is violating a rule of the game with the sole intent of gaining an advantage in that game, in this case, the extra base. The contact is purely incidental to that purpose and not designed to injure. Donovan, on the other hand," and here Kasoff turned just a bit stern, "violated a rule of the game with the specific purpose and intent to kill. What's worse, his violation was committed long before he ever stepped into the batters' box, with time for cool reflection—premeditation and deliberation if you will—whereas the base runner in your example is acting on the spur of the moment. That runner is simply trying to escape a pickle when he breaks the rule. Donovan was creating a game situation—hitting the pitcher—out of his rule violation."

"I understand your position, but those are distinctions without a difference. Judges will recoil from bringing the full weight of the criminal law to bear on games that by their nature carry with them certain dangers. You might as well be asking a judge to sort out a religious controversy: a wall of separation exists between the rules of a game and the laws of society."

"Well, then I say that this is a case where we try to breach the wall, to make some new law. We'll never have better facts with which to impress an appeals panel than these. We've got intent. We've got months of premeditation, deliberation, and preparation. We've got a hitter who knows how to hit the ball where he wants to. We've got no remorse. And most of all, we've got a dead body—a locally popular dead body—and a grieving family. I say we take this to the State Supreme Court if we have to."

B.D.'s expression had evolved from dismissive to thoughtful—second thoughts. This case was unique. It was brutal. If it wasn't illegal, it damn well ought to be. "On a high-profile case like this, we'll have to get Old Show Horse's OK, of course." Kasoff knew that the boss down the hall would have to have his say but wasn't concerned. Chicago's fans would love to see this Yankee prosecuted for killing one of their own. For a politician, it was a no-brainer. Kasoff knew that as long as he had B.D. on his side, Harold Starman would relish the thought of being a Yankee killer.

In less than five minutes, B.D. had returned from Starman's office with a thumbs-up. "Starstruck figured that even if we get bounced out of court, he can always blame the judge. I still think this is a real longshot, but as you put it, let's get the SOB. This will be your case, Bob. I've got full confidence in you. If you need help, extra manpower, investigation, just let me know. And I'll stand behind you if the wall comes crashing down. Good luck."

"Thanks, B.D." And Kasoff went to his office, barely able to wait to begin preparing the search warrants. First, though, he would put in a call to his old friend and consultant of late, Dr. Churikian. "Hey, Pete."

"Yeah, Castoff, what's new on the baseball blotter?"

"Donovan corked his bat! His thirty-four ounce bat is only a thirty."

"Did you say this guy was a physics student?"

"Yeah. Why?"

"You sure he didn't flunk?"

"What do you mean?" The last thing Kasoff needed was a calculating assassin whose plans didn't add up.

"Corking the bat—it's almost entirely myth. Sure, you can swing the bat quicker because it's lighter, but you lose a virtually equivalent amount of power because its mass is decreased proportionately. You can accomplish the same result by choking up on a heavier bat."

"Maybe he just played a hunch, allowed the lore of the game to intrude on dry science." Kasoff was grasping, having come to know something of Donovan's scientific approach to hitting.

"Maybe." But the scientist, not one to speculate, was merely appeasing.

"But that's not all he did. Tell me something. Why does a guy put dimples in the barrel end of his bat, dozens of 'em, I mean, all over the sweet spot and beyond?"

"Well, now that's another story. If you want to improve the aerodynamics—that is, increase the speed of the swing without sacrificing any weight—then you'll increase the power and, in turn, the bat speed. You accomplish that simply by creating a roughened surface on the barrel of the bat. Put little bumps on it. Or dimples, like a golf ball. Bumps, dimples, the effect is the same. You just need to get rid of the layer of dead air that would otherwise cling to a smooth barrel as it's being swung, because that slows it down."

"So that's it! And how much could that increase the bat speed?"

"Two or three percentage points, perhaps as much as five. So

137

if I average out the corking with the dimpling, I guess I have to pass him with a C on doctoring the bat to hit the ball harder."

Kasoff's next task was to contact the DA's office in New York County to have a law officer go before a judge to obtain the requisite imprimatur for a search warrant. By starting with the target's apartment in town, Kasoff hoped he might not even need to use his persuasive powers with Donovan's country constable. All Donovan had to do was consent. If the warrant for the Manhattan dwelling was issued, and were Donovan to be present to witness its meddlesome execution, perhaps he would concur in a request to search his farmhouse in exchange for a promise to carry it out discreetly. Otherwise, it might prove a dicey proposition to convince the Schoharie sheriff to conduct a search of the premises of the village's baseball hero, the noble sentiments of the hamlet's historian notwithstanding. Rather than just mail out or fax the paperwork in support of the warrant as he would in a routine out-of-state search, Kasoff decided he wanted to speak to the Empire State's busiest prosecutor himself.

The Manhattan DA's office had a nationwide reputation for probity. While they would no doubt be as dubious initially as B.D., Kasoff was confident that once they understood what Kasoff already had, they'd realize he had probable cause. He was less sure of Donovan's native county, whose aboriginal name meant "driftwood" but whose denizens were anything but. After all, these were Donovan's roots at which he was tugging. If the slugger didn't consent, Kasoff would simply have to hope that the bedrock values of a Dorothy Ott would permeate the town's citizenry and that the good people of Richmondville wouldn't cut Donovan, or anyone else for that matter, any slack for the mere sake of celebrity.

"Yes, I'd like to speak to the head of the warrants section, please."

"Mike Greenberg here."

"Mike, this is Bob Kasoff, Chicago Prosecutor's Office. I need your help in obtaining a search warrant."

"Sure thing. Just send us a certified copy of the affidavit in support as usual."

"Well, I wanted to let you know what's coming."

"Why, is there a problem?"

"Well, you may take some flak on this one. We're not going to try our case in the press, but word's sure to get out. We're asking you to search the Manhattan apartment of Chris Donovan."

Silence. Then, "The Yankee? What'd he do?"

"We have probable cause to believe he committed a homicide here in Chicago and that certain fruits of the crime may be in his apartment."

"Homicide? What the hell are you talking about?"

Greenberg hadn't even made the connection. Kasoff realized this would take some doing. He attempted to explain patiently what he knew of Donovan's planning and execution of McGinniss's death.

"You guys wouldn't be Chicago fans now, would you?" And then, not waiting for the answer, Greenberg muttered, mostly to himself. "And people think Yankee fans are nuts!" And then, to Kasoff: "Look, if you guys think you can turn a baseball diamond into a crime scene, it's no skin off my nose. We'll do our duty here. That's what reciprocity is all about—" referring to the interstate compact providing that a prosecutor in one state will honor another state's DA's warrant requests, "but all the same, I'd check the water in the Chicago River if I were you. And I'll tell you something: We don't want any publicity on this, either. We've got enough problems."

"How will you prevent it?"

"I know a couple of officers who'll be discreet, no leaks, and a judge who's equally so. Unless Donovan himself blows the whistle, we may be able to keep this out of the media unless and until you charge him. And I'll buy tickets to that."

"Thanks, Mike. And I'll be sure to let you know when the circus is coming to town. Take care."

And with that, Kasoff hung up the phone and prepared to compose his affidavit. But first, like grace before a meal, it was time for his ritualistic cursing of James Madison. Not that Kasoff didn't revere this framer, but that irksome fourth Amendment he had added to the Constitution drove him crazy. Damn it, the nation's secular Bible ought to be about basic governance and fundamental freedoms. Why dwell on the minutiae of what had to appear in a search warrant? Like a mantra, Kasoff silently went through its requirements: probable cause, supported by oath, particular description of the place to be searched, particular description of the things to be seized. Kasoff knew, of course, why Madison had been so concerned about government intrusiveness—those blasted Brits had conducted arbitrary house-to-house general searches of the colonists. No more, said Madison, and he made sure his vow would stick by enshrining the recipe for a search right there in the Bill of Rights. Understandable. Laudable. But it sure added to Kasoff's paperwork.

"Your affiant has probable cause to believe . . . " and here the keyboard clattering halted as Kasoff pondered. Describe the tools of the corking trade, he decided, as Dutch had explained them to him. And whatever may have been used in the dimpling. The smaller the item sought, the better. That would get the searching officers not only into merely all of the drawers but their contents as well. After all, if they're seeking a stolen piano, they can't look under the bed. And a video of McGinniss. Dutch had said that Donovan sometimes made copies of the videos to which he wanted to give some extra study. That would give him access to Donovan's entire video library. Who knew where a few moments of tape of McGinniss might be buried among videotape of who knew what else? Certainly Kasoff would need to have all of the films reviewed.

Sharon, of course, would do the formatting to put the affidavit in final, but he couldn't seem to get her attention. Carol was at her cubicle, gesticulating expansively. Kasoff strode up to them.

"Hey, Mr. K., did you hear that our lotto club won five hundred dollars in last night's three-pick game?"

"Gee, Carol. That ought to just about cover the three days off you're going to get if you don't quit yakking about it and get back to work."

Sharon's remorse was greater than that of the instigator. The search warrant was ready in less than five minutes. One overnight package later and the full force of the law would be ready to spring. There was just one family he wanted to inform first.

The telephone rang four times. Kasoff was about to hang up when the tired voice intervened: "Hello?"

"Hello. This is Robert Kasoff of the Cook County Prosecutor's Office. Is this Ms. Mary McGinniss?"

140

"Yes. Is there something wrong?"

"No. No problem." First things first. "My condolences concerning Mr. McGinniss."

"Thank you," the tone expressing bewilderment, not gratitude.

"If you don't mind, I'd appreciate very much an opportunity to meet with you and the family concerning his death."

With just a hint of rising urgency, Mary replied, "What—what's this all about?"

"It's a little complicated to talk about over the phone. I've looked at it—" he didn't want to alarm her with a heavyweight word like investigated—"and I've learned some things that may interest the family."

"You did say you're with the Prosecutor's Office?"

"Yes."

"All right. I'll have to check with his parents, but how does tomorrow night at eight sound?"

"Fine."

Mary exchanged her address for his telephone number and, a little more than twenty-four hours later, Kasoff sat in Mary's living room surrounded by McGinniss's puzzled survivors.

Kasoff began by explaining to them what he had seen on TV that Opening Day, how his shock and horror had piqued his curiosity, and what he had learned since. He expected one of them to press him as to why they were just now being told, and so he explained how this had been nothing more than his own personal crusade and that nothing was official. Until now. A search warrant was about to be served.

McGinniss's parents were speechless for some time. The nightmares that condemned their sleep to brief interludes would now have new fodder with which to assail their early-morning hours. As the impact of the purpose behind this stranger's visit sank in, the family asked several predictable questions.

"Will there be a trial?"

Kasoff explained that it was premature to speculate. A preliminary examination would be required first.

"Will we have to testify?"

"Probably not." Kasoff noted that such an examination would focus solely on the elements of the crime and whether or not

141

there was sufficient evidence of each element having been committed by the accused to bind him over. It was a polite way of saying that the loved ones of the victim were irrelevant to the proceeding.

"Do you really think he did this on purpose?"

"I try not to inject my personal beliefs in a case. I just go where the evidence leads me." *Try telling that one to B.D.*, Kasoff chuckled to himself.

Thus far, the discussion had been limited to the vagaries of the law. But grief, like wine, soon spills forth one's intimacies. The McGinniss family, having rubbed one another raw with mutual sorrow, reached out to this commiserator.

"That boy was the gentlest soul I ever knew," began Don's mother. "Once he got big and tall, we'd call him the Gentle Giant, isn't that right, Daddy?" And she nudged her husband's shoulder as he nodded while bringing a hanky to his nose.

"He loved my sister," Melanie offered, "as he used to put it, more than all the stars in the sky multiplied by all the grains of sand. That man had more love for a woman than any man I ever met," and then she quickly qualified the remark by adding, "except you, Dad," but she said it more out of respect than conviction.

Now it was Mary's turn to dab her bloodshot eyes. "He really did love me with all his heart. And he showed it every single day we were together. He was as excited about being with me on the last morning of his life as he was the day I agreed to marry him. He swore that if he ever took me for granted I should just put him in a home, because that's how I'd know his mind was gone." And now she laughed through her tears, and a little speck of her saliva flew onto Kasoff's cheek. "Sorry," she said.

"That's OK," he quickly replied. But then, he thought, she hadn't really made a connection with him. Kasoff had always believed he had as much capacity for empathy as anyone—hell, what was he doing in this business seeking justice for victims if he didn't?—but he now found that he was unable to comprehend, not truly anyway, McGinniss's overpowering feelings. Kasoff simply hadn't met the right woman. His eyes saw the glow in this widow's face when she spoke of her late husband and his head understood her words, but his heart lay still throughout. Of course, in his line of work, where sentiment occupies a backseat, appreciating the magnitude of this family's loss even on the purely intellectual level was enough to motivate this prosecutor's zeal to even greater heights of determination.

"Thank you for letting us know what's happening," they collectively told him as he got up to leave. "Please keep in touch if you're not too busy."

"I will, Mary. Nice meeting you. Again, my condolences."

"Thanks again."

*   *   *

June 12. Mary no longer even thought of it as her own birthday. It belonged to McGinniss, and she sobbed at the realization that he never got to see 25 candles on the German chocolate cake—his favorite—she had planned to bake for him. Mary was now 32—and the thought brought her back to the moment five years earlier when he had first confessed his feelings for her. She had been married a year, and there were problems. Victor had been laid off from his job, and the beast of unemployment had driven him to drink. And one night, when he hadn't called to say he would be late, Melanie had appeared on Mary's doorstep. Looking stricken, she told her younger sister that she had seen Victor leaving a bar with a blonde in tow. And that wasn't all Melanie did. Well aware that McGinniss was crazy about Mary and convinced he would be best for her, Melanie had shown up at Auto Tronics one day, found McGinniss, and told him of Victor's betrayal. And Melanie knew that she had done the right thing from McGinniss's unselfish reaction. He was more upset for Mary than hopeful for himself.

McGinniss had wasted no time. That very day, he asked Mary to lunch for that Saturday, the advance notice unheard of since they had started sharing meals at work. He wanted to surprise her by bringing their lunch, he said, though Mary suspected there was more to it. And when Saturday came, she knew she was right. McGinniss was visibly nervous as he suggested they eat in his car. He shared with her a piece of the tomato-garlic bread, but it was the privacy of the vehicle he craved. And, with a trembling voice, he began what for him would be the most courageous conversation of his young life.

"Look. First of all, and most important, I want you to know that I treasure our friendship. I'd never do anything to betray it. But I'm afraid that what I have to say is going to ruin it. So please, no matter what I say, I still want to be friends with you. It would be too painful for words if I knew that you felt you had to distance yourself from me."

At this, Mary wondered if he was about to tell her that he was HIV- positive.

"Melanie," he continued after a pause for breath, relieved that the pounding in his chest was beginning to subside, "she told me what happened with Victor."

Well, that's a relief, Mary thought. This was just going to be a lecture on how Victor was no good for her.

"I might as well just blurt it out." *No such luck*, Mary thought as her eyes widened. "I can't bottle this up any longer." And the renewed thumping in his chest gave his words an urgency that was literal. "I've been hopelessly in love with you for a long time now—"

Stunned, she protested, "But you don't really know me."

"I know you well enough to know that you didn't feel the same about me. Besides, it's good for my self-esteem." To her quizzical look, he answered, "Because I fell for the very best." And then, before she could lodge a final protest, he cut her off. "Now, don't take that away from me. Look, I always figured that you deserved to find a guy that you're as wild about as I am about you. After all, if I couldn't want for you what you wanted, if I couldn't put your feelings first, how could I even hope to be your friend, let alone anything more?" His words were coming quickly now. "And as long as I believed you were happy, I could accept that. But I just can't stand the thought of your being miserable. I don't care what Victor's problems are. He doesn't deserve you. For God's sake, you're the crown jewel of the earth. How could he even think of such a thing? You deserve better. You deserve more. And even though I know what the answer is, I just can't live with the idea of wondering—" he would not be tied to the rack of what might have been—"so just to satisfy myself, I want you to know that I would marry you in a heartbeat." And a tachycardic one at that.

144

And, McGinniss would later tell her, he was sure he knew the answer. That there was no way she could ever think of him as anything other than a friend. And that's why he hadn't phrased it as a question. She wouldn't even have to answer. He assumed she would just say something like, "You're sweet, but—" and she wouldn't need to say another word. The disjunctive would just hang there like an unrequited bridge to nowhere and she wouldn't have to hurt him anymore by giving voice to what they both knew. The answer was "never." And he could go on with his life, freed from the torment of wondering.

But, as he later confided, she shocked him. Stunned him into replaying in his mind's ear her precise words a million times and then some, along with each nuance in her voice. And who could blame him? His confession had taken her aback, all right, but after only a brief pause, she began.

"If you're asking me now, I would have to say no. I can't change my life just like that. Victor and I have had problems. I've always been very comfortable with you. Maybe in ten years if Victor's still running around." And then she paused again, sighed, and said, "Indecision is a decision."

McGinniss was dumbfounded. Indecision? What the hell was there to be indecisive about? This was a suicide mission, but going in at least he knew the deathly rejection would be swift and certain. But what was this? The executioner was dangling before him an escape rope? She loved Victor and she didn't love him. Never would. No chance. No hope. That's how you move on. Sensing his shock and concerned about creating false expectations, Mary recovered and attempted to close the door. "Look, I'm committed to Victor, even if my sister would label it complacency, just as she does whenever I don't jump to follow her advice. I didn't marry him just for the good times. I'm committed to fixing the problems and making it work. Don—" and she looked him right in the eye—"you only live once."

And the lock shut tight. Or at least Mary hoped. She simply had too much character to string McGinniss along as an insurance policy. And realizing this, he just loved her all the more and knew that it would be that much harder to put her behind him, that much longer before she was more a memory than his lifeblood.

145

Too late had his emotions mobilized for the battle, as he now tried to convince her that his qualities would never permit him to commit the atrocity Victor had.

"Don," she cut him off, "don't sell yourself. You don't have to do that." But now she felt the need to console. "Don, I'm really flattered. And you know I think you're really one of the nicest guys—"

"Please, on behalf of all the nice guys, we don't want to hear that we're nice guys." But he was saying it with a smile. "Because we know what's coming after that. It's never, 'Oh, you're a nice guy; where do I sign?' Or, 'You're a nice guy, would you like to come up?' It's always, 'You're a nice guy, but—'" She got it.

McGinniss was now desperate to reassure himself that they were still friends, and he needed to see her smile as proof. "Fifty years from now, if you're all alone in a rest home, can I rescue you?"

"Yes!" And she said it without hesitation and with considerable enthusiasm. And most important of all, with a smile from ear to ear.

Greatly relieved, he then uttered the words that she now remembered on their shared birthday. "After all, when you're a decrepit 81, I'll be a spry seventy-four!" And they laughed as hearty a laugh as they had ever shared. And McGinniss knew that she would still be his Saturday and summertime lunch companion.

And now Mary smiled through the sobs as she sat at his grave site speaking softly to him. They had been married barely a year, and she had, more than she had ever believed possible, grown to love him. And she had so many more memories to retrace, both before and after that day she turned him down that now seemed so very long ago.

11

Judge Martin read over the affidavit in support of the warrant twice. Once in disbelief. The second time to be sure his eyes did not deceive him. "I know it's a crime the way Chicago's teams have played the game for years, but I didn't know they'd started prosecuting opposing hitters for their success against a pitching-poor team."

Sergeant Johnson and Officer Todd chuckled. The judge, with his silvery mane, looked almost as distinguished in his bathrobe as in his judicial garb. The officers had come to his home this evening to assure that no loose-lipped court clerk would get wind of the warrant request. These days, they all knew that the bottom-feeding tabloids would pay big money for inside information on courthouse machinations. As for Johnson and Todd, Greenberg knew they had no use for the media. Two years before, Johnson, a 24-year veteran, had been named by a local TV news's so-called I-team as one of New York's "dirty dozen" cops. The pejorative, with its implication of a cop on the take, didn't even apply. Johnson had made the dishonor roll because he had been named as a defendant in four civil suits that alleged police brutality. But three of them had arisen out of a single incident where he had had to restrain and arrest three young drunk and disorderlies whose uncle just happened to be a personal injury attorney. Their wounds were minor and mainly to their pride, and the city had settled the claims for $1,500 each—nuisance sums because the cost of defending them would be greater—with no admission of liability. But, damn the facts, TV5 had to provide infotainment and Johnson was that week's sacrificial offering to the press god of freedom from responsibility.

Johnson had tried to fight fire with fire. He had filed suit against the station and its I-team leader, Mike Wowland, and thought he had a good case, too. The libel claim was based on the fact that the "dirty dozen" tag falsely implied corruption or illegality when Johnson was guilty of no such thing. But the trial judge had thrown it out in an opinion that expressed sympathy for this honorable man in blue. The court was bound, read the decision, by Supreme Court precedent that protected hyperbole and opinion. "Dirty dozen" was not a provably false fact. Therefore, it was not legally actionable.

That didn't make it hurt any less, especially when the neighborhood kids Johnson used to take under his wing now avoided him and chanted the shameful label as soon as they thought he was out of earshot. At least those innocent children, unlike the hounds at TV5, could be excused from knowing nothing of where Sergeant Johnson had come from and how hard he had worked to earn his badge. Born and raised in Bedford-Stuyvesant, Johnson was watching over five younger siblings by the time he was 14, never having known his father, and able to communicate with his mother only when she was out of detox. Johnson had done such a good job—three of his charges went on to college—that the neighbors had nicknamed him Watchdog. A local patrolman had become a role model, and Johnson had been hooked on police work ever since. Now it was as if TV5 had changed his nickname to Mad Dog. More than once in the week that followed the story, Johnson had looked anew at the trigger on his revolver, contemplating its effectiveness as an instant tranquillizer. But, in the end, he had decided to use the legal system in an effort to restore some peace within.

To no avail. The court of appeals had affirmed the decision, ruling that the judge had correctly applied the cases interpreting the First Amendment. To add insult to injury, TV5, as the prevailing party, was allowed to assess substantial court costs against Johnson, so as to deter anyone else damaged by its I-team from ever attempting to retrieve his or her reputation. It's unwise to pick a fight with people who purchase their videotape by the truckload. If law enforcement cursed Madison's Fourth Amendment, the fourth president would surely be spinning in his grave at the arrogance of those who would hide behind his first one.

No, Greenberg had no fear of Johnson leaking anything to the media. And Todd, who had come to revere Johnson as his mentor, wasn't talking to anyone Johnson wasn't talking to. Now, Martin had stopped shaking his head and began to nod instead. "I don't know if it's a crime in Illinois, but if he did what they say he did in here, the planning and all, they ought to have a chance to prove it." And he scrawled his signature at the bottom.

First thing the next morning, Greenberg called to let Kasoff know the warrant had been signed. He greeted the news with more relief than jubilation. In spite of its routine nature, Kasoff's confidence had continued to wrestle with his doubts that a New York judge would swallow it. The independence of the judiciary notwithstanding, trial judges had to stand for reelection before a woefully uninformed citizenry. The best way to assure one's own defeat was to make an unpopular decision that made its way into the popular press. That was enough to ensure that the opponent would remind the electorate of that one exercise of judicial discretion often enough to sway a sufficient number of voters to deprive that judge of office, much less whatever vestige of His or Her Honor's autonomy might have survived such a capricious means of choosing the members of the third branch of government.

Greenberg had assured Kasoff that one reason Martin had been chosen was the fact that he would not be seeking another term. Still, Kasoff wondered if this jurist would be willing to be remembered as the judge who had authorized a home invasion of a Yankee hero. Now, at least for the moment, he could relax. His quest was moving forward.

The Yankees lost their third straight that night, cutting their first-place margin to one and a half games. Donovan had two hits, but it was the team's fortunes that governed his mood. And so he was not a happy man when the officers knocked. Donovan opened the door just a crack.

"Good evening, Mr. Donovan. NYPD. Sergeant Johnson. We have a warrant to search your apartment."

"What . . . who—what the devil are you talking about?"

"Here's the search warrant—" and he handed Donovan his copy—"signed by Judge Martin. I suggest you open the door and let us begin."

Taken aback, and assuming the suggestion was an understatement, Donovan opened the door wide and stepped aside as he began reading the document, silently mouthing the words as he went along. "Chicago!" he exclaimed when he saw the source.

The officers had already walked past him and were now asking Donovan where he kept his video library. But distracted, his mind racing, Donovan could only point vaguely in the direction of his living room. Soon dozens of videos were being scooped up and placed in boxes Donovan hadn't even noticed the police carrying as they entered. And now, the initial shock having worn off, he demanded, "What the hell's going on? No one's charged me with anything. You haven't told me I'm under arrest, so what the hell is happening here?"

"Like the warrant says, there's a prosecutor in Chicago who believes a crime was committed on April first, that you committed it, and that there is probable cause to believe that there is evidence of that crime in this apartment. We're just here to carry out the judge's order."

Donovan got on the phone as the search moved into his kitchen. "Who is it?" a sleepy Bob Harding demanded. Harding, Donovan's agent and legal counsel, had begun his career two decades earlier as a criminal defense attorney. When one of his old high school buddies made the majors, he asked Harding to represent him in his contract negotiations. Appreciative of the results, his friend had passed Bob's name on to other players, and soon Harding had developed a lucrative entertainment law practice. Bob was happy to leave the criminal law behind. He was tired of representing the mostly guilty, tired of losing, weary of the midnight callers begging to be bailed out before morning, sick of having to demand payment upfront and of receiving cash that too often he'd have to wash off so the bank tellers wouldn't see the adherent traces of white powder. Even so, he'd get funny looks from the City Bank employees with all those large deposits made in small bills.

But in recent years, as his ballplayer-clients found that the big money Harding had negotiated for them bought too many of them tickets to trouble, Bob had reluctantly found himself being pushed back into that netherworld. And he couldn't say no, or the client would go elsewhere for his big-money contract needs. And that's what paid for the stately home in White Plains, the condo in Santa Barbara, and, in another year or two, the private jet. But of all his clients, indeed of all the ballplayers he knew,

Donovan was the one from whom he least expected he'd ever get the midnight call.

"Hi, Bob. This is Donovan. Sorry to bother you this late, but I've got two officers here with a search warrant, and it says they're looking for evidence of a crime I supposedly committed on Opening Day." The Yankee didn't need to elaborate for Bob on the events of that afternoon.

"Omigod. Does the warrant describe what they're looking for? It should, you know."

Donovan didn't but glanced again at the document and replied, "Seems to."

"Yeah, I'm sure they dotted even the *j*s on this one. Well, what's your question?"

"Do I have to cooperate and let them take whatever they want?"

"They can search anywhere the described items could be, and they can take whatever matches the description. It's that simple. But what about your farmhouse? Are they searching there, too?"

Harding waited for the silence on the receiver to abate. Donovan hadn't even thought of that. "I don't know," he finally said with a tone that pled helplessness.

"Well, ask 'em."

"You think they'll tell me?"

"If they won't, you'll know what the answer is."

"Hang on a minute."

Donovan went to the kitchen and asked Johnson if his home in Richmondville was going to be searched. "I understand that's in the works." Johnson had come prepared to execute not merely this warrant but Kasoff's scheme as well. "If you'd like to avoid some of the legal rigamarole, you could consent to the search. I've got a consent form right here. If you'll sign it, we can arrange the search at a time that's convenient for you instead of—" and he spread his arm about as if to say, "Like this."

Left unsaid was the fact that law enforcement would be watching the farmhouse to ensure that no one contacted by Donovan went there to spirit away anything that might be incriminating. Now Donovan asked the officer to hang on as he walked back near his front door and resumed speaking to Harding in a hushed tone, explaining the offer.

151

"Well, they'll be allowed to search only if the Court out there signs the warrant, but since that's likely to happen, you might as well cooperate and see if you can get something in return—like a promise of no publicity and an agreement that if you're charged with anything, they'll contact you before alerting the media. You don't want to have to run a gauntlet from your doorstep. And most important, get yourself a criminal attorney in Chicago. I can give you a couple of names when I get to my office. And don't worry about this. This has all the marks of a grandstanding prosecutor."

Donovan thanked Harding and hung up. He presented the offer to Johnson, after asking and being assured by him that no one had tipped off or would be telling the media about tonight's search. "Would Thursday be OK?" It was an off-day.

"Sure," Johnson replied, trusting that the local sheriff there wouldn't mind. After all, it was a good bet that his hometown's top law enforcement official would prefer to tell Donovan's inquiring friends and neighbors that Donovan had consented to the search, even if it meant a couple of days' delay. At last, with a deep breath, Donovan signed the consent. "I'll be at the farm by noon. You can have your people come by then."

And now Sergeant Johnson, the consummate professional, stepped out of that role for just a moment. "I don't pretend to know what this is all about, Mr. Donovan, but I've followed your career all along, and I think you've been a real credit to the game." And until Opening Day, that had been true. Throughout his career, even after becoming the game's top star, Donovan had exemplified the prototype of the mythical baseball gentleman of yesteryear. After a day game, after showering, when the adrenaline had stopped pumping out its anesthetic for half a dozen groaning tendons, Donovan alone among the players could be found in the runway signing autographs for every last youngster. What's more, on the rare occasions when Donovan's unyielding schedule allowed him to appear at a collectors' show, he alone refused to charge for his signature.

Donovan had remained all these years with the team that had drafted him, even when LA had offered him more money each time he was eligible for free agency. He had never permitted his agent to grandstand for the media in an effort to obtain a bigger contract. After signing a long-term deal several years back that made him deservedly the highest paid player in the game, only to lose the distinction a year later to a couple of rivals not quite his equal, Donovan was asked if he planned to renegotiate. His reply was praised by people all over the country, fans and non–followers of the game alike: "I signed a multiyear contract for millions of dollars in order assure myself lifetime financial security. I knew full well when I agreed to the deal that a year or two later the market price of top-level talent would go up, likely exceeding the amount for which I signed. It would be wrong now for me to renege after having bargained for and received long-term security. I can't have it both ways. If my contract isn't the best, I have only myself to blame. I am honored to fulfill my obligation under it to the best of my ability."

If Donovan did not display exuberance on the field, he didn't trash talk, either. He simply did his job without fanfare and better than anyone else. On occasion, he would quietly compliment an umpire for a good call on a bang-bang play—even when it meant he was out. He had acquitted himself well both on the field and in the court of public opinion. Now, he wondered, would he soon be seeking an acquittal of a very different kind?

The police upheld their part of the bargain. They didn't want publicity anymore than the game's greatest star, considering the sentiment of Yankee fans toward their hero. The Schoharie County sheriff even showed up at Donovan's farmhouse in plain-clothes with a personal vehicle. But, local boy or not, law enforcement was not deterred from the task. Anything close to matching the description in the warrant was seized. Including the single round canister with the flaking aquamarine speckled paint that a sharp-eyed deputy spotted under some old magazines in the attic. All of it was boxed and shipped to the Chicago Prosecutor's Office, care of Robert Kasoff.

Entering the office the following Monday and spotting the dozen TV-sized boxes lining the walls awaiting Kasoff's orders, his first reaction was aimed at his favorite target: "Geez, Carol, how many diet books did you order? Or is this just lunch?" Carol just rolled her eyes. And then to work. "Let's delve, shall we? Sharon, buzz the clerks for me."

Seven law clerks soon appeared. The three who had completed two years of law school's three-year grind would be excused from this project. Their upperclass standing made them too valuable for anything other than advanced legal research. This was a task for the first-year students. "OK," said Kasoff, "I need you first to inventory everything in these boxes by description and, if it applies, date and author. Label everything you do with a date, a number, and your initials. Once that's done, I'll have you start reading or viewing everything we've got, and I'll let you know what you're looking for. We've got only three weeks to complete this, so let's start as soon as possible."

The deadline was purely self-imposed. The All-Star break was 21 days away, and then, following a short trip to Baltimore, the Yankees would return for their only other trip to Chicago this season, barring another play-off confrontation. July 21–23. A three-day window to serve Donovan an arrest warrant without haggling over extradition. In an extraordinary case like this, who knew if he would waive it?

The cataloging went on for more than two weeks, primarily because the clerks had to view each of the hundreds of video-tapes, at the very least skimming some sections and fast-forwarding others to be certain that Donovan's labeling on them was accurate. It was. The John Wayne movie collection was indeed nothing more than the Duke on celluloid. The public television films on topics that ranged from American presidents to the Civil War contained plenty of violence, but no evidence of malice toward McGinniss. If it seemed that the New York law enforcement authorities had been indiscriminate in what they had seized, they would answer that no one would later accuse them of going easy on a target of prominence. They preferred to bend over backward if necessary in service to their own star.

Occasionally, Kasoff would drop by the stockroom where the items were being inventoried to see how the progress was going. Much of this junk, he realized, he would want to have repackaged and returned to Donovan ASAP. It simply wouldn't do to have a prosecutor announce to the world that he was arresting baseball's top player while in possession of his collection of old movies. "Ham-handed" would be the kindest of the media's epithets hurled his way if that occurred. It was on one of his visits to the storeroom that Kasoff spotted the film canister sitting forlornly at the bottom of a nearly emptied box. A chill came over him—mother Donovan's legacy! This film, he would review himself.

It took some doing. No one under the age of 65, it seemed, had the old-style projector that would play this ancient eight-millimeter film. Finally, after a two-day search and calls to seemingly every parent of a friend of a friend, Kasoff got his hands on one. That night, following a brief lesson in the basics of the old machines, he played this bit of history, his curiosity overcoming any ethical qualm. Sure, he had no probable cause to believe this container held any evidence of a crime, and yes, it contained some of the most private moments of a mother communicating with her child, but this case had begun to consume him, and Kasoff needed to learn everything he could about his target. Knowledge is power, after all. That's why, to Kasoff, so many defendants would hide behind the Fifth Amendment right to remain silent, thereby depriving the prosecutor of the opportunity to digest, test, and destroy the alibi. Damn that James Madison again. Never mind that it took the Supreme Court nearly two hundred years to breathe life into those words that prohibit governmental compulsion of self-incrimination, thereby depriving only the most recent generations of the police from coercing confessions.

The film's content was as ironic as it was stirring, and it was just as Dorothy had described. Here was a loving dying mother, urging her young son to embrace life and forever turn away from the violence that she knew would be all around him long after she was gone. And in the defining moment of his life, Donovan had rejected the message, perhaps not even bothered to listen to it, for the film appeared to be in pristine condition, if somewhat brittle considering its age. Instead, Donovan had chosen to stand with his father, pretending to be strong, unaware of what lay behind the facade late one moonlit night so long ago. Like the society in which Kasoff had grown up, the quiet message of peaceful response to evil had been all but drowned out by the constant *rat-a-tat* of violence. Kasoff had come to the Prosecutor's Office to try to contain the latter. For those who embraced violence in any endeavor, and by any means, the People would have their retribution. And Kasoff had determined long ago that

155

it was up to him to do the People's work.

*   *   *

Mary continued to summon the past. Now, she thought back just a few months to the time McGinniss told her the story of when he had first confessed his feelings for her to Melanie.

On a Saturday morning a month before Mary's wedding to Victor, McGinniss had just opened the warehouse door when he saw Melanie, who had just dropped her sister off. Melanie spotted him and waved, and he approached. Mary, running late, had to get into the office, but Melanie lingered. "Mary have car problems?" McGinniss inquired.

"If only. You know what Victor did? He traded in her car for a motorcycle! Why the hell didn't he trade in his own car? What the hell's she going to drive in the winter?"

It did seem selfish, but Mary had never complained about Victor. She had always spoken well of him, even if it seemed she had less to say lately, and it was obvious that she loved him. "I'll tell you," Melanie continued. "I've got my doubts about that guy. You know, if her taste in men was anywhere near as good as his taste in women, she'd have ended up with you."

"Thanks." It was consoling, he thought. "But you can't fault her just because her heart rules her head. I of all people certainly know that. And you know you can't repeat this."

Melanie replied with a knowing look that his secret was safe with her. And he was surprised at how comfortable he was in referring to his most intense and private feelings, even if only to a coconspirator in his dreams. "Just remember, if he turns out to be a bad guy, all she's gotta do is pick up the phone and dial one–eight hundred–I-ADORE-U!" And as she laughed, her face bespeaking an amazed admiration, he added, "Oh, hell, I've got to develop a sense of humor about it."

And that's the way it went. He tried, for a while, to get over Mary, to deny his feelings, to boycott all thought of her, but gradually he realized that to shut them out was to deny the best part of himself. It was futile anyway. She had become, for him, an article of faith. He believed in all that was good because he believed in her. She had long since co-opted his inner voice,

156

becoming his conscience and cheerleader both.

At times, staying positive was easier said than done. A week after Mary's Honda disappeared and reappeared as a Harley, Victor stopped by just as McGinniss was approaching Mary's desk to accompany her to lunch. "I hear Melanie told you I bought Mary a motorcycle," said Victor. Without realizing it, Mary's fiancé was flattering McGinniss—it had never occurred to him that his name would even come up in her conversations with Victor. "She likes it, too," he continued. Was Victor trying to reassure McGinniss or himself, McGinniss wondered as he simply nodded his head. Victor paused and then added with an undertone of irritation, "And you've got your life and I've got mine."

McGinniss felt like he was a kid who has just been hit with a spitball. All he had done in response to Melanie's telling him about the motorcycle purchase was give her a slight shake of the head and a look that suggested he agreed with her doubts about this guy. Had Melanie told Mary, who in turn had passed it on to Victor? And even if she did, wasn't this a bit of an overreaction, especially in front of Mary? And before McGinniss could say anything, not that he had a clue as to what he would say, Victor continued, his voice rising, "If you have a problem with me, let's settle it right now," stepping forward so as to emphasize the immediacy of his challenge.

Now McGinniss was getting angry, but not from the beet red embarrassment he felt in his cheeks. "Look, I have too much admiration for your taste in women—" he liked Melanie's line— "to respond to that in Mary's presence. But I would hope that you would think enough of her that you would never do anything to make her feel as uncomfortable as she so obviously is at this moment." Even out of the corner of his eye, McGinniss had easily noticed the pained expression on Mary's face.

Whether disarmed or merely outwitted by McGinniss having taken the high road, Victor backed off the confrontation by turning to Mary. "Come on. I'll take you to lunch." And so he did, leaving McGinniss to ponder whether Mary's future happiness would be because of or in spite of the man her heart told her to marry. If luck was what was left over after subtracting that which is deserved, Victor was indeed the luckiest man on earth, thought McGinniss.

Eventually, McGinniss consoled himself with what he had to admit might be a bit of self-deception. Perhaps Victor reacted as he did because he felt threatened by McGinniss. And maybe that was because Mary went home at night and spoke fondly of him: "Oh, Don did this today. Don did that today. Don really made me laugh today. Don has a chance to be a big leaguer someday." What guy worth his salt wouldn't get sick and tired of hearing that crap?

For McGinniss, the wedding reception was anticlimactic. He had already ruled out asking Mary to dance in light of Victor's behavior. He did take to the floor for one number with Melanie. "So, do you really think you can make the majors?" she inquired.

"I sure hope so. Coaches say I've got all the tools. I just need to tame 'em."

"Don't we all. And after Auto Tronics, when you no longer get to see Mary so often?"

"I don't know. I do know—" and here he looked around to be sure no one else would hear—"my feelings are forever. But I'm determined to be happy, even if it kills me."

"In spite of yourself. And after baseball?"

"Not sure yet, but I guess I'll invest my money in cloning research. One day, years from now, if a couple of guys in white lab coats knock on Mary's door and ask for a tissue sample, tell her to be generous with 'em."

And they laughed. "You're the one they should clone, Don McGinniss."

One more keg of consolation to go, he thought as he thanked her.

12

"Well, what've we got?" Kasoff demanded of the clerk when at last all the diggings had been sifted through.

"Not much. The guy sure liked movies. Westerns and war pictures mostly. And a small tool kit we cataloged. Oh, and this—" and the neophyte handed Kasoff an anatomy book. "Check out the bookmark." Kasoff opened the text to the page it identified as its reader's final focus. The skull! And there, bright as day, was the yellow highlighting that described its contours, size, and, most important, density, thickness, and sutures—those locations where the bones of the skull fuse together. Those bridges are the weakest links in the brain's protective armor. And there, circled in red pen, was the vulnerable area of the right temple. Donovan might just as well have drawn in cross hairs.

"This we keep. Let's get the rest shipped back to Donovan pronto. I've got myself an arrest warrant to prepare tonight." Kasoff wasn't about to trust this ministerial task to Chicago's men in blue as was customary, both to prevent leaks and for his own personal satisfaction. "Hell, I can even fill in my own description of the accused. I'll be seeing him on the tube tonight. Batting third in the All-Star game. Good work," and he gave the clerk a thumbs-up that she would long remember.

"B.D., we've got to talk. I think we're ready to go on the Donovan thing."

B.D. rolled his eyes. Though he had given Kasoff the green light, he still had his doubts, and those flashed continued caution. "OK, what do you have?" And he motioned Kasoff to sit down. Taking his own seat, B.D. swiveled it over to his speaker phone. "Al, can you get in here?" B.D. wanted a second opinion. A moment later Green joined them. "Bob thinks he's ready to go forward with the Donovan case. Let's hear what he's got."

Kasoff, having been tested this way before in sensitive or difficult cases, began confidently. "OK, here's a rundown of our evidence on the elements of a murder charge. We've got a guy who

159

has studied for months the victim's windup to see where his head is exposed and vulnerable."

"How do you know that?" Green interjected.

"The lab guys say that certain sections of the tape were played hundreds of times more than other portions. The heavily played parts all correspond to the part of the victim's follow-through where he is most defenseless. They can point to microscopic striations in the film to prove this.

"We've got a guy who apparently—"

"Apparently?" B.D. raised his eyebrows.

"—who clearly studied another section of that tape in order to learn how McGinniss was tipping his pitches. We haven't yet figured out how he did that, but the wear marks show unmistakable evidence of multiple replays from the time McGinniss would begin looking in for the sign until the moment he would begin his windup. It's particularly striated in a spot that captures the victim from a center field camera with a telephoto lens as he is gripping the ball just before he begins to rock-and-roll. And we all know that if he's tipping his pitches, Donovan knows what's coming, and maybe where it's coming."

"Well, somebody better figure out how, or we've got nothing on that score," chimed in B.D.

"We've had an expert, an old Chicago pitching coach—remember Toby Wyatt?—take a good look at the film, and he thinks he'll have it nailed down soon."

It was Green's turn. "You mean that even a local guy—a biased witness—hasn't figured it out yet?"

"We're working on it."

"I thought you were going to tell us what you've got, not what you're hoping for," B.D. cut to the chase.

"I'm not all the way there yet," Kasoff had to concede. "Of course, we've got the vow of vengeance and his ecstatic reaction to his success on tape. We've got a perpetrator with a physics background who knows how fast a bat will propel a ball. A guy who's studied anatomy—we've even got his book—and knows the sweet spot on the skull as well as he knows it on his war club. Right at the squamosal suture of the temporal bone. It's the thinnest portion of the skull, and that particular suture doesn't fuse before age thirty—and sometimes not at all. And a coroner's

160

report that lists that spot as the point of impact. All this from the best place hitter in the game.

"And, most of all, we've got the bat. He dimpled it, like a golf ball, for extra bat speed. More bat speed, more velocity transferred to the ball. An X ray proves what I was sure of. Cork. Because he thinks that will increase his bat speed as well. We've got motive. We've got means. We've got a wrongful overt act."

"You know my feeling on that, Bob. Breaking a rule of the game is not the sort of act that will support a murder prosecution."

"And I still say it ought to be."

B.D. paused and began to shake his head just slightly back and forth, as though watching the scales of justice to see which way the evidence tipped. Green just tapped his fingers. He wasn't yet ready to go out on a limb on this one. At last, B.D. spoke. "Damn it, what the hell are we here for anyway if it's not to put coldblooded killers away? And that's exactly what this was," his voice rising. "We may not have a snowball's chance on this one, but it's just flat out the right thing to do. You want to seek an arrest warrant? You've got it. Let me just run it by Starman. Even though he authorized us to go forward, he's got to be kept informed so he'll be ready when the story breaks. Our surest ticket to oblivion is to let him get caught by the media with his pants down."

Kasoff smiled. He knew the pol would be pleased at the opportunity to do the popular thing. Now, Green decided it was his turn to speak. "Fair enough, but we might as well draw straws right now to see who'll be Starstruck's scapegoat if this thing blows up on us," he warned.

"Come on, Al. Can't you suspend practicality for a moment? Go with your heart on this one, not your head," B.D. counseled.

"Last time I did that, she took everything but the shirt off my back." Green wasn't buying B.D.'s customary equanimity this time.

Kasoff, pointing to B.D., replied to Green. "Ah, don't mind him. He suffers from equatorial disorder." To quizzical eyebrows, Kasoff added, "He's always on an even keel!"

And all three enjoyed the hearty laugh of relief when a weighty decision has been met squarely and resolved.

As the trio got up to go out for lunch, Green had a fresh inquisition for Kasoff. "All right, Bob, it's time for the all edibles team. You know, fruits, vegetables, the works," Green challenged. "No repeats."

"Gotcha. OK. Let's see. I've got Johnny Oates catching with Herman Franks second string. My pitcher has got to be Bob Lemon—"

"A Hall of Famer—"

"Over Bob Veale or David Cone. OK, outfield. Zack Wheat—"

"Another member of the Hall."

"Jim Rice is tempting, but Sam Rice is also in the Hall and you said no repeats. And the third outfielder is Willie Mays, you know, as in corn."

"That's your second whole grain with a mispelling. That's a deduction."

"Well, Wally Berger or Johnny Grubb just don't make it, so I'm sticking with Say Hey. Third base is Eddie Mayo. Shortstop, Dick Groat."

"Groat?"

"Sure, as in buckwheat groats. You never heard of kasha? All right, second base. Kevin Bass. First base. Now, bear with me on this one. Harmon Killebrew."

"Kille-what?"

"Sure. Killebrew. As in chug a beer."

"Novel, but no dice."

"OK, OK. Hang on a minute. I've got it. Johnny Hopp."

"Who the hell is he?"

"Are you kidding? He played nearly fifteen years, with a lifetime batting average just under three hundred."

"I'll take your word for it. Let's see. That's three Hall of Famers, four if I count Willie and five if I let you throw in the Brew. Your best yet."

With lunch over, it was time for B.D. to speak once again with the top dog.

"Hell, yes, you can go after his ass and then some." B.D. had hardly begun to explain the evidence—much less the baseball-sized holes in the case. "I saw the film of that SOB threatening McGinniss last year. You prepare the copy and I'll be glad to call the news conference."

162

"Well, I'm not sure we want to go public just yet. I'd like to wait at least until after he's served."

"Well, whatever then. You just let me know when we're ready."

"Thanks, Harold." And B.D. left the office of the prosecutor, shaking his head.

"The copy," he muttered to himself. "It's all just PR to him. Heaven forbid he should ever read a brief." Still, B.D. knew that, for once, Starman's bent was right on target. B.D.'s statement would have to justify for the world the warrant Kasoff was preparing to seek.

Kasoff had just put the finishing touches on the legal equivalent of "Play Ball!" It was the document that would crank up the machinery of the justice system—to be witnessed by a capacity crowd.

In the name of the people of the State of Illinois, County of Cook, you are commanded to arrest and take into custody one Christopher Donovan [and the physical description was right out of the Yankee's media guide], six feet, two inches, 210 lbs., brown hair, brown eyes, left-handed, and bring him before Magistrate Stuart Meadows for arraignment on the charge of murder in the first degree, to wit, the killing of a human being, with premeditation, deliberation, and malice aforethought, one Donald McGinniss on April 1, 1997, at or about the hour of 1:15 P.M. at Chicago Stadium, by means of striking the head of the said victim with a blunt object, i.e. a batted baseball.

Kasoff would be pleased to sign this one himself and present it to the magistrate personally in order to authorize its execution. Stuart Meadows was well known as a big Chicago fan, but Kasoff knew that would do him no good on this score. Unlike some of the other judges, Meadows had a firm rule with his clerk that under no circumstances was any lawyer allowed to leave ball game tickets gratis for him. If he chose to attend a game, he would mail away for the ducats or stand in line at the box office like anyone else.

Still, Kasoff was convinced Meadows would be on his side. Before his appointment to the bench, he had long been an antiviolence activist. Whether protesting the hated war of the sixties,

163

the death penalty, or the havoc produced by drunk drivers, Meadows was a confirmed pacifist. Republicans had howled in a protest of their own when a liberal governor had appointed him to this entry-level post in the judicial branch, threatening to hold hostage the chief executive's budget until he agreed to throw his support behind a state constitutional amendment that would give the state legislature an "advise and consent" role concerning judgeship appointments equivalent to that of Congress at the federal level. Heaven forbid that an attorney who had not spent his or her career defending corporate America or prosecuting its poorest citizens should ascend to such a position.

But Meadows had performed admirably. Even his critics respected his integrity. Kasoff knew he could count on Meadows to reveal nothing until the appropriate time and that his visceral opposition to violence would make him amenable to the due process Kasoff had in store for Donovan. Kasoff was right. It took him longer to walk over to the courthouse than to await the magistrate's authorization. Meadows said nothing while signing it, but Kasoff appreciated the gleam in the judge's eye as he returned the document.

Within thirty-six hours, the warrant would be served, Donovan would be taken into custody, and the battle would begin.

B.D. readied the ramparts for the siege. The first line of defense was the receptionist. "Look, within the next day or two you're going to be swamped by calls from the media demanding to talk to Starman, Kasoff, myself, or anyone else. Hang up. Just hang up on them. I'll handle them on my own time. You got that?"

"Are you indicting another judge?" Eighteen months before, when the office charged the popular Judge Joseph Lombardi with accepting a bribe, the switchboard's circuits had been overloaded.

"No. It's bigger than that. And for the media people who show up here, we'll have guards in the lobby preventing access. If any do get through, you call Security first and then me. Got it?"

"Sure. But can you tell me what's going on?"

"Just turn on the morning news day after tomorrow."

The Yankees' plane arrived from Baltimore shortly after dinner the next night, the team having completed a sweep with that afternoon's victory. Donovan had had three hits, and the Yankees were on a roll again, stretching their lead to five games. After a period of adjustment, Donovan was getting used to the headaches. His doctors had predicted last fall that he might develop them weeks or even months later. He had been pain-free all winter, but they had begun soon after Opening Day. His real concern, though, was the doctors' other forecast. He might even develop a seizure disorder as a result of the beaning, which might not show up for a year or two. If so, he would require medication that would dull his extraordinary reflexes just enough to disqualify him from stardom, if not major-league competition altogether. It was funny, though. Donovan had a hunch that the headaches were not related to the beaning.

With B.D.'s concurrence, Kasoff now hand-picked the two officers, Jeff Franzen and David Obringer, who would serve the arrest warrant. Like the police who had conducted the search of Donovan's apartment in Manhattan, these two could be counted upon to be discreet. The plan was to apprehend Donovan just after 11:00 P.M. Too late for the night's local news shows to get wind of it, and past the deadline for the early edition of the morning paper. The milk and cookies edition, as Kasoff derisively referred to it, because it went to bed so early—when children were devouring their bedtime snacks. At precisely the appointed hour, the uniformed officers identified themselves to the hotel desk clerk.

"Room eight-o-two," she revealed in response to their asking his whereabouts.

"Strictly routine," they assured her. They were merely following up on his complaint about the loss of an equipment bag. "Is he alone?" And Obringer said it with just a hint of the sly smile that suggested they merely didn't want to catch him at an embarrassing moment.

"He's booked in a single, but I don't know for sure," and she didn't, though she returned the knowing look borne of experience with putting up ballplayers and the young women who loved them, if only for a night.

The officers turned and strode toward the elevators. Officer Obringer fingered the warrant as it sat snugly inside his breast pocket while he silently rehearsed how he would remove and present the order. If the procedure was conventional, the suspected felon was anything but. At last, the bell signaled the eighth floor, and a sign pointing toward the room number greeted them. "Must be the last one on the right."

"Nearest the emergency exit stairwell."

"Not near enough."

The door for 802. No sound within, but a crack of light escaping through the door sill. The knock. Twice. Footsteps. The peephole darkens. Through its fisheye lens, there is no mistaking that these are police. Chain removed. Deadbolt undone. Doorknob rotates, and Donovan opens the door to his temporary home, no longer private. "Evening, Officers. What can I do for you?"

"May we come in a moment?" The police preferred their conversation not be overheard by the strapping young man—probably a teammate—who had just left 805 to get some ice.

"Sure, what's up?" The officers sensed that Donovan, who had a pretty good idea what was up, was attempting to project a calmer comportment than he felt.

"Are you Christopher Donovan?" The question was purely a formality. Obringer had seen more than one *Sports Illustrated* cover in his day.

"Yes."

Obringer executed flawlessly. He removed the arrest warrant from his pocket in one sweeping motion, and announced sternly and solemnly, "I have a warrant for your arrest. Come with us."

"For, for what?"

"For murder in the first degree."

And before Donovan could sputter a protest, Franzen placed him in handcuffs.

"Nothing personal you know, just department policy."

"Murder! I didn't murder anyone." But by this time, Franzen was already reciting his Miranda warning and Donovan decided to heed it.

As they began to lead him from the door, Donovan recovered just enough to ask for a moment to "get my things, call my manager, and let him know."

But these men played it by the book. Murderers don't get such quarter, however momentary. Celebrity scores no points with these guys. Hell, who's more deserving of all that big money anyway—these prima donnas who get to play a boys' game for half the year and a man's game—golf—somewhere warm for the rest of it or big-city cops, who put their lives on the line every day for a pittance by comparison and who, instead of being cheered, take it on the chin every time one of their number succumbs to the pressure and goes bad, beating a citizen or going on the take? "Just do as we say and there'll be no trouble. Come with us," is all Obringer says, but it's enough to stifle Donovan's efforts.

As Donovan is led down the hall, the Yankee catcher happens to open his door. "What the—" and he rushes back into his room to buzz the Yankee manager.

"It won't be long, now," Franzen sighs, anticipating the frenzy about to burst.

Fortunately for the officers, the hotel was only a few minutes from police headquarters, which gave them a head start on the parade of notepads and cameras that would soon be forming. Donovan was booked like anyone else—mug shot, fingerprints— and then given an opportunity to make a call. It was after midnight in Evanston when the telephone rang in Mark Wingo's bedroom. Normally a night owl, Wingo had turned in early after a mostly sleepless night twenty-four hours earlier on the redeye from LA. Groggy to begin with and annoyed at the intrusion, he snapped into the receiver, "Who is this?"

"Chris Donovan, Bob Harding in New York suggested I call you."

It took a moment for the name to register. *Nothing good ever happens after midnight*, Wingo thought to himself, but then, with the flash of recognition, he felt a sudden surge to alertness. What the hell did the Yankee star want?

"Look, I need an attorney. Harding recommended you. I've been arrested." Donovan never was one for small talk.

"Arrested? For what?"

"Murder." The word didn't register, not from Donovan's lips. "They want to say I murdered McGinniss on Opening Day just for getting a hit off him."

Wingo doubted that Donovan was a drinker, but what the hell was this?

"Hello," Donovan demanded of the stunned silence at the

167

other end. "Can you help me or not?"

"I'm afraid not, at least if you need help right away. I have a big trial beginning day after—what day is this?—oh yeah, tomorrow, right. I do know another guy in town who's top-notch, though. Harold Weinstein's his name. He's a tiger. Expensive, though. And uh—" and now he hesitated.

"What?"

"He's a little off-beat, not the straight arrow you are. Judges consider him a pain in the ass. But juries love him."

"Is his office downtown?"

"Yeah, on Wacker. It's easy to remember. Wiley Weinstein on Wacker." The sobriquet was more clever than accurate. Aside from his unconventional appearance—no handicap in a trade where one goes to work for society's outcasts—Weinstein had a reputation for playing it straight, if tough and sometimes from the hip.

"Thanks," replied the Yankee, too preoccupied to acknowledge the attempt at humor.

Donovan was led back to his cell. There would be no bail tonight. This was, after all, a capital case. The one concession the Chicago PD had made to his celebrity status was to give him a solitary cubicle away from the holding pen of thieves, drunks, and male prostitutes. In the morning, he would be arraigned and then the issue of bond would be raised. Donovan would try to get in touch with Weinstein first thing in the morning, to avoid even a temporary court-appointed attorney. From what little Donovan had heard, he knew they were chronically overworked and understaffed. The fact that he had always voted for the politicians most eager to cut such legal services mattered nothing to him until now.

At 8:30 A.M., a sympathetic guard allowed Donovan a second call. "Baker, Weinstein and Mott," chirped the female voice on the other end.

"Harold Weinstein, please."

"May I ask who's calling?" The disconnected voice was no longer singsong.

Donovan took the cue. It was time to make an impression. "Chris Donovan, the New York Yankee."

In a heartbeat, the barrister took the call. On his way into

168

work that morning, he had switched from public radio to the all-news station for its traffic report "on the threes." At 7:52, he had caught the tail end of the 7:50 sports update: "We repeat: The big news in the sports world this morning..." Dramatic pause. "New York Yankee superstar Christopher Donovan..." Another pause. "Arrested here in Chicago. The charge...Murder. The victim, Chicago pitcher Don McGinniss. Details at the top of the hour and again on our next report at eight-twenty."

"Holy shit!" Weinstein screamed to himself in his hermetically sealed luxury car. And he almost hit the vehicle in front of him as the stop-and-go snaking line of cars came to another halt. Then, thinking of Donovan's agent, Weinstein moaned in sympathy, "Oh, the endorsements." If fame was fleeting, bankability was all that and mercurial, too, and no one needed a wind sock to know which way a murder charge blew. But now, in his office, he assumed the dignified mien that every cold-call client expected.

"Harold Weinstein here."

"Yeah, this is Chris Donovan. Mark Wingo recommended you. If you've heard the news this morning—" Donovan had overheard it himself on the jail radio.

"I have. I'm sorry to hear that."

"Anyway, I'm supposed to be transported to the Circuit Court before nine-thirty for an arraignment. There'll be a whole busload and I understand they're saving me for last, so if you've got some time this morning, I'd like an opportunity to meet with you before my case is called."

"Sure thing. I'll meet you in the holding area at nine-thirty and they'll give us a conference room, I'm certain. Oh, just one thing you should know up front."

The fee, Donovan guessed, and correctly at that. "I bill four hundred dollars per hour plus expenses. In a capital case, I usually work with an associate, who's an additional two hundred. Our investigator is ninety dollars per hour, including travel time, plus expenses. Normally, I require a ten-thousand-dollar retainer up front in a murder case."

Assuming Donovan was eminently collectable, having earned millions in his career, Weinstein, contrary to his custom with the typical cash-and-carry criminal client, would have been willing to wait a week or two for the initial check, but before he could say so, Donovan replied, "No problem. I'll see that my agent wires it to you today."

"OK. Thanks. See you then."

At exactly half past nine, Donovan was ready to meet his counselor, but there was no sign of him. A few minutes to ten, Weinstein ambled up to the holding area, sugar doughnut in one hand, the sprinkles from which had spilled onto his suit—even on his left shoulder for heaven's sakes, thought Donovan—briefcase in the other.

"Sorry that I was detained, but I knew you'd be here well past ten. I checked with the court and found out there's a long call this morning."

Doctors and lawyers, thought Donovan. *They're never just late. They're always detained. Like it's always someone else's fault that they mismanage their time.* Of course, it had not yet dawned on this efficiently built baseball machine that, in his current predicament, he had no use for his efficacy.

At Weinstein's arrangement, a deputy led them to a conference room. Donovan said nothing but fixed his gaze on the diamond chip gleaming back at him from the advocate's right ear, surrounded as it was by long, unkempt curly brown hair. Donovan's contempt for the bejeweled modern ballplayers was spilling over to this stranger, but he told himself, and Weinstein, "Wingo recommended you highly."

Weinstein flashed the perfunctory smile that accompanies the well-meaning compliment heard so often its impact has been dulled.

"But let's get something straight right off the bat. I don't like lawyers. Never have."

"That makes two of us."

But Donovan, as usual, was not about to be deterred. "As far as I'm concerned, you guys twist the facts to suit your own purposes and you just prey on the misfortunes of others."

"Yeah, yeah. The same way that doctors prey on the sick and teachers prey on the ignorant and truckers prey on the freightless. By the way, I charge time and a half while I'm being insulted. Now, shall we get to work?"

Donovan had to admit to himself that he had a grudging respect for a guy who challenged him with a straight fastball

170

right down the middle like that. "Fair enough."

"OK, I've read the arrest warrant. You'll be arraigned today. That means the charge will be read to you and you'll be asked how you plead. Naturally, I'll speak for you and indicate 'not guilty.' Then I'll request bail. The prosecutor will oppose it as they do in every capital case, but the facts of this one are unique, so I think we've got a real shot at something as low as fifty thousand dollars, so long as—I'm assuming you've never been in trouble before?"

"No, sir." Donovan wanted to begin talking about the case, but Weinstein cut him off.

"Not yet. I want to see the reports. Then we'll talk."

"What reports?"

"The coroner's report and, more important, the case report which the detective on the file completed. It summarizes the expected testimony of the witnesses for the prosecution."

To Weinstein, following this protocol was critical. He needed to study the prosecution's case in order to determine its weak points. Then he could point these out to his client. Only then would Weinstein ask the accused what happened. And even then, only after pointing out all of the possible defenses. As in, "OK, you're charged with rape. You can defend in several ways: consent, alibi, insanity; now, suppose you tell me what happened?" To critics, this was an invitation to criminal defendants to perjure themselves while their attorneys remained only in the most technical sense unaware of the fabrication. In this way, the lawyers would skirt the ethical bar against presenting evidence knowingly tainted by falsehood. To the defense bar, this was simply the best way to present their clients with the evidence against them in order to set the stage for plea negotiations as well as to refresh their clients' memories of the events. After all, many such crimes are committed in a fog of drugs, including alcohol.

"What kind of a judge do we have?"

"Crusty old sort. We've had our battles over the years, but I believe he respects me. Name's Taft."

"Is he a Chicago fan?"

"I doubt it. The only thing he reveres is the history he'll never make. I'll tell you, though, he's got guts. He won't give a hoot that the prosecutors are pressing a popular cause." To the defense bar, the other side was known only as prosecutors, never the People, and that was on a good day, when they weren't being ridiculed as persecutors. "Anyway, we'll be asked at the arraignment if we waive a preliminary exam. Of course we won't. I don't see any way they can prove probable cause to believe a crime was committed. And without that, you can't be bound over—case dismissed. But we'll hit those details harder after today."

Hit, Donovan thought. He might not be doing any hitting tonight. And, "My God," he wondered aloud, "will the Yankees suspend me pending the outcome? Will the league?"

"I don't know, but you can check with the team this afternoon, assuming we're allowed to post bail, and I'll have your agent check with the Commissioner's Office."

"Thanks." Donovan was still contemptuous of Weinstein's appearance, but he did seem to know what he was talking about between the white lines. Oddly, though, he unexpectedly realized that the headache he had been enduring just before the police took him into custody had disappeared soon after and, in spite of the stress of the previous eleven hours, had not returned.

Insofar as his professional obligations were concerned, Donovan needn't have worried. In response to an urgent inquiry from Yankee brass, the Commissioner's office issued a terse statement within minutes of Donovan's posting bail. After a brief reference to the arrest, it continued:

> The fate of Mr. Donovan is in the hands of the judicial system. Under that system, all persons are presumed innocent until proven guilty. Until such time, any punishment would be premature. The Commissioner's Office and the American League will therefore await the outcome of the legal process before considering what action, if any, is warranted against Mr. Donovan. Furthermore, the Yankee ball club firmly believes that the tragic event of last April 1 was nothing more than a terrible accident.

That bail hearing Donovan had won in a walk. Kasoff had a commitment in another courtroom on a critical suppression motion in a major drug case, and anyway, it behooved the DA's office to allocate its assistants' time efficiently. That meant that a rookie prosecutor would cover arraignment day, it being an exercise in simplicity. Three times the young assistant DA referred to this case as involving a capital crime, and three times Judge Taft interrupted to remind him, "That hasn't been established yet." Ominously for the People, the first time, Taft went on to mention that "normally, there is no question that a crime has been committed and the issue boils down to who the perpetrator was and, for the purpose of bail, the likelihood of flight from the jurisdiction, and so forth. But that's not this case, counsel."

Weinstein had spoken merely to assure the Court that Donovan wasn't going anywhere the rest of the Yankees weren't and the prosecutor could keep tabs on his whereabouts by the simple expedient of reading the sports section. Taft needed no convincing, and Weinstein had been around long enough to know that when you're ahead, you shut up and run for the elevator. Taft set bail just as Weinstein had predicted, at $50,000—the statutory minimum in a capital case—and made it personal, so Donovan wouldn't be chained to a bondsman.

The preliminary examination was set to begin in two weeks. Taft set aside three days for the proceeding, including the inevitable defense motion to dismiss the charges at the conclusion of the testimony. Donovan was greatly relieved when Weinstein told him his presence wasn't required throughout. The first week of August involved a key four-game series against Boston.

*　　*　　*

As for the courtroom, it was packed. Media had already arrived from much of the country. A number of Chicago fans, eager for all the revenge due process could muster, also attended, if only in the back row well behind the privileged press section. If it weren't for the fact that Taft, as the longest serving judge, was eligible to invoke a grandfather clause allowing him to bar cameras from his courtroom, the whole nation would have seen the dubious look His Honor exhibited each time the DA mentioned murder.

Donovan was able to get to the ballpark in plenty of time for batting practice even if he did miss some of his self-imposed pregame regimen. As the next several days unfolded, Donovan discovered that for the first time in weeks he was headache-free.

His batting average had slipped dangerously close to the .300 level—for Donovan, unlike his brethren who played the pastime, .300 was a floor, not a ceiling. Now it began to climb again, rocketing up to .358 after a doubleheader against Oakland where he went 10 for 11 on a day when the Yankees scored 31 runs to sweep. Though they won 11 of 15 in that stretch, Boston and Baltimore kept pace and both remained within striking distance, behind 4 and 5 games, respectively.

During this judicial interlude, and in the middle of a home stand, that same anonymous phone booth outside the stadium was the spot from where a call was made to TV11 in Chicago. "Greg Townsend, please," said the voice as his dialing hand fingered the business card. After identifying himself, the caller was put through.

"Mr. Donovan. Thank you so much for calling. What can I do for you?"

"You remember our conversation in Detroit?"

"Sure do."

"Good. You can use it. On-the-record. For attribution. The whole bit."

Greg's heart was pounding, partly out of frustration. *Damn, why didn't he let me record it?* Greg thought.

Anticipating the reaction, Donovan went on. "No doubt you made detailed notes the minute I left the table."

"Well, sure. But it's not on tape." For this generation of the press, the absence of a video or audio recording was the equivalent of a court hearing without a reporter: it was as though it never happened. Mere note taking was no substitute for trust long since lost in a business whose stock in trade is speed in spreading the story at the expense of accuracy.

"Well, so what? I gave you the whole story. My attorney tells me the media in Chicago are killing me. They've already got me convicted. If I make a public statement now, people will just see it as the squealing of a rat caught in a trap. Besides, he's ordered me to maintain my silence. But you can tell the public what they need to know—before any overzealous prosecutor dreamed up these trumped-up charges. I told you the way it really was. You're sitting on an exclusive. Now get it out there before I get lynched for crying out loud."

174

"I'll certainly talk to my program director. Thanks for the call. I'll see what I can do. If we run it, I'll let you know. Thanks again."

It never even occurred to Greg that Donovan had forbidden taping because he had calculated—correctly—that he might be prosecuted and wouldn't want to be trapped by his own recorded words if events required a bit of historic revisionism on his part. This way, he could get his side out there and still maintain deniability if any portion of the report became inconvenient.

*　　*　　*

The fortnight following the arraignment was not headache-free for Kasoff. Preparing his list of witnesses was easy enough, but the logistics of planning their arrival in the courtroom were getting complicated. Nothing produces a burning gut more quickly for the trial lawyer than when the judge orders the advocate to call the next witness. When the lawyer steps to the door, opening it a crack, then wide, the witness damn well better be standing out there, the typical sequestration order barring these participants from sitting in on the proceedings until they have completed their testimony. If the hallway is empty, the entire symphony screeches to a halt, no matter how frantically the advocate waves his arms when he beseeches the Court for more time.

One of the two deputies from upstate New York who had conducted the search of Donovan's home had just retired and gone fishing. Where? A lake in that region. Which one? No one knew. That left only several thousand from which to choose. The other deputy had just undergone open heart surgery. No traveling would be allowed for six weeks. An adjournment from Taft was out of the question, mainly because of the speedy-trial provision of the Sixth Amendment. Madison strikes again.

At least the officers who had searched the New York apartment were all set to appear. Dutch promised to show up, but Kasoff had made a commitment to him that he would issue Dutch a subpoena to cover him, and so far the process servers had managed to miss him. The batboy who had retrieved Donovan's bat was needed as well, but New York law, which applied in

175

the case of a subpoena served in New York, required that a minor be served by handing a subpoena to a parent or guardian. And his parents were in Europe, according to what a neighbor told the process server.

Rodriguez, who Dutch had said had the McGinniss tape until Donovan called San Juan for it, had been subpoenaed, but he hadn't responded to the "please call to confirm" message on the accompanying letter. Kasoff fretted that Rodriguez might take his chances with a contempt citation rather than give testimony that might hurt a teammate. Kasoff had no idea what the big first baseman would say, but the preliminary exam was the time to find out. That way, come the trial—if it came—Kasoff would know Rodriguez's answers in advance and therefore whether he was worth calling. Perhaps, just perhaps, Donovan had confided in his teammate his reason for wanting the film. At least Evans, who had taped Donovan's infamous threat, was lined up. So was the coroner and, finally, Pete, the physicist, whom Kasoff had since formally retained as an expert to explain the dynamics of a moving ball striking a swinging bat and—subsequently, if a split second could be thought of as something other than simultaneous—that ball then striking a human head.

On his way into the office one morning after a night tossing and turning these difficulties over in his mind, he overheard Carol and Sharon discussing an old musical. Kasoff brightened. "I love that one. You remember the timeless lyric, 'There is nothing like a dame . . .'"

"Watch it, Mr. K.," interrupted Carol. "You might be able to get away with the 'fat' smart remarks, but gender harassment is unlawful."

But, as always, Kasoff was ready, "This from a woman whose most charitable appellation for the average male is numb-nuts!"

Sharon laughed and even Carol smiled a surrender as she shook her head. And Kasoff wasn't through. "Would you like your touché here, or shall I wrap it for you? And will that be cash or charge?" Now he was laughing as he made his way to the office while thumbing through the telephone messages Sharon had just handed him. "Media, media, media, media," he repeated as he glanced at each. "Great. No calls yet today. I can get straight to work."

176

The morning's good start continued. His investigators reached the batboy's parents in Europe, who agreed that his grandmother could accept service on their behalf. Late the night before, Dutch had finally been served following a Yankee game. Even Rodriguez had faxed a note acknowledging service, though that afternoon his attorney would offer Kasoff an affidavit attesting that Rodriguez had no material information on the homicide and he would therefore move to quash the subpoena if Kasoff attempted to enforce it. Lacking a factual basis to contest that assertion, Kasoff acceded to excusing Donovan's teammate from the legal process. Otherwise, he knew, he would be accused of a fishing expedition.

But, best of all, another such expedition had mercifully concluded. Deputy Aaron had come home. They weren't biting up in the Finger Lakes region, and so now he called up Kasoff to inform him that he had made a discovery on a return visit to the Donovan barn. When copies were faxed to Kasoff, he took one look at them and knew that another visit with Pete was called for. The case indeed was beginning to add up.

Kasoff knew, of course, that this was a prosecution where making a strong presentation out of compelling facts would not be enough. The legal briefing necessary to prove that these facts constituted the crime of murder would have to be first-rate. With B.D.'s blessing, he had assigned the task to the best brief writer in the office. Their newest hire, Angela Newson, had been on the job less than six months, but she had spent two years clerking for the Seventh U.S. Circuit Court of Appeals, and the word out of that court was that the judge for whom she worked, a brilliant judicial conservative, had grown to trust her to write drafts of key opinions in criminal cases. And his editing consisted of not much more than a note that would say: "Ready final."

The elements of the crime of murder having evolved from English common law, Kasoff's instruction to Angela had been to pull out all the stops, check the university library for cases not only from England but throughout the British Commonwealth as well as all U.S. authority for any remotely similar prosecutions. Somewhere, some bloke must have played a game that wasn't cricket.

Two days before the hearing was set to begin, Kasoff read a

draft of Angela's brief. And he liked what he read, even appreciating the irony. After she scoured the entire Western world for the most telling precedent, it turned out that the best cases were close to home. As the hours to the courtroom confrontation dwindled, it wasn't only Donovan who was peaking.

For Weinstein, there was actually not all that much to do. He, too, had farmed out the legal briefing to the topnotch writer in his office—a young associate named Jason Diamond. Weinstein's forte was the courtroom action, but a preliminary exam didn't call for much on his part. After all, these exams required the People to prove the existence of a crime and that his client probably committed it. The law didn't require him to do anything. He certainly wouldn't be calling any witnesses—that would just give the prosecution a road map for his trial defense. He would just cross-examine the prosecution witnesses to see where they were vulnerable and where they weren't so at trial he would know where to bob and where to weave. Much of the cross-examination at the exam would be based on Weinstein's ability to think on his feet—the stock in trade of the criminal defense attorney.

The People, of course, had a constitutional obligation to turn over any information that tended to exculpate their target. Weinstein had received nothing from Kasoff but hadn't really expected to. Everyone knew what happened here. It was a simple matter of putting it on record and then arguing the law. And judges, of course, have the exclusive province to decide all questions of law. Weinstein was convinced that Donovan would stay out of jail because he would never have to submit his fate to a jury of Chicago partisans.

Kasoff was riding high the night before he was due in Taft's courtroom until he got a call from Carol telling him he should tune in to TV11's late news. One of their prime-time teasers showed Greg bragging about an exclusive interview with Donovan. "You're kidding!" shouted Kasoff into the phone, assuming Donovan had just spoken to Greg. "I can't believe Weinstein would let him do that." And, of course, he hadn't.

At 11:26, after twenty-five minutes of promises at every break in the newscast trumpeting an exclusive interview with startling revelations, Greg came on camera to rehash what Donovan had told him in Detroit months earlier. It wasn't that

Kasoff was worried that Donovan's side of the story would affect Judge Taft—if anything, pressure on him to rule for Donovan might cause him to tilt the other way—but it was galling that Greg's program director would choose the night before the hearing to air an uncritical and incredible expression of Donovan's viewpoint. But Kasoff knew to expect it from contemptible TV newscasters. On second thought, contemptible would be a step up. It was too kind a description. These people were a ceaseless drain on the reservoir of thoughtful discourse.

*　　*　　*

The summer following his freshman year, McGinniss began to come into his own on his American Legion League team as he built on the no-hitter he had pitched that spring for his school. He cut his bases on balls by nearly half, although starting from a lofty two per inning, they were still excessive. Nevertheless, this was a major improvement, especially considering that his fastball was flying harder than ever. For every nine innings pitched, he averaged 17 strikeouts. And, better than that, he was becoming known as a pressure pitcher. With men on and in a tight spot, usually of his own making through a combination of walks and wild pitches, he would stalk to the back of the mound and stuff the ball in his glove, intently staring at it. Then, he'd break the trance with a sudden stomp of his left foot as he wheeled around and practically pounced on the rubber. His next pitch would invariably be his fastest, and the batter, woefully overmatched, would nearly always strike out with a swing that lashed out as blindly as if trying to swat flies in the dark. Everyone thought the ritual that preceded the pitch was designed to focus McGinniss's concentration. They didn't know that, for him, this was actually an exercise in self-distraction. He would summon the extra shot of adrenaline he needed to blow the ball past the hitter by calling to mind what made him angriest. Victor! And McGinniss drove the hitters to distraction.

By August, McGinniss had led his team to the final statewide play-off round: a best of three series against perennial power Peoria. In game 1, McGinniss struck out the side in the first inning. In the second, he walked the first two hitters. And then disaster struck. On a wild pitch, McGinniss ran in to cover the plate as his catcher raced to the backstop to retrieve the errant fastball. It was nothing he hadn't done that season a dozen times before, but sandlot fields aren't like those in the pros. Not only is there no grass infield, but also the diamond itself will have its assortment of flaws. Conditions are so far removed from the majors that you'll often see the fielding percentage of the top infielders rise with each promotion through the minors right up to and including the show. On this field, on this day in Peoria, not six feet in front of the plate, a three-quarter-inch peak of Midwest granite nosed above ground. Like an iceberg, nearly a foot of it lay just beneath the surface. If your cleats hit it, it wasn't going anywhere; you were. And as McGinniss loped in, his right shoe struck it, causing him to fall forward and to the right, landing on that leg on an unforgiving earth, hardened as it was by the dog days' sun.

McGinniss cried out from the pain. His ankle was turned at a sickening angle of nearly 90 degrees. Ice was quickly obtained from a nearby concession stand, and McGinniss was at the hospital within an hour. Surgery would be required to repair a bimalleolar fracture. As the surgeon on call explained it, "Those round bony prominences on each side of your ankle—you broke both of 'em." This meant that both of the long bones in the lower leg had been fractured. Until they went in, the doctors wouldn't know how much damage there was to the joint space or the cartilage. And as serious as the bone breaks were, the key was the cartilage. It acts as a shock absorber between the bones that make up the joint and permits them to move free of any excess friction. If the damage was extensive, he might never pitch again. It would simply place too much stress on the joint. The remaining weakened cartilage would wear away; bone would rub against bone. The pain would be so disabling that additional surgery would be necessary to fuse the joint. That would eliminate all motion in it, causing a limp. Forget about pitching with a fused joint.

And McGinniss wouldn't get an immediate answer to what lay within this dark cloud over his future. The swelling would have to go down first. Otherwise, there was a high risk of skin breakdown and secondary infection following surgery. Icing would be the technique chosen to reduce the edema. It might take twenty-four hours. It might take ten days.

McGinniss would just have to lie there, bedridden, until then. In the meantime, the nurses offered McGinniss a self-administering morphine pump—morphine!—in anticipation of the severe pain in which he would find himself.

McGinniss had also complained of a headache. He figured it was just the stress of the situation, but because he seemed a bit fuzzy in his history of how he landed, the emergency room physician had ordered an MRI to rule out the possibility of intracranial injury in the event McGinniss had struck his head in the course of his fall. He was wheeled into the radiology room, where half a dozen separate films, each showing several slices, were taken at a cost of nearly $200 each. As McGinniss expected, the scan showed no sign of injury. What a shame that, aside from being shipped with the remainder of his records to Northwestern University Hospital in Chicago where he would eventually obtain his follow-up care, these all but gold-plated films would be left to gather dust.

McGinniss was certainly in a good deal of discomfort—that's how doctors always label pain, no matter how piercing—as he lay there waiting for the ice to do its work. Even though the pain had left *severe* in the dust and was gaining fast on *excruciating*, McGinniss wouldn't use the pump. He wanted to experience this pain. He needed it. It would come in handy later. And as he awaited his fate—his baseball future depending on the condition of a measly ounce of white gristle between his tibia and his astragalus—he would distract himself with fantasies of Mary and her smile. And he enjoyed his thoughts that night.

But by 5:00 A.M., it was a different story. With each beat of his heart, the ankle throbbed with overwhelming distress. McGinniss could tolerate it no longer. He took to the pump, like a suckling child, and maxed out on his prescribed dosage within the hour.

And the relief it brought was comparable only to the doctor's good news less than twenty-four hours later. The swelling had subsided enough to go forward with the operation. Several screws and a plate were required, but the surgeon's prognosis was hopeful. The damage to the joint had been minimal. The doctor had been able to reapproximate the bones to their original anatomical positions. McGinniss would wear a cast for three months and could then begin non-weight-bearing exercise of the leg to begin restoring the atrophied muscles. By four months, he should graduate from crutches to a cane and begin weight-bearing. Running or other heavy exertional activities would be out for a year. If the hardware began to irritate with weight-bearing, it could be removed, but that would set the timetable back a few months. If everything went well, within eighteen months McGinniss might—might return to full function.

And that was supposed to be good news? McGinniss, as Melanie had said from the first time she met him, might be mature beyond his years, but the thought of hobbling around for a year to this nineteen-year-old athlete was a searing pain no narcotic could ameliorate. No baseball. No work—at least none on his feet. And no opportunity to see Mary. McGinniss made up his mind—the physical agony was enough. He would have to find ways to distract himself from missing out on the opportunity to pitch. And as for Mary, the time had come for weaning. He would have to find a way to forget about her. As soon as he was discharged from the hospital and driven back home by his parents he wrote a letter to Mr. Nagy at Auto Tronics to let him know he would be disabled for at least a year. If there was room for him to return part-time after that, great. If not, he understood. As it turned out, McGinniss went back for one final stint the following summer. Next, he enrolled in extra classes. Mary did call him when she heard about his accident and said she would try to get over to visit, but, busy herself, she never did. That fall and winter, McGinniss threw himself into his books. With nothing else to do, McGinniss was now getting the most out of his education.

Meanwhile, his recovery went well, even better than expected. After the cast was removed, his now spindly legs began to reassume their muscular form as he soon built up to over an hour per day of weight-resistance exercise. He reveled in the exertion, telling himself that if he could overcome this, he could get over Mary, too. X rays showed complete healing of the fractures. The orthopedist in Chicago into whose care McGinniss was transferred allowed weight-bearing a month early. By March, he was walking without a limp and with only occasional discomfort from the hardware. In June, McGinniss was allowed to test the ankle with some light jogging. Soon, he was throwing again, too.

By that August, his rehabilitation was complete. He could run a mile without pain, and the mound was again familiar territory. He even got to pitch in four sandlot games as summer waned, the first two in relief, the last two as a starter, pitching five and then seven innings without pain. His doctor warned him that it might be another year or two before he would know whether the reconstructed joint would become arthritic. If he could modify his delivery to place less stress on that joint, he would have a better chance of avoiding that outcome. McGinniss would try this but quickly found that he couldn't give up his trademark. For him, the high leg kick and thundering follow-through weren't merely most comfortable for his mechanics. This was his mental edge over the hitters. There was one thing about his pitching he would try to modify, though. In his last game that shortened summer following sophomore year, he found himself in a tight spot—and thinking of Victor to provide him with that extra push. McGinniss would have to force Victor out of his mind and focus instead on something else that made him angry in order to supply that burst of adrenaline.

In his junior year, McGinniss returned to the school team and, after the first few games, seemed his old self on the mound. Though control remained a problem, he was striking out more hitters than ever, and now his fastball was clocked at 97 mph. There were occasional twinges of pain in the ankle, but the doctor's prognosis was benign. The scouts who had given up on signing McGinniss, knowing he planned to complete college first, came back around, and he learned why after one particularly impressive shutout where he walked only three, his all-time low for a complete game. Now that he had suffered and recovered from a severe injury, couldn't he see how easily his chance to play in the big leagues could be lost? "Sign now and we'll have you in the majors before you know it. Stay in college and who knows? One more injury could end your career and you'll always wonder what might have been."

"I'll always wonder what might have been, anyway," McGinniss barked back, the scout having no idea that this pitcher was

183

referring to a very different pursuit. McGinniss concealed at that moment the pain he felt. Mary was still creeping into his thoughts despite his self-denial. He recovered himself, apologized, and told the man from Kansas City that he still planned to finish school first. The recruiter left, but it was McGinniss who sighed with dismay. However pleasant, school and sport were mere diversions from what he really desired. It had been nearly a year since he had seen Mary, and still she popped into his thoughts daily. He would have to redouble his determination to relegate her to the ancient history section. If only there was a way to concentrate on not thinking about the one thing, the only thing, he really wanted.

"If you can't accept the fact that you will never, ever be with her, you'll never be able to live your own life." He began repeating this bromide to himself each time she came to mind. He even tried to imagine her with serious character flaws that perhaps he had been too blinded by his emotions to discern. But McGinniss could only come to laugh at his own futility. Angel or otherwise, the portrait was going nowhere. He could only hope that time would cause its colors to fade, its rich texture to disintegrate.

13

"Oyez, oyez, oyez. Please rise. The Circuit Court for the County of Cook is now in session, Judge Richard Taft presiding. Draw near and you shall be heard. Please be seated and remain silent until your case is called." The bells of the cathedral across the street were completing their ninth chime as the clerk concluded her solemn call to order. When it came to starting court, Judge Taft did not tarry. If your hearing was set for 9:00 A.M., you were present ready to proceed at that moment, or you better bring a toothbrush when you finally arrived, because your contempt citation might include an overnight in the pokey. Most of the circuit courts had dropped the old formalistic opening, but Judge Taft insisted that his court clerk call it out the way it had been done for decades, decades ago.

Kathleen Schmidt had played this role for nearly 20 years, at her desk immediately to the left of the bench. She knew all of what the younger attorneys would refer to as his peccadilloes and what she would characterize as his standards. Once, a dozen years earlier when she was on maternity leave, a substitute clerk had taped several of her favorite cartoon clippings—the sardonic ones whose basic message is, "What the hell am I doing here and why on earth do you think I can help you?"—on the side of the bench that bordered her desk. As Judge Taft entered the courtroom, the 9:00 A.M. bells couldn't conceal his growl when he spied the offenders. Before the dirgeful echoes had ceased, the cut-outs were in the nearby trash bin and their champion had shrunk a full foot lower in her seat. "This is a court of law, not some dime-store service desk," he hissed at her the moment the morning recess arrived. And Ms. Schmidt's replacement was relieved that her pregnancy was without complications. In Judge Taft's court, the majesty of the law was presented in full ceremonial headdress.

And whether or not it made for justice—and lawyers always disagreed on that when it came to this particular jurist—it seemed to work. Litigants were on time for his morning call, unlike other courtrooms where lawyers would wander in well after 9:30 knowing that, likely as not, the judge hadn't taken the bench yet. And this courtroom generally remained silent as well—of course the bailiff, taking the judge's cue, saw to that. And so it abruptly hushed now, in spite of the fact that it was a standing-room-only throng, as Judge Taft instructed the clerk to call the case that everyone present, including dozens of journalists, knew was on the docket. The chief judge had offered Taft his courtroom, the largest in the building, to accommodate the crowd better, but Judge Taft wouldn't hear of it, just as the chief had anticipated. This was Taft's way of saying that in the neutral eyes of the law, there was nothing about any case that called for special treatment, even on so collateral a matter as the capacity size available for the spectators. And the gathering would not have access to their laptops. There would be no keyboard clacking, not in this courtroom, anyway.

"*The People of the State of Illinois versus Christopher Hedrick Donovan.* Docket number ninety-seven four-one-six-o-o-seven."

"The clerk will read the charge."

"The People charge that Christopher Hedrick Donovan, on the first day of April 1997 at or about the hour of one-fifteen P.M., at Third Street and Stadium Way, on the premises of the Chicago Stadium Authority, did willfully and intentionally, and with malice aforethought, commit murder upon the person of Donald Michael McGinniss by means of blunt object, to wit, a baseball, which he forcefully struck with another blunt object, to wit, a baseball bat, violently into and upon the head of McGinniss . . . The defendant has pled not guilty to the charge."

"All right. This is a preliminary hearing. The issue is whether there is probable cause to believe that the crime charged was committed and that the defendant committed it, sufficient to bind over the defendant for trial. Does the prosecutor wish to amend the charge to add any lesser-included offenses?"

This was a key strategic decision, and Kasoff was prepared for it, having discussed this one late into the night with B.D. If the evidence was insufficient to demonstrate the probable cause requisites for murder in the first degree, the case would be dis-

186

missed and, pursuant to a wrinkle of Illinois's code of criminal procedure, Donovan could not thereafter be charged with a crime less than murder-one unless the People, not later than the outset of the preliminary hearing, amended the charge to include such lesser offenses. Here the additional crimes could include voluntary manslaughter or second-degree murder. After much debate Kasoff and B.D. had decided that this was an all-or-nothing case. If the judge wasn't buying their view that this was a crime, he would dismiss all charges anyway, including the lessers. If he sided with them, they would have all of the elements of a first-degree murder charge and be in the strongest possible position at trial. At that point they would let the defense have the Hobson's choice of whether to ask the court to instruct the jury that they could convict Donovan of a lesser charge. Unlike the People, the accused retained the option right up until the case went to the fact finder to decide whether to gamble on compromise. This gave the defendant the opportunity to evaluate the strength of the People's case vis-à-vis its own before exercising the option.

Kasoff rose—one never addressed the Court, especially this Court, while seated, even for a one-word reply—and stood tall with the confidence instilled by a decade of courtroom confrontations. "No, Your Honor." Ms. Schmidt shifted nervously in her seat. If she could hear the scribbling of fifty or more pens in the gallery, so could Judge Taft. And she was sure it would not be long before the jurist and the journalists, made adversaries by their divergent views as to whether free press or fair trial was the Holy Grail in the Bill of Rights, would be tangling.

"Are the parties ready to proceed?"

"Yes, Your Honor," Kasoff responded as he bobbed up again.

"Yes, Your Honor," echoed Weinstein as his client sat impassively, having been amply advised what to expect this morning.

"The People will call their first witness."

"Thank you, Your Honor," and Kasoff instinctively moved toward the podium, as if it was a strategic base of operations. "The People call Vladimir Novikoff."

Two hundred pairs of eyes turned back toward the door behind the gallery as the bailiff posted there opened it for the short middle-aged man who now entered and made his way toward the witness box to Judge Taft's right, where, just before

187

reaching it, the clerk interrupted him in order to administer the oath. Immaculate in appearance, the witness presented himself in a solemn and deferential manner. After having him identified for the record, Kasoff proceeded.

"Mr. Novikoff, were you employed as the chief video technician for the Chicago baseball club on April first, 1997?"

"Yes, sir."

"And were you videotaping the first inning of a baseball game that day between Chicago and the Yankees at or about the hour of one-fifteen P.M.?" Now, this was certainly a leading question, but at a preliminary exam, the prosecutor is granted leeway in the conduct of direct examination. Because he or she needs only to establish probable cause, impatient judges prefer the expedited testimony that such questions provide. Besides, Weinstein wasn't inclined to object to what would be the easy part of the People's case. Everyone knew the facts. Weinstein would make his stand on the law.

"Yes, I was."

"And have you brought that videotape with you today?"

"Yes."

"And have you viewed it since playing it?"

"Yes."

"And does it accurately reflect what you observed on the field that day?"

"Objection, Your Honor. There is no foundation that this witness looked at the field through anything other than his viewfinder, and so there is no foundation that he can attest to its accuracy." Weinstein wanted to let Kasoff know he would be no pushover. Of course, to the reasonable laymen present, the interruption was nonsensical.

"I'll withdraw it, Your Honor," replied Kasoff. Apparently, the objection had merit only to those schooled in the mysteries of the seamless web.

"Proceed."

"Sir, would you describe briefly how you observe the field of play as you're videotaping the action?"

"Certainly. When I tape a game, I work with an assistant. He looks through the viewfinder while I watch the field. I tell him when I want to zoom in to get an isolation shot, when to back off to take in the whole field, and so forth."

"Thank you. I'll ask you again. Does the videotape which you have brought here today accurately reflect what you observed on the field that afternoon?"

"Yes, it does."

"And on April first, where were you and your assistant positioned?"

"We were behind third base."

"What particular views of the game does that vantage point provide you?"

"With our zoom lens, we can get a good close up of a right-handed pitcher in the stretch position. We can also see close plays at first base."

"Mr. Novikoff, did you film anything unusual that day?"

"Yes, sir."

"We've set up a TV with a VCR here," and Kasoff pointed to the jury box, otherwise vacant for this proceeding. "Would you please play back what you and your assistant filmed?"

The courtroom quieted as the humble man expertly began the tape.

"Please tell us what we're seeing as you begin to play it."

"OK." The click of the "play" button could be heard in the back row. "I've cued it up to one-fourteen P.M. precisely, as you can see on the monitor. Here we see McGinniss beginning his windup, and we can't see the hitter in this shot, but in a second we'll see the batted ball—there it is!—" And the spectators gasped, as if seeing it again for the first time. As McGinniss went down, Mr. Novikoff hit the "pause" button.

"Now, you'll see as we zoom into the mound, the batter running toward first, we lose him for a second or so, and then the camera zooms in behind first," and the witness hit the "play" button again. "OK, there's the foot of the runner in the background as we're zooming. Now, the lens focuses behind first base and we'll see the hitter. There!" "Pause" button again.

Frozen in time. Arms aloft. And Donovan smiling from ear to ear up at the great blue sky above. A close-up. No mistaking the emotion revealed. Kasoff, well aware of a picture's worth in words, had few now. "Nothing further of this witness. I would ask that the reporter mark the tape as People's Exhibit One and

I move for its admission."

"No objection, Your Honor."

"Exhibit One is admitted."

Weinstein had only two points to make, and he succeeded. Rising, remaining at his chair, he inquired softly, "Mr. Novikoff, when my client hit that ball, did he run anywhere other than where every other batter runs when he hits the ball?"

"No, sir."

"He didn't hit the ball and do a dance at home plate, did he?"

"No, sir."

"And did he touch first base?"

"I believe he did."

"And, sir, you don't claim to know why he smiled afterward, do you?"

"No, sir."

"He might have been smiling at the thought that he had managed to overcome his beaning and return to the game he loved, isn't that true?"

"Objection, Your Honor. Speculation."

"Sustained."

But Weinstein didn't care. The press would know what the answer was, and this would be a victory in the court of public opinion, so important to his client. More critical to the legal outcome, the judge would know as well that the TV image that had so transfixed the Prosecutor's Office offered no window into the questions of premeditation, deliberation, or malice, issues of Donovan's soul.

"Thank you. Nothing else." Weinstein didn't need to hit home runs at this hearing. Singles would suffice.

After Novikoff was excused and Judge Taft had ordered Kasoff to "call your next witness," Kasoff himself walked to the courtroom door, opened it, and announced, "The People call Paul Jones." A diminutive and visibly nervous adolescent stepped forward and was escorted by Kasoff to the witness box, where the customary preliminaries were observed before Kasoff resumed.

"How old are you, Paul?"

"Fourteen."

"And where were you on April first at one-ten P.M.?"

"I was at Chicago Stadium."

"And what were you doing there?"

Paul brightened as he swelled with pride. "I'm a batboy for the Yankees." The press gallery stopped writing for a moment, as if collectively shaking their heads and thinking, *You're so young.*

With each question, Paul would look directly at Kasoff. As the boy answered, he would turn his gaze toward Donovan, who returned just a hint of a reassuring smile, as if to say, "It's all right, Paul. You just tell the truth and I'll be out of this fix in no time."

"Did you see the defendant bat that day against Don McGinniss in the first inning?"

"That was the only inning played that day." And the gallery laughed at this pup who nipped with common sense at Kasoff's legalistic ears. Even the prosecutor had to smile as they reddened.

"Thank you. I stand corrected. Did you see the defendant bat against McGinniss that day?"

"I sure did."

"Where did he get his bat from?"

"Well—" and here Paul's tension reasserted itself as he paused and stammered, "I, I know he didn't get it from the bat rack because I know what bat he uses, and I would've handed it to him. So he must have brought it himself from his locker."

"Objection. Calls for speculation," interrupted Weinstein, and Paul jumped with fright, partly at the commanding voice but largely from apprehension that he may have done something to hurt his hero's cause.

"The Court will allow the answer to stand but notes counsel's objection."

Kasoff resumed. "In general, when a batter completes his at-bat, is there anything that you do with the bat?"

"Yes."

"What's that?"

"It depends. If he strikes out, he brings the bat back to the dugout with him, and I return it to the rack while doing my best to keep my distance." More laughter. "If he hits the ball, as soon as the play is over and I see the umpire call time, I run out to home plate, grab the bat, and take it back to the bat rack."

"And on this day, in the first—the only—inning, is that what

191

you did with the defendant's bat after he hit the ball?"

"Pretty much. Only when I got back to the dugout, Dutch—he's the hitting instructor—asked me for the bat."

"And did you give it to him?"

"Sure. I'm just a kid." And the courtroom really broke up now, as if, they all thought, *adolescents always obeyed their elders. If the game could accomplish that, it really hadn't lost its magic.* And the press would have a new headliner to accompany its lead. If the kid kept it up, his picture might even go above the fold.

But this wave of laughter crashed well short of shore, for it was abruptly brought to a halt by the banging of Taft's gavel. "One more outburst like that and I'll clear this courtroom!" he bellowed, and even the seasoned journalists sat up a little straighter, their body language acknowledging the respect the judge demanded. The noise had also concealed the murmuring of two veteran sportswriters in the back row. They realized the prosecutor would be following that bat for a reason.

"Did you ever see the bat after that?"

"No, sir."

"Thank you, Paul."

"Am I done?" he replied, boyhood innocence beaming, and this time the gallery's chuckles were stifled.

"No questions, Your Honor," said Weinstein.

"Yes, you are, son. Thank you." And Kasoff returned the youth's smile.

Dutch was the next witness. The two writers in the back turned over their notebooks, convinced they would need a full fresh page.

"Please describe your position with the Yankees."

"For thirty-two years I've been their hitting instructor."

"And what does your work involve?"

"I study the hitters for flaws in their swing. I tell 'em what I see. I suggest corrections. I study the opposing pitchers. See if they're tipping their pitches. Remind our hitters what to look for against them, and any adjustments to make against 'em, like stance, choking up, shortening the swing. Once in a while, we even brush up on bunts."

Close followers of the game smiled and nodded knowingly. The Yankees' offense was built around the three-run homer.

Every year, they would be last in sacrifice bunts and the league leaders in hitting into double plays. But beyond that, the game's die-hards knew that, these days, the bunt was but a relic of baseball's glory years. In the business that the game had become, there was just no money in sacrificing one's self for the cause.

"Do you use videotape to assist you in carrying out your responsibilities?"

"Yes."

"Can you describe the video facilities?"

Weinstein rose. "Your Honor, it seems we're getting awfully far afield here. How does the Yankee video library relate to the crime charged?" Weinstein knew, of course but he was hoping Judge Taft, notorious for requiring attorneys to stay on point, would cut off this line of questioning as rapidly as he did the laughter of a moment ago.

No dice. "Mr. Kasoff, do you intend to tie this up?"

"I do, Your Honor. Before I move on to the specific videotape that I'll be seeking to introduce, I simply wanted to avoid the foundational objection that I knew my esteemed colleague would otherwise make." Kasoff always enjoyed a response that took his opponent's most recent objection and stuffed it back up his ass.

"All right, but next time let's wait to see if the objection is made, shall we? Now, let's get to it quickly."

Dutch then went on to describe the comprehensive Yankee video library, the system for culling key excerpts, and their study by the coaching staff and players, including the off-season requests.

"Speaking of the off-season, did the defendant have a routine he would practice relative to the video library?" Kasoff was confident that Taft would appreciate the significance of this line of questioning. Demonstrating that a suspect varied from the habits of which he was a creature was often a crucial brick in the erection of a solid murder case.

"Yes. Each October, Donovan would order videotape of forty pitchers. He would study them all winter at his home in upstate New York, and then return them on the first day of spring training."

"Did the defendant vary from that habit last winter and, if so, how?"

"Yes, he did. In December, he ordered a single videotape. It was on loan to Jaime Rodriguez in Puerto Rico." And in response to Taft's inquiring look, Dutch volunteered, "He's our first baseman. Donovan obtained it from Rodriguez and kept it until he reported for spring training."

"And what was portrayed in that videotape?"

"That tape contained two hours of pitching moves of Don McGinniss." Murmuring in the courtroom again. This time it stilled itself as soon as Taft began to reach for his gavel.

"And is that videotape here in the courtroom today?"

"Yes," and Dutch pointed to the envelope in which he had brought it to Kasoff and which now sat on the prosecutor's table.

"Your Honor, we've marked this as Exhibit Two. I don't intend to play it at this time—" and as he said this, you could sense some of the air let out of the spectators, so many of whom came of age as the TV generation—"but," turning now toward Dutch, "why don't you describe what's on it briefly to acquaint the Court with what it will be reviewing?"

"The film shows Don McGinniss in his windup and pitching from the stretch against a variety of different hitters. It shows his pickoff move to first base. And—" here Dutch hesitated and displayed just a hint of a sheepish grin—"it also shows close-ups of McGinniss gripping the ball, staring in for the sign, tugging his cap, those sorts of things."

"And what's the purpose of obtaining and preserving those close-ups?"

And Dutch revealed the reason for his hesitation. "We're looking for something that will tell us if he's tipping his pitches so our hitters will know what's coming. There's no rule against it as long as we restrict ourselves to the league-authorized camera locations and angles," Dutch hastened to add, in deference to the forum in which he found himself—one whose rule book with which he was unfamiliar—this summer morning.

"Thank you, Mr. Vandiver. Nothing else."

"Mr. Weinstein?"

"Thank you, Your Honor. Mr. Vandiver. You've seen hitters beaned before who've never been the same since, is that right?"

"Yes."

"Most of the time, unless it harms their vision, it's the fear of getting back in the batters' box that ruins their talent, isn't that so?"

"That, or the severe headaches that often follow." And Donovan, sitting there watching his coach, realized he had been headache-free ever since his arrest.

Ignoring the last portion of the answer, Weinstein continued. "Well, when fear is the overriding factor, a player who can overcome that fear is a hitter who has the best chance to return to form, right?"

"I suppose, yes."

"And if that hitter has something to study that may help tell him when the pitcher is going to throw that high hard one inside, he doesn't have to be so fearful anymore, does he, because he'll know in advance when it's coming, right?"

"This game is not that simple, counselor."

"Well, that sort of study will help, won't it? Otherwise, why bother with all those videotapes in the first place? Right?"

"The study will help, I'll agree with you on that."

"You certainly wouldn't fault one of your players who'd been beaned if he spent the winter studying the pitcher who beaned him so he'd be less likely to have it happen again, would you? In fact, you'd encourage that sort of thing, wouldn't you?"

"Objection. Compound."

"It is compound, but I'll take the answer, counsel."

"If that's what he's doing, no, of course I wouldn't fault him."

"In fact, for all the money your club pays these players, it's something they ought to take upon themselves to do, isn't it, to help them perform at their peak?" A man so dedicated to the game as Dutch, who had played it for peanuts back in the days when the owners had the players on a short leash, could hardly agree more. But he never got the chance to say so.

"The Court will sustain its own objection to that question as irrelevant. Move on, counsel."

"That's all right, Your Honor. I've made my point." And to the gallery, indeed he had.

For just a moment, even Dutch appeared shaken by his own words, embarrassed that he hadn't thought of the innocent explanation that Weinstein had so readily coaxed out of him. But then he remembered the doctored bat, no sooner than

Kasoff retook the podium.

"Excuse me, Your Honor. There was one other area I wanted to cover with this witness." Kasoff hadn't forgotten; it was just that he wanted Weinstein to finish his cross-examination first. Kasoff had anticipated that his adversary would make exactly the point he had. Rather than have this witness leave the stand on a low note for the People, Kasoff had decided to save the best for last.

"Mr. Vandiver. What happened to the defendant's bat after McGinniss went down?"

"I took it from the batboy and stored it in my locker until I turned it over to your office back in June."

"And why did you decide to retrieve it?"

"In a word," and here he paused, "cork. Cork and dimples." The gallery again erupted, and was not stilled until three strikes of the gavel.

"Explain that."

"The last day of spring training at our facility in Florida, I noticed four wine bottles in Donovan's partially opened locker as I walked past it after the final exhibition game had ended. Donovan doesn't drink, so I asked him who they were for. He told me it was a gift. That didn't make any sense to me. After all, this is the day we're packing to head north. Who the hell—pardon me, Your Honor—" Dutch turned white from his breach of etiquette, but the judge understood that the coach had merely transported himself back to that locker room, with its own vernacular.

Dutch exhaled when the judge merely nodded in his direction, and continued.

"Anyway, who would want to travel up north for Opening Day in Chicago with four large glass bottles if they didn't have to? Now, Donovan is usually the last one out of the locker room. But on this particular day, I couldn't locate a pair of my sunglasses after I had packed and gone back to the hotel. Thinking I'd left them behind, I returned to the park and retraced my steps in the area around my locker. I never did find them, but as I looked around, I noticed a faint fruity aroma near the sink. I looked at it and noticed one little red droplet near the faucet. I dabbed it with my finger and tasted it. Sure enough, it was wine. A few minutes later, I walked past Donovan's locker and I saw a few small shavings on the floor. They felt like cork. I went to the nearest waste-basket, felt around underneath the lid, and found them."

"Found what?"

"The empty wine bottles." Stirring in the gallery.

"And what conclusion did you draw from these observations?" Anyone could connect the dots, but Kasoff wanted this repository of the game's lost integrity to draw the picture.

"Donovan corked his bat." The journalists were scribbling frantically now, especially the sportswriters. If this hearing produced nothing else they'd have a great story for weeks: baseball's best player caught cheating!

But Kasoff, as usual, had no interest in headlines. "And what about the dimples?"

"I noticed those when our batboy handed the bat to me. Never seen 'em before on a major-league bat. I recently double-checked the rule book, and the rules forbid it."

"Did you bring a copy of the rule book with you?"

"Yes."

"Could you point out for us, and read into the record, the rule in question?"

"Yes... 'A batter is out for illegal action when he uses or attempts to use a bat that, in the umpire's judgment, has been altered or tampered with in such a way as to improve the distance factor or cause an unusual reaction in the baseball. This includes bats that are filled, flat-surfaced, nailed, hollowed, grooved or covered with a substance such as paraffin, wax, etc.'"

"Mr. Vandiver, why does a hitter cork or dimple his bat?"

"Makes the ball go faster and farther. Better chance of hitting safely."

"So a line drive is hit harder than it would be otherwise?"

"Yes."

"Or, at least, is that the prevailing view in the baseball world?"

"Yes."

Kasoff had to leave himself a little wiggle room here. The scientist would pooh-pooh this as largely myth, at least as to the cork. Kasoff was more interested in showing what Donovan believed. It was his state of mind, after all, that was pivotal on the issue of malice.

"Sir, are you familiar with how someone would go about corking a bat?"

"Yes."

"Please describe it."

And the batting instructor explained how one would make a through-and-through cross-cut near the top of the barrel, ream out a hole up to ten inches long with a diameter of about three-eighths of an inch, and plug the channel with cork, tapering it down lengthwise with a paring knife if need be in order to make it fit. Then, the barrel end would be glued back on. Now, with Dutch's help, Kasoff opened the bat to reveal its guilty secret. And four plugs came bouncing out right onto counsel table, one of them rolling almost right up to its owner himself. And oh, how the shutter fingers in the gallery itched to hold a camera.

"Thank you. No further questions, Your Honor, though I would ask that the bat be marked as Exhibit Three A and its corked center be marked as Exhibits Three B through E. And I move for their admission."

"No objection"

"They will be admitted."

"Mr. Weinstein?"

"If Donovan corked his bat, or dimpled his bat, or waxed it for that matter, that would be a violation of the rules of the game?"

"Yes."

"Do you know of any law against it?"

"Objection, Your Honor. This witness is not qualified to render a legal opinion."

"Sustained." Kasoff knew that Taft understood Weinstein's point, but Taft went further. "Mr. Kasoff, will you be presenting this Court with any authority for the proposition that doctoring a bat for improper advantage in the playing of a baseball game violates a law of the state of Illinois?"

Kasoff did not want to answer this question, at least not yet. "Your Honor, we'll be submitting a brief on all of the issues in this case at the conclusion of the testimony."

"Counsel, you needn't tell me what I already know. Is it the position of the People in this matter that such doctoring or altering of a bat violates Illinois law? Yes or no?"

Trapped, Kasoff could only beg the Court for some time. "Your Honor, I'm not prepared to answer that question here and now, but I promise the Court that our brief will address this."

Taft scowled but said nothing as the gallery snickered at the prosecutor's discomfiture. Even Donovan, who had remained stone-faced throughout this colloquy, allowed himself the faintest hint of a smile. And a woman in the last row of the audience, shunted to a far corner by the media mob who had arrived after her, sobbed softly as she clutched her handkerchief. The healthy fetus she carried was blissfully unaware that she felt as though the life was draining out of her.

Weinstein had concluded his questions and the court broke for lunch. "How's it going?" asked B.D., though he knew the answer from the way Kasoff came trudging through the door.

"Taft has it in for us in this case. Our only chance at a bindover is to convince him on the brief, and even that's looking like a long shot now. Meanwhile, the only thing Weinstein hasn't neutralized is the acid in my stomach."

Kasoff then went to his office and did a quick run-through of his notes for the afternoon's witnesses. And the support staff knew enough to keep their distance. For at such times, there was only one priority. Every other case, every other matter, was an intrusive distraction. A subordinate who dared breach Kasoff's wall of concentration would be met with at best a withering glare.

The two-block walk back to the courthouse gave Kasoff five minutes of reflection he would just as soon not have had. God, how he hated to lose. He had injected himself into this controversy— indeed, he had created it, and on a national stage, no less—and now Taft was going to send him down in flames. He could see the media now, picking over his bones. It wouldn't be enough to report Donovan's vindication; they would have to resort to questioning Kasoff's motives. How else would they sell their newspapers? He did it to make a name for himself to run for office, they would say. He did it because he's a frustrated Chicago fan. He did it to sell the movie rights. Damn those bastards. No one would ever report the real reason—he honestly believed it was the right thing to do. If Donovan's mother couldn't succeed in teaching her son nonviolence, Kasoff would be the one to shout out that lesson into the whole wide wilderness.

And so reaching the courthouse door was actually a relief. But it was to be short-lived. When he checked back in with the clerk, Kathleen informed him that the judge would like to see him in chambers—alone. Kasoff agreed—what choice did he have?—and went off to report this to Weinstein, compelled by ethical protocol to inform his opponent of the Court's request for an *ex parte* communication. Kasoff located Weinstein, along with his client, in an alcove near the elevator. Weinstein readily indicated he would not object. As Kasoff left, Weinstein saw that his client had that "what kind of home court justice is this and why the hell aren't you objecting to it?" look on his face. But before Donovan could utter his protest, Weinstein soothed him.

"The only time Taft talks to an attorney privately on a case is to pound on him. Kasoff is dreading having to go in there. Taft is gonna tell him to dismiss this case or risk sanctions. You watch."

Donovan was only partially mollified. "But doesn't this give Kasoff a chance to change the judge's mind without your being there to prevent it?"

"Taft isn't doing this to listen, only to lecture. I've been there. We've all been. Trust me." At last, Donovan appeared assuaged.

The two of them then turned and headed toward the courtroom. They nearly arrived in time to get a glimpse of Kasoff slowly making his way past the clerk toward the door to chambers, lips pursed, right hand clutching a legal pad just a bit too tightly, but as Donovan came around a corner, he bumped into the woman with the handkerchief. "Pardon me," he said, and, spotting her delicate condition, redoubled his apology. "I'm so sorry." Having studiously avoided the local press and the broadcast news, Donovan was undoubtedly the only one in the courthouse that day who didn't recognize the widow. So he thought it odd that, instead of acknowledging his apology, she quickly turned away.

"Don't you know who that was?" inquired Weinstein.

"No."

"That was Mary McGinniss."

Donovan grimaced. In all his singleminded preparation over the past winter, somehow the thought that there might be survivors, let alone loved ones, had never occurred to him. And as the afternoon session wore on, Donovan began to think that

200

his doctors might well be wrong in linking his recently-quiescent headaches to physical injury from his beaning. Because now, one returned.

Meanwhile, in chambers, Kasoff was getting a headache of his own. Taft was indeed giving him an earful. The judge had heard nothing that even remotely suggested that a crime had been committed. Where did Kasoff think that he was going with this case? "Have you got anything else? Do the words *malicious prosecution* mean anything to you?"

They certainly did. Even though prosecutors in Illinois were clothed with absolute immunity from any civil action for money damages by an accused vindicated by the courts, the Illinois bar association had set up a special ethics subcommittee to review complaints of unfair or abusive prosecutions. The panel of distinguished members of the bar had the authority to recommend sanctions against an offending prosecutor ranging from reprimand to disbarment, plus monetary fines ranging up to $10,000, payable out of their own pockets, not those of the taxpayers, leaving aside, of course, the fact that it was the taxpayers who paid their salaries in the first place.

The DA's offices hated this check on their otherwise unbridled discretion to initiate a prosecution. A study had shown that, five years after its inception, virtually every assistant prosecutor in the county's metropolitan area had had at least one charge filed against him or her by some disgruntled target of the DA. To Kasoff, this was proof enough that criminal defendants were getting more process than they were due. After all, one would not expect to see a random pattern of complaints if the bulk of them had merit. Instead, most would be lodged against whatever small number of prosecutors sometimes went too far. And, in fact, most were dismissed without any finding of wrongdoing. Still, if a complaint was initiated by a judge, as Taft was now threatening, the subcommittee would feel bound to take a serious look at it. And Kasoff had been in this profession long enough to know that his energy stores were sometimes no match for his determination. He could fight just so many battles, and every foot soldier, much less his general, knew that a two-front war was a losing proposition.

Kasoff felt that he had to argue his case then and there, but

Taft wouldn't hear of it. Not without Weinstein present and without a record. Kasoff could only assure the Court that it would be persuaded that this was a good-faith prosecution after all of the evidence and briefs were in and the arguments concluded.

"For your sake, I hope so," warned Judge Taft as the church bells tolled 1:30 and he rose from his desk to inaugurate the afternoon session.

"Call your next witness," and the proceeding resumed.

"The People call Sergeant Johnson." The officer explained that he had led the search of Donovan's Manhattan apartment. "And did you find any of the items for which you were searching?"

"Yes, sir."

"And have you brought those items with you here today?"

"Yes."

"And in whose custody have these items been maintained since the search was conducted?"

"I have maintained them under lock and key in our evidence locker with the exception of a single day when they were signed out by a Dr. Parsons."

The sergeant then described for the record, just as he did in every such case, the procedures for bagging, tagging, logging, and storing physical evidence.

"Your Honor, I would ask that the reporter mark as People's Exhibits Four through Eight the items this officer has brought with him."

After the pause in the proceedings while the reporter affixed the stickers, the sergeant described the evidence. "Exhibit Four is a nine-inch carbide blade, sixty teeth, for a power saw. Exhibit Five is a paring knife. Exhibit Six is a tube of Super-glue. Exhibit Seven is a twelve-inch drill bit, diameter three-eighths inch." Each was still contained within its individual plastic bag.

"Have any changes been made in any of the exhibits while in your custody since each was first collected?"

"No, sir."

"No cleaning, brushing, or wiping, for example?"

"Correct, there was none of that."

"I notice a number of fine bits of material resembling sawdust inside the bags, with the exception of the one holding the glue. Was that present on these tools when they were found in Donovan's apartment?"

"Yes."

"Thank you. Nothing else."

"Mr. Weinstein," intoned the judge.

"Thank you, Your Honor. Sergeant, do you have any idea how long these bits of material had been present on any of these tools?"

"No."

"Or where they came from?"

"No." Johnson had been around long enough to know that as a cop, you didn't utter one word more than necessary at the direction of a defense lawyer.

"Or who had last used these tools?"

"No."

"Did you dust them for fingerprints?" Weinstein assumed, correctly, that the officers had handled the evidence so as to preserve any prints.

"No." No need to, at least not yet. Their mere presence in Donovan's apartment would establish probable cause that he had used them last. If and only if Kasoff got to trial would he incur the expense of a fingerprint expert.

"You mentioned that you found this carbide blade," as Weinstein held the bag containing it aloft. "Did you see a power saw?"

"Yes." It had struck Johnson as unusual to see such a piece of equipment in the high-rent district, but he wasn't about to volunteer that.

"Is there some reason the saw was not seized?"

"We took photos of it."

"And where are the photographs?"

"They didn't turn out."

"What do you mean, they didn't turn out?"

"You'll have to ask Officer Todd that. He was handling the camera."

It wasn't the first time in Weinstein's experience that the men in blue had blown a photo op. Normally, this sort of thing had a perfectly innocent explanation, but it was the sort of blunder around which Weinstein could always weave a web of doubt.

One screw-up begets another, he would argue to the jury. But, he knew, it wouldn't be enough to negate probable cause. "Nothing further at this time," he concluded.

"Next witness, Mr. Kasoff."

"Your Honor, the People call Benjamin Parsons, Ph.D." The professor explained that he was a materials expert who had spent a day examining the sawdust in the evidence bags.

"Sir, did I ask you to compare these bits of material with People's Exhibits Three A through Three E?"

"Yes."

"And would you please describe your findings and opinions, if any, within a reasonable degree of scientific certainty?"

"Certainly. The fine bits of material on and around People's Exhibits Four, Seven, and Eight are ash."

"As in lumber?"

"Yes, the hardwood."

"Continue."

"Exhibit Five, the paring knife, contains residual bits of cork. The ash sawdust matched the ash wood found on People's Three A, the bat. The cork on the knife matches the cork, marked as exhibits Three B through E, found inside the bat."

"Thank you."

"Cross-examine?"

"Sir, can you tell us anything about the relative elasticity of a bat and ball that strike each other—an official major-league hardball I mean?"

"I've not done any measurements, nor have I been asked to in this case, but certainly the elasticity of a baseball would be many times greater than the bat."

Kasoff immediately assumed that he recognized Weinstein's strategy. The defense lawyer would attempt to play off this expert on materials properties against Kasoff's physicist. If Weinstein could get this witness to render opinions that contradicted those of Dr. Churikian, he might create reasonable doubt at trial just by showing that the People's own scientists disagreed.

Weinstein continued. "And is that one of the variables that one must control for if one wishes to determine the speed of the bat off the ball?"

"I would assume so, though we're getting a bit out of my field here."

"Does the presence or absence of cork inside the bat change its elasticity upon collision with a baseball?"

Parsons, sensing trouble ahead, became even more cautious. "I've not been asked to examine that, counselor, and I would not want to speculate."

Kasoff now realized that his first instinct had been wrong. Weinstein was more interested in the causation issue. If Weinstein could show that the doctoring of the bat made no difference, then Kasoff's red flag was nothing more than a red herring. Parsons had stymied the defense for now, but Kasoff knew he might have to switch gears. The corking, granted, may have been unimportant in the outcome and the dimpling only minimally so, but both certainly went to Donovan's malignant mental state. Clearly, the Yankee believed that this loaded bat would help him do away with his nemesis. Still, Kasoff fretted. Without an overt act that made a substantial difference, the pejorative label of the thought police would continue to stick to him.

"Nothing further of this witness, Your Honor." Weinstein would revisit this issue with the physicist.

"Call your next witness."

"The People call Dr. Jagdesh Patel."

"Dr. Patel. Did you conduct an autopsy on the body of Don McGinniss on April second, 1997?"

"Yes, I did."

"And would you please describe for the Court the cause of death and the significant findings as they pertain to it?"

"Certainly. The cause of death was trauma to the brain as a result of blunt force from a moderate-velocity impact."

Kasoff appreciated the irony of the description of speed as "moderate," but he knew, as did his opponent and the Court from their years of experience with the scientific descriptions of death, that such a velocity was distinguished from the speed of a bullet. Any object striking the skull with force sufficient to break it would produce fractures whose characteristics would differ depending on its speed.

Patel continued. "The object was a baseball weighing approximately five and one-eighth ounces with a circumference of approximately nine and one-eighth inches. This was by history." This meant that the coroner was relying on what was reported to him, as distinguished from his own observations. Like the box score that makes no distinction between the line drive hit and the Texas leaguer, you can't tell in the autopsy whether the fracture was caused by a baseball or some other object of similar size and speed.

"Pertinent findings included a severely depressed complex fracture at the squamosal suture, that is, where the temporal bone joins with the parietal." This placed the impact point just above and in front of the ear. "Five distinct fracture lines emerge across the skull from the area of depression, which is approximately three-quarters of an inch in diameter and nearly one inch deep. Fracture fragments penetrated brain tissue, causing intracranial hemorrhage in the temporal lobe of the brain. Additional fragments tore a meningeal artery along with a cerebral vein, both in the dura mater. This caused profuse bleeding, leading to hematomas both epidurally and subdurally. Death was virtually instantaneous. As an incidental anatomic variant, the victim's temporal bone was just two millimeters thick, versus about three in the average adult male. Its density also appeared below average. Ordinarily, these variations would be of no clinical significance."

"What effect, if any, would such variants have on the outcome here?"

"This portion of the victim's skull is rather like a boxer's glass jaw. It will fracture with surprising ease."

"Thank you. Nothing else." Ordinarily, Kasoff would be content to rest this aspect of his case with such testimony, knowing that the law did not excuse a perpetrator who employs deadly force merely because his victim is more susceptible than the average person to the effects of that force. The one who swings his fist will not be heard to complain that his victim's nose was too easily bent out of joint. But Donovan hadn't swung a fist, and Kasoff wanted his old physicist friend to point out that the defendant had taken murderous advantage of the anatomic anomaly.

But first, Weinstein would have his chance to cross-examine. And, of course, in the courtroom, every stroke has its counter.

Weinstein was quick to strike back. "Dr. Patel. Do you have any evidence that this defendant had any awareness of this preexisting vulnerability at any time prior to this tragic accident?"

"I wouldn't know anything about that."

"Thank you." Kasoff kept his smile to himself. He was about to introduce evidence suggesting that Donovan had incorporated such an assumption in his preparations.

"The People call Officer Earl Aaron." Aaron, the erstwhile fisherman, had been flown in from Richmondville the night before. He brought with him a letter-size manila folder whose contents were sparse from its slender appearance. After Kasoff laid the foundation that Aaron had acted on the authority of the consent-to-search form signed by Donovan, the officer explained that he had returned to the defendant's home once after the initial search, this time to make a more thorough inspection of the barn. There, on a shelf, sitting amid a pile of old newspapers, were several sheets of writing paper that contained a series of what appeared to Aaron to be higher math problems. He wasn't sure. It was gibberish to him. "Anyway, I took them with me and stored them in an evidence locker, just in case. I got busy with some other things and forgot about them until you—" and here he pointed to Kasoff—"called me a week ago to ask if there might be anything else. I told you about these math notes," and now he held them aloft, "and at your request, I faxed copies to you. Two days later, you asked me if I could bring them here and testify. Naturally, I agreed."

"Thank you. Nothing else."

The papers were marked and admitted as Exhibits 8A through F.

"Cross-examine."

Weinstein obtained the documents. "May I have a moment, Your Honor?"

"A brief one."

The lawyer walked back to his seat and huddled with his client. In the first row, spectators were able to discern Donovan nodding ever so slightly amid the whispers. Then, Weinstein rose. "No questions, Your Honor."

"Next witness."

"The People call Joan Hammond." The witness took the

stand. "What is your occupation?"

"I'm a graphologist, a handwriting analyst."

"Have I asked you to examine and analyze several documents which have now been marked as Exhibits Eight A through F against these exemplars which I am now handing to the reporter to be marked as Exhibits Nine A through C?" Ah, subpoena power. Kasoff had compelled production of Donovan's bank deposit slips of the previous winter from City Bank so as to permit careful study of his scrip. He could have required Donovan to submit handwriting samples, but did not trust the slugger to refrain from modifying his penmanship. Every graphologist will tell you that a collected standard sample beats a requested standard any time.

"I have examined both sets of documents."

" Please outline for us what you did."

"I have compared the handwriting on the exhibits with the standards in terms of their form, line quality, and arrangement. On the matter of form, I looked at the shapes of the numerals and letters, their proportion or relative height, their slant, and the angles, straight lines, and curves. In terms of line quality, the amount of pressure placed on the pen is revealed by characteristic pen markings. I also examined the beginning and ending strokes of particular numerals or words because they give clues as to identifying pauses and speed. Finally, in terms of the arrangement, I am looking for the spacing between numerals or letters as well as their alignment relative to the base line. For example, Abe Lincoln had a signature that was like a flight of stairs, with each letter a bit higher than the one preceding." At the mention of Honest Abe, Taft perked up. The gallery remained somnambulant.

"And what did you find?"

"Based on my comparative analysis, it is my opinion that the author of Exhibits Eight A through F was also the author of Exhibits Nine A through C."

"And whose signature appears on Exhibits Nine A through C?"

"Chris Donovan."

"Thank you." Weinstein had no questions. Based on his conference with his client, he would not be contesting authorship.

It was now 4:30. Quittin' time per collective bargaining agreement for clerks and court officers. Taft's kingdom was one of limited sovereignty after all. "Court is adjourned. We will reconvene tomorrow at nine A.M."

14

Kasoff reached his office in time to commiserate with B.D. and Green. "Man, that damned Taft ripped me a new asshole today," he began. Kasoff wasn't generally one to be profane—it wasn't the offensive nature of the speech to which he objected; it was its imprecision with which he took issue. English was far too rich a language not to mine just the right word for every occasion. But there was something about the combat of the courtroom that sometimes caused him to succumb to the language of the streets. "I could use a drink." Another rarity.

"Come on, that stuff causes brain damage," needled Green.

"Brain damage? Just from a Cabernet?"

"Sure. You ever hear of fetal soda pop syndrome?"

"All the same, I need to unwind even if the price is ten points off my IQ."

Half an hour later, they found themselves at a nearby tavern. Kasoff was still reliving the day's lowlights, muttering about not having a prayer.

"Jesus. You really do need to unwind. Speaking of which, how about the all-religion team?"

Now Kasoff smiled, as if transported back to simpler days. "Religion. Hmmm. OK, I've got some good names, but they're mostly nobodies."

"I'll go easy on you today."

"OK, here goes. Mark Grace at first over Luke Easter."

"Mark and Luke along with the last names. I like 'em. Those are double-word scores."

"Second base. Johnny Temple over Johnny Priest or Max Bishop."

"Never heard of 'em, but they're great names."

"Shortstop. Jose Pagan. Third base. Harry Lord. Pitching. Howie Krist. Catcher. Lance Parrish."

"Finally, a real ballplayer."

"Outfield. OK. Dave Pope, Wally Moses, and Ike Blessitt."

"Blessitt?"

"Sure. He played a couple of games for the Tigers one year."

"God bless it, Kasoff. You've done it again."

Morning broke with bright sunshine, and Kasoff's disposition was refreshed.

"Good morning, counsel. Are you ready to proceed?"

"Yes, Your Honor."

"Call your next witness."

"The People call Dr. Pete Churikian." Kasoff had spent parts of three evenings with his old friend going over his anticipated testimony. Unlike most forensic experts retained by one side or the other in a legal battle, Churikian was a virgin, having never testified as an expert before. The DA knew he would need everything going his way for this prosecution, and that included an expert pure as the driven snow, not someone his opponent could label as a whore. Now the physicist, at Kasoff's behest, spent just a few moments summarizing his education and professional background and then explained that a batted ball aimed at a person presented a rather simple physics problem. He had indeed been well prepared. Having been given the speed of the pitched ball as well as the speed of the swinging bat that met it and knowing the distance to the target, as well as the density and thickness of that target, one could calculate the likelihood that the ball would shatter the target.

Kasoff invited the scientist to run through the numbers on the available blackboard. Churikian explained that a pitched ball loses about 1 mile per hour for every 7 feet it travels toward the plate. McGinniss's release point had been 56 feet from its front edge, where the bat met it. At that spot, the ball was traveling at 98 mph. Based on extensive review of the videotape, the ball appeared to have been hit flush by a bat being swung at a speed of 90 mph, an extraordinary 10–15 mph more than the typical big leaguer.

"Now, calculating the speed of the ball off the bat requires application of Newton's second law—" this case was no mere falling apple! "The force in pounds equals the mass multiplied by the acceleration. Before we get there, though, we first have to determine the speed of the ball off the bat. This requires use of what is known as the coefficient of restitution, or the COR."

Weinstein was baffled as he sat there. Why spend time on this when viewing the video would reveal the speed? But Kasoff wanted to prove what Donovan could have and would have known in advance of his deed.

"And what is the coefficient of restitution?"

"Stated simply, a collision between bat and ball uses up energy in the form of friction. A hardball has more elasticity than one might think. It is literally crushed to about half its normal size during the collision. Even the hardwood bat is elastic enough to compress about one to two percent. The greater the elasticity, the greater the force generated internally by the object that is struck. A child's Super Ball, for example, is very elastic; that's why it bounces so high. A lump of clay, on the other hand, has virtually no elasticity, so that it will stop dead upon being bounced."

"This is all very interesting, Your Honor, but what has it got to do with the crime charged?"

"I'll tie it up soon, Your Honor."

"Well, let's be quick about it."

"Continue, Doctor."

"In addition, there may be some minute slippage between the ball and the bat during the collision, which also expends some of the energy. As a result, the coefficient of restitution is a number that takes into account this expended energy, which has the effect of reducing the speed of the ball as it leaves the bat. The higher the coefficient, the greater the amount of retained speed off the bat. Technically, it is the ratio of the velocity of the ball bouncing off the bat to the incident velocity and equal to the square root of the proportion of the energy retained in the collision. In general, nearly two-thirds of the energy is lost to friction."

Kasoff was squirming. No jury would ever understand all that. Of course, at trial, Pete could put on an elaborate show and tell to illustrate his points. If he got to trial.

"And how do you know what that number is here?"

"The baseball rule book indicates that the COR of an official league baseball must be point-five-four-six."

"And have you formed an estimate of the speed of the ball off Donovan's bat independent of reviewing the videotape?"

"Yes I have."

"And what is it?"

"One hundred sixty-four miles per hour."

"How did you come up with that?"

"The mass of the bat is thirty ounces, and of the ball, five ounces. The COR is point-fifty-five. The pitch is thrown at ninety-eight miles per hour, and the bat is swung at ninety miles per hour. The speed of the ball after impact is calculated as follows. First, you multiply the weight of the bat by its speed and then multiply the product by one-point-fifty-five, that is, the COR plus one. Then, you add that to the following. First, take the speed of the pitch and multiply that by the product of the COR and the weight of the bat less the weight of the ball. Do you follow me so far?" No one did, but Weinstein was taking copious notes. "Finally, you divide the number you get by the sum of the weight of the bat and the ball. Here that makes the denominator thirty-five."

"And what was the actual speed, as revealed by your study of the videotape?"

"That was easy to determine. It took just under one-quarter of a second for the ball to travel fifty-six feet. That means it traveled at an average speed over that distance of one hundred sixty-four miles per hour, just as I calculated. Of course, the ball would travel a few miles per hour faster in the first portion of its journey and a few miles per hour under that when it struck the pitcher."

"Doctor, have I asked you to consider what effect, if any, the dimpling in the bat that has been identified as Exhibit Three A would have on these calculations?"

"Yes."

"Please describe that for us."

"Certainly. A normal bat is not aerodynamic. When you swing it, a thin layer of air clings to it as it moves through space, creating a drag on it and thereby decreasing bat speed. By dimpling the bat, the layer of air against it is decreased."

"And what effect would this have on the bat speed?"

"The dimples can increase it by up to five percent."

"Are you now ready to apply Newton's law?"

"Yes. We know that the mass of the ball is five ounces. Actual-

213

ly, it may exceed that by up to a quarter ounce, so my number is a bit conservative. We multiply that by the acceleration in feet per second. That number is two-forty-one. The force is therefore four-o-two psi. But because a baseball is round, only about three-quarters of an inch actually makes contact with its target. Because of this concentration of force, we are actually measuring the pounds per three-fourths inch, so to convert to psi, we divide four-o-two by point-seventy-five and we end up with five thirty-six.

"In conclusion," he added, it was his professional opinion, within a reasonable degree of scientific certainty, that this amount of force was more than sufficient to fracture the skull, based on old studies that showed that a baseball delivered at as low as 425 psi on a cadaver bearing normal anatomy is enough to fracture it. "And that doesn't even take into account the fact that not only is this skull abnormally thin, but the blow was delivered at the suture, which hadn't even closed, thereby striking the weakest point."

Now Kasoff turned to the papers marked during the testimony of Officer Aaron.

"Dr. Churikian, could you please examine People's Exhibits Eight A through F and tell us if you recognize the data therein, and, if so, please explain them."

"Sure. The math notes and symbols on these documents contain physics problems which compute a variety of speeds of a batted ball striking a target some fifty-six to sixty feet away based on a set of variables. The target itself is a human head assumed to have several variables of its own, one of which shows its bone thickness to be as thin as two millimeters, plus the scalp, of course."

"And what do these problems reveal by way of solutions, if any?"

"The author of these documents knew his stuff. He determined that a batted baseball could be made to strike a pitcher at a speed as high as one hundred sixty-five miles per hour and that, if the target's skull was two millimeters or less, it could fracture it severely."

The chroniclers of this game of numbers would see to it that these would be printed in every paper in the country within 24 hours.

Weinstein rose to begin his questioning. At this stage, he wanted Churikian to educate him. Now that he knew what formulas the scientist had used, was there any margin for error in the data? What were all of the variables? Might there be some he hadn't thought of? Weinstein needed to know step by painstaking step not just what Churikian's conclusions were but also each brick in the foundation for his opinions. Then Weinstein would take the data to his own physicist for independent—the prosecutors would call it biased—analysis. If the case ever went to trial, Weinstein would be well equipped to make his points with Churikian and sit down. Those questions would be answered with a simple yes or no. Today Weinstein knew there was nothing he could do to erase the specter of probable cause in the physics link in the People's chain of evidence. So, he would let Churikian have free rein, as long as every number and symbol he wrote on the chalkboard was read into the record.

It took Churikian more than two hours to explain it all as the eyes of the gallery glazed over as one. And when he was through, the wiggle room was a wash. He established the immateriality of the cork but also elicited what Kasoff had planned as his cherry on top at trial: because McGinniss was moving forward down off the mound at 9 mph as he completed his follow-through, the combined total collision speed was actually 173 mph.

After lunch, Special Agent Jeremy Petersen then took the stand, looking even younger than his 26 years. It took him 20 minutes to explain the minutiae of microscopic analysis of videotape for wear patterns. It all boiled down to dust, which is carried forward into the tape with each pass. Each time it scratches, ever so slightly, the film, until after several hundred passes one can discern deterioration in its quality. He wanted to tell the story of how he had stumbled into this field, but a preliminary exam, he knew, was bare bones. The dog-and-pony show would have to wait for the jury trial. It was a good yarn, though. It even kept the judge patiently attentive.

When he was sixteen, he had taken a job at a video store. Before he had cleared his probation period, he noticed that whenever a customer—and it was always a male patron—complained about the quality of a tape, the film was invariably from the hard-core porn section. After several such returns, he began

215

asking the men just what the problem was. His curiosity was taken for impudence by the adults, who were unrevealing, but one night a carload of eighteen-year-olds with the same complaint eagerly replied, "Man, every time the movie gets to a juicy part, the picture quality goes to hell." Of course, that was the edited version he would repeat in court, never mind the whole truth. Anyway, as Petersen would tell it, he decided to check a few of the films and, sure enough, the customer, as always, was right. So Petersen developed a hypothesis. Perhaps the pornographic high points were being played and replayed by the viewers, so that those portions of the film were subject to premature wear. He began subjecting the tapes, along with control samples of videotape known to be worn out, to microscopic analysis. And he proved his theory. The wear patterns on the control samples matched up almost precisely with the pornographic highlights. The customers were playing these excerpts to death. And Petersen, all in the service of the scientific method, got more than just an underage peek at this prurient perk.

In any event, it was Petersen's opinion that the wear marks on the McGinniss tape clearly demonstrated two distinct spots where the tape was played hundreds of times more than the remainder of the film. The first was of McGinniss's delivery and follow-through from a game played in Chicago the previous fall. The other was a close-up taken that same autumn from a center field camera in Detroit that showed McGinniss from behind staring in for the sign and beginning his windup.

Petersen, having cued up the first of the two, now played it for the judge while Kasoff, on a separate monitor, ran once more the film of McGinniss's final pitch on Opening Day, until the images on the two screens matched. Whatever sense of triumph Kasoff may have felt when the twin tubes were shown to portray identical images of McGinniss storming down off the mound was turned to dust as Judge Taft winced and tilted his head slightly as if to say, "So?"

Petersen also played the film from Detroit, but even Kasoff had to admit to himself that, for now at least, its significance was lost on him. He had given Dutch an extra copy and asked him to view it, but up to this point, the game's best hitting instructor could only conclude that Donovan must have spent hours studying it before he spotted McGinniss tipping his pitches. Dutch was unable to discern for himself what his best hitter had found. As for the former Chicago pitching coach consulted by Kasoff, he had no clue, either. Kasoff had since followed up with Chicago's current coaching staff, as well as the veteran hurlers on the club. All were equally baffled. For now, this thread would remain loose, and Kasoff would just have to hope that the additional time before trial would prove productive in solving this mystery.

Weinstein had no questions for Petersen. The Court, with one look, had summed up his testimony better than the advocate could.

Kasoff closed out his case with Greg's colleague—Robert Evans, who had goaded Donovan into his infamous threat of the previous fall. The video was marked and admitted as Exhibit 10. Weinstein's cross was simple. He elicited Evans's provocation in an effort to show the remark was made in anger on the spur of the moment. And for the first time in this proceeding, a section of the gallery—the broadcast media—was with Kasoff on this point.

Ordinarily, a display of a defendant livid in living color would be the summit on which to rest one's case. But Kasoff wasn't stupid. Taft had been openly disdainful of his case, and all Kasoff had left now was to submit his brief and argue against Weinstein's motion to dismiss. He was about to tell Taft that he had no further witnesses when the clerk handed the judge a note. His Honor then announced that court would be adjourning early due to a judicial conference just convened by the Chief Judge for the balance of that afternoon. Court would reconvene at 9:00 A.M. To Kasoff, it was a relief. In the morning, his mind would be clear and again hopeful, for the toughest part of a trial lawyer's day is late in the afternoon, when the mind frets over every question not worded quite right, every witness that varied even a little from what was expected, every ruling that went against the side of the angels. And most of all, the regret over every question not asked. Even though overnight sleep during such proceedings was fitful and abbreviated, mornings brought on fresh ideas as well as a resupply of stamina to continue the battle. Yes, Kasoff would much rather wait until morning to begin to set his sights on the next phase of this case.

But there was still the bleakness of this afternoon to get through, and it was not yet 3:30. Kasoff packed up his briefcase slowly and maintained a stoic, "No comment," as he wended his way through the crowd of reporters that followed him down the courthouse steps and beyond. The shouted questions had begun before the courtroom door had closed behind him. Kasoff was actually pleased that one of these jackals had still been just inside the courtroom when he shouted, "Are you going to appeal when Taft throws out your case?" Although the judge had already left the bench, Kasoff was hopeful the jurist had heard it, knowing he needed all the help he could get before this contrarian.

Finally, escaping the pack, Kasoff trudged through the lobby of his office not noticing the visitor sitting there. As he reached Sharon's cubicle, she informed him, "There's a man out there who's been waiting over an hour to see you."

"He doesn't have an appointment. Tell him I've got bigger fish to fry."

"He says he can help you get Moby. Is that big enough?"

"Huh?" replied Kasoff with a look that said, *Don't keep me in suspense.*

"He says he can help you with your case."

Kasoff peered warily past the cubicle and now noticed the earnest-looking young man in the white lab coat. He didn't look like press, but who could be certain these days? Carol, previously filled in by Sharon on the mysterious visitor, now walked by and piped up. "Gee, here's a shock. A guy in a white coat finally coming for Kasoff. What took them so long?" And then, noting Kasoff's careful scrutiny of the stranger, she added, "Now, don't get paranoid."

To which Kasoff shot back, "Only my real enemies think I'm paranoid. My imaginary ones understand." And then, "Well, things can't get worse. I might as well go meet this guy."

For once, Carol had the last word. "Be sure and write us. That is, if they allow you any sharp objects." Kasoff turned back and smiled at her as he went to greet the man.

"Hello. I'm Bob Kasoff. What can you do for me?" Kasoff said it with a smile as he extended his hand, but he was serious about getting right to the point. After all, every minute of the balance of that afternoon and evening would have to be devoted to reviewing the briefs and preparing for the morning's argument.

"Nice to meet you. I'm Dr. Frank Albertson."

"So says your coat."

"That's why I'm here."

"Huh? Well, come on in. I can only give you a few minutes," replied Kasoff, having no clue as to where this was going.

"Thank you. This won't take long. I'm a first-year resident at Northwestern University Hospital. Last year I interned there. One day in December, the chief resident asked me to go down to radiology to retrieve an old MRI on an elderly patient. He needed it to compare with a current one for some reason or other I forget. Anyway, I walked into the room where they store the patient films, alphabetically, of course, and there was a gentleman there wearing a white coat like I am. I assumed he was a doctor. He took a film out of its jacket, held it up to the light for a moment, and then pulled the report out and read it. When he saw that I was looking through the same section of the alphabet that he was in, he turned away, as if he wanted to avoid contact."

"Where were you looking?"

"In the *Mc*s. But that wasn't all. You see, when he lifted the film to the light, he did so only briefly, and with a blank look on his face. I knew something wasn't right. I asked him if he needed help. He declined without looking at me. But when he turned to go, I saw the name on his coat."

"And?"

"It said: 'Dr. Baker. Dr. Charles Baker.' I knew Dr. Baker. It wasn't him. He then left the room. I went to find a house phone to call Security, but by the time I got ahold of them, he must have gotten away, because they never found him. I didn't know if this guy was dangerous or what, but I decided that Security should know the name of the patient he was interested in, just in case. So I returned to radiology and found the film jacket askew with the report still sticking partly out of it—he'd left in a hurry—and I noted the name on the report in case he was a patient so Security could watch for this guy."

As usual, Kasoff was a step ahead. "And the name was McGinniss."

219

The young doctor's eyes widened in amazement. "Right! Don McGinniss. Security asked me to make out a report, so I did. Here it is," and Albertson handed Kasoff a folded-up report that summarized the incident.

"Can you identify the stranger?" Kasoff certainly had.

"As a first-year resident, I'm incredibly busy. I'd been up for thirty-six hours. But when someone's picture is in living color on the front page of the paper at every newstand in town, even I notice it. And the guy I saw posing as a doctor that day is the guy I saw with his picture plastered all over town yesterday. I'm no baseball fan, but even I know his name is Donovan."

"You're certain?"

"Certain as a sleep-deprived resident can be."

"And the report and film he was looking at?"

"Sorry. I can't bring that. Doctor–patient privilege, you understand. But I'm sure you could subpoena it."

"Did you happen to read the report of the film study yourself?" Kasoff wasn't sure he wanted to subpoena it to court if it wasn't going to help him.

"I just glanced at the name. But when he held the film up to the light, just from the brief look I got, it was obvious that it was of the skull. And anyone reading the report would learn whether or not the study showed any abnormalities, along with their locations."

That's it! Kasoff exclaimed to himself. *Now we've got Donovan committing criminal acts to obtain information to assist him in carrying out the murder. No doubt the report told him the weak link in McGinniss's skull.* "But how the hell would Donovan have known to look there?" Kasoff wondered out loud.

"I don't know. But I do know that the local professional teams have their athletes undergo physicals at our hospital to clear them for play. Maybe Donovan knew that and just played a hunch."

Sure, thought Kasoff. The year before, Chicago's third baseman, Joe Mallory, had become a free agent and signed with the Yankees. Donovan could have asked him. "If I give you a subpoena, can you be in court tomorrow at nine A.M. sharp?"

"Uh, sure. I'll have to clear it with my chief resident, but a subpoena, sure, it'll cover me. I thought this might help." And the doctor again displayed eyes as wide as those of the pediatric patients he saw.

"It can't hurt," replied Kasoff with uncharacteristic understatement. "Oh, and this judge insists on starting right on time. Don't be detained."

"The chief will understand. He's a big fan."

"I'll be back in a few minutes with your subpoena," and upon exiting, "Sharon, I've got a rush here."

And what a rush it was for Kasoff. "Oh, and, Sharon, when you finish, call our friend at the phone company and have him check all incoming and outgoing calls for the months of October and November last year between Joe Mallory—" whose off-season home remained in nearby Evanston—"and Donovan's home in Richmondville."

Within a few minutes, Kasoff handed Dr. Albertson his subpoena and added, "We'll serve a *duces tecum* subpoena tonight on the hospital's record custodian to supply the McGinniss film and report. I'll put a note on it that their appearance is excused if they'll supply you the jacket to bring with you. Can you check with them on that later tonight?"

"Sure."

It would be a long night for Kasoff as well as an early morning. He sent the doctor on his way, order to appear in hand, and practically ran down the hall to B.D.'s office.

Beaming, Kasoff excitedly informed his boss, "Lightning has struck. A one-in-a-million shot has just paid off."

"What's up?"

"Tomorrow morning, that damned Taft is going to hear proof positive that Donovan broke into a hospital, stole property, and invaded the privacy of a patient in order to gain critical information that he knew would enable him to kill McGinniss."

"Stop arguing your case for a moment and tell me the unvarnished facts."

Kasoff repeated his conversation with the resident. B.D. interrupted. "Wait a minute. He didn't break into the hospital."

"He broke into an area off-limits to the public. As soon as he opens the door to the radiology library, that's a breaking. Add that to the theft of the coat—"

"You have proof the jacket wasn't given to him?"

"I'll have that by the time we're in trial. For now, Dr. Albertson gives me probable cause to believe that he stole it. Plus, with the invasion of a patient's privacy, you've got three distinct crimes he committed in furtherance of his one-man conspiracy—"

"An oxymoron."

"I'll grant you that. But now he's no longer committing a killing simply by playing by the rules, or even breaking only the rules of the game. Now, he's committed two felonies and a misdemeanor in order to carry out his plan."

"Hang on now, Bob. You know as well as I do that the felony-murder rule doesn't cover this situation." It was true. The felony-murder rule was designed to enable the state to charge a criminal with murder for a death that occurred in the course of committing a felony that carried with it a high degree of risk to life. If an armed felon robbed a bank and a guard, in the course of attempting to stop it, accidentally shot and killed a teller instead, the robber could be charged with murder of the teller. The notion was that the felon has no cause to complain that he had no intent to kill where he commits a crime that has a natural tendency to endanger people's lives. But here the felonies were not committed in close proximity to the death and were not the sort of crimes that were inherently risky to life and limb.

"Still," B.D. continued, "at least we've got another arrow in our quiver. We can take the position that the felony-murder rule should be expanded to cover this situation as well as pursue our original argument. This case will ultimately be decided by the Court of Appeals, if not the Supreme Court, anyway. Who knows? If they won't buy a Chevy, maybe they'll take the Ford. But we'll have to ask the Court for permission to amend the charge. At least it's not a lesser offense. That we'd be barred from raising now. And we'll need some supplemental briefing on this of course."

"I know. I'll be asking Angela to start on this right away. The question is, will Taft even let us have additional time?"

"You put that witness on in the morning and he's got to give it to you. Hell, even if he won't and you just make the argument orally tomorrow along with an offer of proof, the record will be protected for appeal. Good work, Bob."

"I can't take credit for this one. The doctor just fell out of the sky." If it even occurred to Kasoff, he would never admit that it was the press he detested so deeply that had flushed out this witness with its floodlights.

"He wouldn't have been there to fall if you hadn't been there to catch him. Hell, you're the only one who's ever believed in this case. Now you've actually got a chance to win it, or at least try it, and make some good law in the process. And even if nothing else comes of this, it'll be a cold day in Hell before another sports figure ever dreams about doing serious violence to a competitor."

"Thanks, B.D. I'll let you know what happens."

"Let me know? Hell, I'm going to be over there myself listening to the arguments. Buzz me when you know about what time they'll start."

"Sure thing."

"Don't you wish?"

When court convened the next morning, Judge Taft was just sitting down when Kasoff rose to announce, without fanfare, "Your Honor, I have one more witness." Knowing that the judge was even less fond of surprises than delays, Kasoff hastened to add, "Who will take no more than fifteen minutes."

Taft harrumphed a, "Proceed, counsel," that suggested resignation more than protest.

"The People call Dr. Frank Albertson." Some in the press gallery groaned, assuming this would be simply more elaboration on the cause of death. Several had gone so far as to begin a draft of their postmortem on the proceedings, a requiem that would include a funeral pyre for this prosecutor's ambition.

So the fledgling doctor, carrying a large off-white envelope, took the stand and told his story. The MRI report, six years old, revealed McGinniss's anatomic variant as the coroner had described it the day before. When Kasoff asked the doctor if he could identify the interloper in the radiology department that day, he pointed to Donovan and said firmly, "That's him, sitting right there."

Several reporters scribbled furiously, but many more bolted from the courtroom to get on their cell phones to their papers or stations. Anyone in the hallway knew immediately what every compulsive gambler wishes he could divine: the content of tomorrow's headlines: "McGinniss's Medical Records Rifled by

Donovan." "Records Caper Enabled Donovan to Kill." "The Line Shot Heard round the World." The bailiff had to step outside to quiet them. But the deadline hounds were missing the real story inside. For the first time, Kasoff had something other than Taft's undivided disdain. Now he had his attention.

For several years in the late seventies, Taft had sat on the board of the hospital in an unpaid capacity. The business community saw nothing wrong with it, but he had taken a lot of flak from one quarter. The plaintiffs' trial bar had had the temerity to begin filing blanket motions to disqualify him in any civil suit brought against the hospital, and the Chief Judge eventually had to prevail upon him, privately, to surrender his board seat. It was, the Chief Judge gently pointed out, interfering with Taft's responsibilities on the bench, in violation of the canons of judicial ethics. While the thought that what he viewed as community service could somehow be seen as a threat to his impartiality rankled him, his respect for the Chief and the appearance of propriety had finally persuaded him to step down. As the faithful thought of their houses of worship, Taft thought of hospitals. Both brought comfort to the afflicted. As the sanctity of the confessional was the soul of the former, so were the patient records of its secular equivalent. Invading the privacy of either, particularly for nefarious purposes, was, in Taft's view, the epitome of evil.

Weinstein, who had entered the courthouse that morning with a bounce in his step and a smile, kept a close eye on Taft as this neophyte told his tale, and Weinstein's own face began to register concern equal to the judge's interest in this witness. When it was Weinstein's turn, he decided to attack where he knew every criminal case was most vulnerable: eyewitness identification. As a defense attorney, he loved to tell juries in closing argument the story of the national news magazine that, several years back, put a close-up picture of a Gulf War soldier in profile on its cover in the midst of that conflict. He actually kept a copy of the magazine so he could display its clarity and ample size to his rapt, if captive audience. Anyone could see at a glance how easy it was to identify the young warrior. Then, Weinstein would take out a second issue of the magazine dated two weeks later, and point out the portion of the "Letters" section devoted to readers' correspondence on that cover story. After a dramatic pause, he would tell the triers of fact that there were seven—count 'em, seven—letters from seven different families thanking the magazine for putting their son on the cover! If loving parents in the comfort of their own living rooms couldn't distinguish their own flesh-and-blood from that of a stranger, how on earth could the poor victims of this robbery, that rape, this burglary accurately identify their victimizers? He wouldn't even have to mention the good lighting in that living room or the time for review and reflection, let alone contrast it with the victim's mayhem-encumbered glimpse.

And Weinstein's argument was effective. Unless there was solid physical evidence tying his client to the crime, that contention produced an acquittal every time. Oh, sure, the prosecution would follow Weinstein in rebuttal by claiming that the criminal's image was burned into the victim's brain as if by a branding iron, never to leave or fade. But when all was said and done, the burning brain theory did nothing to singe reasonable doubt, and so Weinstein's clients would walk the path shown them by those well-worn magazines.

Weinstein began innocently enough. "Are you a baseball fan?"

"Not really."

"'Not really.' Does that mean you don't go to games?"

"Right."

"Don't watch 'em on TV?"

"Right."

"Don't check the baseball coverage in the sports page?"

"Right."

"Do you subscribe to any sports magazines?"

"No."

"Before last fall, ever see any pictures of Donovan to your knowledge?"

"No."

"So, before last fall, you didn't know who Donovan was, did you?"

"I'd heard the name, like I'd heard Babe Ruth's name, but it never really meant anything to me."

Weinstein hadn't been hurt by the answer, but he was nevertheless disgusted with himself for not fully closing the exits before springing the question. "Before last fall, you wouldn't have recognized Donovan if you saw him on the street, is that true?" That's the question he had meant to ask.

"True."

"Once you realized that day at the hospital that you were dealing with an intruder, you were concerned about it, right?"

"Sure."

"You wanted him caught, right?"

"Right."

"That was important to you, right?"

"Sure."

"And so you wanted to give Security the best possible description, right?"

"True."

"And that's how you felt when you completed the incident report, right?"

"Right."

"And so you wanted to prepare an incident report that would be as accurate and as complete as possible, right?"

"Right." No holes in the net now.

"May I see the incident report you completed?"

"Sure." And he handed Weinstein the document.

"There's a box near the bottom for 'Unauthorized entry,' and if that's checked off, as it is here, you're supposed to describe the situation, is that correct?"

"Yes, sir."

"And there's a line for 'Description' of the intruder, you see that?"

"Yes."

"And you entered some information in there, true?"

"Yes."

"And you wrote, and I'm quoting now, 'White male, approximately six feet to six feet, two inches tall, two hundred to two hundred and twenty pounds, brown hair,' right?"

"Yes."

"And that's all you wrote, right?"

"Yes."

"Nothing about glasses?"

226

"True. But he wasn't wearing any."

"But you didn't note: 'No glasses,' did you?"

"No. I didn't think it was necessary." A witness who volunteers anything on cross-examination is a witness who quickly finds himself out on a limb. Weinstein now detoured to chop it off.

"Well, you didn't know who would be following up on your description in attempting to locate this intruder, did you?"

"True."

"Well then, didn't you think it would be helpful to the investigator to know whether he or she should be looking for someone not wearing glasses?"

"I guess I just didn't think of that."

"Well, you certainly know the significance of noting negative findings in a medical examination, do you not?"

Kasoff intervened. "Objection, Your Honor. Irrelevant."

"Sustained."

The expression on Taft's face told Weinstein he had won the point, if not the objection. The judge, after all, knew the answer without having to hear it. The branch removed and cleared, Weinstein now continued his line of attack. "There is nothing on the incident report's description of the intruder regarding facial hair, true?"

"He had no facial hair." Albertson was not one to be deterred. He would make his points as he thought necessary in order to prevent what he perceived as Weinstein attempting to paint a misleading impression.

But the canvas belongs to the inquisitor. The witness is a mere palette, allowed to reveal only those hues the brushmaster chooses to emphasize. "Would you please answer my question? Is there anything in the incident report concerning facial hair or its absence?"

"Nothing."

"Did you make any note regarding whether he was balding?"

Kasoff had had enough. "Objection, Your Honor. The report provides the best evidence of what was noted."

"I'll withdraw the question, Your Honor, and rephrase it. Did you make a mental note at the time as to whether the intruder was balding or had a full head of hair?"

"I remember he had brown hair. It may have receded a bit."

"That's not my question. I don't want to know what you're attempting to recall for us today. I want to know if you made a mental note of the intruder's hairline when you saw him last December?"

"Not that I recall."

"Nothing about his complexion in the report?"

"True."

"Or any distinguishing characteristics?"

"True."

"Well, can you recall for us today, did he have any distinguishing characteristics?"

"Not that I recall."

"And if you look out into the courtroom this morning, how many men fit the description that you gave in your report?"

"Several. Including your client." Titters from the gallery. Weinstein ignored them. He had more.

"And the description that you supplied in the report is the best description you could give at the time, wasn't it?"

"I wouldn't say that. I didn't think about inserting every little detail like you just mentioned."

"Well, did you at least tell anyone in Security any of these additional details so they could help catch the intruder?"

"Not that I recall."

"And did you ever hear any more about this incident after that day?"

"No." This answer invited a two-pronged follow-up.

"So, apparently, the general description you gave was insufficient to apprehend the intruder, true?"

"I don't know."

"In addition, the fact you never heard anything more about it indicates that you never had any reason to remind yourself or otherwise commit to memory the identifying features of this intruder, true?" Weinstein was gambling here a bit but believed it was a good bet.

"I remembered him well enough to recognize him immediately when I saw the newspaper photos." Albertson was holding his own.

"Nevertheless, you resumed your busy schedule?" Weinstein was back on safe territory and confident that this line of inquiry would negate the point this witness had just scored.

"Yes."

"Now, from that day some eight months ago until this week when you saw the newspapers, is it fair to say that you remained a non–fan of baseball?"

"Yes."

"You still never saw Donovan's picture to your knowledge?"

"True."

"Now, you were an intern through when, the end of June?" Weinstein knew that new doctors begin their hospital residencies in July. Within weeks their exhaustion is outflanked only by their terror, their field of ignorance stretching to the horizon as it begins to dawn on them that it will be half a lifetime before they're fully familiar with the expansive territory. Yet miraculously by midwinter their confidence is soaring. Never choose the waning days of summer to be wheeled into the emergency room.

"Yes."

"And then you began your residency several weeks ago, true?"

"True."

"And whether you're an intern or a resident, you've got an extremely busy schedule, right?"

"Right."

"You'd see dozens of patients each day, wouldn't you?"

"Usually."

"You've probably seen several thousand faces since last December, right?"

"True."

"Probably several hundred would match the general description you provided in the incident report, true?"

"I doubt it would be that many."

"Well, then, how many would it be?"

"I don't know. A few dozen, perhaps."

"A good number anyway, true?"

"As I said, perhaps a few dozen. I don't know what a good number is."

"In any event, have you seen some of your patients on repeat visits?"

"Yes."

"Ever see a patient and then check your previous visit's chart note only to realize that you were confusing this patient with another?"

"I don't know. I don't recall."

"A person who, like yourself, works with people gets used to the idea that some people resemble others, right?"

"I suppose so."

"Ever have the experience of getting a glance at someone, even someone you know, and you're about to say hello, but as the person gets closer, you realize it's not the individual you thought it was?"

"Sure, haven't we all? But that's not what happened here."

Weinstein ignored the rejoinder. "Haven't we all indeed?"

"Your Honor—" Kasoff rose, but Taft intervened.

"Just proceed with your examination, Mr. Weinstein, and leave the editorializing to the gallery, shall we?"

"Thank you, Your Honor. Isn't it true, sir, that for the better part of a year, you had absolutely no reason to bring to your mind's eye the face of that intruder until just the other day?"

"True."

"And in that time, you saw thousands of faces in that very same hospital setting?"

"Objection, Your Honor. Asked and answered."

"Sustained."

Had this been the trial, Weinstein would have sat down now, content to deliver his news magazine coup de grace in his summation. But here he was willing to ask a question to which he did not know the answer, knowing he had nothing to lose. After all, he was sure that Taft was already convinced there was probable cause to believe that Donovan was the intruder. That didn't seal the issue for the People, but in case Taft did decide to run with this and was going to issue a bind-over, at least Weinstein would know the answer in advance of trial to the inquiry he was about to make, which would go to the ultimate issue of reasonable doubt.

"Sir, how can you be certain that the man in hospital attire you saw for a brief moment the better part of a year ago at a time when you were preoccupied with your own work was the man you see here today dressed in civilian clothes?"

"Well, as I have said, I was convinced it was him when I saw his picture in the papers, but seeing him here today, I'm even more certain."

"Yes, but how?"

"That day in the radiology lab, when he realized I was watching him, he gave a little tug at his earlobe, unconsciously like a nervous habit. When I began testifying here today, as soon as I mentioned that I worked at the hospital, I saw him do it again, the same way, right here as he was sitting before me." In an instant, the witness had wiped away the shroud over the portrait, so carefully draped there by the cross-examiner. It was as if the work had been restored to the condition it had been in when its original paint was still tacky. In court, as in art, presentation of the finest detail is the mark of the master.

Murmuring in the courtroom. Weinstein knew that even for the purposes of this hearing, he had asked one question too many, though he consoled himself with the thought that Kasoff would have learned this by the time of trial after fully sanding this witness and thereby would have brought out this fact in his own examination anyway. Still, the doctor's answer would do nothing to dissuade Judge Taft from allowing the case to go forward.

"No more questions, Your Honor," Weinstein concluded, and Kasoff concurred.

"The People have no more witnesses, Your Honor." The telephone records would have to wait for trial. There was simply no time to talk to Mallory to determine the content of any conversations he had had with Donovan, and without that, the records were meaningless.

"Does the defense wish to call any witnesses?" Defendants always had the right to do so but rarely exercised the opportunity except in the most unusual case, where a witness could blow away the prosecution's case so convincingly that the People would be persuaded to drop the charges or, at the very least, convince the judge to dismiss. Aside from that, the defense bar viewed these examinations as nothing more than a way to discover the vulnerable points in the prosecution's case. Of course, if no such weaknesses presented themselves, this was a signal to the defense to become receptive to plea negotiations.

"We have no witnesses, Your Honor."

"All right, we'll break a bit early for lunch and return a bit early—at one P.M., to begin the arguments."

Kasoff rose. "Your Honor, the People are certainly prepared to argue the case this afternoon, but we would appreciate it very much if the Court would be willing to permit supplemental briefing and perhaps additional arguments in light of this morning's testimony. We believe that this witness, whose existence concerning which we had no way of knowing about until yesterday—" and Weinstein knew what was coming—"requires us as advocates for the People and as officers of the court to request that the charge be amended to include a felony-murder complaint, which we believe will be sustainable under an appropriately expansive interpretation of that rule, which we will expound more fully upon in our additional briefing."

"Your Honor, on behalf of my client, we vigorously object. By no stretch of the imagination, as Your Honor is well aware, has the felony-murder rule ever been applied in this type of situation. Any such amendment would therefore be futile and should not be considered, let alone granted. The prosecution seeks here not merely to expand upon precedent, but to shatter it."

"At least we won't be shattering anyone's skull." Kasoff knew it was a cheap shot, but sometimes it was necessary to remind the Court of the reason everyone was here. Weinstein immediately objected, and of course, Kasoff quickly apologized to the Court. And then it was Judge Taft's turn to speak.

"Gentlemen. This hearing itself has been a precedent-shattering proceeding. As long as we've come this far, I'm in favor of making as complete a record as possible for the Court of Appeals. I know the loser will be going there anyway. The People's motion to amend the charge is granted. It shall be filed and served on opposing counsel within three business days. The People shall file their supplemental brief within fourteen days. Defendant has fourteen days thereafter to respond. The People may file a reply brief within seven days after that."

As Taft spoke, the lawyers were scribbling as fast as the press had during the testimony. "Oral argument will be conducted fourteen days after the defendant's brief is filed. My clerk will call you with the precise date and time. Have you got that, counsel?"

"Yes, Your Honor," was the reply, in harmony. And the lawyers, to themselves, agreed on something else. The jurist they knew was behaving a bit too benignly. And, for once, they couldn't read which way he was leaning.

As Donovan left the courtroom with his counsel, he exhaled a sigh of relief. The serpentine legal proceedings would drag on well after season's end before Donovan would ever find himself confined in this venue again, and then only if Judge Taft ordered him to trial. Good thing, too. He had missed the last two games, each of which the Yankees had lost by one run, so their lead was down to three games over Baltimore, with Boston just one more off the pace. With less than two months to go and half a dozen games remaining against each of the contenders, the Yankees needed Donovan almost as much as he needed them. Leaving the courthouse for the fresh air of August—a cool breeze was blowing from the north for the first time since early June—Donovan's exhilaration was cut short by the headache that suddenly returned after a four-week hiatus. That and a commissioner who Donovan soon learned was weighing the doctored-bat revelation.

15

As McGinniss matriculated through his junior year, aside from his successful return to the diamond while wondering what might have been, he saw it as a time to get serious, not that he had ever been frivolous, even as a five-year-old. His major was business. He gave up intramural basketball—no sense risking injury if he didn't have to. His parents persuaded him to accept their largesse, and so he concentrated on his studies without working a part-time job. Classes went well and he aced most of them. From time to time as he walked across campus he would receive strange looks. He knew it was because he had been caught exhorting himself aloud to "stop it." That was his way of fighting off thoughts of Mary that would creep into his free moments. Reminders were ever present. The young woman who sat near him in his marketing class with the identical hairstyle. The co-ed who wore the same coat as Mary. The songs blaring out of the student union that evoked a memory of being with her when he had first heard the tune. Still, as the year concluded, he began to believe that he might eventually come to terms with the idea that he was destined never to spend his life with her, though the thought of never seeing her again was still impossible to accept.

Meanwhile, a year after Melanie had spotted her then-unemployed brother-in-law straying, she had begun to discern that things were far from idyllic with Mary's marriage, even though Victor had got back to work and the couple had attended counseling. She wouldn't say anything, but Melanie was sure she could see it in Mary's eyes. She knew that Mary wanted children, yet after two years of marriage none were on the way. One spring Saturday while the two were shopping, Melanie decided to broach the subject as they sat down for lunch.

"So, Mary, any news yet in the baby department?" She made sure to ask it cheerfully, as though she had no suspicion that anything might be wrong, lest she put Mary on the defensive.

234

"I don't know-w-w," and Mary drew out the last word, as though she wouldn't anytime soon.

"Well, if you don't know, who does?" Melanie inquired playfully.

Now Mary's voice dropped and her cheeks sagged a bit as she dropped her eyes. "I don't think that Victor wants children."

"Oh, Mary—"

"Or, I should say, any more children."

"What?"

And now she would drop the bombshell. "I found out—he didn't tell me—that he already has one on the way. In three months."

By Melanie's quick reckoning, it was obvious that fidelity had not been Victor's watchword even since he had sworn off other women after his last transgression. And right in the midst of counseling for that very issue. Oh, the deceit!

"I confronted him about it. It was an old girlfriend. They had gotten together again for just one night."

"And he used the lame excuse that it was just so spontaneous and all." Mary's already pained expression grew, and Melanie knew she had hit it on the nose. "Do you know what Don would say about this?"

The name startled Mary and she suddenly raised her bowed head with a look that combined resignation and fondness.

"He'd tell you that a guy who really loved you would never dream of doing that because he would feel that the thought of hurting you would be too painful to bear. That's what Don would say."

Mary didn't doubt it, but to her sister she simply replied, "How do you know that?"

"Because that's what he told me the last time Victor strayed."

"Well, I haven't given up on Victor changing his mind about children, and about being faithful, for that matter. There's hope."

"Hope triumphs over experience when the heart rules the head." And Mary's heart ached. And Melanie's head ached for her.

*　　*　　*

Back at the office, Kasoff ticked off yet again what he had on Donovan as B.D. played devil's advocate. "Malice: Donovan knew his action had a high probability of causing death. Premeditation and deliberation: he planned this for months. We've got a felony committed in the course of the planning. The break-in at the hospital yields Donovan a crucial piece of evidence. His act of doctoring the bat was not only a violation of the rules of the game but was done with the intent to increase the speed of the deadly projectile. And not that we need it, but we've got motive: revenge for the beaning and against the baseball establishment itself."

"And yet," B.D. replied, "the whole is less than the sum of its parts. Any hitter who bats less than four hundred, and that's all of 'em, can't—" and here he made quotation marks with his first two fingers on each hand in order to emphasize his next word— "*know* anything about where or even whether he's going to hit any particular pitch."

"Hang on, B.D. I've been thinking about that. Suppose Donovan goes up to the top of the Sears Tower early on a Sunday morning when there are very few pedestrians. He tosses a lead pipe out the window and correctly assumes there is just a ten percent chance that he'll hit someone. But he defies the odds, and a death results. Can't he be prosecuted for murder in some degree?"

"Sure."

"Well, then, it's not the certainty of hitting the target that's important. It's the deadliness of the delivery device. As long as the means used is reasonably calculated to bring about the expected result—death—what difference does it make if he hits the target ten percent or one hundred percent of the time?"

"But tossing the lead pipe is itself criminal, so the result is not important except as it defines the degree of guilt. Here there's no crime in hitting a baseball as part of a game. So I think you're rightly held to a standard that requires you to show not only intent—which I'll concede we have here—as opposed to mere expectation, but that the means used was virtually certain to bring about that intended result. And so what defeats you is the law of averages—batting averages."

"So we've come full circle."

"Say what?"

"That was my first thought in this case. We would need to show certainty. But the certainty I've focused on has been the probability of death if he succeeded in hitting the target. I've been overlooking, maybe because I wanted to, the probability of hitting the target to begin with."

"OK, so where does that leave us?" Only the tapping of his pen broke the silent void Kasoff knew he had to fill.

"Maybe here. It should be enough that he attempts—hell, he tried his damnedest—to hit the target, as long as he knows that striking it will be deadly. After all, he was certainly going to get more than one shot at it over the course of a season, wasn't he?"

"Sure," said B.D., the rise in his voice matching Kasoff's growing intensity.

"That's it, then!" And Kasoff slammed his palm down on the desk, the pen flipping up end over end, shooting beyond his doorway until it landed somewhere out of sight.

"And the kick is good!" replied the old football star.

But B.D. wasn't through. "As for the felony-murder rule, you and I both know that it's limited to deaths which occur in the course of the commission of felonies that are inherently dangerous to life. He didn't rob the radiology lab rat at gunpoint, and McGinniss's death didn't occur until months later. Doctoring a bat may draw a suspension from the game, but not a prison sentence. As much as I hate to admit it, to the extent—" expect bad news whenever a lawyer begins an opinion this way—"we have to rely on this old rule of the common law, I'm afraid we're going to fall short here. And when we do, Starstruck will be scrambling for so much cover—I don't care what he said earlier—there'll be nothing left of your ass . . . or mine."

"Are you suggesting—"

"Damn right this could cost us our jobs. But, hey, I'm behind you on this no matter how it turns out." Kasoff merely nodded his thank-you in the unspoken language that passes between people who know each other as they know themselves.

Meanwhile, ever since the revelation, sports headlines all across the nation had been screaming about Donovan's tainted bat. Never mind McGinniss's death. This baseball icon was now viewed as having feet of clay. Any number of columnists were beating the bushes for evidence that Donovan had resorted to

237

such cheating before. So far, nothing of the sort had turned up, but that didn't stop the writers from suggesting now that there was less to Donovan's success all those years than met the eye. The Hall of Fame, it was now said, was a foregone exclusion.

In an effort to calm the protests, Donovan issued a press release, flyspecked by Weinstein, assuring his fans that this was the only incident where he had ever "failed to abide by the noble standards of the game." But this only fanned the flames when Donovan refused to submit to journalism's version of a witch trial—a TV press conference where reporters, posing as high-minded trustees of the game's integrity, could take potshots at the star. This was one grandstand before which Donovan would not appear. To no avail, Greg, along with every other reporter, requested an interview, exclusive or otherwise. Donovan natu-rally blamed his silence on his lawyer's instructions, just as Weinstein had advised, but his reticence satisfied no one else.

The Yankee brass, anxious to tame the distraction so it could get on with the business of winning a pennant, persuaded Dutch, after some reluctance, to issue a statement that made it clear that as the hitting instructor, he had never before seen any indi-cation of Donovan having cheated. But still the media storm showed no sign of abating. This was one tempest that only a more salacious story could tame—one that would excite even the jaded press down in New Orleans. Yes, it would require some guy being caught in a motel room with not merely a dead woman but a live man, too. No such luck—this week.

The commissioner was being pressed to act on the affront to sportsmanship, especially by the owners whose teams were in the hunt for a play-off spot. He ordered an investigation, even retaining his own sleuths to talk to the parties involved. Wein-stein wouldn't let Donovan speak, of course, but the batboy, Dutch, and several Yankee players were interviewed, and a copy of the transcript of the pertinent portions of the preliminary exam was ordered and read by the commissioner personally. And now, for a change, he invited the media in to chew on this bone.

Squinting before the bright lights, baseball's lord of lords began reading: "'As you know, the Commissioner's Office has been carefully monitoring developments in the pending legal proceedings in the city of Chicago against Chris Donovan of the

238

Yankees. Based on the presumption of innocence, we have refrained from taking any action in the matter to this point, and we will continue to so refrain until that matter is concluded, at least insofar as the criminal charges go. But those proceedings have revealed not only actions that the law is considering but a serious violation of baseball's rules, specifically, the use of an illegal bat during a regular season game. I therefore conducted an independent investigation into these allegations, and I have concluded that Mr. Donovan did in fact use such an illegal bat last Opening Day in Chicago. Therefore, in accordance with the authority vested in me by the baseball owners, I am hereby ordering that Mr. Donovan be suspended without pay for a period of ten games, beginning tonight. Mr. Donovan is not to accompany the team or practice with it for the full term of this suspension. In accordance with baseball's collective bargaining agreement with the players' union, Mr. Donovan has a right to appeal. If he chooses to do so, an expedited hearing will be scheduled within forty-eight hours.' Now, I have only a moment or two to answer questions."

What the hell is his hurry? wondered the press gallery, but the first question posed aloud was, "Sir, what about Donovan breaking into that hospital's radiology room to check McGinniss's X rays? Are you going to take action on his invasion of another player's privacy?"

"We view that as a matter for the courts in the state of Illinois. Depending on the outcome of those legal proceedings, we will revisit the issue of any appropriate disciplinary action."

"Sir, if Donovan was doing all these things in revenge for being beaned the year before, shouldn't he be banned from the game for life? After all, doesn't it look to you like he was trying to kill McGinniss, and breaking the rules of the game at the very least in order to do it?"

"As I have stated, baseball will refrain from drawing any conclusions about the tragic death of Don McGinniss until after the legal proceedings terminate. At that point, there will be ample time to review that matter."

The reporter wanted to follow up, to make the point that baseball didn't need to wait for the wheels of justice to grind to a halt before taking action to assure the game's integrity, but the commissioner was already doing his usual sidestep away from the podium.

Donovan didn't concern himself with the endorsement contracts that were drying up and turning to dust. For him, the game was everything. He certainly didn't need the money, and in any event he had always imposed upon himself a single rule that had strictly limited those opportunities: he had to believe in the product and actually use it before he would agree to pitch it. And he had anticipated a suspension. And that appealing it would be useless. They had him dead to rights. He was hoping that it would be five games, seven maybe, but the thought of ten games was torment: the last three were against Baltimore. And the Yankee pitching was struggling. Though the dog days of August were over, sore arms were showing up like fleas in a kennel. True, with the coming of September, rosters could be expanded. But with more than half the teams still in the running for a divisional title or wild card berth, few had worthwhile talent with which they were willing to part for future consideration. And with the recent expansion of the number of teams in each league, pitching was hard to find anywhere, particularly in the Yankee farm system. Indeed, the talent pool was shrinking. American kids simply had too many diversions to grow up with the single-minded dedication to become the best of all ballplayers. The national game was past its time. Now, teams were finding that the favorite drink of their best scouts was rum—quaffed each night on some steamy Caribbean island as they scoured the unkempt fields of the Third World for the next baseball hero—it was a search of rough diamonds for that diamond in the rough. So, aside from a veteran journeyman—a polite term for another team's cast-off—the Yankees would have to go with what they had.

As that pivotal series approached, Baltimore and Boston both managed to win five of seven, two better than the hated Yankees. On September 10, the team would start a stretch of twelve games consisting of two three-game sets—home and home—against the two rivals. The Yankees clung to a slim one-game lead over Baltimore, two over Boston. On the ninth, the Yankees' number-two starter found that the recent cortisone shot in his pitching shoulder was not the cure for the inflamma-

240

tion in his rotator cuff. One of its tendons ripped in the seventh inning as he delivered an overhand fastball, and that was the last one he would throw for at least a year.

In the heat of a pennant race—though baseball's purists refuse to dignify the diluted road to the championship with the phrase that connotes the all-or-nothing, nail-biting, season-long excitement of those bygone days—the contestants will tell you that hitting is contagious and so are slumps. One guy starts pressing at the plate, and soon the guy batting behind him is trying to do too much to make up for his teammate's slippage. A few guys start hitting, and soon it's the opposition that's choking as they begin to sense the invincibility of their streaking opponents. While the race is on, guys who never finished high school and whose chief cultural contribution is to spit tobacco will suddenly wax poetic about teams of destiny and of players reaching deep for peak performance.

But step back from the race, and just look at the statistics. Year in and year out, over a long season, they look remarkably similar, for both individual players and the teams as a whole. Oh sure, a .250 hitter may have a break-out year when he hits .300 and a pitcher will suddenly learn to control the split-finger, elevating himself from a .500 pitcher to a 20-game winner. But no one hits .600. No team ever wins 130 or only 30. The players are ruled by the numbers, and not vice versa. Draw the bell curve, and those on its fringes are in the minors or the Hall of Fame. There's a balance of nature by the numbers.

With one exception. Since the twenties, the Yankees had risen to the top so often that more than six centuries would have to pass before every team could qualify for the World Series as often as that Gotham dynasty. So as the Yankees came to bat in the first inning of the first game in this crucial series with Baltimore, the screams of every fan in Poe's hometown cried out, "Nevermore!" at least not in their collective lifetimes, anyway.

And the local heroes didn't disappoint. In game 1, to the strains of the roaring crowd, Baltimore hit the Yankees with a big five in the first, leaving the champs to play catch-up. Baltimore hung on for a 6–4 win. Game 2 proved to be one of those epic struggles that fans look back on as a season's turning point, as though any one game could be statistically any more significant than any other. The final was 4–3, but the game was even closer than the score indicated. For nine innings, the teams remained scoreless. Now, as every fan knows, the Sunday doubleheader and the twi-nighter—except as part of a makeup game—had long since been eliminated from the schedules by the owners. After all, why provide fans a double feature when they'll pay the same money for a single game? But tonight the fans would see the equivalent of two full games. In the tenth, each team scored a run. And then the hitters resorted to that extra-inning effort that so often occurs in baseball marathons. If the leadoff hitter is retired, the next two batters simply swing for the fences in an effort to put an end to it. For the pitcher with a change-up, this is a godsend. The opponent who is overswinging is easily fooled by the off-speed stuff.

And so it went. A scoreless eleventh, twelfth, and thirteenth with plenty of strikeouts on both sides. In the fourteenth, the Yankees' leadoff hitter got on. The next batter, a left-hander, was given the hit sign in an effort to poke one through the expanded hole between first and second, the first baseman being forced to hold the runner. As frequently happens when a hitter is just trying to make good contact—"Don't try to kill it," they're urged from Little League onward—the ball clears the fence. Suddenly, the Yankees were up 3–1, and the pall in the park was palpable.

But Baltimore's heroes retied it with back-to-back doubles, a groundout to the right side, and a long flyout. Again the pitchers took command. Fifteen, 16, 17 innings. By the top of the eighteenth, five Yankee pitchers were icing their elbows. The Yanks got their leadoff man on that inning, but the next batter flubbed that neglected orphan of the hitters' repertoire, the bunt, popping it up, so that it backfired into an easy double play. And so the Yankees were soon retired in their half of the eighteenth.

The bottom of that frame would go down as one of the most bizarre in Baltimore franchise history. The Yankee reliever, pitching his fourth game out of the last five, didn't want to waste any pitches, but he walked the leadoff hitter on four straight. And then the pitcher promptly picked him off. The next batter hit a solid single to left. And he was immediately picked off as well, in spite of the vigorous protests of the Baltimore management that the Yankee pitcher was balking on his throws over to first. The fans couldn't tell whether it was their language or gestures, but the rhubarb ended only after the hometown manager and pitching coach were ejected.

And a pitching change was made, the Yankee hurler having nothing left in the tank. Kirk Caldwell was rested, not having taken the mound in more than a week since making his major-league debut in a mop-up role to close out a laugher. But he wasn't ready, at least not for the pressure of a divisional race. After throwing the first pitch a foot outside, he hit the batter with his next one. Baltimore's best base stealer, Jimmy Smith, shook off the pain in a forearm that would be bruised in the morning and trotted to first base. Caldwell tried to keep him close. But his third throw over there was the harm. It caught Smith leaning, all right, and he would have been out if the rookie's throw hadn't skipped wildly toward the right field side of the bag. By the time the ball could be retrieved and fired back into the diamond, Baltimore had the winning run on third.

Three straight pickoffs, defying the game's statistical baron, who had rebelled at the arrogance of the final effort, and the result was the winning run only 90 feet away. Only once before, and not so many years ago, had a pitcher successfully picked off three consecutive runners in a single inning, and the Lord of probability was not about to permit it to happen again. After all, in a million years no one would believe that even a million members of the primate world could ever pound out *Hamlet* twice.

Caldwell, his concentration confounded, threw six straight outside the long-shrunken strike zone and was pulled before he could do any further damage. Shattered by the experience, he had barely finished toweling off after his postgame shower when the pitching coach assured him that, yes, Columbus would be a fine place in which to live for at least another year.

With runners at the corners, the Yankees now brought in their last resident of the bullpen. Wade Wilson was ordinarily a middle reliever, which translated at contract negotiations from management's standpoint meant that his stuff wasn't good enough to start or close out a game. Wilson promptly threw a strike but then completed the free pass to load the bases.

The next man up was Baltimore's number-nine hitter, a great-field, light-hitting shortstop with a keen eye. Though his batting average had never exceeded .250 in his eight-year career, his on-base percentage was always around a hundred points higher because of his ability to work the pitcher for a walk. The crowd noise told the story, alternating between cheers and oohs with each pitch as the count went to 3 and 2. The runners, of course, were moving on each of the next five two-strike foul balls. As the seconds ticked by between each delivery, the noise of the faithful rhythmically waxed and waned. Meanwhile, Baltimore's lead runner, the only one who mattered, noticed that the Yankee pitcher didn't even check him before beginning his windup. And so, Smith became more daring each time Wilson threw home.

As the eleventh pitch was pending, Smith—who, as a member of the base stealers' elite, had a standing green light—determined that he would try to beat the ball. Naturally, he would need a huge head start, and a running one at that. He got it. The pitch, a fastball right down the pipe, was delivered. As the batter, a left-hander, began to swing, the ball, bat, and runner all converged over the center of the plate. Along with the catcher's glove, the man behind the mask having moved up to extend his reach when he saw the runner about to slide in.

It was as though four screaming ambulances had arrived simultaneously at an unmarked intersection. The catcher caught the ball. The runner beat the throw. The pitch was a strike. The batter had missed. Who had the right-of-way? Now, it was the umpires' turn to convene, with players and coaching staff alike buzzing around them, trying in vain to argue their cause. But the game's referees don't have to stand for election, much less abuse, and so the lobbyists for both sides were shooed away while the judges deliberated.

Did the third strike on the batter take precedence over the runner sliding in safely? At last, the ruling, and it brought the house down. Yes and no. True, the rule book stated that the batter would be called out and, should that be the third one of the inning, the run didn't score. But it wasn't that simple. The catcher had interfered with the batter's opportunity to hit the ball cleanly. The batter was awarded first base on catcher's interference. The run scored. The home team was victorious.

It's a cliché among baseball's followers that a heartbreaking loss like that has a spillover effect, though the cold truth of the statistics does not bear out the sentiment. But it happens just often enough to perpetuate the folklore, and the next night's game was one of those. Baltimore pounded the Yankees, 15–2. Sweep! And a new division leader.

Back in upstate New York, the barber's neighbor noticed that the barn lights were burning later than ever. Donovan had barely had enough time to watch his teammates on the tube. He was at his batting cage 10, 12 hours a day, hitting, changing the speed settings, and hitting some more. He spent his remaining time studying videos of the Boston and Baltimore pitching staffs. No way was he going to lose his timing during the layoff.

And he didn't. The ten days in solitaire had cleared his mind to concentrate on maintaining his excellence at striking a bird-sized speeding ball with a wooden club. Over the next nine games against the two contenders, Donovan would go 19 for 35, plus eight walks, including six home runs and 24 runs batted in. The Yankees won eight of them, losing only their final game against Boston. When the dust had settled, the Yankees had a two-game lead over Baltimore and a four-game bulge over Boston. Strange that Babe Ruth's curse should still hang over Beantown in an age when all the owners were constantly making player moves with both eyes on the bottom line. At least Boston's hard-up honcho had the financing of a Broadway play in mind when he had sold the young Bambino to the Yankees all those decades ago. Today's owners had neither the pull of a cultural bent nor the push of financial desperation motivating such moves. Just greed unfettered by frail excuse.

Only a dozen games remained. It was looking more and more like Donovan would get another shot at postseason play and maybe even the Series. All that marred the moment for him was those damned headaches that seemed to assert themselves with increased vigor each time he hit safely. Twelve games against the also-rans, and the Yankees mopped up, winning 11. They conquered the division going away, by 6 games over Baltimore. On October 1, the team could look forward to the opening play-off series. The opposition, once more, would be furnished by Chicago, with the winner playing the victor in the Texas–Baltimore series. As Baltimore was the wild card team, those fans got a reprieve. No longer trapped in the winner-take-all glory of an honest-to-goodness pennant race, the city's fans could take comfort this year in the fact that the owner's scheme to fill the cash registers with an extra week of TV revenue had got their heroes into postseason play. The city fathers responded with a pre-playoff parade and pep rally for the pretty good. Baltimore, after all, could at least be crowned the best mediocre team in the league.

16

Senior year. McGinniss's final lap for his B.B.A. Mary remained a daily memory, and he was still training himself in dealing with it. He could handle thinking of her smile and a remark he had made oh, so long ago to provoke it, as long as he kept it brief. Don't, under any circumstances, conjure up her voice in the mind's ear. That made it all too real, and the stomach-churning sense of longing for her would begin. Well over a year and counting, and he could still replay whole portions of their conversations in his head. He would have to let that go if he was going to take her advice, but this posed a dilemma. Could he, should he, surrender his fond memories of her, deny his feelings? They were the best part of himself, he knew. If he was only going to live once, shouldn't he live the life he desired? And weren't those feelings a big part of that life? Wouldn't he be denying the most important part of who he was and what was important to him if he renounced those emotions? Yes! Even the death of a loved one doesn't bury those feelings. No one would dream of telling anyone not to visit the final resting place of departed family no matter how many years had passed since their deaths. He would find a way to embrace his feelings, as he had once and only once embraced her, without letting them gnaw. And he would celebrate the emotion of—yes, he could even say it now—unrequited love. He would take what was positive and good about this dilemma and use the energy generated to accomplish every other dream he ever had.

And he aced his classes that year, graduating with honors. And he had a superb year on the school team as the scouts outnumbered the small contingent of fans who followed the team. Meanwhile, Chicago, an improving young franchise, had traded away its aging slugger the year before to obtain a top-10 draft pick in order to position themselves to select McGinniss. Don had done nothing since then to scare them off. In the June draft, just as he was turning 22, McGinniss was fitted with a Chicago cap and signed a $7.5 million contract, $1 million of it upfront, with the balance payable over the next three years. And half was guaranteed. His father, though a rube in the business world, had a sharp sense of what his son's best interest was, as well as his market value, and had even acted as his agent.

McGinniss, instantly the top prospect in the organization, was promptly shipped out to Chicago's AA team in Springfield for seasoning and was all but assured by management that if he progressed as expected, he would be pitching AAA the following year, with the possibility of a September call-up at that time. Then, the year after that, if all went well, McGinniss would be slated for the show.

McGinniss reveled in the improved competition. Some of the players were ex-major-leaguers on their way down. They were the ones with no second career upon which to fall back. Others were solid prospects. The remainder had reached the limit of their potential but were needed in order to round out the rosters to provide entertainment for the big towns and small cities for whom they played. The coaching was better as well. McGinniss was getting his best advice yet in fine-tuning his mechanics, though his control remained a problem. But even though he was now a professional and had been paid a handsome advance, he couldn't shake the rattling to his self-confidence provoked by his bouts of wildness. Pitching every fifth day through the end of the season, McGinniss had gone 11-3 with an ERA under 2.50. In 18 starts, he had pitched 138 innings and struck out 177 but walked 124. For him, the only number that mattered was the last one. He had to bring it down. As for the losses, there was only one of any real consequence, and it wasn't to be found in a box score. Still, there was consolation in knowing that he would be promoted next spring.

McGinniss enjoyed the camaraderie in the dugout and didn't even mind the eight-hour bus trips—he would spend them reading a book—but after joining his teammates a few times for postgame entertainment, he knew he didn't have much in common with them beyond the white lines. The booze, the riverboat casinos, the townies, none of it appealed to him. He swore it all off the night the featured exotic dancer at a strip club took center stage. *Oh, my God*, he thought, *she reminds me of Mary.* And he remembered the vow he had made to himself: *Seek out the best of everything. That's her gift to you. Now start living up to it.* And so, when he had an afternoon to kill, he would find a museum. On nights off, he would seek out a local theater troupe performance or read the classics. And he would smile to think that Mary was his guiding spirit in these enriching endeavors.

But as McGinniss was setting his sights higher, Mary's were falling. Having married once at twenty-one, an age when passion rules reason and the thought of settling is abhorrent, Mary was, as she closed in on the completion of her third decade, now stricken with the realization that the second man about whom she had felt so passionate would never put first whatever love he had professed in return. The charm that drew her to him was rooted more in self-love than mutual adoration. And it sapped her love for him right out of her, imperceptibly at first, but reaching critical mass over the most minor of events, like the single grain of sand that, when added to the small mound of its compatriots, suddenly causes the entire hill to collapse. Marriage as chaos theory.

They were at the zoo on a sunny Sunday. As they strained through the crowd to get an unobstructed view of the penned-in wildlife, from time to time an opening would appear with just enough room for one. Three times, Mary would later tell Melanie, Victor took that spot for himself instead of inviting Mary to occupy it, leaving her to fend for herself. And three times, though she kept this to herself, she flashed back to her zoo trip with McGinniss, when he had been so caring. That was it for Mary. The emperor hope had no clothes. Life was too precious to share one's bed while maintaining separate souls.

Within a week, Mary had filed for divorce, resolving to Melanie that she was still plenty young enough to find and fall in love with someone who was capable of reciprocating. Melanie wasn't so sure, but for now, she would keep quiet her conviction that her sister's best chance at a good life—not to mention the good life—was to settle for McGinniss. Except for a brief comment Mary made when his signing bonus was reported in the papers, his name rarely came up anymore. Melanie would bide her time a bit. Let Mary rediscover just how hideous the dating game could be. Melanie had noticed, after all, the broad smile that crossed Mary's face when Melanie showed her the news article. "He's got a real chance, doesn't he?" she had inquired. To herself, Melanie had replied, *Just as soon as you swear off the search for Prince Charming.*

McGinniss, traveling through every two-horse town in the Corn Belt, knew nothing of this, of course. He wasn't about to make a pest of himself by contacting her. And he took comfort in knowing that if lightning ever did strike, Melanie, as his staunch ally, would communicate the intelligence to him. Besides, in spite of a religious upbringing, McGinniss was a skeptic on the question of whether Heaven existed, much less heaven on earth. To accept the thought of going through life without Mary was something he could learn to live with. To fantasize about the possibility of a possibility was to court the dread of new disappointment. After all, she had shown absolutely no interest in him before Victor. What difference would her divorcing the cad make? At his age, the thought that a woman would be willing to settle was as incomprehensible to McGinniss as the prospect that he would ever forget about her. And so he had buried alive eternal hope, and deeply.

And he did date, though the second dates were few and far between. At first, he worried a bit that he might not be able to tell which women were interested in his money since the publicity surrounding his signing bonus. But the gold diggers were so transparent that he soon found his fear was groundless. Typically, if the evening began with dinner, before the salad bowls were emptied, his date would be asking about it. And the questions presupposed a fair amount of thought. "What was the agent's cut?"

"My father was my agent." This reply would always bring a beaming smile, like that of the fisherman who realizes the source of the tug on his line is bigger than expected as he reels it out of the water.

"Did you put most of it in mutual funds?"

"No, slot machines," he would deadpan, and for just a moment he would encounter the dead silence of the tardy prospector who's told the vein has just been exhausted.

One such woman had been so bold as to ask what kind of money he was earning on his investments. Thoroughly disgusted, McGinniss replied, "I don't know. Why don't I give you the name and number of my accountant so you can find out?" He thought that would be enough to bring the evening to a mercifully brief conclusion. Instead, concluding that the rate of return must be an impressive one if it required the consultation of an expert, she cooed as her reply, "Would you like to spend the night?"

"Now I know what's meant by the term *naked avarice*," he muttered, but she didn't hear him. Still, no matter how turned off he was by their greed, he always managed to tell them, "Thanks for a great time," just before he would add, "but no thanks."

But as he would head back to his motel from these misadventures, he would be struck by the same sense of emptiness and longing he remembered from his intramural basketball days. Compared with all the other women he had met, he placed Mary far above a pedestal. Then, after a moment or two, he would shake himself back to the present, soon to fall into bed and sleep it off.

Meanwhile, Mary decided to return to school at night, enrolling at the local community college to study computer programming. And she found a new job as assistant office manager at the downtown corporate headquarters of Chicago's biggest bank. Aside from fetching coffee for the boss from time to time and picking up his dry cleaning down the street, it was a step up for her. And in her business suits—no one could tell that she shopped at secondhand stores and never paid more than five dollars for an outfit, though the real price to pay was the living nightmare that one day she would walk into the office wearing something a coworker or, worse, the boss's wife had previously donated—she was rather fetching herself.

Mary, as well, had no shortage of dates. The suitors fell into two distinct categories. Those who insisted they loved their work and who were always plotting and scheming to get ahead. And those who professed to hate their jobs, who ruefully admitted that they had sold out for the money or were awaiting a better opportunity on which to pounce. Both groups had two things in common. They couldn't stop talking shop, and they wouldn't quit pawing at her. After a dozen or so such wrestling matches, she started saying no to the offer of the night out, instead of waiting 'til night's end. It was simply more efficient. This way, she would only have to say it once.

Thus ended another year, one in which Don and Mary, living separate lives, had more in common than either realized. New Year's Day found McGinniss on a flight to Puerto Rico. Chicago had big plans for their investment that year. He was placed on the 40-man major-league roster and was assured a spot in the starting rotation for Chicago's new AAA affiliate, Des Moines. And, more than anything, McGinniss was looking forward to that September call-up. In the meantime, the team had asked him to attend a three-week winter instructional league in San Juan. He couldn't get over it. Here he was, having been made a millionaire at this tender age, and the employer who had made it possible was merely "requesting" he spend 21 of Chicago's worst-weather days in the Caribbean doing what he enjoyed most at their expense. Whatever it was about the game and its riches that spawned in its participants a sense of entitlement, it was beyond McGinniss to fathom. He had packed his bags so quickly that he had forgotten to include his briefs.

The hitters down there weren't fully prepared for him, either. Thrilled at the opportunity to pitch to his best competition yet—consisting not only of top minor-league prospects but also a number of rookie and sophomore big-leaguers, McGinniss was throwing harder than ever. Ninety-seven, 98, even 99 mph. And his ball had movement on it. He was striking out one of every three batters as the coaches assured him that he was only a few too many walks and wild pitches away from the big time. Striving for excellence, McGinniss would draw on thoughts of Mary for inspiration. She was wired deep into his brain, as much a part of him as any of his emotions. And she would pop into his mind without his ever attempting to summon her, as the sight of a single flower evokes memories of spring. And he was learning control. He was able to limit her presence in his mind's eye to just a moment or two. He could enjoy sipping the memory without suffering its hangover of emptiness. And he vowed if he could control this powerful desire, he would learn to control his power pitches.

But hope and reason are no match for reality. McGinniss

began the season at Des Moines wilder than ever as his walks kept pace with his strikeouts. When he took a little off his fast-ball to try to improve his pitch placement, he discovered that the better AAA hitters were good enough to put his mistakes in the seats behind second base. McGinniss tried to convince himself that his problems were due to the unusually cool and wet spring in the Midwest—he figured the chill was affecting his all-impor-tant grip on the ball—but that fear went out the window with the warm weather on June 7 when he walked eight batters in the first three innings and had to be pulled after surrendering his second grand slam, two blows whose force was matched only by the impact his glove made against the back wall of the dugout when he finally reached it following his long walk off the mound. His record to that point: 1-4 with 42 walks and 45 strikeouts in just 39 innings. An ugly 5.31 ERA.

But he had reached his nadir. After talking his manager out of a demotion to the bullpen, McGinniss came back just five days later and pitched a two-hit shutout against Indianapolis, thrice striking out Cincinnati's number-one draft choice, a prospect labeled "can't miss." And McGinniss issued only three free passes. After that, he was on his way, throwing seven straight complete games, winning six, and giving up only nine runs while averaging a respectable four walks per game without giving up anything on his strikeout per innings pitched ratio. By mid-August, the word in the organization was out: within a fortnight, McGinniss would be in the show.

Everyone in Chicago's management, indeed everyone who followed the game's top prospects, wanted to know how McGin-niss had so suddenly turned his season around. Had a flaw in his mechanics been corrected? Or did he reach back internally and draw on some mental reserve? The truth was, it was a simple telephone call back in June. The voice was immediately familiar. "Melanie! This is a nice surprise. How's everything in Maryville? And how'd you find me?"

She explained that she had spoken to his father, who had given her his number at the apartment in Des Moines. "Happy Birthday," she added. He was touched by her thoughtfulness, no less so because she had the benefit of a sibling tickler system. And now his emotions swung back to the present.

253

"I don't know how happy it is. I'm another year older and my career is going down the toilet." And he explained his recent mound woes. But Melanie had just the tonic.

"I understand from your father that you've got a day game in Des Moines on the tenth and you're off on the eleventh, with a game in Indianapolis on the twelfth. Care to help celebrate two birthdays a day early here in Chicago? It's practically on the way."

If McGinniss didn't travel with the team, it was at his own expense, but that was a small price to pay to accept this bolt from the blue. "Sure. Who-all's coming?" he replied, assuming that Victor would be among the attendees.

"Just a small gathering." She wanted to save the best part for last. "Oh, by the way, did you know that Mary's divorced?"

The electric news surged through McGinniss as quickly as the neurons could transmit it, as hope, foolish but indestructible, rose from the permafrost. He managed to sputter, "I'm really sorry for whatever pain she went through." And he meant it, placing, as always, her well-being before his. But Melanie, knowing that McGinniss had earned the right to indulge some feelings of his own, played to his ambivalence.

"Oh, come on. You know she's better off without him."

"No, really. If I can't put her feelings first, especially over something like this, I'm not even worthy of her friendship." But having been invited to consider his own feelings, he allowed them to edge gradually forward. "How long ago did this happen?"

"She left him just over a year ago."

And disappointment quickly arrested the newly freed hope before the latter could barely stir. A year! More than enough time for her to become involved with someone else. McGinniss was reeling now, angry with himself for not calling her and yet feeling a sense of betrayal that her sister, whom he had thought was his ally, hadn't tipped him off long before. Melanie, perceptive as always, immediately noticed the change in tone of the voice on the line and quickly explained, "Look, when she broke up with Victor, she was still convinced that the great love of her life was out there waiting for her. It took a while, but she realized that the dating scene was a disaster. For a while now, she's sworn off men. But I'm sure she'd be happy to see you. The rest is up to you. I don't know if she'd ever be receptive to anything more than your friendship, but no one ever treated her like you did. So what do you say? Do I order two birthday cakes or just one?"

"Chocolate's my favorite," he beamed. But then hope's mirror image reasserted itself as he reflected out loud, "I can't afford to finish in second place again. This time, it would kill me."

"Second? I thought nice guys finish last," she teased. And she had just one more question. "Seriously, now, how often do you think of Mary these days?"

"How often do I get on a hotel elevator? How many miles do I ride on a bus? How many moments of idle time do I have in the course of a day?"

"Oh, it can't be that bad."

And then they hung up, each one looking forward to Mary seeing him.

If McGinniss slept two hours that night, it was more than he needed and as much as he would get in the next three days—the longest 72 hours of waiting he would ever endure.

June 11 at last. Melanie had said 7:00 P.M., and he had intended to arrive on time, unfashionably or otherwise. Since morning, he had eaten only a piece of toast and a small glass of juice, and he had barely been able to contain his excitement enough to keep that minimal sustenance down.

A band of heavy thunderstorms was moving in on Iowa's capital that morning, making air travel iffy. No way could he afford to be stranded. By car, only five hours separated them. Time to rent one that he could drop off at O'Hare. As he drove it eastbound through the farms of western Illinois, he contemplated the paradox. It had been three years since he had seen Mary, and yet as much as he had missed her every one of those 1,100-plus days and nights, it was as though he had seen her just last week. After all, in his mind he visited with her daily. He had ceased the self-flagellation for dwelling on the hopeless and his inability to get over her. Now, he took pride in his feelings. After all, falling for the very best had to say something terrific about him. And now, at last with an opportunity to see her once again, the overwhelming sense of longing for her, the intense emotion he had kept tucked away on an out-of-the-way shelf in his mind, came flooding forth. All he wanted was to be with her and make her happy and put her first and see her smile and hear her voice and give her a big hug—no, more than one—every day. And for the first time since his childhood, he felt tears run down his cheeks, and he laughed a nervous laughter at himself, right there all alone in the vehicle, because he didn't know if they were tears of joy or wistfulness or anticipation or all three. And he drove past the late spring's budding corn fields in wonder at this swirl of emotions that, like the havoc created by the twisters that abruptly set down on this peaceful land, he could neither tame nor fully grasp. And, at last, he found a way to chuckle at his predicament. When he would first lay eyes on her tonight, which of his body fluids would escape? Depends®. He now laughed out loud.

And he had a million things to say to her. God, how would he ever get it all in? And yet he was so much more interested in what she had to say, what she was feeling, what was important to her. *And remember*, he told himself as the freeway sign for Chicago brought him back to reality, *this is a birthday party for her, others will be there, and what gives you the right to think she'll even be interested in talking to you for more than a few minutes about matters superficial? Out of sight, out of mind, never in her heart to begin with. You're just an old friend. One of . . . who knows how many. Remember, if you can't look at things from her point of view, you're not deserving of her anyway.* And he sighed, the emotion having receded back into its receptacle. After tonight, he feared, it might require a burial more permanent than nuclear waste. After all, as bad as her husband and the subsequent loneliness must have been, the thought of McGinniss as the alternative must have been worse. Otherwise, he would have heard from her, and long before now. However, could it be that Mary had asked Melanie to call him? *No. Stop it. Don't do this to yourself. Just enjoy this one evening for what it's worth. Don't you dare exhume the ghost of false hope.*

As he reached Melanie's street, he noticed that aside from the trees on her block being a bit taller, things looked pretty much as they had that first time five years earlier when he had driven Mary here after her car had broken down at D'Amico's. And when Melanie answered the door with a broad smile, she remembered. "Aren't you that serial killer who picked up my sister several years ago?"

"You can't prove that," he beamed back, suddenly feeling 17 again at the memory. And as he entered, another face poked itself out of the kitchen.

"Hello, stranger." And Mary's voice was no longer confined to his dreams.

"How you doing, Mary?" And he approached her and gave her a hug. Immediately he felt a sense of relief, though it was quickly tinged with a sense of self-concern. Mary looked different from his memory of her, and he didn't feel an immediate emotional connection to this woman now standing before him. She had put on about twenty pounds, and he had not expected that, nor especially the changes the extra weight had created in the outline of her face. If the crow's feet weren't yet prominent, they had certainly taken root. Her haircut was different as well, and for some reason she seemed shorter than he had recalled her. For a few moments, he wondered if his emotions were all memory and no feeling. And he worried as well—could he really be so shallow that a few changes in her appearance would shake his love for her? Hadn't he tested his feelings for her in these past years by silently imagining her in every hell possible, with horrible disfigurement, for example, and hadn't he passed all his own tests with flying colors? He's standing on a dock. She's swimming nearby. A shark is about to attack her. Of course he jumps in to save her, even if he knows he'll be surrendering his own vital flesh.

And didn't he know himself better than this? He had been so certain of his feelings for her. How could he possibly react this way or, more accurately, fail to react? He could feel the adrenaline leach right out of him as he relaxed. Whoever this woman was before him, and whatever he had become in the meantime, his concern was now overtaken by the confidence that he could easily talk to this person. Unraveling the emotions frees the tongue.

And as it turned out, there was time for talk. The party was limited to her family—parents, sister and brother-in-law, as well as an older brother McGinniss had never met and his wife, plus the children of both Mary's siblings. And her Aunt Ruth, her mother's older sister, now 76. In her youth, as Mary had once told McGinniss, Ruth had looked out for Mary's mother the way Melanie watched over Mary. It seemed to have worked. Mary's mother had married a good man after turning down a bum she was too blinded by love to recognize, and Ruth had been instrumental in the deprogramming. Melanie and Ruth had become kindred spirits over the years, each recognizing their shared gift of good insight and sound judgment when it came to the opposite sex. "It's like panning for gold, only harder," Ruth would explain. "Too many of the nuggets turn out to be—well, let me put it this way. 'Worthless' would be an undeserved compliment. A financial and emotional drain, that's what they are. Find one that doesn't glitter too brightly, that looks like it would be solid underneath. Then you can at least hope for the best. But if it's not working out, run for your life. Just don't have any kids until you know."

It didn't take McGinniss long to realize, happily, that Melanie had orchestrated this evening in his honor. Not only was he seated next to Mary at dinner, but also the hostess-turned-conductor had arranged it so afterward everyone would fall back into the woodwork somewhere, leaving Mary with McGinnis in the living room to talk.

And they spent well over an hour catching up with each other. McGinniss told her about school and his parents' pride upon his graduation. And, of course, baseball. Yes, he explained, but without an ounce of bragadoccio, he was hopeful of making the majors the following year, if not that September, in spite of his recent slump. Somehow, the sound of her voice was balm for its sting.

And Mary described the downfall of her marriage with an intimacy that transcended the years of separation from the younger man before her. "The first year we were married, I assumed that if I could just make everything right for us, Victor would be happy. And we would be happy. And so I made sure that everything was just the way he wanted it. You know, the little things. I volunteered for the chores he liked least. I only worked part-time so I'd have time to make our home just right for him when he walked in at the end of the day. Like my mother treated my father before women had more choices. But, gradually, I real-

258

ized I was powerless to make him happy. Whatever it was that drove him, it was purely from within. There was nothing I could do that would make him content with me and only me. And then when he lost his job, it was as though all my efforts meant nothing. He was oblivious to me and all I tried to do. Like the song says, 'The answer lies within.'"

"That one must have been before my time."

"Not if you count your cradle and crib years. And speaking of age, he was older by a few years. He wasn't going to change. Not for the better, anyway. Like Melanie says, men aren't fine wine. They don't improve with age."

"So you left because you knew you'd be hurt?"

"No. Because I knew eventually I wouldn't be. I'd become hardened to it. And that scared me. I'd be giving up life's greatest gift if I allowed him to give me an emotional lobotomy. No, I left to save myself, because I couldn't save him."

And they began to reminisce. "Do you remember that insufferably arrogant woman who came in one time and treated you like dirt?" he asked her.

"Oh, right," she recalled immediately. "She was the wife of the owner of one of our biggest distributors and some kind of mistake had been made on their order."

"Right. And I happened to walk up front just as she was starting to get into it with you. And I can't remember exactly what she said, but I do remember that her demeaning tone suggested that she thought you were some type of lesser being."

Recalling herself what had followed, Mary laughed. "And I remember what you said to her. And I couldn't believe you said it."

"Well, you know how there are some things you'll say as a teenager that you'd never dream of saying when you're older but, nevertheless, you're, like, really proud of?" said McGinniss, as though his twenty-third birthday, now just hours away, qualified him to speak as a sage for the ages. "I used an old baseball expression that applies when a mediocre player thinks he can replace a star."

"So that's what that comment was all about."

"'You couldn't carry her shoelaces,' I said. 'Who the hell do you think you are?' I said. And then she complained to my man-

259

ager. I can't believe I didn't get fired for that."

"I couldn't believe it, either."

"And once, just once, I gave you an order, and you actually obeyed it. Not that I'd be one to order you around," he quickly recovered. "Do you remember?"

"No."

"There's no reason why you would, but I do. We went to lunch, and you squirted some moisturizer on your hands. But a bigger gob came out than you intended. So you're vigorously rubbing your hands together to absorb it, but your hands are a bit dirty from handling the mail. So I'm watching this ooze between your fingers turn from white to gray to black, and I say, 'That's disgusting. Go wash your hands.' And you're rubbing and rubbing, like Lady Macbeth you know, and I say with finality, 'Go wash your hands!' And you did! You got up and washed your hands. You could've said, 'Back off; who the hell are you?' But you didn't."

Mary now replied, "Well, maybe I agreed with you."

"Oh, no. You were content to keep rubbing and rubbing." And Mary marveled at the clarity of his memory of this silly moment, but for McGinniss, it was one of a countless number he had replayed innumerable times, for it never failed to bring a smile to his face.

"And then there was the time you set me up with the best straight line in the history of comedy and I let it pass instead of giving you the punch line, and I've always regretted it." It was so damn easy to talk to her now he couldn't believe it. "One of Victor's classier friends, you told me, mentioned to you that he thought he recognized you as a dancer from some topless joint. And you looked at me and said, 'Can you imagine me as a topless dancer?' Now, you could have said, 'Can you believe he would think that of me?' But no. You just had to say, 'Can you imagine me as a topless dancer?' Well, I've seen my share of old movies. Can't you just imagine Groucho with his cigar popping up out of his grave to say, 'Well I'll try!' But I just let it go. Back then, I was mortified at the thought of mentioning to you anything remotely sexual."

"*Remote* is exactly the word these days." And suddenly McGinniss was back to feeling like the awkward teenager. He was, of course, pleased at this obvious signal confirming Melanie's briefing that Mary wasn't dating anyone but fearful of ruining the evening's friendly fun by asking her out. Fortunately, she placed a hold on his discomfiture by using the pause to announce a bathroom break. And as he sat there in the empty room, it now occurred to McGinniss that in this brief reunion the emotion had all come flooding back. As she spoke to him and looked at him and responded to his smile with her own, Mary was still exactly the woman he had fallen so hard for, and the old feelings, which he had struggled so long to keep at bay, reasserted themselves more powerfully than ever.

Melanie soon pounced at the interlude. "So how's it going?" she inquired with a facial expression that told him this was no mere greeting.

"It's a blast. I'm so grateful you invited me."

"So what's it like to see Mary after, what is it, four years?"

"Close enough." And, in this brief time, McGinniss already had given the question some thought. "Think of a place you visit when you're young. The most beautiful spot you've ever seen. You look around, you see the trees, the meadow, the mountains in the distance, maybe even a rainbow. And you tell yourself, 'I'm always going to remember this moment, this spot. How perfect and wonderful it is. I'm going to burn it into my brain, every detail. The sights, every sound, the aroma.' And as the years go by, you do remember. Every one of those details that you possibly can. You're convinced your memory is every bit as perfect as this place. Years later, you return to that same spot. And what you discover is that no matter how tenaciously you clung to every nuance of that precious place, you realize it was impossible for your senses to retain entirely the lushest green you'd ever seen, the bluest sky, the gentlest breeze. And so you realize that the place was even more wonderful than your memory could imagine. That's just an inkling of what seeing her again is like."

"Don McGinniss. I decleah," replied Melanie in a mock southern accent as she pretended to fan herself from going faint, "you take my breath away."

And they enjoyed a good laugh just as Mary reentered, wondering, "What's so funny?"

"Oh, Don's just telling me about his travel adventures." And

Melanie shared with McGinniss the knowing look of the private joke that was tinged with anticipation. "By the way, Don," Melanie went on, " how many years separate you and Mary?"

"Let's see now. If I take her age and start subtracting . . ." And here he began conspicuously counting with his fingers.

"All right, that's just about enough," Mary responded with feigned annoyance.

"Hang on; I need both hands here," and they all burst into laughter as Mary slapped at the seven digits now standing at attention.

As Mary sat down, Melanie got up to go, begging off Mary's suggestion to stay with the excuse that she had birthday cakes for which to make final preparations. As she left, the sibling in charge signaled a secret thumbs-up to McGinniss, who smiled furtively so as to maintain the privacy of the communication. "So where are you living now?" asked McGinniss. Mary answered that she had an apartment just north of downtown. "I remember that you once told me that you wanted to live in a big house with a lot of land, enough to support a couple of llamas."

"Well, you know, when you're young you dream the foolish dreams of your heart. As you get older, reality intervenes and you dream with your head."

"Or you don't dream at all. If that's what turning thirty does to you, I'm not sure I want to. I'd rather dream with both, and turn those dreams into reality."

"And what is it you now dream of, Don McGinniss? To be the best there ever was?" asked Mary, quoting a line from an old baseball movie.

McGinniss just chuckled and kept the direct answer to himself. It was much too soon to be blunt. Still, the heart has its ways of making itself heard, however obliquely.

"No. To be with the best there ever was."

It was time for the cake. And after the candles cooled, after the wishes, and the crumbs abandoned in their paper plates, it was getting late. And McGinniss wasn't simply going to say good-bye and wonder when or if he would ever see Mary again. In the old days when they worked together, he had feared he would lose her friendship if he ever pressed for more. Now, what was there to lose? If he didn't ask her out now, he would probably never see her again. If he did, she might say no, but he'd be no worse off.

"Say, would you like to go to lunch Monday and spend the afternoon together? It's an off-day for me and I'll have some time and—" here he felt he was beginning to stutter—"for companionship," he hastened to add, the old fear of coming on too strong resurfacing.

"Companionship," she repeated, striking a contemplative pose. "There hasn't been much of that lately. Sure. Where would you like to go? And don't say Lukens'." And she laughed.

"Tell you what. You pick the place. I'll be by at noon if that's OK. What's your address?"

"Noon is fine." And she gave him her address. Now he smiled as she led him to the door.

Just as he turned to go, fear seized him. What if she had to cancel and, with his baseball schedule, he never got another chance to see her again this summer, let alone who knew when? And so he just had to say one more thing. "Now, you take good care of yourself," and the slight wave of his hand in the direction of her once-slender waist told her this was no mere social good-bye. She tried to give him a perfunctory, *Sure I will,* with her eyes, but he wasn't buying it. "No, really. Look, if more pounds meant more years, I'd say bon appetit. But the opposite is true." He didn't want to hurt her feelings, and it was a bold subject to raise after so long a separation, so he chose to end on a lighter note.

"Remember, you once told me that I could see you in a rest home in about half a century. I'll be damned if you're going to stand me up with the lame excuse that you've been dead for ten or fifteen years!" And now Mary's self-consciousness dissolved in their mutual laughter. "But, seriously, I want to see you live down to your potential. And, besides, I've got to do something to jolt you out of your sibling-described complacency!"

And McGinniss wasn't through. "You know, I thought about just leaving my wallet here or maybe tossing it in your purse, but I figured you'd never fall for that one again." And he laughed.

And now she did, too, after a mock, "Hey, wait a minute!" And after he said good-bye, she replied, "Monday. See you then. Oh, and I had a real nice time tonight." It was not an afterthought.

263

As it turned out, McGinniss really was thinking about his wallet at that moment, though not about parting with it. He couldn't wait to check his copy of the team schedule. As he got into his car, he turned on the dome light and pulled it out, searching as never before for the off-days. Another Monday, he noticed, and a Thursday—no, that was going to be a makeup, he now recalled, for an earlier rainout, damn!—and the Monday after that, but he'd be in Louisville then. Too far to drive. But he could catch a flight. Lucky him. Not many minor-leaguers could afford to travel at their own expense. Then there was the league's All-Star game. The way he had been pitching, he had no chance of being selected. Three precious days in a row. But just six in the next four weeks.

"Whoa!" he exclaimed as he tried to rein himself in. "Let's not get ahead of ourselves here. She said OK to one lunch. So far, this is a one-time companionship thing, remember?" Damn that hope! As he drove to the airport in the opening hour of his twenty-third birthday to catch the late flight to Indianapolis, he alternated between spasms of euphoria when he would sing his lungs out to the rock on the radio and bouts of foreboding, fearful for himself at the prospect of adjusting once more to despair once Mary quashed his hopes again, as he was still so sure she would. But he just couldn't help himself.

That was the day his remarkable turnaround on the mound began. In a century of major-league baseball, its thousands of pitchers have had an infinite number of ways in which to psych themselves up for their next battle. In the old days, booze and superstitions figured prominently. In recent decades, hypnotherapy, biofeedback, and other techniques designed to place mind over matter had taken hold. Rituals were followed, from mealtimes to workout regimens. McGinniss now realized what he needed. He'd do just fine every fifth day if he could see Mary every seventh. For now, anyway.

And, lo and behold, he did. One by one, she consented to each of his Mondays off. They spent the time talking, walking through her favorite parks, talking, having lunch together, and talking. McGinniss kept telling himself he couldn't be too intense with her. *Don't scare her off*, he thought. And so he would avoid the heavy subjects unless and until she raised them. But his eyes

264

betrayed his true feelings. He'd gaze into hers so intently as he spoke that she would unconsciously do his blinking for him, like the listener who rubs his mustache when the speaker has a food particle on his own.

And laughter. He equated keeping her amused with holding her interest. This didn't come naturally to him. In school, he had been the guy who, after two or three wisecracks by his buddies, each of which drew increasingly raucous laughter, would spit out the line that was one too many, the one that led his friends to change the subject.

He would begin by poking fun at himself. A safe subject, he concluded. "Do you remember the office Christmas party when you sneaked me the vodka tonics—underage as I was?"

"I remember that they were more vodka than tonic."

"And I asked you to dance and you shot me down. And I couldn't figure out whether you just didn't want to dance with a fall-down drunk or you didn't have any rhythm. So which was it?"

"Both," she replied as she began to laugh at the memory.

"Well, I'm stone sober now. Whattaya say we go out to the parking lot, blast the radio, and see if I can teach you how to shake it?"

"Fat chance," she said through the laughter. And she told him how much he amused her.

"Well, sure. I've had several years to prepare this monologue. Call me next week and I'll bore you to tears."

She would have laughed again, but her mind had raced ahead to a question. "Say, why did you leave that party early, anyway?" It struck her as odd, knowing in retrospect how he had felt about her.

"Are you sure you want to ask a question to which you may not like the answer?"

Mary was taken aback, but she had gone too far down this road to retreat. "I think I can handle just about anything five years after the fact. I did handle a divorce after all, not to mention everything that led up to it."

"Oh, right," and he flashed with embarrassment, feeling, for perhaps the first time, every one of those seven years younger than she. "I was talking to you. Someone got your attention and you turned your head. I had you in profile right in front of me. And the booze said, *Kiss her. On the cheek. Just a peck. You can tell her it was a platonic kiss if she seems startled. Go ahead. Do it.* And even through the fog of my inebriation, I can remember myself just beginning to tilt my face forward toward you. Then I caught myself. I had just enough control left to know that I was out of control. And I told myself, *I've got to get out of here now. Before I blow everything.*"

"That's sweet. But I would've bought it, you know."

"Bought what?"

"The platonic part."

"Oh, hell, in my drunken state even a peck would've come out as a big sloppy wet one." And they shared a big smile. "Besides, the best part of me that just wanted to be your friend felt bad for you. I knew guys were always hitting on you—or at least that's what I assumed. Hell, when it came to the female form, evolution reached its end point with you. Not that it was particularly important to me, but even with the passage of geological time, no body will ever be better." He said it matter-of-factly, as the strictly empirical observation he was convinced it was, ignoring her protests to the contrary.

"And I didn't want to be like that. I wanted to show you how much I liked you for the person you were. It was just my bad luck—" and here he hesitated, knowing he was violating his self-imposed rule against coming on too strong—"that I got hung up on you. Sorry."

"Don't ever apologize for your feelings. You've said a lot of nice things to me. No one's ever said all the nice things to me that you have." And now Mary herself hesitated.

"And does that part of yourself still want that?"

McGinniss looked at her in silence for a moment, unsure if she was inviting him to say he wanted more than her friendship—she already had that, didn't she?—or hoping to cut off right here any possibility of anything more than what he shared with her at this moment. He was deathly afraid of answering the most important question ever put to him but knew he would have to respond to her as he always did—guilelessly.

"Look, you know how I feel. It didn't happen overnight. But once my emotions fixed on you, I knew then that the feeling was overwhelming and forever. I'm as powerless to change it as to jump out of my own skin. And I know you'll never feel the same way. But I know this, too: You've been a very positive force in my life. The feelings I developed for you were so wonderful that they taught me at a young age that life was basically wonderful. And so I look for other things that are wonderful because they remind me of you. The truth is, you're the best person I've ever known, bar none. In fact, the more people I get acquainted with, the more I appreciate—no, more than that, treasure you. As much as I love you, I like you even more. And I'm really proud of the way I feel. In fact, I shudder to think what my life would be like if I had never met you. I'm sure there would be a black hole in my soul that I wouldn't have a clue how to fill. There hasn't been a day that's gone by in the last five years when I haven't thought of you. I talk to you in my mind all the time. I'll be alone driving somewhere and suddenly I'll realize I have this goofy smile on my face because I know I've been thinking of you." He wouldn't tell her of the occasions when, as he was aching to see her, tears instead would well up. It was one thing to shout a celebration of his feelings, but he had no right to lay the poignant stuff on her, thoroughly blameless as she was for his predicament.

He continued. "Or I'll miss my freeway exit because I'm daydreaming of you. And even though I didn't see you for years, it seemed like days—it should be more like decades if I really missed you, right?" And with this she nodded agreement. "But you were with me all that time. I mean you were right there. And so for me, seeing you again was like resuming a telephone conversation after being put on hold."

"But, Don," and now she repeated her protest of years earlier, "you don't really know me. And, besides, how do you know that we'd even be compatible?"

"Well, that's a catch-twenty-two." He now smiled. "After all, if I agree with you, it means we're not compatible. If I disagree, then we're already arguing about it." And they shared a laugh, but only for a moment. "But, seriously, if I don't know you, how did I know, now that I've seen you again recently, that you would not have dyed blond hair or gaudy jewelry? How do I know that you would never have thought of cheating on Victor? How do I know you'd never violate hospital visiting hours, let alone the law? How did I know, even before Melanie told me, that you would still have dreams of falling in love again instead of settling?"

He paused, but not long enough for her to initiate the reply she had no idea how to begin, beyond a sardonic, "God, she has a big mouth." Then he resumed.

"You know, when you married Victor, I felt bad for me. I wanted you to be happy and I was glad you seemed happy, but all I could dwell on was my own incurable emotional disease. But once I learned that he wasn't worthy of you, I realized I was being selfish, and I felt bad for you instead. Which was worse? I wondered. To have the person you want, but to suffer his betrayal, or not to have the person you want, but to enjoy otherwise the charmed life I've had? But—" and here he still felt the need to retrieve something of their relationship—"I'm capable of being your friend. Of confining myself to the subjects that friends talk about, along with a few laughs. To refrain from this subject from here on out. Now that I've said what I have to say, we can get past it."

"Look, Don. This isn't easy for me." *Oh no*, he thought, *she's going to say she just can't handle seeing me.* "It's true I'd like to fall in love again. I'm only thirty. Who wouldn't? And it's also true that while I like you dearly—" and here her face expressed the sympathy for the victim of love unrequited—"I'm not in love with you. But that doesn't make it simple." What was she saying, he wondered intently. "The truth is, the door's open a little bit. I know you really love me and I'm sure you'd be wonderful to me. But don't you deserve more?"

He was already shaking his head. "More? How could I ever want more? Don't you realize that your most enduring—I mean endearing—well, both really, enduring and endearing quality is the fact that you have no idea just how special you really are? Just as you once told me, appropriately enough, 'Don't sell yourself,' my response to you is, 'Don't sell yourself short.' "

"And what about ten years from now? I might come to regret settling and go middle-age crazy and hurt you terribly. I couldn't live with myself if I did that, and you deserve better."

"I'll take my chances, believe me." And his heart leaped just to hear her voice the possibility.

"And what about twenty years from now when I'm getting old and gray? Are you sure a younger woman won't turn your head? I've been through that once more than I care to already."

"No way. They're not making them like you anymore. Besides, the aging process is very kind. You see, women age at the same rate that men lose their visual acuity. So, for us guys, everything just sort of blurs together and we never even see the wrinkles and pockmarks, so you look as young as ever." He was smiling again now, and it was contagious.

"And how do you know all this at your age?"

"I just try to see life from your elderly point of view."

"Careful, before I belt you with my cane, young man." And they enjoyed another laugh, but only briefly, as Mary returned to the subject at hand. "I don't know. I have to think about it. I have to satisfy myself that I can be fair to you as well as myself."

"I know that. I won't pressure you. Take all the time you need. I've waited nearly five years. I can wait fifty more if I have to. We can continue to see each other as friends as often or as infrequently as you're comfortable with. And I mean it. I can stay away from this subject, and I will, unless you raise it. Fair enough?" And he extended his right hand to shake hers, as though this were nothing more than a business proposition.

"Fair enough." And she met his grasp as he met her gaze.

They continued to see each other about once a week through the balance of that summer, and McGinniss kept his word. Mary found herself looking forward to their meetings more and more, though she continued to think of him strictly as the dearest of friends. McGinniss had just received word that Chicago would not be calling him up that September. In his previous start, he had informed the pitching coach of a slight twinge in his shoulder as he finished the eighth inning. As a seven-figure bonus baby, McGinniss was too valuable an investment to risk. Management knew that if he were promoted to the big time now, he would be too tempted to overthrow in an effort to impress. That could result in lasting damage. Better to put their young star on the shelf 'til spring. McGinniss concurred. Though he believed his ankle had healed solidly, he had heard the story of Dizzy Dean. Ol' Diz had tried to come back too soon following a knee injury. His mechanics were thrown off as a result, causing seri-

269

ous injury to his pitching arm. He was never the same after that.

Of course, McGinniss knew the alternative was no small consolation. If he wasn't going to Chicago to pitch, he could at least go home to see Mary. Yet he worried. If he began asking to see her more often, would she back off? If he didn't, would he drive himself crazy? McGinniss would use the time to enroll in a couple of business courses with a view toward an eventual master's, but that, along with his exercise routine wouldn't be enough to occupy his time.

McGinniss decided it was time for some advice from the sage. He picked up the phone. "Melanie, how have you been?"

"Great. I've been thinking about you." This sounded hopeful.

"Well, to get right to the point, I could use some advice from you."

"On our favorite topic, no doubt." McGinniss chuckled. He knew that she had been busy lobbying his cause.

"No doubt, indeed. Can we meet for lunch on the second?"

"Sure. Why don't you just drop by here? Is twelve-thirty OK?"

"Of course." Hell, 3:00 A.M. would have been fine.

The next day, McGinniss drove up to Melanie's home at 12:15, telling himself that he didn't like to keep people waiting for him but too excited to await the appointed hour. He needed to hear Melanie's view. Could his hopes ever be realized or, having long since concluded that he would never forget Mary, would he nevertheless be forced to banish her back to the furthest netherworld of his mind? And oh, what would that do to his dreams, much less his nightmares?

After the greetings and a bit of catching up, Melanie didn't take long to broach the subject herself. "Well, Mary told me all about your conversation. She's a tough nut to crack, but I think she's weakening. It's a shame that money doesn't impress her, with you being touted as a sure-fire major-leaguer—" Melanie laughed a little as if to give an exclamation point to the preposterous notion. "But then if the dollar bill turned her head, I guess you wouldn't be interested in her. She really just needs, I think, to satisfy herself that she can live contentedly with you. I try to tell her, 'Look, what have you got to lose? If it doesn't work out, you can divorce him.' But she has too much integrity to be anything less than fair with you. And she insists on taking seriously the idea of commitment. If you weren't such a damn nice guy, I don't think she'd be putting herself through this."

And they both paused for breath a moment. "Give her a little time, Don."

"Oh, I'll give her more than a little time. If the last several years prove anything, they prove I'm quite capable of delaying gratification." And he smiled.

"Tomorrow night, we—that is, she and I—are going over to visit Aunt Ruth. Mary's always respected her advice. I have a feeling that before the evening's out, your name will come up." Melanie beamed back a smile that told him that within the next 36 hours another member of Mary's support system would join the effort to make McGinniss's dream come true.

"Thanks a lot, Melanie," was all he could say. And all he needed to.

Aunt Ruth had lived a full life in her three-quarters of a century, her wisdom along with her inner strength fortified by tough times so very long ago. Her mother had died in childbirth when Ruth was twelve. Her father followed six years later, leaving her as the oldest of five, with four kids to support and raise at a time when Roosevelt's New Deal took a counterpunch from the recession of '38. A year later, she was jailed for six months for forging a birth certificate for her sixteen-year-old brother, Buddy. She was convinced the recently declared war in Europe would eventually ensnare America, and she reckoned that if Buddy could just be made two years younger—and he certainly looked it, frail for his age as he was—he would avoid battle and live to see the peace. But that was a time of no excuses and very little money, let alone a constitutional right to counsel. And no time off for good behavior. And so Ruth served every last one of those 182 days.

But it turned out that she was right. Buddy, his true age revealed to the authorities, was shipped off to the Far East in January 1942 at the age of nineteen and was never heard from again. Decades later, when the last Japanese soldier finally emerged from his hideout on a God-forsaken island in the South Pacific to learn of the war's end so many years before, Ruth thought again of Buddy and allowed herself, for only a moment, to rekindle the hope that maybe he, too, was on some long-lost

271

Asian island, surviving on snakes and cassavas while holding out for rescue.

And now, having listened in silence to Melanie as she discussed Mary's life through her own eyes, Ruth now leaned slowly forward and sadly told Mary this story. Told her niece of her sorrow at the loss of her little brother and how it had been so magnified each time an MIA was found, right down to that last enemy warrior. Each flicker of hope dashed was more painful than the one preceding.

Ruth had only two questions for Mary. "Are you sure he really loves you?"

"Yes."

"Will he give you a good life, and I don't mean financially?"

"Yes." With each answer, Melanie was nodding more vigorously than her sister.

"Mary," the elder now said sternly as she sat up and looked her straight in the eye, "You can find your peace with Don McGinniss. You might hold out forever and never find anyone better for you. Mary . . . you only live once."

Ruth's last words hit Mary like a cold shower, and she shivered to think that she had given McGinniss that same reminder just a few years earlier. Mary's pained expression told her aunt that she was far from making up her mind, but Melanie knew that now at least it would be an even struggle. Mary's head was no longer helpless against her heart. Reason now had a fighting chance.

"Thanks, Aunt Ruth. I'll sleep on it," she finally said.

"Here, before you go. Let me give you this." And she removed the locket from around her neck and placed it in Mary's hand.

"Oh, Aunt Ruth, I couldn't."

"No, I insist. I've had it for more than fifty years, and now it's time to pass it on to the next generation of O'Briens."

Mary didn't need to open the pendant to see its inscription, for its words were seared into her brain. At a family gathering when she was eight years old, Mary had spotted an old family photo of Ruth and Buddy with their parents. Mary had asked who they all were, and upon being told by Ruth that the boy was her little brother, her child's curiosity had gotten the best of her. This was Thanksgiving, after all, yet her putative uncle was

272

nowhere to be seen. "So, where is he?" she inquired with the insistent exuberance of the innocent.

At that moment, Ruth had brought her face in close to the child and intoned in a hushed voice, "Buddy died, honey." Mary had instantly shrunk back in her chair, mortified, shortly to be soothed by Ruth's kindly words that the child never forgot.

"Here's the last thing I ever received from him. Before he disappeared in the war." And she opened the locket. "Here, read it," she offered.

"'For my dear sweet sister. Always, Buddy.'" Even as a child, it struck Mary as brutally unfair that *always* could mean never again. And she realized that her aunt feared that McGinniss would soon be out of her life for good if Mary turned him down now. She hugged Ruth a teary thank-you.

The ride home with Melanie was silent until Mary suddenly blurted out a question, as a scream pierces the still of the night: "How do I respond to a feeling I don't share whenever he tells me he loves me?"

Melanie could only reply with a question of her own: "And how will you respond if no one ever tells you that, or at least no one worthy of believing?"

"But won't I grow to resent him, even to hate him, for not being able to feel what he feels for me?"

"Only if you decide to hate yourself for being treated as you deserve."

The night was silent once more. There would be no answers this evening but much for Mary to contemplate.

Two days later, Mary called McGinniss and suggested they meet that Sunday at the Elk Grove preserve, an urban park large enough to contain them if they chose to walk for miles. Early-morning joggers could spot an occasional deer darting across the trail, yet the nation's biggest airport was so close by that the sound of its behemoths on takeoff from Runway Number Five would drown out every lovers' discourse on the park's south side.

"Should I bring a picnic lunch?" was McGinniss's way of asking how much precious time she would grant him.

"Better bring dinner, too," she chuckled. And McGinniss now knew this would be no ordinary meeting.

Once again the excruciating wait. Three days until the day of rest, but there was none for this prayerful suitor. His ears were peeled to every weather report each of those days. *It just couldn't rain, it just couldn't*, he begged the gods and the radio with equal fervor. Finally, 11:00 A.M. at the south-side parking lot, right where they usually met, near the family of fenced-in elk. The day dawned bright and sunny, warm for the third week in October, though clouds were forecast, with a chance of showers by midafternoon. Eleven-ten and still no sign of Mary, who, like McGinniss, was habitually early. Two people who would rather be kept waiting than impose the dead time on others. Where was she? Had something happened? He called her home but got only the machine. At last, he saw the familiar blue Chevy approach.

"Sorry I'm late," she announced as she locked her car. "My washer practically blew up this morning and I had soapsuds all over my utility room."

McGinniss smiled with relief. Once again, the mundane triumphed over the sublime, if only temporarily.

"Let's walk for a while," she announced, and they began a trek down a trail that would take them past more than two miles of forest followed by a meadow with picnic tables and a play area. McGinniss began with his usual lighthearted banter but soon noticed his companion was in a pensive mood, which he now reflected himself. His thoughts took him back to the first time she had introduced him to this park. The way the trail meandered through the woods, it could be difficult at times to tell if one was near its end or its beginning. And as they walked now, he could discern no more from her silence. At last they reached the clearing.

"Why don't we stop here awhile?" she suggested.

McGinniss spread out the blanket, and as Mary sat down, she noticed two toddlers, a girl and a boy, playing in a sandbox not far off. Typically, by now, McGinniss would be into the edibles—he'd even gone out of the way this morning to pick up some garlic-tomato bread—but this time, hunger didn't beckon. He took only a few swigs of mineral water, to counteract the dry mouth.

"Don, we need to talk."

Immediately McGinniss perked up, for her tone did not suggest finality.

Out of the corner of her eye, Mary noticed that the little boy was now stealing a kiss on the forehead from the little girl.

"Sure," was all he could muster.

"We've been good friends for a long time now, so I know I can be frank with you."

Uh-oh, he braced himself.

"Male ego."

"Male ego?" He drew a blank, which she now began to fill in.

"We need to talk about male ego and how it handles one subject we've never discussed."

The little girl was now throwing a dirt ball at the little boy. Mary expected that the child would now start crying, but he just stared at the object of his misguided affection, as if experiencing love's first betrayal.

McGinniss didn't have to inquire. He knew that topic was sex. Now it became clear to him. "Let me guess. You're wondering how I'll handle it if we're together, but the thought, not to mention the act, of making love to me is no big thrill for you." Mary nodded quickly, thankful for his spelling out what she didn't want to but wary that she had already inflicted a wound that would leave a permanent scar. But she had to get it out now. After all, the truth was, she felt no more passion for him today than the day five years earlier when he had convinced her that he was not a homicidal maniac.

The little boy got up and walked away, back toward his family. When his companion realized he was not returning, she began to call out to him. But she didn't know his name. And he just kept going. He never looked back.

McGinniss was grateful for the opportunity to allay her fears. "I've thought of that. And I'm really relieved that you're getting this out in the open. I even thought of raising the subject for you, but I was afraid of appearing presumptuous, let alone scaring you off for good." They both heaved a sigh of relief as he continued. "Look, I realize that I'm not going to light up the sky for you like the Fourth of July. But I'll always put your needs and wants first, and I'll be loving to you in ways that are far more important than the act itself. And I'm in no hurry. Frankly, I'd rather wait awhile."

Now, Mary looked at him quizzically. No guy had ever said that to her before. But she knew that McGinniss was too sincere for this to be merely a well-rehearsed monologue. He went on to explain. "Look, if we were to make love now and you're not too thrilled about it, I have to believe that it would be pretty easy for you to break it off. But if we start seeing each other a lot and you see that we're getting along real well, then even if the sex isn't great for you, I'm hopeful that you'll be happy enough with the other aspects of our relationship that you won't want to throw it all away. Because whatever you want for your own personal fulfillment I will help you achieve. Whether it's a family or a career or both, or whatever you want."

"Don't you think you'd grow resentful if I wasn't interested all that often? Or, worse yet, feel that your male ego was being attacked?"

"Look, the best way that I can answer that is to tell you something I never thought I'd get the chance to. Do you want to know something? In all the time we worked together and after, not once did I ever have a dream about you that was the least bit sexual. You'd think that as much as I adored you, if I couldn't have you for real, at least my subconscious would let me pretend," and he smiled. "But I knew it wasn't something you wanted and so it was unthinkable to me."

Mary shook her head in wonder as McGinniss continued. "And do you want to know what drew me to you? It wasn't your body. If that had been it, I would have been attracted to you immediately. Oh, sure, you struck me right away as a person I'd like to get to know. But it took awhile. And I'm convinced that the qualities you have that hooked me were simply that you are the most well adjusted, sincere, reasonable, normal, nice, fairminded person that I've ever known. Can you believe that? An eighteen-year-old guy, at an age when emotions and hormones are out of control, and that's what attracted me to you! And I was right all along. I've never heard anyone say a bad word about you. That's what's important to me. When it comes to sex, you won't have to worry. You won't even have to say no. I'll know the answer as I know you."

And she smiled, because she believed him, and because, for

the first time, she began to think that might be enough. Thrilled with her reaction, McGinniss now sought to dispel what little was left of the tension. "Besides, marriage is like a hockey game. Scoring is only about two percent of it." And they laughed, followed quickly by her rejoinder.

"Yeah, but the rest of it is just a lot of going back and forth and pushing and shoving and you're lucky if you don't get your teeth knocked out."

The laughter was louder now, until McGinniss placed his right hand on her left shoulder, caressing ever so softly her cheek with his thumb as he smiled. "And I promise you that your bicuspids will die of old age."

Now, he embraced her, a big friendly hug that reminded her of the sense of security she used to feel as a child wrapped in her father's embrace. And maybe, just maybe, she thought, she could be happy with this man. McGinniss went on. "And I promise to hug you every day of your life, several times a day, big ones." And then he partially withdrew, placed one hand under her chin, and looked intently into her eyes. "My God, I love you so deeply," he said, with everlasting conviction.

"Careful," Mary replied, "Or you'll convince me I don't deserve you."

"Now that's the one thing you're bound to fail at."

"You are wonderful, Don."

"Oh no, the only compliment I ever want from you is for you to admit that I have the world's best taste in women." And they shared another smile.

Still, Mary wasn't yet sure about the happily-ever-after stuff. "Can we take things a step at a time?"

"Of course. Above all, I want you to be comfortable. Just as long as you promise to tell me if you're not."

"It's a deal, Don." And the rest of the afternoon flew by as they walked arm in arm. The toddlers had long since rejoined the comfort of their families. And the rains never came.

As fall turned to winter that year, McGinniss and Mary saw each other almost daily. He kept his promise, hugging her at every opportunity. And one night just after Christmas, as he embraced her to say good-bye, he noticed something different in her response. And this time, he did not let go.

The next morning, he announced with mock seriousness, "Well, at least now you'll find out if everything I've said up to now has just been part of a five-year scam to have my way with you just once and then not call again."

"Isn't it a bit soon to be so irreverent?" Mary pretended to scold him.

"But I've shared so much with you for so long," he replied as he pointed to his left temple—the one that was not yet a target of another's wrath—"that I guess I jumped ahead of myself." He smiled and embraced her again, his powerful arms no match for the esteem in which he held her.

As she would later look back on it all through the looming fog of her grief, she couldn't even remember the details of his marriage proposal. All she recalled was that right after the New Year, he had given her an engagement ring. The wedding would be a small one—on the last weekend in February, just before he would have to report for spring training. She remembered that McGinniss had written his own vows, and she even knew them by heart—he had had them laminated after penning them, like the driver's license he had tossed into her purse years before, only this time the words identified what was in his soul.

"It's said that the more worthwhile in life something is, the longer and harder it is to attain," he began, before the small gathering of family and dearest friends. "And by that standard, waiting less than six years for Mary qualifies as life's biggest bargain. Mary," and now he paused as he continued gazing into her eyes, "I love you more than anybody has ever loved anybody. All I want is to do whatever makes you happy. All of my happiness will be derived from that. And in one sense, I'm doomed to fail. Because no one on this earth can give you everything you deserve. But I will treasure every day of the rest of my life just to have the chance to try." And as the tears began streaming down his cheeks, she began to cry as well. Then they both began to laugh as Melanie gave them a thumbs-up. And they were pronounced husband and wife exactly fifty-seven weeks before they would be separated for all eternity.

The opening of spring training made for a short honeymoon, though Mary did join McGinniss in Florida for the balance of the exhibition season. McGinniss experienced no hint of arm trouble, but this was a year when Chicago felt it could challenge for the pennant, having signed two top free agent pitchers to megabucks long-term contracts. There would be no youth movement this spring, and anyway, team management felt it was wise to give McGinniss more seasoning. His poor start of the previous year, coupled with his arm problem, was cited. Besides, in spring training his old devil, wildness, continued to assert itself. One more year on the farm would help him. Then, the consolation call-up in September. Next year would be his year. Mary seemed more disappointed than her husband. But he reminded her how he kept things in perspective. If he could wait nearly half a dozen years for her, he could handle one more season riding buses in the bushes.

When spring training ended, they moved to Des Moines, renting a small ranch home. There wasn't much point in decorating it, as they would only be there a few months, but McGinniss did have one request. "We'll need a two-by-four in every room of the house," he deadpanned.

"What on earth for?" wondered his bride.

"Because if I ever do anything that upsets you, I want you to have one handy in order to whack me right here," as he pointed to his forehead. Mary laughed as he swept her up and hugged her. The third time that morning, no less. But a year later, she would cringe at the memory of the target he had selected.

As the days in Des Moines turned to weeks and spring to a hot summer, Mary came to realize that life with McGinniss was better than she could have imagined. In spite, not because of, his road game absences. Whatever her youthful romanticized dreams, her feelings for this man were developing into a deep and abiding love. If, for her, it was still short on passion, this was more than made up for by the knowledge that they were truly soulmates, with complementary needs and desires. For the first time, she experienced the security of the certainty that her spouse's contentment was derived entirely from her mere being. There was no need to impress, no pressure to produce, nothing to change. And, most of all, no cause to worry whether she was making her husband happy. It frightened her to think how close she had come to rejecting this life in foolish pursuit of some dream that now seemed so futile, even immature. She needed

279

this man as he needed her. And now she knew that she really loved him as well.

Sure enough, on August 31, McGinniss got the call. He and Mary moved to Chicago in a heartbeat—Mary had been living out of boxes in anticipation of the summons so the two could take flight at once—direct from Corn Field International Airport or whatever the hell it was. McGinniss would spend the next 30 days with the team, confident that he could prove to management that the minors were a thing of the past for him.

September 1. At 2:00 P.M., McGinniss was issued his first major-league uniform for that night's game. The team was in second place, only half a game back. This meant that McGinniss would be consigned to mop-up work out of the bullpen for now. Left unspoken was the implication that once Chicago either clinched or had been formally eliminated from the race McGinniss might get a start or two.

As the culmination of a dream goes, McGinniss was surprisingly serene as he put on the official game dress. He had, after all, long since grown accustomed to his way of keeping things in perspective. *It's great, but it ain't Mary*, he thought to himself. On opening night—his opening, along with half a dozen other farmhands—his action was confined to an occasional stretch at the end of the bullpen bench. The game was a close, low-scoring one, so he never got the call to warm up.

As it turned out, the race for the wild card went down to the wire even after McGinniss's new team fell half a dozen games behind division-leading Cleveland. At last, his team emerged victorious for the final play-off berth. But the plan to bring McGinniss along slowly went up in smoke when Chicago's two big-money pitchers faltered in the season's final week. Eight million per year is no balm for a fraying rotator cuff or a split finger that's mysteriously lost its way. The rookie got a hint of what might be coming when he was placed on the postseason roster to replace the monied ace who had been put on the disabled list. And now, after pitching just 12 major-league innings, 6 of them in a couple of laughers on which Chicago was on the short end, against the Yankees, McGinniss found himself penciled in to start against that very team in game five of the second round of the play-offs. The winner would go to the Fall Classic. McGinniss had given up only one earned run in those two outings, striking out nine while walking six. Only Donovan had ripped him hard.

Though still susceptible to fits of wildness, McGinniss already stood in baseball's spotlight. Everyone who followed the game knew that they were watching mere previews of the next major attraction. No one threw that hard anymore, at least not American kids. It wasn't like the old days, when farm boys developed powerful upper-body strength from heaving bales of hay all day long. Until baseball beckoned early in this century, who even knew those rural youth of yesteryear had transferable skills? These days, the only lifting most kids did was of the fryer baskets at their fast-food jobs. That and, of course, the remote.

Donovan did not, to put it charitably, share the sentiment of the baseball world for McGinniss. He had come of age as its golden era was ending. It was a time when a pitcher had to learn the tools of his trade, including control of both self and one's pitches, in the minors first. No mastery, no majors. Nowadays, the greedy owners rushed along kids who simply weren't ready to play the game at its highest level. Donovan, who played it better than anyone, was incensed at the debasing of the currency of his realm. McGinniss didn't belong in the show, let alone the play-offs. He hadn't paid his dues. He didn't deserve the chance to succeed against the powerful Yankees, who had.

The fact that McGinniss now held off the Yankee hitters for seven innings mattered not one whit to Donovan. McGinniss simply hadn't shown the consistency so integral to playing the game as it should be played at this level. The rookie had already walked six of Donovan's teammates and thrown two wild pitches, in spite of the 2–1 lead he nursed into the eighth. At any moment, Donovan knew, McGinniss could uncork a wild one or, for that matter, a series of them, like the holiday fireworks that suddenly flew askew into the horrified crowd.

Each time he stepped to the plate, Donovan dug in against his opponent just as he always did, ever more resentful. The man who insisted on always booking a nonstop flight because he didn't like the odds of too many takeoffs and landings wanted no part of this wild man. As far as Donovan was concerned, he was risking his life each time he planted his feet. But there would be no baling out, no stepping into the bucket, for him, in spite of the danger.

And so when McGinniss beaned him, the rage, having festered, was no longer self-contained. And as the dizzy spells wore off only that winter, much too late to participate in the championship series, Donovan had devoted his rigid self-discipline to a new diamond endeavor.

Oddly enough, as only Mary knew, once that fateful pitch had been delivered, McGinniss didn't really disagree with Donovan. For weeks that off-season, McGinniss doubted himself, telling Mary he had no business being in the big leagues with his control problems. She had tried to assure him that if the team felt he belonged, then he did. But McGinniss knew that the owners were grading on a curve. There were only a few hundred ballplayers with the skills to play the game at this level, as his father had told it, but now, with so many additional teams in the league, their ranks had swelled to more than a thousand. In the old days, half of them would be AAA players. Another quarter would be grateful to accept a pay cut so long as the uniform on their back identified them as major-leaguers. Now, some of these guys were making millions, whether or not they were earning it. And it made a conscience-stricken McGinniss feel like a fraud.

It took Mary several weeks to bring him back to where he could return to the frame of mind he would need entering spring training. "It was only one pitch," she would say over and over again. "You can work on your control all this winter and in Florida. And if you're still not ready, tell 'em you'll spend more time in Des Moines."

Taken aback, McGinniss replied, "No one ever does that. It's unheard of."

"Yeah, well you've got a moral sense that other people don't. And if that's what you need to do to satisfy yourself, you do it." This, plus the fact that his letter of apology to Donovan was returned unopened, helped put McGinniss back into the competitive state he knew he had to have. And Donovan himself supplied the icing when, just two days after McGinniss discovered his apologia had been stamped RETURN TO SENDER, Donovan broadcast his threat over the airwaves, the one that, less than a year later, would be booked as evidence. McGinniss could be true to himself by requesting the demotion if he wasn't ready. Meanwhile, he would work harder than ever this winter and spring to become worthy of his exalted position.

Before the tulips were up, Mary would rue the day she had helped rescue his career. And now, this thirty-one-year-old woman, one month from single motherhood, found herself at his grave site placing a wreath. It was six months to the day after her husband's death. Twenty-six weeks of dwelling on the past in an effort to block out the pain of the present.

17

The interlude between the preliminary exam and the hearing date on Weinstein's motion to dismiss allowed the respective legal combatants to catch up on other matters. Both would leave the brief writing to their research attorneys. Both gave similar instructions: Check out every reported case that involved athletes charged with any crime or tort committed on their fields of play. Look for felony-murder prosecutions where the underlying felony was relatively remote in time to the homicide. Come back with a solid draft of a brief for final review with copies of all cited cases attached. When the opposition brief arrives, read every case cited and do a memo pointing out any distortions of the rulings. And do it all at least three days before the court-imposed deadlines in order to assure timely review and filings.

Weinstein's initial brief in support of his motion to dismiss was simple enough, as Kasoff expected. There was no illegal act at or immediately before the death and therefore no crime. Kasoff anticipated, correctly it would turn out, that Weinstein would save the more complex and subtle aspects of the legal analysis for his reply brief to Kasoff's response. This naturally left the prosecutor at a disadvantage. Not only did he have only one chance to lay out his arguments in support of his offensive strategy for prosecution, but he also had to tackle the reply of the defendant before he would have a chance to see it. Sure, he'd have another opportunity during oral argument to dismantle Weinstein's reply brief, but one couldn't count on that. At times, Taft had been known to allow attorneys to argue at length, to "make your record, counsel," only to read his opinion—obviously prepared in advance of the lawyers' verbal pyrotechnics—from the bench. Yet, on other occasions, Taft would engage the lawyers in lively debate, playing devil's advocate with both, and then take the matter under advisement before issuing a carefully worded tirade that passed for his idea of the deliberative process.

Kasoff's intermission was Donovan's highlight film. Over the next two and a half weeks, the game's top star would lead his team to play-off victories over Chicago and Baltimore. In the city of last spring's homicide, Donovan's war club would prove far more powerful than the nightsticks carried by the police who again ringed the field. So many threats on the Yankee star's life had been made that the league considered requiring all fans to pass through metal detectors, until someone did the math and concluded the lines would be almost as long as those snaking toward the women's rest room doors at ballparks all over the country. Can't have that. And so the authorities contented themselves with posting "profile spotters"—those law enforcement personnel trained to pick a drug courier or terrorist out of a crowd based on appearance—at each entrance gate. That and all carry-in items—coolers, cushions, thermoses, whatever—were barred. Several fans were apprehended, too, though once they were escorted to the stadium offices, the bulge in their jacket lining or pants turned out to be nothing more hazardous than 100 proof. The booze was confiscated, of course, but the miscreants were relieved they were being allowed entry, even if it meant settling for the stadium's overpriced suds.

Donovan was kept insulated from the hubbub with the use of an alias, a phony beard, and a separate hotel. An unmarked car with tinted windows would pick him up each morning in the hotel's underground garage and deliver him to the ballpark. As long as Donovan could run through his pregame routine, this cocooned existence was just fine with him.

In the spring, a power hitter's shoulders and wrists are as fresh as the breeze that blows away winter's sclerosis. By Memorial Day of any given year, several sultans of swat may find themselves on a pace that if maintained throughout the balance of the schedule would break the single-season home run record. But as summer takes hold, those rippling muscles begin to tire. Throughout baseball's Golden Age, by Labor Day the record was always safely ensconced high above the trails blazed by mortal hitters. Donovan had never challenged the record. His hallmark was consistency, not spring's burst of color that fades with summer's wilting sunshine. And now, in the play-offs, he outdid even himself as he defied the calendar. In the five-game series against

Chicago, Donovan hit five homers, including two in the decisive game that were instrumental in the Yankees' 7–4 victory. The Baltimore series went to its maximum of seven games. In the first four, Donovan had five hits but no dingers. Then, he took over. In game 5, he hit one. In game 6, two more, and in the pennant clincher, 3, 2 of which were hit into the teeth of winter's calling card as the temperature plunged from 70 degrees at game time to 42 degrees three and a half hours later when the final candle was blown out on Baltimore's chase of the champs.

This time, Donovan would finally play in the Series. Game 1 was set for 8:26 P.M. EDT on October 18, just a few hours after Taft would be expected to rule on his attorney's motion, unless the jurist chose to take the matter under advisement. Donovan was counting on the system's glacial pace to continue. Even then, Taft's decision might come down before the trophy was presented. For the Yankees' opponent was Montreal, and the weather forecast was nasty until next May. But for Donovan, more important was the legal outlook Weinstein had given him weeks earlier. As he had listened impatiently at the time while his counsel had run through what Donovan concluded was part cover-his-ass boilerplate that didn't apply, his concentration, so finely honed on the diamond, had wavered. What was that Weinstein had said about not being allowed to leave the country if lightning struck and he was bound over?

*   *   *

The church bells announced the passing of the half hour past the lone chime of 1:00 P.M. as the buzz in the courtroom, now well trained to the habits of its presider, hushed itself. Judge Taft took his seat. The case was called. The attorneys stood and placed their appearances on the record. Weinstein approached the podium.

"May it please the Court, my client, Christopher Donovan, and I have looked forward to this day. Finally we have an opportunity to tell this Honorable Court why, in no uncertain terms, the People should be sent packing on this case. Your Honor, this case takes me back to my first day in law school. The very first Latin phrase that my esteemed professor, Norman Fletcher,

taught us. Apparently, my brother at the bar—" and here he nodded toward Kasoff—"was absent that day."

There were a few chuckles in the room, but Kasoff remained
impassive. He knew what was coming.

"There is," Weinstein continued, his voice now rising for
emphasis, "no objective *actus reus*. Now what do I mean by
that?" The journalists in the gallery, who had been expecting a
snappy punch line, certainly wanted to know. Except for the *New
York Times* legal correspondent, they had no clue.

"Mr. Donovan's behavior, his actions on the field on the date
in question, betray no guilt of any crime. He did nothing more
than every other ballplayer on that field who steps into the batters' box tries to do: hit the ball solidly. Viewed objectively that is,
from the standpoint of any observer judging his actions up to and
including the instant of the tragic impact—and we certainly concede this is a terrible tragedy and our hearts go out to the McGinniss family—Mr. Donovan did absolutely nothing wrong.
Nothing illegal. That's the core of this case regardless of how
many legal gymnastics the People attempt to put this court
through.

"Consider for a moment these examples." And now Weinstein
would play to the crowd behind him. "A man has sexual relations
with a girl—excuse me, a young woman—over the age of consent, though he believes that she is underage." This certainly got
the attention of the press. "Has he committed a crime? No. Of
course not. Every court in the land would conclude that his mental state is irrelevant if the act actually committed is not prohibited by the criminal law.

"Or consider, a man smuggles Irish whiskey across the border in violation of customs requirements." Another example dear
to the hearts of those in the gallery. "Only it turns out that what
he thought was the genuine article was only a mislabeled local
brew, a pale imitation, and not subject to duty. Can he be prosecuted for violating the customs law? No. Because regardless of
his subjective intent to break the law, an objective view of what
he actually did reveals the commission of no crime. Once we
understand this, we know that the People in this case come up
empty in the *actus reus* department."

Kasoff, who knew the inscrutable Taft as well as anyone, recognized by now that this was shaping up as one of those arguments where the judge would allow the attorneys to ramble. Still, Kasoff expected this would not be a case of a prewritten opinion. Surely Taft would want to mix it up with the lawyers before the hearing was concluded. After all, this issue wasn't argued every day. Even a veteran judge, perhaps especially a seasoned jurist who had seen it all, would appreciate a change of pace from the run-of-the-mill auto theft trial and bail revocation hearings.

Now Weinstein summarized Kasoff's case before the prosecutor could in the hope that his slant on the People's evidence would defuse the damage Kasoff could wreak on Weinstein's argument. "What is the People's case, Your Honor? A pitcher beans Mr. Donovan. By the way, is he punished for that? For deliberately driving him off the plate by aiming a missile at his ear? Of course not. Nor should he be." Brief pause. "Six months later, six full months, Your Honor, Mr. Donovan steps into the batters' box, just as he has more than eight thousand times before. He digs in as he always has. He studies the pitcher as he always has. He swings the bat as he always has. He hits a line drive, as he does only three or four times out of ten. And the line drive strikes the pitcher, as occasionally happens. All pitchers know it can happen. All fear it. But all go out there because they understand that it's just part of the game. It's one of the risks they assume every time they deliver a pitch.

"The hitter knows it, too. He doesn't need to sit down and calculate physics equations to figure it out. He doesn't need to study videotape of the pitcher's windup. And he certainly doesn't need to x-ray a pitcher's skull to know that a line shot can all but take the hurler's head off. Incidentally, however, let's suppose for a moment that a hitter did all those things. After all is said and done, what would he have to conclude about his chances? In the history of major-league baseball, not once has a pitcher been killed by a batted ball. Not once in all of the millions of pitches that have been delivered to the best hitters on the planet for over a century from a distance of less than a mere sixty feet, six inches. In other words, anyone who even contemplated such a deed would have to conclude that his chances of ever succeeding were astronomically small.

"But let us stipulate that it may well be impossible for a pitcher to react in time to get his glove in harm's way between the line drive and his head, notwithstanding that it has never once occurred with fatal consequences. If that is so, then let us prosecute Abner Doubleday. He's the one who started it all. Blame him for the short distance between the pitchers and their opponents. And their opponents are armed, all right, with baseball bats. Deadly weapons. And all according to the rules. And depending on the strength of the batter and the weight of his wooden weapon, the batted ball can reach the pitcher in little more than the blink of an eye, whether or not the bat has a thick handle or a thin one, whether it is thirty-four ounces or thirty, or has cork in it or dimples or whatnot. There is simply no time for the pitcher to react. So if we're going to prosecute this hitter, we're going to have to move the mound back. Maybe pitch from second base. If the law is going to step in, that's what we'll have to do. And that will put an end to this great game. This court cannot, this court should not, put a man on trial for his life just for getting a base hit. Thank you, Your Honor."

It was an argument even Kasoff could appreciate. In his summation, Weinstein had managed to weave Kasoff's evidence into his argument in a way that cleverly belittled each piece of the puzzle. For a moment, Kasoff thought back to the spring day, which now seemed so long ago, when B.D. had first OKed the go-ahead on this case. Once again, Kasoff knew he had his work cut out for himself.

Kasoff knew he would have to meet the legal challenge head-on, but he would take the scenic route to get there. In this respect, he was pleased that Taft was playing the passive adjudicator. To begin, Kasoff would remind the Court that the law granted athletes no special dispensation. As he rose to approach the podium, the crowd was still buzzing about Weinstein's argument, as it does after the cheering dies down following an especially long home run.

"Your Honor, in the case of *Nabozny versus Barnhill,* our Court of Appeals held, and I quote, 'Organized athletic competition does not exist in a vacuum. Some of the restraints of civilization must accompany every athlete onto the playing field.'" That quieted the crowd.

"Your Honor, from time immemorial, civilizations have had among their foremost concerns restrictions against the taking of another's life. And make no mistake. That's why we are here today. Because the facts of this case, when viewed in the light most favorable to the People as this Court must view them for the purpose of the defense motion here, demonstrate, if they demonstrate anything at all, that the defendant, for a period of six months up to and including April first of this year, operated as a conspiracy of one, so to speak, in order to carry out the deliberate, premeditated murder of the victim here, a twenty-four-year-old husband and father-to-be—and let's not ignore the magnitude of this tragedy, because what this case is really about is the death of a human being, one Don McGinniss.

"And while the law does examine acts—and I'll get to that issue in a moment—it also considers the accused's mental state, the *mens rea*, as I recall from the second day of law school. Perhaps my worthy opponent decided one day of law school was enough. He apparently missed that lecture." Pause, to accommodate the titters in the audience. "And here, the evidence of the defendant's murderous mental state—malice, if you will—is as plain as the nose on my face. You know, often, Your Honor, we don't have a window into the accused's state of mind. We are forced to infer intent from the nature of the conduct. Blow up a bank vault to obtain money, and we infer malice from the inherently dangerous nature of the act, so that we prosecute for murder if a death results from the blast, and we ignore the perpetrator's protestations that he was only in it for the money, that he didn't mean to hurt anyone.

"Here, we don't need to infer anything. The defendant expressed his intent at every opportunity. On videotape, for all the world to see, last fall. Alone in his farmhouse all winter, plotting the deadly trajectory on paper with the aid of more videotape. Breaking into a hospital's records section, where some of the most private information on all of our lives is housed, for the express purpose of discovering the victim's anatomic weak link, clearly a criminal invasion of the victim's privacy no less than an unlawful entry. How's that for an *actus reus*, incidentally? And finally, the day of the deed itself. The defendant, the best place-hitter in the game's history, hits it right where he wanted to,

290

right where he planned all along."

Up to this point, Kasoff knew the issue had not yet been truly joined. Each advocate had merely argued to his own strength, Weinstein focusing on the deed and Kasoff primarily on the intent. Now, Kasoff knew he had to address Donovan's conduct.

"Turning to the issue of Donovan's actions pertinent to the date in question, Your Honor. We first have the overt act of doctoring the bat to consider. While it may be true that the victim here consented to assume the normal risks inherent in the game of baseball, he certainly did not consent to his opponent violating a rule of the game for the purpose of increasing the speed of the ball off the bat."

"But, counsel, is the rule against the doctoring of a bat designed as a safety rule or only to secure the better playing of the game as a test of skill? As the Restatement of Torts would suggest, only the intentional violation of the former should be subject to legal sanction."

Kasoff knew that the Court was quoting from Weinstein's reply brief. If the reason for the rule's existence was merely to promote a greater test of skill, like the intricate rules that separate a balk from a good pickoff move, its violation couldn't be considered as creating a hazard to the health or safety of a participant.

"I believe the rule was designed to serve both purposes. Sure, it's there to ensure that home runs aren't too easy to hit, but I believe it also serves an important role as part of that delicate balance between the ordinary hazard posed to the pitcher in throwing to his opponent from such a short distance on the one hand and the advantage to the batter in being able to cause the ball to travel only so far so fast off the bat on the other."

"Have the People shown that a legal bat—and by that I mean a bat that complies with the rules of the game—would have made a difference in the outcome here?" It was obvious to Kasoff that he was losing this argument. It was time to get the train back on track.

"Your Honor, for purposes of the defense motion, I don't believe that's pertinent here. What's important is that this is another in a whole series of overt acts in furtherance of a one-man criminal enterprise to accomplish a killing. And accomplish it this defendant did."

Now Taft posed the question that struck at the heart of the prosecutor's case: "Counsel, you referred a moment ago to the defendant acting as a conspiracy of one. Are you suggesting that the law of conspiracy should be expanded to apply to this case?"

That was precisely what Kasoff's brief had argued, but Taft had phrased the query in a manner that suggested Kasoff's contention was going too far. In the law of conspiracy, the commission of any overt act by any co-conspirator in the course of the conspiracy is itself punishable. Kasoff would not answer the question as he would expect a witness to—with a simple yes or no. His response required some explication.

"Your Honor, the defendant wants to keep the focus on a single strand, the line shot itself. I believe this Court should view the entire woven web. If we tie together all of the strands, from last autumn through that winter and up to the date in question, we certainly have at least one unlawful act in furtherance of this conspiracy—the break-in at the hospital. Parenthetically, I would remind the Court, as it is no doubt already aware, that a breaking need not involve the use of force or violence. The mere act of opening a door of another's property to which the perpetrator has no right of entry qualifies as a breaking under our law.

"Now, in a traditional conspiracy, all members are criminally responsible for all acts committed in furtherance of the conspiracy. If that is true, why isn't it even more compellingly so—" his voice was rising now—"that an individual who goes about committing all of the acts in furtherance of a criminal plan should be responsible for the entire criminal enterprise. We need not call it a conspiracy if the Court is not comfortable with the application of that concept to these facts. But even considering the single strand of the hospital break-in, the defendant's examination of that MRI film and report is the moral equivalent of casing the bank. Find the soft underbelly and strike there."

"But doesn't that beg the question, counsel, as to whether the actions of this defendant on the date in question amount to an unlawful act?"

Kasoff felt cornered. From day one, he knew that this was the weak link in his line of argument. But now, he was ready. "Your Honor, I believe that where the end achieved is the intentional violent killing of a human being, the law should step in and say, 'Mr. Defendant. If you do anything—and I mean anything—unlawful that assists you in carrying out that objective, we are going to prosecute you just as we would if the killing itself was carried out by unlawful means.'" And here, Kasoff stopped for a moment, as if to savor his next words as he took careful aim with his final, most telling arrow—the one he had waited all summer to fire. "Otherwise, Your Honor, the means justify the end."

For a moment, the courtroom was silent except for the scribbling of the reporters, who now had their sound bite, the spell broken only by the 2:00 P.M. church bells. The jurist who knew it all, who had heard it all, rubbed his chin with his thumb and forefinger. To himself, Kasoff allowed a smile. His point had hit home. Taft had no more curves to throw on this paramount portion of his argument. After letting his last words sink in, Kasoff made his anticlimactic request for relief: deny the motion for dismissal. B.D. indulged himself a smile as well, for his associate's argument was a compelling call to arms for the law to impose its majesty on the morally opprobrious.

"Any rebuttal?"

Weinstein rose. "Thank you, Your Honor. Let's get back to reality here. Let's get back to reality." Weinstein immediately wanted to prick the balloon. "I guess it's left to me to point out that the People should be addressing their arguments to the legislature. For more than a century, the law of criminal conspiracy has required two or more conspirators. If my worthy opponent finds that limitation too constraining, let him go to Springfield and convince our lawmakers to change the law.

"For more than a hundred years, the felony-murder rule has required that the act that results in death occur in the course of the commission of the felony. A felony committed months earlier, if that's what the hospital snooping caper amounted to, doesn't qualify. What's more, the felony must itself be inherently hazardous to life. Rape. Armed robbery. Kidnapping. Looking at someone else's medical file hardly risks anyone's life or limb. Just imagine. A businessman who cheats on his tax returns will be prosecuted for murder when his accountant drops dead of a heart attack a year later when the IRS comes knocking, suspecting him of complicity in the fraud. There are reasons for these rules, Your Honor. This Court's task is to follow them. Not bend, twist, fold, spindle, and mutilate them to satisfy the urges of an overzealous prosecutor. We move for dismissal."

"Thank you, counsel. This Court will take the matter under advisement and will issue a ruling within two weeks. You will be notified by my clerk to appear when I am ready to release my opinion and order."

And that was it. There was nothing more for Kasoff to do except to see whether the Court would vindicate him or side with the opponent who had just uttered the epithet most hated by prosecutors, the one that would grace the headline of New York's number-one tabloid the next morning.

Weinstein left the courtroom and immediately placed a call to Montreal. It took a few minutes to get Donovan in off the practice field. "What happened?" asked the star.

"Taft has always been a tough nut to crack. I can tell you what the law says he should do, but predicting what he will do is like trying to forecast which way the wind will blow next week. But he's promised us a decision within two weeks. My guess is he'll take the full fortnight to issue an opinion. He's often impatient on the bench, ready with his judgment before the lawyers are, but he didn't appear that way today. I think he actually intends to give this one some thought."

Donovan was half-pleased. At least that timetable would put off further proceedings until safely after the Series. On the other hand . . . Donovan drew a deep breath. "Hmmm, doesn't sound too promising, does it?"

"Let's not jump to conclusions. As I said, he's unpredictable. But in my opinion, he's more likely than not going to go our way."

"Listen, just in case he rules before the Series is over, and if it's against us, what was that you told me before about leaving the country?"

"Oh. If he decides to bind you over, he's bound to revisit the bail question, one of the traditional conditions of which is that the defendant agrees not to leave the country. But your situation is unique. I'm sure you'd be allowed to travel to Montreal to complete the Series. Besides, even before a bail hearing, we would seek an emergency stay against further prosecution until plenary review of Taft's decision by an appellate court."

"Whoa. I'm just a ballplayer. Could you translate that for me from the legalese?"

"It means we would ask a higher court to stop the prosecution until it has a chance to rule whether or not Taft was correct in deciding that your act could be prosecuted at all. A decision on that issue would likely take at least a year or more in the absence of an expedited review, which I don't see happening here."

"And I can play ball until then?" The steely baseball star was reduced by the vagaries of the law to the child's plea of, "Just one more hour, Mom, please?"

"As long as the appeals court grants our request to enjoin the proceedings until it's ready to issue its decision on the merits. The alternative is the worst-case scenario."

"Damn right. We have no intention of being forced to return to Montreal for a game six, anyway."

Weinstein laughed. "Glad to see you've got your priorities in order." And now the barrister let the game's brightest star get back to honing his skills.

Simultaneously Kasoff and B.D. were just getting back to the office. "How'd it go?" inquired Green. "I wanted to be there, but someone's got to keep a lid on the run-of-the-mill mayhem in this city," he needled.

Kasoff described the scene, noting, as Weinstein had, Taft's uncharacteristically patient and almost somber demeanor.

Green replied, "You know, Edna in the cafeteria was telling me the same thing just this morning. Taft hasn't been his ebullient self the past week, she says. Comes in, eats his eggs, reads the paper without his usual running commentary on everything under the sun. The gusto's gone lately, she says. You know him better than I do. What's eating him? You think this case is weighing on him?"

"I don't know. That wouldn't be like him. Maybe he's not feeling so good. I thought his color was a bit languid today. He may have a health problem."

"Yeah, maybe those eggs have turned Benedict on him."

"Oh hell, he'll outlive us all. But all the same, we better drink to his health for at least another two weeks. I sure don't want to have to do this all over again, not that trying to educate a new judge isn't a challenge."

"Especially if you enjoy butting your head up against a brick wall it's not. Well, good luck on the outcome. Oh, by the way—how about the all-financial team?"

"What? Oh, hell, I've got no time for that now."

"Come on; you've been working too hard. I'll even allow repeats."

"All right. Let's see. Norm Cash at first. Dave Cash on second. Ernie Banks at short. Don Money at third. Jim Price catching. Pitcher. OK, Wes Stock or Kid Nichols. In the outfield. Hmm. Barry and Bobby Bonds. And Bobby Loane."

"Not bad, even if I do have to take your word on the last one."

As B.D. and Green were entering their offices, the phone rang. "Greg Townsend for you on line one," said Sharon.

"All right, put him through," replied Kasoff as he rolled his eyes.

"Hey Castoff. Nice work."

"Were you there?" *What a stupid question*, Kasoff told himself.

"Outside, with the video press pool. Our sports guy was in the courtroom taking notes. He transmits them to me and I do the story. He's furious that I'm horning in on his sports acreage, but, hey, our producer's right. This is more than just a sports story. And I am the local news reporter, after all."

"What can I do for you?" replied Kasoff, well aware that the sun would never set on Greg's basking in self-importance.

"How about an interview on this? You know, a peek at the behind-the-scenes stuff that gets you ready for your courtroom performance." Kasoff was already grimacing. "Maybe a prediction on the outcome. A little good publicity wouldn't hurt you."

"Yeah, well with Taft it won't help, either. He's from the old school, Greg. He actually believes that the lawyers who appear before him should confine their arguments to the record in the courtroom and in each other's presence. Something about due process, I think. Thanks, but no thanks." Leave it to the media, thought Kasoff, to bring him to the defense of such a jurist.

"Well, I hear stories that if Taft throws this out, Starman will be looking for scapegoats. And you've got the biggest horns. With some favorable press—hell, maybe I could make it a series with

296

a bio of you—by the time he comes head-hunting, you might be too big for him to toss you overboard."

Oh, the power of the press, thought Kasoff sarcastically to himself. "Hey, Greg, can you spell *grandiose?*"

"Huh?"

"Look, if the bell tolls for me, your puff piece isn't going to make a dime's worth of difference." Greg's uncharacteristic silence told Kasoff his one-time friend was hurt. "Look, I'm afraid there won't be any interviews on this case. But if I did one, you'd get first crack. After all, you did get me some valuable insight into Donovan's motive."

A mollified Greg now recovered. "OK, thanks a lot."

"By the way," asked Kasoff, "what's your feature for tonight?" the prosecutor feigning interest to put the finishing touches on the contrition."

"A department store makes shopping more convenient for its customers."

"No kidding."

"Well, got to run, Castoff."

"Good-bye," replied the prosecutor, and suddenly he wasn't in quite such a hurry to receive Taft's ruling.

* * *

The victim's widow, after placing her wreath, had heard the news on the radio. In two weeks, she would know if the perpetrator of her husband's killing would stand trial for his action. Her reminiscences of her short time with McGinniss had got her through these past six months. She still had the holidays to dread and the coming of next year's spring, with its anniversary. And she remembered now his telling her how much each May reminded him of her. "The flowers are back out and everything's so green and beautiful and it all reminds me of your smile. And your eyes." And now they teared up again.

Of her brief marriage, she pondered the cliché that time flies. Looking back, our memories can flip through the weeks and months of a calendar in the blink of an eye. It is only in retrospect that time takes wing. Looking ahead, real time marches on, but it cannot take flight the way our memories can race

297

through the past. Mary was 32 years old. The life expectancy tables gave her another 53 years. In the blink of an eye, she remembered another cliché—you only live once. God, how she needed McGinniss to say that to her now. Somehow, she would have to bring herself to believe the very words of which she had once reminded him. Otherwise, how would she ever walk the next half-century's road without stumbling?

In the history of the World Series, only two kinds of events have delayed the pomp and circumstance. Earthquake and rain. The momentous and the mundane. Now, with the first championship series to be played in a city where its play-by-play required translation, a third would intervene. No sooner had Donovan returned from the clubhouse telephone than he saw the artificial field of green before him turning white. The snow didn't stop for nearly 24 hours. Ten wet, heavy inches. And the 9 days set aside for the Fall Classic—the seven-game maximum plus two open dates—were up to 15 before a single pitch was thrown. A cold blast of air following the snow wiped out play on the nineteenth. The blanket wasn't going anywhere without help from a brigade of volunteer shovelers. The twentieth dawned with bright sunshine, but benevolence is a sometime thing from the weather gods in Quebec's late October. By game time, a freshly falling sleet was making the turf treacherous. And so it was another night when no one left the dugout.

The next several days revealed Mother Nature's varied autumn offerings, but this was no color show, as every type of storm buffeted the ballpark. Rain. Snow. Sleet. Hail. More than once as a quartet. Finally, on the twenty-third, the skies cleared.

Once the anthems had been played, it was the opposition for a change that tormented Donovan instead of his old headaches. Montreal's ace, Luis Gomez, threw a wicked screwball. Donovan, of course, had done his usual homework on this opponent, but watching ain't swinging, and no one in the American League threw that pitch anymore. As Gomez was a righthander, his ball would tail away from Donovan's left-hand stance. In theory, it was no different from facing a left hander's curve ball, but with an opposite delivery point and ball rotation, the screwball managed to make Donovan look silly. Three times he fanned, twice with men in scoring position. His last time up, with his team down, 3–1 in the eighth, Donovan tapped a harmless dribbler back to his adversary, who easily tossed him out.

Back in Chicago, Weinstein had turned on the game. A Yankee hater all his life, he was hoping that the jurist who held his client's fate in his hands was getting a firsthand glimpse of how helpless even the game's top hitter could look flailing away in vain at a pitcher's masterly deliveries. *It's the mistakes that kill,* he thought, reminded of the medical malpractice cases handled by his partner. *But at least on the diamond the damage is strictly self-inflicted. Anyone can see that a pitcher who's in command of his pitches will always have the upper hand. Like Zeus, he stands above all, firing lightning bolts from his mound. Each triad that zooms across the sturdy rubber pentagon on its way into the catcher's mitt strikes down one of the enemy, sending him on a long, lonely journey whence he came, descending into the dugout of humiliation until, nine comrades later, it is time to try again. If all a Donovan could do was profit from the pitcher's mistakes, how could he possibly intend anything by a swing other than to try to make contact? How could one condemn a soul for success in a struggle in which he is so wretchedly overmatched?* But Taft had no time for the luxury of such reflection. He was doing his own research on this one.

Down one game to none, the Yankees came back with fury on the twenty-fourth, scoring 11 runs in the first four innings en route to a 13–4 victory. Donovan had a double and a single as the fabled champs banged out 16 hits, including three home runs. The travel day having been eliminated by the snow, the Series was set to shift to New York for games 3 through 5 beginning on the twenty-fifth. The contestants split the next two games, leaving it a best-of-three series. And then the weather once again got the best of both. Rain won out the next four days. An attempt had been made on the thirtieth to get under way, but the appearance of a rainbow that had signaled the tarp's removal was, in a reversal of biblical proportions, followed by a deluge that sent the network executives scurrying to fill their prime time for the sixth evening in little more than a week. Baseball's bigwigs, meanwhile, worried that the TV moguls might insist on a discount for rain delays in the next Series television contract. As they left the comfort of their sky boxes for their limousines ten minutes ahead of the public-address announcement of the post-ponement, they never even saw the shivering fans' umbrellas barely fending off the wind-driven water, consoled only by the thought of the rainchecks in their pockets.

At last, sunshine returned on the thirty-first, though the ballpark offered up only a vacant stare in return. Another night game, naturally, even if the temperature had dropped to 41 degrees by the opening pitch. But the play far exceeded the elements, as the players betrayed no sign of rust. For a few hours the grandness of the game was on display at a level not seen since its glory days. A perfectly executed suicide squeeze. The hit-and-run timed to perfection. A stolen base earned after six pickoff attempts, the runner refusing to surrender an inch of his daring lead, and evading the tag on a pitchout, no less. A cleanup hitter fouling off eight straight pitches, as if he knew all along that the ninth one would be a mistake right in his wheelhouse whose trajectory would be rudely interrupted seconds later only by the facing of the third deck. A rally-killing double play choreographed by the Bolshoi. Each team mounting a comeback and then another comeback, the seesaw game hanging in the balance on every pitch. And when it was all over, rather than one team having defeated the other, it was more accurate to say that it was simply the team entitled to bat last that won. Thirteen to 12 Yankees. Thirty-four hits and not a single error or unintentional walk.

As Kasoff watched, transfixed by the perfectly played cliffhanger, now he, too, hoped that Taft was tuned in. The hitters seemed to have their way against their mound opponents. The electric golf cart that brought in the relievers from the bullpen would need a charge. No matter who took over, the hitters soon sent him to the showers. Who could argue that the batters were not in command?

The teams were to travel to Montreal in the morning for a night game on November 1. Not even the temblor-delayed Series of '89 could fracture October's grip on season's end. For the first time in baseball history, the game's youngest fans could watch the first inning or two of the Series—bedtime would intervene thereafter—while eating their Halloween candy.

18

November. This was the month when the days grew too short and cold for comfort yet offered none of the consolation of knowing that any of the worst was past. For all of winter lay ahead. It scarcely deserved to be classified with its benevolent next-door neighbor, October, as autumn. If the calendar's denizens could organize and form a union, surely November's predecessors would demand a separate bargaining unit. The first day of this miserable 30 would be an eventful one. Nearly every hour.

Mary McGinniss had been asleep for only a few moments when, at 12:30 A.M., a stabbing pain jolted her into consciousness. "It's time." She gently nudged her sister, with whom she was staying in these final days. Within twenty minutes, she found herself being wheeled into the labor and delivery room, where she was quickly surrounded by the obstetrics team, which did all the right things medically but was utterly unable to diminish her sense of aloneness at this moment. Shared intimacy is a protective garment against life's inclemencies; loneliness conspires with the elements to freeze the soul. For the next 22 hours, each perspiring push forward would be offset by a backward-looking sigh as the sweat turned cold.

Donovan was in the clubhouse studying his videotapes well past 1:00 A.M. The Yankees' plane was due to take off at 8:00 A.M. for the forty-five-minute flight to Quebec's biggest city, but the night's fog had only thickened as the clock ticked on November's opening hours. Donovan began to fret at just how much time he would miss from his pregame routine while stranded on a runway. And even this was not the worst case scenario.

In his study, it was shortly after 2:00 A.M. when Taft turned off the light. His opinion was complete. He lay down to get a few hours' sleep but then remembered he needed to do just one more thing. At 3: 02 A.M., he reached for the phone.

Shortly after 4:00 A.M., Kasoff stirred, not for the first time in those early hours. Now, he surrendered to the insomnia and got

301

out of bed. Today was day 14. The judge was never tardy. This had to be the day. Kasoff was sure he would receive a telephone call in less than five hours from Taft's clerk requiring counsel's presence. This was one opinion, he was convinced, that Taft would not be sending through the mail.

The press knew it, too. The broadcasters began setting up shop outside the courthouse shortly after 5:00 A.M. and were testing their equipment long before their anchors were in makeup.

Weinstein was an early riser, but he didn't usually receive calls at home at 6:00 A.M. Trouble is cast with a late-night hue. By this hour, his clients were sleeping it off as Weinstein would begin his calesthenics. So it was easy for him to guess correctly that the caller was Donovan. "I haven't heard anything from you," said the star.

"That's because I've heard nothing myself."

"Today is the judge's self-imposed deadline. Do you think things will be delayed again?"

"Knowing Taft, I doubt it, but I'll call over there this morning to see what's up."

"All right. I'm on my way to the airport—"

"You guys didn't fly out last night?"

"Too foggy. It looks worse today, though. I'm afraid I'll be sitting in the damn airport all morning."

"What's the forecast? You're not going to get postponed again, are you?"

"As long as they can get us there by six P.M. or so, we'll play."

"It must be tough to keep your edge through all these delays. Hell, it's worse than me having to waste half my life waiting around in courtrooms."

"After waiting half my life for this, I don't even notice. I just use the extra time to prepare."

"Well, remember the first rule about dead time: there's an inverse relationship between the amount of work you bring along and the amount of time you wait. So take lots to read."

"I'll have enough to keep me busy. But let me ask you—worst-case scenario, as you put it. The flight is delayed. Suppose Taft rules this morning and it goes against me. Is there any way they can stop me from going to Montreal?"

"Very remote that Taft would do that. If he tried, we'd be in the Court of Appeals seeking an emergency stay within an hour. On the other hand—"

"You guys kill me. Never a straight answer. Do they teach you in law school that you can charge twice as much if you give two different opinions even when they're mutually exclusive, so that both are worthless?"

"Hang on, Mr. Donovan. This isn't exactly a routine case. Taft is as immune as any judge to outside influences, but who can guarantee what steps he'll try to take if he does rule against us? I doubt it will come to that, but let's cross that bridge if and when we come to it."

"I won't be crossing anything if this damn fog doesn't lift."

"Oh, sure it will. And good luck tonight. Say, do you want me to call you at the park if I get the decision today or would you rather I not interfere with your focus if I don't have to?"

"You might as well call. Better I hear it from you than from ESPN in the clubhouse or, worse yet, some reporter sticking a mike in my face. God knows I got in enough trouble with that once already."

The call came in to Sharon at precisely 8:30 A.M. In her nervous excitement, instead of transferring the call she knew Kasoff had been awaiting, she accidentally cut off the judge's clerk. Instantly she was reminded of a day more than three years earlier when she had done the identical thing, although on that occasion the source of the tension was the fact that it was her first day on the job. As she already had inadvertently erased a portion of one of Kasoff's dictation tapes before she had transcribed it, her debut had not been auspicious. Confiding her mistakes that first day to Carol had produced only a shaking head in response. Sharon, fearing she had nothing in common with her next-cubicle neighbor aside from proximity and her stomach churning from her errors, had gone into Kasoff's office at day's end to confess that perhaps she wasn't cut out for the job. She hadn't forgotten his reply.

He had already proofread and signed several documents she had prepared, and he took the opportunity to contrast her work with that of her predecessor. "She had been here nearly ninety days when I asked her to type a summary of a witness statement that referred to the victim as having suffered a gunshot wound.

303

When I got it back, *wound* came out as *womb*. It flew in under the shoddy spell-check radar, of course. Well, this certainly wasn't the first such error she had made—command of the English language was not her strong suit—and so I took the document to her and told her to find the mistake in it or I would sentence her to read *Thirty Days to a More Powerful Vocabulary*. So she starts to read it, and she reads past that line, so I give her a hint. 'No,' I say, 'it's in the first paragraph.' So she rereads the passage, slowly now, and she gets to the last three words. 'Gun shot womb,' she says out loud, and then muses a moment. 'Should *gun shot* be one word?'

"Now," Kasoff had told Sharon on her opening day, "If you can keep those two straight, you'll make it just fine." It broke her up and saved her day, and her job. And as she grew more confident, Carol's initial disdain disappeared, and the two had become friends. It struck her that one stern word from Kasoff would have been the difference between staying and finding something else. She knew, too, that the average boss has no insight into how powerful is the impact on the subordinate of the demeaning tone. The hostile word hangs on far longer in memory's vault. But Sharon had made a place for Kasoff's soothing words.

Now, she got the clerk right back on the line. He simply told her that the judge wanted to see both counsel at 9:30 A.M. if possible. Seeing her boss just walking past, she repeated the request, to which Kasoff gave a thumbs-up. All she had to do was confirm Weinstein's availability, which she immediately did.

The two combatants approached the courthouse from opposite directions but arrived at the same elevator simultaneously. After a brief minuet of, "You firsts," they shared the short ride to the third floor. The car doors opened and all Kasoff could do was shake his head. "Either this is a mob of press or they're auctioning off the antacid concession just outside Taft's door," he said. The adversaries now shared a common goal of swimming upstream against this tide of tabloid flotsam to get into Taft's courtroom. "The bailiffs must have given up," he muttered, and Weinstein nodded.

At the appointed hour, Taft appeared before a packed house. Somebody's cell phone began ringing. Everyone expected a scowl from Taft followed by who knew what, but the judge just smiled benevolently, for he was always delighted to be able to donate the latest technology to his favorite charity. The court officer confiscated the offending device. Among the gathered throng, some twenty-five index fingers felt around inside twenty-five pockets to ensure that the power was off on their own equipment, the owners so apprehensive they dared not remove the offenders from their hiding places in order to make the much simpler visual check.

The case was called. As soon as appearances were placed on the record, Taft began to read. "'This case is before this Court on a motion to dismiss the People's charge of first-degree murder against the defendant Christopher Donovan. The defendant was arrested and charged with the said offense arising out of a baseball game played within the city limits of Chicago, in Cook County, on April first of this year, during which it is alleged that the defendant, with malice and with premeditation and deliberation, intentionally caused the death of one Don McGinniss by means of the following instrumentality, to wit, a baseball bat, which he used, the People allege, to strike a baseball delivered by McGinniss in the course of the game, thereby hitting that ball back at McGinniss such that it struck him with deadly force against his skull, fracturing it and thereby causing his death.'"

Kasoff didn't have any children, but he knew the feeling of the expectant father. Each time a jury deliberated, he paced, unable to maintain extended concentration on anything else until the jury returned. But this was worse. This time, he had waited two weeks, and now the judge was holding up the envelope, letting the tension build as he described the game's events, reciting the facts everyone well knew, before announcing the winner.

Next, Taft summarized the positions of the two sides. With nothing to write home about thus far, the journalists in the gallery betrayed their short attention spans by shifting in their seats as the yawning spread among them. Lethargy's version of the wave. At last, the judge moved beyond the preliminaries.

"The criminal law is generally clear and well established. It is not for this Court to change it. That is left to the legislature." Kasoff felt as though he had just been stabbed, while Weinstein inhaled deeply the air Kasoff could no longer breathe. "However," and now the tide ebbed from Weinstein back toward Kasoff. *The contrarian will come through!*—he shouted in his mind. "The common law," Taft continued, "is like a glacier. At times it retreats, on other occasions, it advances. In either event, its movements are judge-made. On the precise matter at issue here, we deal with no statutory law, the cardinal rule of which requires the judiciary to divine the intent of the legislature whenever possible and apply that intent to the facts of each case. But the felony-murder rule and the law of conspiracy grew up out of the common law, that is, judge-made law, and have developed over many decades in this state.

"In an 1867 case, a bank robber fired shots as he fled the bank he had just held up, causing a stagecoach to stampede in panic. A little girl was trampled to death as a result. The felon did not intend to kill her, but his actions demonstrated such reckless disregard for life that the felony-murder rule was born. Our Supreme Court ruled that he would be held to have intended the expected consequences of his actions. Anyone back in 1867 knew that gunshots at close range would cause a horse reflexively to panic. On this basis, the robber was found guilty of murder. The malice, premeditation, and deliberation he evinced in committing the bank robbery were transferred to the death.

"Thirty years later, another bank robber provoked a guard to attempt to foil the scheme by shooting at him as he fled. It was admitted by the People that the guard had fired his gun in violation of bank policy to refrain from shooting at robbers when customers were present. An innocent bystander was killed by a ricocheting bullet from the guard's gun. This time, the felony-murder rule was broadened to include not merely those events which are expected, but also those which are reasonably foreseeable. In short, the rule was augmented to fit the facts of the case because to do otherwise would have defied common sense. At bottom, judge-made law, to maintain its legitimacy, must reflect the common wisdom of the community. The alternative would have been to exonerate the robber of the killing and rely on the legislature to pass a new law to cover the situation the next time. Such a course, however, not only fails to do justice in the individual case but cedes the chief realm of the judicial branch—the doing of justice in individual cases—to the legislative branch.

This task, the legislature is not equipped to perform.

"Here, the defendant did not merely foresee or expect the prospect of death, there is probable cause to believe that he specifically intended it. But, the defendant argues, he cannot be held responsible because the underlying felony was committed at another time and by itself posed no risk of harm to the victim. The defendant would limit this Court to viewing a mere snapshot or two when the complete film—his entire course of conduct—must be examined in the context of the resultant harm.

"In order to do so here, we must look to the law of conspiracy. In a vein similar to that of the felony-murder rule, the common law of conspiracy has developed over many decades. Today, a conspirator is guilty of all illegal acts performed by any of his co-conspirators in the course of the conspiracy.

"In the case at bar, the People argue that this is a case where the common law of felony-murder and conspiracy intersect. If one individual, rather than a group, commits a series of acts, at least one of which is unlawful, in furtherance of carrying out a homicide, it defies common sense to exonerate that individual merely because the unlawful act itself was not inherently dangerous to life or committed at the time the life was taken. The entire course of conduct, if carried out with the intent and means of committing a homicide, should be subject to the scrutiny of the criminal law. Otherwise, whereas a co-conspirator could be held responsible for murder merely for supplying to the actual killer, at a remote time and place, the murder weapon, for example, in spite of having no further involvement in the crime, a single individual who hatches and carries out an entire scheme to commit a homicide has committed no wrong in the eyes of the law as long as the actual act of killing is somehow carried out in a 'lawful' manner. Such an anomaly the criminal law cannot stand.

"Therefore, it is the opinion of this Court that the felony-murder rule may be expanded in the common law to include nonviolent crimes remote in time and place from the killing if, had the non-violent crime been committed by a conspirator in the course of a conspiracy, such a conspirator could also have been held responsible for the resulting homicide. And provided also that the perpetrator had the specific intent to cause the victim's eventual death at the time of the commission of the crime as well as at the time of the act causing death. This extension of the felony-murder rule is consistent with the history and intent behind that rule and its legal cousin of conspiracy.

"Applying this rule to the case before this Court, it is clear that this defendant had the intent to kill. Therefore, the required element of malice is present. Similarly, there is ample evidence in the record of premeditation and deliberation. The overt act of breaking into the hospital records room to study the victim's most vulnerable spot to target is a qualifying underlying felony for the purpose of applying the felony-murder rule, because had it been committed by a co-conspirator, that co-conspirator could have been held responsible for the subsequent taking of the victim's life. Hence, when Donovan took McGinniss's life, a fact undisputed by the defense, the defendant was in effect carrying out the roles of both conspirators. Seen in this perspective, the defendant's dual role is especially incriminating.

"That the action of the defendant that was the immediate cause of death occurred on a field of sport is immaterial to this analysis. Twenty years ago, in the case of *Hackbart vs. Cincinnati Bengals:* Judge Richard Matsch of the federal district court in Denver considered a tort claim brought by a football player who, while down, was intentionally struck in the back of the head from behind by an opposing player, in violation of the rules of the game. Judge Matsch wrote, and I quote: 'There is no discernible code of conduct for NFL players. The dictionary definition of a sportsman is one who abides by the rules of a contest and accepts victory or defeat graciously ... That is not the prevailing attitude in professional football. There are no Athenian virtues in this form of athletics. The NFL has substituted the morality of the battlefield for that of the playing field, and the restraints of civilization have been left on the sidelines.'

"Then, Judge Matsch denied relief to the plaintiff on this basis, although he took care to limit carefully the application of his ruling, as follows, and again I quote: 'I have considered only a claim for an injury resulting from a blow, without weaponry, delivered emotionally without a specific intent to injure, in the course of regular play in a league-approved game ... '

"Two things are particularly compelling about the judge's ruling as they apply to this case. First, even in a contact sport such as football, Judge Matsch limited his ruling to cases where there was no evidence of a specific intent to injure. That is assuredly not the case here. But far more important is the fact that Judge Matsch was reversed! The Court of Appeals squarely held that the game of football carries with it no license to commit acts of violence. Virtue, Athenian or otherwise, will not be relegated to the sidelines in this courtroom.

"Therefore, it is ordered that the defendant be bound over for trial on a charge of murder in the first degree. Would counsel please approach the bench?" Taft now had to bang his gavel and threaten to clear the courtroom before the din would die a slow death. At sidebar, the judge broached the subject of scheduling the bail hearing to follow. Weinstein was noncommittal.

"Not until we see what the Court of Appeals does with this, Your Honor."

"That's your prerogative, counsel. But, now that there is a judicial finding of probable cause on the record, I intend to revisit the bail issue immediately."

Weinstein was stunned. There would be no opportunity to seek a stay before Taft imposed his conditions. Now, the judge continued. "This, after all, is a capital case, and so of course I will not permit your client to leave the country until the terms of bail have been set."

It was 10:00 A.M. exactly. Aware of the morning's weather in New York, Weinstein could not assume that the judge's point was moot. "May I have a few moments, Your Honor? I'd like to attempt to reach my client to advise him of these developments."

Turning from sidebar, the jurist announced for the record a 15-minute recess. By this time, only the lawyers were left in the courtroom. The entire gallery had completed its stampede into the hallway, either typing furiously on their laptops or shouting above the crowd noise into those pesky personal phones, now freed from their subterranean prisons.

Anyone looking for a sign of exultation in Kasoff would search in vain. Success, even the sweetest variety—the unexpected victory—brought relief only. If it was grudgingly admitted by the defense bar that this DA was not one to gloat, it was simply because he didn't feel the desire to. Victory, like virtue, was its own reward.

309

Weinstein reached Donovan just in time to learn that not five minutes earlier he had been pulled off the plane, which was still sitting at the gate, and taken to a conference room. In fact, Donovan had been just about to try to reach Weinstein when his phone rang. The long arm of Judge Taft's early-morning intervention had asserted itself. Well before 6:00 A.M., his trusted ally had acted. Sam Kucinich was about to retire as the FAA's regional director. Based at La Guardia Airport for the last 36 years, he had attended undergraduate school in the forties with Taft at Columbia, where they had become the closest of friends. Sam was widely appreciated for his probity, and there were no leaks of sensitive information out of his office, whether it involved terrorist threats to wreak airport havoc or the progress of a crash investigation. Through the FBI field office in Chicago, Sam had received word a few hours earlier that Taft did not want the Yankees' plane to leave U.S. airspace that morning until one of the confirmed passengers was first removed. Sam had finally located the pilot to inform him of this court order, which, the captain was told, was to remain highly confidential. The pilot's response had been to laugh.

"Someone's going to a lot of trouble to do what the pea soup out here is already sure to do."

But Taft would take no chance trusting the elements. The plan was to delay the flight until 10:00 A.M.—nature's mist had simply obviated the need for a maintenance problem to serve as an appropriate pretext. Then, as soon as the judge's decision was on the record, the Yankee would be yanked off the flight.

Once Donovan described the events of the preceding minutes, it took even less time for his counsel to put two and two together. Weinstein was dumbfounded at what he was convinced was Taft's breach of judicial discretion. In effect, the judge had tipped off an arm of the Prosecutor's Office—forgetting for the moment that the FBI was a separate law enforcement agency—to assist in apprehending his client. All without notice of the decision, much less an opportunity to be heard, never mind that there had been no known signing of a bench warrant. For a moment, Weinstein felt dizzy with anger as the pressure mounted between his temples. It was a tough-enough business when everyone played by the rules. Keeping up with the ones

310

that judges made up as they went along, let alone responding to them, was like groping one's way through a nighttime battle zone. The sudden flash would immediately concentrate the warrior's attention, but it was impossible to develop a counterstrategy without knowing the source or location of the next offender.

But Weinstein had no time to contemplate which judicial canons Taft may have violated or how his grievance to the judicial tenure commission might read. He had a client who had to get to Montreal and perhaps only minutes to act. "What explanation did they give you for pulling you off the plane?"

" 'Come with us.' That was it. They had uniforms, and I knew it had something to do with this, so I went. Can you get me the hell out of here?"

Weinstein couldn't reply that he was still reeling any more than a hitter can tell the umpire he's not yet ready to return to the batters' box following a brushback. Nor would it do simply to rail against this breach of due process. "Look, I suspect that the judge is simply reminding us who's boss. He probably just wants to set the bail terms before you're out of the country. From his point of view, playing the devil's advocate for the moment, the Series ends in Montreal and, for all he knows, you may want to retire right after that down to some South Seas island where there's no extradition treaty."

"So that's why they confiscated the grass skirt in my luggage. Look, you and I both know that's ridiculous. My plans for the off-season are the same as always. I can live with just about any bail terms that will allow me to finish this Series and return home for the winter. If they want to tether me, that's fine."

"With your economic status, the dollar number will be awfully high. Maybe five million, ten percent cash. Before you cross the border."

"I can have that wired in no time. What else?"

"You'll have to return to the States right after the Series. No additional traveling without court permission—not even to Disneyland if you win. That's at a minimum, I'm sure." Weinstein was regaining his bearings along with his confidence as he dispensed the type of advice he was so accustomed to giving. "Look, we're on a short recess. I can represent to the Court that I've talked to you and that you're agreeable to all of the conditions we've discussed. In the meantime, before I hang up, make sure they'll let you continue to use your phone to make the wire transfer arrangements."

A moment later, Donovan reported the affirmative reply. "Thank Heaven for small favors," the Yankee muttered.

"Great. I'll call you back as soon as I learn the amount that's set so you can make the arrangements. Fair enough?"

"That's what I hired you for. Looks like you're about to earn your money."

"I'll be in touch real soon."

Weinstein returned to the courtroom, where Taft soon reappeared. "Your Honor, I've had an opportunity to speak to my client." Taft betrayed just a hint of a smile, well aware that the counselor could not have found Donovan at an altitude where use of those hated cell phones was prohibited. "And he is prepared to waive personal appearance at a bail hearing if the Court wishes to impose the conditions at this time."

"Have the People had an opportunity to consider appropriate terms?"

Kasoff answered with one eye on the Court of Appeals, for he knew that Weinstein would be over there within the hour. Pushing too hard for stringent conditions would only increase the chances that his opponent would get the higher court's attention. The real war, after all, was about getting this case to trial. This was a skirmish irrelevant to the outcome. Every general must know which battles not to choose. And so, Kasoff was careful about what he wished for, lest Taft grant it.

"Your Honor, the People would suggest that bail be set at one million dollars—" a rather ordinary sum in a capital case where affluence was in the dock. Ignorant of Taft's early-morning machinations, Kasoff requested that Donovan be ordered to return to the jurisdiction of the court within 24 hours of the conclusion of the World Series and be required to provide the Court at that time with an address and telephone number as to where he could be reached at all times. Because Donovan's barn contained material evidence of the one-man conspiracy, Kasoff requested that the defendant be ordered to refrain from making any modifications in or about it. Taft nodded his head throughout the litany, and when Kasoff concluded, Weinstein offered no objection. Donovan's defender relaxed. A moment too soon.

"Counsel, I believe you've omitted one condition, perhaps the most vital. Mr. Weinstein, can you show cause, if any there be, why this defendant should not be immediately enjoined from repeating the activity that brought him here pending trial?"

Weinstein was known for being quick on his feet in the courtroom, but these words took a moment to sink in. So! Taft's objection to allowing Donovan on the plane was not merely geographical. He actually intended to forbid Donovan from batting in a major-league game until trial. The whispers in the gallery grew to a steady buzz as the realization hit home throughout the courtroom.

What's more, this put Weinstein in a very delicate position. He had to assure the Court that the deadly line shot would not be repeated without conceding that his client's conduct on April 1 was any different from what it would be this evening. If Opening Day was truly an accident, one could hardly guarantee that such happenstance would not be repeated. Yet without such assurance Taft was certain to issue the injunction.

Weinstein decided to play strictly to the Court of Appeals. It was obvious that Taft was out of control and was going to beat him whatever he argued. "Your Honor, there is no evidence and no reason to believe that the tragedy of last Opening Day, which was a one-in-a-million circumstance however one views it, will be repeated or that Donovan has any motive or desire to see it repeated. At this stage, we are simply required to assure this Court that the defendant will appear for trial."

"Counsel, as you know, in a capital case, this Court has the right, indeed has the duty, to take into account the prospect of danger to the community in the setting of bail conditions. Now, if what the People allege is proven true, and if what this Court has determined there is probable cause to believe is true, then Donovan represents a danger to opposing pitchers over the course of the next forty-eight hours. Therefore, it is the order of this Court that the defendant shall not be allowed to step into a batters' box against an opposing pitcher pending the trial of this matter. This hearing is concluded."

If Taft had his way, Donovan would be reduced to the status of a pinch runner in the most important game or games of his life, hardly his forte after fourteen years of his knees' taking a pounding, especially on artificial turf, where concrete resides less than a thumb's length below Monsanto green. Even the plastic version of the game is one of inches.

In the game of baseball, there was once an unwritten rule against a hitter showing up an umpire over a called strike. The hitter might step out of the box a moment and might complain the pitch was too high, but he would make his objection without turning around and facing the man in blue. Only the catcher would be privy to the protest. The crowd would remain unaware. As the coarser grains of a more permissive society have eroded that custom, fans have been witness to heated nose-to-nose displays between umpire and hitter, often resolved only when the game's enforcer points a thumb in the direction of the offender's clubhouse.

Now, as Weinstein began to turn away from counsel table, he indulged in the courtroom equivalent of an in-your-face home plate rhubarb. "Miss Reporter, please supply me an expedited copy of the transcript for appeal," he said, making no attempt to rein in his voice below that of a stage whisper. But it was pure theater all the same. He would be at the appellate court with his emergency application well before the record would ever be available. His protest, even the gallery guessed, was simply an expression of his disdain. Taft knew it, too.

"Careful, counsel, or I'll find you in contempt of court."

"Not of it—" and now Weinstein went beyond the pale—"for it." Weinstein all but spit the rejoinder. The bailiff, anticipating Taft's next words, was already beginning to move toward the reprobate with one hand on his cuffs, but Taft raised his hand in a stop signal to his deputy when Weinstein added, "After this morning's antics as I slept." Permitted to wheel around and walk out unmolested, Weinstein was more convinced than ever that Taft's hands weren't clean enough to mete out a swift judicial blow against such impertinence.

Now, the contemnor had to bring his client up-to-date. "The good news is that you can go to Montreal. The bad news is you can't bat again until trial." After Weinstein convinced Donovan that he did not have a bad connection, the counselor spent the next several minutes assuring him that the Court of Appeals

314

was bound to stay temporarily that portion of the judge's order in time to assure Donovan's full participation in the remainder of the Series.

"It looks like the fog here is beginning to lift. What do I do?"

"Tell 'em your attorney has an order allowing you to travel with the team and that they can verify it either by calling Taft's courtroom or by giving me ten minutes to obtain a copy of the order and fax it to them." Weinstein gave Donovan the number of the judge's clerk. "Now, get on that plane and call me right back if they give you a hard time."

"You'll be the first one to know."

"Fine. I'm on my way to get that SOB reversed."

Weinstein knew he had the option of first seeking out the Chief Judge for relief, but that particular jurist was known as loath to second-guess his colleague. And so Weinstein walked across the street to the appellate court. There were 36 judges on this bench. Their typical assignment, after being broken up into random three-member panels every third week, was to hear and decide appeals from final decisions of the trial courts in both criminal and civil matters. Because oral arguments in such cases were staggered, there were always judges available to consider emergency requests for relief from decisions of the lower courts that did not involve a final order. These interim rulings, known as interlocutory orders, mostly involving procedural matters, could frequently preordain the ultimate outcome on the merits, so that an advocate who lost such a decision would naturally want quick redress before proceeding further in the lower tribunal. It would be too late once the clay entered the kiln. But the doors of this emergency appellate avenue were barred except to those whose clients would suffer immediate and irreparable harm if the error was not promptly rectified. Hence, for example, evidence suppressed on the eve of trial could be examined anew on an emergency basis by an appellate judge before the jury was sworn.

Kasoff had agreed to meet Weinstein within 15 minutes to check in. As Weinstein entered the courthouse, trailed by a gaggle of journalists, he transformed himself from the righteously indignant foe of injustice to the humble supplicant. The change took place unconsciously. He had been at this work so long that the role-playing had become second nature.

Drawn by lot, the available judge was Howard Wagner, a thoughtful straight arrow in his late sixties. Weinstein had not initially been an enthusiastic supporter of his. Wagner had come from the DA's office and that, after all, would likely spell trouble for those of Weinstein's clients who appeared before him, but Wagner had turned out better than expected. Once, early on while still a trial judge, he had confided to Weinstein during plea negotiations on a case that the toughest part of his job was fending off the pressure from his old pals in the Prosecutor's Office who expected him, as a former colleague, to favor their cause. "When you take the oath of this office," he had said, "you have to forget where you came from." *Good for him*, thought Weinstein, and from that time on, he had been a Wagner backer. He was convinced that the judge would be incensed at Taft's overreaching.

And he was right. The hearing took all of 10 minutes. The offending condition was ordered stricken. As long as the bail money was wired by 5:00 P.M., Donovan would be given the green light. Weinstein now informed his client, whose plane, having safely arrived across the border, had discharged its passengers by 1:00 P.M. The electronic funds transfer was accomplished by midafternoon.

Meanwhile, Green was counting on his colleague being ready for a break. On their way to lunch, he began, "OK, I've got it. How about the all home and garden team?"

"Home and garden?" Kasoff was laughing now.

"Sure. You know, things found in a garden or in a home, around the home . . ."

"Fair enough. Of course I go with Pete Rose at third base and Daryl Strawberry at first."

"Those are gimmes."

"Donnie Bush at short. OK, let's see. Around the home. Alan Bannister at second. Phil Roof catching. And my pitcher, oh, you'll love this one. Tommy John!"

"Yes!"

"Over Jimmy Key and Dennis Lamp. OK. Outfield. Hmm. OK. Don Lock. Back in the garden with Billy Bean."

"They're nobodies."

"Hmm. I'll have to get back to you on my third outfielder."

"You're kidding. You? Stumped?"

"Only at the moment. I'll come up with someone."

"But you're missing the most obvious choice."

"How about Al Kaline, as in the batteries?"

"Sorry, that's too much of a stretch." Kasoff wasn't about to admit that this taunting was getting under his competitive skin. "Just gimme a little time. I'll figure it out."

By 4:00 P.M., Donovan was stepping into the batters' box for his first round of batting practice. Strange, he thought, for the first time in weeks he had not the slightest hint of the headaches that had been present ever since Weinstein's prediction at the outset of the preliminary exam that he would never be bound over.

* * *

All afternoon, mother and fetus remained stable. The fetal heart tones were within normal limits, as was Mary's blood pressure. Contractions remained about five minutes apart, however, and dilation was not yet complete. Melanie, fearful that her sister would suffer prepartum depression over the absence of McGinniss, wouldn't leave Mary's side. Fortunately, Mom now appeared to be doing well, musing about the baby instead of mourning the father. At 8:25 P.M., from the TV over the neighboring bed came the strains of the national anthem. Melanie asked Mary's roommate to lower the volume for fear that her sister would hear the name that had rendered this moment more bitter than sweet.

* * *

His head cleared of its aching, if not the burden of legal uncertainty, Donovan started strong and got better from there. He doubled home two runs in the first on a gapper to left-center and followed that with a solo homer in the third. Then, he reprised his home run trot with a three-run shot in the fifth. Three at-bats, six RBIs, and a 6–3 lead for the Yankees after six. But the Yankee relief corps wasn't up to the task in this penultimate game. To the reporters in a postgame interview, their pitching coach would blame the 37-degree weather, but privately he believed that the pressure had affected their rhythm. By the top of the ninth, the Yankees trailed, 8–6. And they went out 1-2-3, the final one made by Donovan himself, on a screamer down the first base line that was speared by Montreal's tall and lanky first sacker. The Series was tied at three. And the dreary weather forecast for the next twenty-four hours was in stark contrast to the excitement and anticipation in both clubhouses.

*   *   *

Meanwhile, Mary's labor had intensified that evening. With each stabbing pain, she concentrated her mind for the next push. Only later would she realize that for the first time since McGinniss's death she had been so focused on the present that she had gone several hours without a conscious thought of him. And then, with a final effort, she suddenly heard, "It's a boy!" And now, her own tears dwarfed those of his first cry. As the newborn was brought up for her to embrace, she saw in his tiny eyes a reflection of a 24-year-old photograph she had first seen just a few months earlier. "It's Don," she whispered to no one in particular. "He's Don," now out loud. And the combination of joy and sadness was at once overwhelming as hope and despair. And she laughed and cried, and she could not tell the difference.

Soon, to Melanie, Mary turned and said with unaccustomed solemnity, "I'm going to name him Don."

"Don Junior," Melanie beamed. It was a statement, not a question. Mary merely smiled.

*   *   *

Across town, Weinstein was spending that evening with his partners, collectively shaking their heads over Taft's actions. "I can't believe he would order law enforcement to detain a person without notice to his counsel based on a decision he hasn't yet put on record." But insofar as Weinstein wanted to nail Taft for unethical conduct, this was the seething of frustration that was futile. For the devil's advocate nagged within. What's wrong with

318

a judge deciding to prevent a defendant concerning whom there is probable cause to believe has committed a capital crime from leaving the country? And if the departure is imminent and therefore requires immediate action, why shouldn't the judge take that action, especially where the parties have already been heard on the issue and the Court is all set to announce its decision? The jurist had simply outflanked him. As for Weinstein's own visceral courtroom response, well, it's the stuck pig that squeals the loudest. At least the appellate judge had set Taft straight while setting his client free for the time being.

"But that opinion! Shameless bootstrapping. I mean, just because there is an underlying felony, the death is transformed into murder? And that's forgetting for the moment its nonviolent nature. This time, the Court of Appeals is bound to reverse him. Donovan will never go to trial. We'll file an immediate appeal coupled with a request for a stay of prosecution pending a decision. The only question is whether we should go ahead and file a grievance against Taft as well."

Weinstein's second thoughts were now reinforced by his partner. "What do we have to lose, except the goodwill of every other judge in the county?"

"But if we don't do it, we invite the rest of 'em to cheat due process along with our clients. Do we really have a choice?"

"Will this really benefit Donovan or only some possible future client? Because if it's only the latter, right now our duty is solely to our current client, and a good-paying one at that. And suppose we lose the grievance as well as the appeal and the case goes back to Taft for trial? He'll be gunning for us all the more. It's just too chancy."

"I guess you're right. It's just not worth the risk." Sometimes, seeing the forest for the trees requires one to look beyond its poison ivy ground cover.

Weinstein filed his notice of appeal the very next day, while his client was taking early batting practice. The brief would be due in six weeks on the expedited criminal appellate track, the People's six weeks thereafter. As anticipated, the Court of Appeals granted the stay of prosecution pending resolution of the key issue on appeal: was there indeed probable cause to believe that a crime had been committed in Chicago Stadium on

April 1, or had Donovan merely hit safely? Another Opening Day would come and go before the litigants would have an opportunity to argue their case before a three-judge panel, and it would be next autumn before a decision could be expected. Still, this was a full year less than the standard appellate backlog for civil cases. In the meantime, Donovan would be free to play ball wherever the schedule called on him to be.

Game 7 was on tap. Sportswriters were bemoaning the fact that the commissioner would not even consider moving the game up to a daytime start. The temperature was forecast to dip below freezing by 9:00 P.M., and the long-range forecast foretold only an early winter. But the commissioner's hands were tied. TV commercials, after all, had been sold based on prime-time rates. Preempting the soaps wouldn't merely infuriate America's daytime TV fans; corporate America wouldn't stand for it. The show must go on. As scheduled. And so the hearty fans hunkered down in their parkas and quilts, except for the three bare-chested knuckleheads in the bleachers who, numbed by their pregame alcohol, were sure the cameras would capture them even in the farthest reaches of the park.

Each team was going with its ace. Both had had plenty of rest with all of the postponements, but that was a mixed blessing for the home team. Gomez's screwball was best when he was a bit tired. When feeling strong, he would tend to overthrow and would lose the movement on his ball. He also was most effective in parks where the grass was nature's own. Artificial turf, as in Montreal, didn't sufficiently slow up some of the grounders that would otherwise be gobbled up by his steady but unspectacular infield. But no matter. In game 7, there is no time for redemption. If Gomez came out anything less than his sharpest, the manager would send him to an early shower pronto.

Donovan, having planned all along for the possibility of a game 7 in spite of his prediction to his lawyer, had used the time off to study videos of the entire Montreal pitching staff, for any of them might get the call from the bullpen for this ultimate game. The Yankee video operation didn't skimp on filming the senior circuit's mound men. In this day of free agency, who knew where any given player would be hanging his cap the following spring? Donovan had watched tape of Gomez pitching when he was fresh, when overworked, on grass, on turf, you name it. He would be ready.

An hour before game time, a light drizzle began to fall. The tarp was rolled out onto the field just as the first snowflakes began to accompany their warmer brethren. Ten minutes before the first scheduled pitch, precipitation was continuing, but it was light enough that the umpires, in consultation with the league presidents, decided to go forward. The home team took the field, the anthems were sung, and play commenced.

The Yankee first inning began with promise. A single and a walk followed by Donovan digging in. Two pitches later, the play would unfold so quickly that the TV announcer's eyes would be deceived. "Line shot—speared by Gomez!" He had got that much right. For the first time since Opening Day, Donovan had sent a rocket back through the middle right at the pitcher. But this time, his opponent's glove was the bulls-eye. "He wheels and fires to second, back to first, a triple play!" Well, not quite. The second base umpire ruled that the shortstop missed the bag, and the first base ump ruled that the phantom tagger's throw had pulled the Montreal first baseman off the base. In two blinks of an eye, the second triple play in World Series history had been reduced to a routine O-fer in the box score. The home team's fans groaned that they'd been robbed, but to the Dorothy Otts of the world, the game's virtue was on display. It wasn't enough merely to look good while playing it. Completing the task correctly and with precision was the requisite for success.

In spite of the reprieve, the Yankees were unable to score in the first, and that set the pattern for the next five innings, played in a steady light rain that was turning to a wintry mix. In spite of the layoff, Gomez's screwball was effective, and the grounders the Yankees were pounding into the turf were taking big charity hops into the gloves of the Montreal defense. To start the seventh, Montreal was forced to introduce a new pitcher into this scoreless tie, having pinch-hit for Gomez in the sixth in an effort to get something started. The first man the reliever would face would be Donovan. The Yankees had had only one baserunner since the opening inning—Donovan had walked leading off the fourth—and he had been erased in a double play. Now, after falling behind three and one, the home team's fresh hurler would

321

want to make the star earn his way on base. And Donovan had his checkbook ready. With a vicious cut, he pierced the snowflakes all the way to the scoreboard above the second deck in right field. Donovan and his team were now nine outs away from the game's top star being fitted for his first Series ring.

Far from the stricken crowd, Dorothy Ott saw, as she had so often before, how the game, so great and glorious, could at once be so oblivious to the virtue—or lack thereof—of those who played it. For she, too, had followed the proceedings in that courtroom in Chicago, and had come away with the conviction that there was more to Donovan's season-inaugurating hit than met the eye. It would be up to her neighbor—the shrine down the road—to pass judgment on Donovan's eventual application for admission. Five years after his retirement from the game, ballots would be distributed to the sportswriters who record moments great and small, inquiring whether Donovan and lesser lights of the game were fit for immortality in baseball's Elysian fields. The scribe as Saint Peter.

All that would have to wait, of course. For now, the Yankee bullpen would be called upon to hold the tenuous lead. Their manager would play it safe. He would dance with the guys that brung him, never mind the debacle of game 6. That contest was ancient history. His set-up man, if all went well, would pitch the seventh and eighth, and his closer would then slam the door. "Don't fall behind the Yankees after six," was every commentator's mantra. "You can't catch 'em against those two." In the entire season, only once had the Yankees lost when leading after eight.

Chris James was a "stuff" pitcher. Half a dozen different windups, five different pitches thrown at a variety of speeds. Hitters rarely saw him more than once in a game, so it was almost impossible to make adjustments for all those variations. And his ERA showed it. In 96 innings, it was 1.24, and, more important for a reliever, he led the league in fewest inherited runners scoring. No cheap victories for him, bought with the currency of inflating his predecessors' ERA while depriving them of the chance for the W.

James was warming up as the last raindrops turned to snow while the winds picked up blowing in from left. It's an ill wind that blows in on the team that needs a long ball to tie. And he did his job in his two innings of work, setting down all six while fanning four. The slim lead held up into the season's final regulation frame.

In the old days, a manager would stay with his hot hand, and James would have taken the mound to begin the ninth. But in this era, when a top closer earned in excess of $7 million per year, an owner would justly wonder if the man was not called upon to preserve the precarious when everything is on the line. And so James knew he was through for the season when he walked off the mound to complete the eighth.

The Yankees' multi-million-dollar man out of the bullpen was Dave Frankel. Originally from Brownsville, he was no fan of winter sports; even less did he like summer's games played when the days were short. And it showed. He walked the first batter on four pitches. Normally, when Frankel would take the mound in the ninth to uphold a narrow lead, his manager would shut down the bullpen for the night, figuring no one could second-guess him for sticking with his best. But in a concession to the night's all-or-nothing fever—what else would bring out 46,000 fans to sit for more than three hours, humbly accepting every insult nature could hurl their way?—he chose to inoculate himself by having two other guys ready. One was the number-two starter; the other a lapsed closer they had picked up the year before as insurance in exchange for cash and a no-name to be identified later. As the game's richest franchise, the Yankees could well afford to scoop up the worthy discards of any owner bawling about a cash flow crisis.

One more baserunner and he's out of there, the Yankee manager told himself. And he was right, though not as he had foreseen. As the flurries intensified, Montreal pinch-hit for their shortstop. Brian Bonham was a twenty-nine-year-old veteran who had once shown promise as the game's next Donovan. But what Bonham had in native ability he lacked in dedication, and the game, policeman of its virtue, had soon defeated him. After a sensational rookie season, hitting .333 with 33 homers, he had asked for and received a uniform number to match. But this moth was too enamored of the flame of adulation. Just three years later, he found himself in a Midwest league bouncing along

323

on far more buses in the bushes than he cared to and drinking more than his share in every town along the way. A coach down there, an old-timer who had seen the syndrome before, had played counselor, and, gradually, Bonham had stopped taking advice from bartenders. Now, after a four-year absence from the show, he had managed to work his way back to his first full major-league season in the last six. As a part-time player, in 200-plus at-bats, he had managed to hit over .300 once again, with 11 home runs. Most important for every pinch hitter especially, pressure situations didn't faze him, not after the baseball hell he had been through. Now, he had a chance to achieve a Lincolnian last full measure of redemption.

As Frankel was ready to assume the stretch position, winter's blanket was already beginning to cover the turf. No way could the umpires stop play. Winter's immovable object had met summer's irresistible force. The snow wasn't going anywhere, and there was simply no precedent for postponing or suspending a World Series game in the bottom of the ninth. This one would be played to its conclusion. No matter that the carpet was beginning to look as though Mother Nature was preparing for Santa's arrival. The only concession to the elements, with the approval of the league presidents, was to bring forth a box of dusty orange baseballs for the umpires. Once the game's laughingstock when its most irreverent owner had experimented with it a quarter of a century earlier, this brightly colored ball now merited the deep appreciation of the hometown crowd. Their prodigal son would have an easier time picking it up against the snowy background as he awaited its arrival at home plate.

Donovan stood sentry in left field. In fourteen years, he had long since learned how to tame the wind that plays tricks with fly balls. He knew how to use his glove as a shield against the glare of a sunny high sky to snare a high fly that plays eclipse with the fiery orb. He knew all about keeping one's footing in the rain by maintaining his body weight in line with every stride. But snow. He had never had such an opponent, not while playing summer's game. For in the spring, winter's last-gasp flurries signal postponement; the schedulers know that summer's promise beckons with its bigger crowds.

Now, as the flakes surrounded him like so many stars and the playing surface all around lost its green, Donovan felt at sea. No boatsman, this expert at taking the measure of the opponent's fly ball was now reminded of how he had been struck by the difficulty of judging distance out on the water when he had accepted a teammate's invitation to climb aboard his yacht one March afternoon down in Florida. For the first time since his rookie year, this star of stars was fearful. Bonham was a right-handed pull hitter. It might fall to Donovan to defeat the elements and Montreal both.

As usual, his instincts on the field were accurate. Frankel's first delivery was laced toward the gap in left-center. It was clearly Donovan's ball. His counterpart in center had no chance. In good weather, it would be catchable on the run, provided the fielder got a good jump and went all out.

There were baseball spikes designed for the best bite into artificial turf—Donovan and the Yankees had them of course—but none made with a snow-covered carpet in mind. It simply was not a foreseeable use. Donovan saw the ball heading to his left and began sprinting to the spot where he was sure his glove would intercept it. A slip slowed him for just a moment. But then, in attempting to make up for it, he lunged too soon and slid forward on winter's mantle, his momentum carrying him 20 feet or more on the slithery surface, as the ball skipped past, just out of his reach. Bouncing all the way to the wall. Donovan scrambled up, slipped again, and finally found his footing, racing back to the remote territory invaded by this orange sphere. His partner in center field, who had closed the gap in anticipation of a back-up role, just managed to beat him to the ball as it caromed off the wall at the 385 mark.

Bonham may have squandered his stardom, but just as speed can't be taught, it's not lost before one's third decade is history, either. He was nearly halfway to third as the ball was just being picked up, and the runner ahead of him was tying the game as the center fielder was poised to fire it in to the relay man. And now old devil winter triumphed over summer again. For years, people would argue about it. Did the ball slip out of the outfielder's hand on account of the snowy moisture on it, or did he, in his haste, simply fail to get an adequate grip before attempting to hit the frantic cutoff man? No matter. The throw went no farther than a duffer's drive and was just as wildly off the mark. Donovan, on his knees at the warning track, could only watch helplessly. Bonham scampered home before the Yankee short-stop could get his hands on the ball, and the city known for the Stanley Cups of its own national pastime now treasured the trophy that, for the first time in history, would reside in this city on the Saint Lawrence.

In a heartbeat, Donovan knew he would never get this close again. Back in his hometown, Dorothy turned off the TV and wondered if the famous native son would ever succeed in redeeming himself in the only game that mattered. Now, she sat down to write a thank-you note to that nice young man pictured in her Sunday *New York Times*—the one captured standing outside that Chicago courtroom. The same one who had helped her plant the begonias that had just been snuffed out by the previous week's frost.

And in America's Windy City, rooting for the enemy of their enemy, the fans applauded the result and looked forward with greater expectations for Donovan's next trial, as he had proven himself beatable in this one.

19

It was several days after Mary left the hospital with her son—she was staying at Melanie's—when her big sister noticed the official-looking document while tidying Mary's room in Mary's absence. The birth certificate. Melanie glanced at it lazily, expecting to see nothing more than the routine information. Then she noticed that the spot in which to insert a "Junior" or Roman numeral was left blank. *That's funny*, she thought. *Mary named him Don*. And then she saw the entry under the first name. To her horror, it was not Donald, as in McGinniss's given name. No, when this child was to be formally addressed, he would be called, of all things, Donovan. "Donovan! His father's killer!?" she screamed at the empty room. Was this a joke? What revolting evil had possessed her sister? Had her grief driven her mad?

Melanie's anger and agony were evident when Mary walked in. "What?" she inquired of her protective sibling. "What is it?"

"What the hell is the meaning of this?" Melanie thrust the offending paper at her.

"What?" Mary repeated, though she now suspected the source of her sister's wrath.

"How could you? Donovan? Donovan?" Melanie's voice was rising with every syllable.

Mary exhaled and replied with a calm that disarmed her sister. "Yes, I named him Donovan. After Chris Donovan—but wait," as Melanie attempted to renew her protest.

"Of course I'll honor Don's memory for the rest of my life. But somehow, I need to heal, too. I thought long and hard about this even before he was born, just in case it was a boy. The idea finally came to me when I decided to do something I haven't done since we were kids." Mary paused a moment, then continued.

"I prayed. I mean, I literally got down on my knees and begged God to help me handle this. For weeks, I thought my prayers had fallen on deaf ears." For now, she skipped the part where she had first admitted to God that she recognized how neglectful of her faith she had been and, therefore, how undeserving she felt of even so much as a hearing at this late date. Especially because she was using the occasion to seek succor for herself and not another in need. "But as I went into labor, it came to me. I have a plan. Donovan won't have the luxury of playing ball forever. Don used to tell me that when he was on the field, it was like taking a vacation from every worry, big or small, he ever had. Mostly, he would say," and here she shone the smile of memory, "about me. As long as he could play ball, he would say, he knew he would be OK. Before we got together, he feared turning forty. Not just because, he explained, he would measure his dreams of me against the reality of his life, but because he would no longer be able to enjoy playing the game that set him free, if only for a few hours, from life's disappointments.

"Anyway, after Donovan retires, if not before, what he did is going to eat away at him. From everything I've read and heard about him, he led an exemplary life before he killed my husband. So he must have a conscience. And there will come a day when I appeal to it. I will find him and introduce him to my son, the son who will never know his father because of what this man did. And I'll tell him his name is Don. And he'll say, 'After his father.' And I'll reply, 'No, Donovan. After you. I named him in tribute to what was good in you. In tribute to everything you forgot on that dreadful day.' And he will stare at me in disbelief, and then the truth will sink in with a horror more painful than your own reaction a moment ago. And it will hurt him. God, it will pierce his conscience like no trial, no conviction, ever could. And only then will he begin to rue that day. That day of so much promise, when Don and I still had so many dreams. And I will tell him that I never got the chance to tell my husband that he was about to become a father. But I won't sound bitter when I say it, only as empty as I feel right now. And Donovan will begin to feel what I have felt all these months." Now, Mary exhaled again, this time with relief. "And that's why I named him Donovan."

Now, grief met understanding as the two embraced and wiped each other's tears. "For God's sakes, Mary, naming your son Donovan is the maternal equivalent of tattooing the killer's name on your forehead." But her tone bespoke resignation and she even betrayed just a hint of a smile as the sisters found solace in each other's arms.

*　　*　　*

A couple of weeks later, Weinstein was in his corner office organizing his outline to assist his associate with the brief on appeal. His door was closed. The DO NOT DISTURB button was blinking on his phone. This meant no interruptions shy of the doomsday asteroid. Not from support staff, not from clients, not even from his partners. And then his junior one returned early from a suppression motion at the courthouse. And barged right into Weinstein's inner sanctum. "Haven't you heard?"

"Heard what?" Weinstein looked up with concern. Surely this breach meant grave news.

"Taft was found dead in his chambers this morning. It looks like a stroke."

"Jesus." And then, once the shock has worn off, the desire for detail takes over.

"Who found him?"

"The bailiff. Apparently, when Taft didn't appear at the threshold to his chambers at exactly eight-fifty-nine, the officer looked in on him. He had been sitting at his desk and keeled right over onto it. No pulse. Nothing. They tried to revive him, but it was too late. The courthouse is closing up. Funeral's Tuesday at Holy Redeemer."

"Well, at least we won't have him hearing the case if it ever goes to trial." Self-interest is slow off the mark at a moment of tragedy but soon makes up the difference as it overtakes its jump-started cousin, curiosity.

The tributes at the funeral, like the body in the coffin, were appropriately overdressed for the occasion. Neither the effusive praise nor the judge's best suit could camouflage his frailties of body and mind. The Chief Judge spoke of his diligence and dedication. One of his ex-law clerks described his humility and patience in chambers—leaving unspoken the absence of those qualities in the courtroom. Kasoff, sitting next to B.D., whispered that the only thing missing was an appellate judge to pay

329

homage to his scholarly opinions. Like the church steeple that survives its town's wartime carpetbombing, somehow the results Taft reached would stand alone against the higher court's consistent annihilation of his judicial reasoning. When, sure enough, a judge of that esteemed court was introduced to say a few words, heads turned toward the two prosecutors as they shared the stifled laughter of a couple of schoolboys.

Afterward, the Chief Judge announced that there would be an informal gathering that evening at the courthouse in the judges' lounge for members of the bar who wished to remember the jurist. "I'll bet Starstruck suggested it." B.D. nudged Kasoff. "He wouldn't dare miss an opportunity like this to schmooze." Kasoff nodded agreement. Still, convention required their attendance, and they joined more than a hundred fellow members of the bench and bar for the occasion.

Taft's clerk was there, of course, reciting the litany of events that preceded the fatal moment. "Yes, he seemed fine that morning, in fact, better than for the several days prior. No, he hadn't complained of anything before he was found." Everyone, naturally, wanted to know the signs that presaged the tragedy for the sake of reassuring themselves that it couldn't happen to them. "No, we didn't hear anything unusual. When the bailiff looked in on him, his head was on the desk to one side." And now the telling assumed a solemn, almost reverential character. "His eyes were still open, but glassy. There was just a bit of blood under his nose. And his coloring, of course, was gone. We knew right away. The bailiff hollered, and I came in at once. We first set him down on the carpeting—I'm sure I twisted my back." And now the joke that signaled that we were back in the present; it wasn't us, thank God. "It should be easy proving I'm entitled to workers' comp, lifting a body that size." And the laughter of release followed, more raucous than the line deserved.

"The bailiff tried CPR, and I called nine-one-one, but he showed no response."

"Had there been any signs? You said he wasn't feeling well," inquired one member of the bar who appeared old enough to have a stake in the answer.

"He had complained of some headaches and nausea the last week or two. We told him to see a doctor, but you know how stubborn he is. He thought it was just a bug that would pass. Last Tuesday—no, Wednesday—he'd stood up from his desk and complained of dizziness and that his right arm felt funny. We persuaded him to call his doctor, but he wouldn't go into emergency. The doctor thought it was no big deal. Lots of people feel dizzy when they get up suddenly, especially older folks, he explained. He even had a term for it. *Ortho—*"

"*Orthostatic hypotension.*"

"That's it. How'd you know that, Mr. Weinstein? Anyway, from what I understand now, his doctor believes he probably had one or more ministrokes in the last week or two. TIAs, they're called. That one I remember."

TI attacks, Weinstein repeated to himself. That might explain why Taft went over the line, even for him, and yet recoiled when Weinstein gave him the perfect opportunity to lash back. Still, a portrait of Machiavelli would be a fitting epitaph, he thought.

* * *

By now, the trading of Taft war stories was in full swing, at least amid the small groups that were sans a jurist. His previous year's clerk amused one gathering when he related Taft's explanation for the rot that has pervaded America's media in recent years.

"He told me that everything started going to hell in this country when I was around five years old. That some member of the press had had the gall to ask the First Lady how often she slept with her husband. Instead of giving the reporter a hostile glare, he told me she just replied, 'As often as possible.' It was his theory that that's what opened the floodgates. From then on, every person with a sexual thought, particularly a deviant one, couldn't wait to tell all on the talk shows that were only too happy to accommodate 'em. People were so damn busy watching that drivel that they had no more inclination to read. So the papers started playing catch-up, and before you knew it, according to Taft, we were up to our keesters in trash. He really believed it, too." So this was it. The man who fancied himself as the last bastion of decency had fallen.

Weinstein, spotting Kasoff, needled him as he would never dream of doing if they met each other in this very building during business hours. Somehow, night brings a candor not common to the officers of the court in broad daylight. "Say, Bob, how are you going to uphold that opinion when the bootstrapper is no longer around to hold his own?" Kasoff, unfazed, smiled and shook his head.

"How have you been, Bob? I haven't talked to you ever since you denied my client a deal last spring." It was Alicia.

Kasoff drew a blank. "Sorry, I don't remember that."

"Oh, sure you do." Alicia didn't appreciate just how preoccupied he had been. "He was charged with a couple of armed robberies. Cristoff ended up trying it for your office. Got a conviction, too. My client was sentenced to a thirty-year minimum. You refused a plea for eight to ten."

"Sorry, I'm drawing a blank. But, tell me, did he do it?"

"You know I never ask my clients that. The jury sure thought so, though. Took 'em less than an hour to convict."

"Good thing I turned down the deal, then."

"You'll be a hard-ass 'til you die, won't you, Bob?" She softened her opinion with a smile, but she meant it. So did he.

Nearby, another member of the bar was recalling the time she was trying a child custody case. Her client, the mother, was a banker attempting to retain her three children against the efforts of her lawyer-husband who had selected a new trophy. On the stand, the mother was testifying concerning her salary and fringe benefits, in order to drive home the point that she was easily able to support the children. "When Taft heard mention that the bank offered a four-o-one K, he interrupted my direct exam to inquire as to whether she self-contributed to it in addition to the employer's share. She answered that she didn't and did not volunteer that she was intending to next year, after she paid for her kid's braces. Then he asked if her employer matched her contributions over and above its basic share. She answered yes. 'And what's the match?' he asks. 'Twenty-five cents for each dollar,' she says. So Taft explodes, 'You mean to tell me that your employer is offering you a tax-free, risk-free twenty-five percent rate of return on any investment you make and you've not taken advantage of that, and you're a banker no less?' My client was mortified. She barely whispers her admission and he demands that she speak up, so she repeats it. When I finish my direct a few minutes later, he announces to my opponent that he is free to cross-examine if he wishes, but Taft is prepared to find on the basis of what he's heard that my client is unfit because she must suffer from a severe case of instant gratification to turn down such an offer and today's youth need to learn how to delay it. So I try to interrupt to rehabilitate my client, but Taft won't hear of it. She won't be allowed to contradict her own testimony through the suggestions of her lawyer, he rules. Talk about equal justice. So we take him up to the Court of Appeals and we get him reversed. One of only three times that year, I think. Unbelievable."

Now it was Green's turn. "Several years ago, you may remember that Antonelli"—the elected prosecutor—"got a hard-on for going after the topless joints in town. And, you know, getting a TRO in one of these cases is next to impossible on account of the First Amendment." A TRO, or temporary restraining order, can be obtained on short notice from a judge without giving the other side an opportunity to object or even be heard where immediate irreparable harm is likely to result if the relief is not granted, provided the petitioner also shows a good probability of eventual success once the full case is heard in court. The order is typically entered for three days while the adversary is notified of a hearing date that must be scheduled at the earliest possible opportunity for a proceeding known as a request for a preliminary injunction. Once that hearing is concluded, the TRO is either dissolved or extended in the form of an order enjoining the offending activity. Because the First Amendment provides for freedom of expression, prosecutors find that it is extremely difficult prove a legal right to close down a topless bar and therefore next to impossible to establish the requisites for a TRO.

"We had given up on even trying to get 'em in these cases. Even Taft, guardian of virtue that he was, had stopped granting them after the Court of Appeals had spanked him two or three times. But one week, while Taft was on vacation, we had a visiting judge from a small town downstate, where the home folk have no such entertainment, and he's a Bible-toting moralist worse than Taft, so Antonelli decides to strike. He has me file for a TRO to close down the Booby Trap as a public nuisance and tells me to dress it up with allegations of prostitution on the premises, of which we had some anecdotal evidence, but nothing we could prove. The hayseed grants it and returns to someplace south of Peoria three days later. Taft returns. I go to him and let him know we need to schedule a hearing on our request for a preliminary injunction following our TRO petition. He doesn't look at the file but simply assumes the TRO request was denied. So, of course, sleaze slayer that he is, he wants this hearing set as soon as possible in an effort to close down the joint"—a judge has a better chance of being affirmed if he's first given the other side a chance to reply rather than just granting the TRO. "He gives me a date three days hence. That Thursday. Then I happen to mention that the visiting judge had granted the TRO in this case. The Booby Trap had been padlocked for three days. Taft knows that if it stays shut much longer, it'll be out of business. He'll win the war without ever having to suit up his armor. Suddenly, he rechecks his calendar. Thursday is no good, he now realizes. In fact, with his backlog from his vacation, he's stacked up like O'Hare at rush hour for the next four weeks. 'Sorry,' he says with a wink. The joint remains shut down. By the time the hearing date rolls around, the owner is busted, he can't even pay his attorney, and I get my injunction without ever having to argue the First Amendment issue. And Taft practically dances all the way back to his chambers." All heads were shaking, but not in amazement, for the story line was familiar.

"Did you ever hear how his first court clerk got fired?" The speaker was an old-timer, who now kept his small audience of much younger lawyers rapt—as he once did with juries in his prime, before he had to give up the strain of trial work. "Back when dating services first started mass mailings, a male client of mine kept getting their ads. His wife was suspicious. 'I never get any. Why do you keep receiving 'em?' she would nag. She was convinced he must have contacted at least one in order to get on their mailing list. He would just reply, 'How the hell should I know? They mail 'em to everybody.' 'Not me.' And they'd go round and round. Turns out, he did do something to get on the list, but not what she thought." His audience drew nearer now. "A few months earlier, he had been arrested for soliciting a prostitute and the prosecution was out of this court. There were hundreds of 'em, clogging the docket, and many of 'em repeaters. Somehow, Taft's clerk got the idea that these johns ought to think about getting a real date. So she contacts one of these services and they agree to buy from her the case lists of every guy busted in the city. She turned the money over to the county treasurer's office, too. But when Taft found out, he was furious. Packed her things in a box and left it outside the courtroom, where she found it on her way into work. All he ever said to her was that he'd be damned if his staff was going to play pimp to those bums. Funny postscript, too. That was the last year that the Circuit Court staff was nonunion." For the younger generation of lawyers listening, the only puzzle was why hadn't the clerk kept the profits of her entrepreneurship?

Toward evening's end, several barristers found themselves debating Taft's fundamental contradiction. The man committed nearly every deadly sin on the bench to uphold the virtues before whose altar he knelt. He was arrogant. Impatient. Brimming with self-righteousness. These were the words missing from the eulogies of the day that now, as the hour approached midnight, were bandied about. And all in the service of tossing process aside to achieve the desired result.

On his way out, Kasoff again ran into his worthy opponent and, competitor that he was, couldn't resist the last word. "I think we'll win this one on appeal," he told Weinstein. "And then we'll all get to see Donovan in the dock." Posturing by a prosecutor knew no time of day.

"Come on. Get serious. It's too bad Taft won't have a chance to see his winning streak broken. This time he gets reversed. No question. McGinniss's death was just a tragic mistake."

Kasoff, in deference to the informality of the occasion as well as the hour, allowed himself to muse. "One day, believe it or not, I'm going to leave the DA's office. If I end up losing this case, it may be sooner rather than later. And I may decide to practice what your partner does." He was speaking, of course, of medical malpractice cases. "At least when a doctor buries his mistakes, we can hold him liable in a court of law." So much for the tragic mistake. Both men laughed, for different reasons. Kasoff for the way he had made his point; Weinstein, convinced that Kasoff's efforts were pointless.

In the morning, Kasoff returned to the Sisyphean task of catching up with the accumulated telephone messages. Now, he came across one he wished he had returned a week earlier. Keeping victims informed, and in a timely manner, was one of the commandments posted on his wall, for heaven's sakes. "Hi, Mary. I'm sorry I didn't get back to you sooner. You're wondering what's next and how much longer, right?" Kasoff had long since learned that it was a more efficient use of his valuable time to pose the question of the caller than to wait for the other party to grope for the right words.

"Well, I've read the papers, of course, but I know I can count on you for the reliable information."

"The Court of Appeals has decided that we must wait for their ruling on the appeal before we can go forward with the trial. That was expected. If they decide that the conduct does not amount to a crime, there'll be no trial. And we won't get a decision for nearly a year. In the meantime, Donovan is still bound by the conditions of his bail, though he's basically a free man 'til then."

"Do you think you'll win?"

"I don't know. This case will certainly get their attention. To a large extent, it may depend on the three judges we draw at random for the panel. We won't know who they are until a month before oral argument is scheduled, and that won't be 'til next summer. Aside from filing briefs, both sides basically just sit and wait 'til then. I'll let you know if there's anything new, though."

"Well, whatever happens, thanks for all you've done. I'm going to Don's grave site today, so I'm glad you called me back. I—" and here she hesitated—"I talk to him when I'm there. I know that sounds silly."

"No, not at all. I understand."

" I just think that if it helps me, why not? My sister thinks I need to begin thinking about moving on. But I'm not ready to yet. I'm sorry; I don't mean to ramble and take up your time."

"That's OK, Mary. When it comes to something like this, you go with your own feelings, not someone else's." Kasoff had listened to enough victim's families that he knew more than a little about grief counseling.

"Why, thank you. Maybe one day you can join me at the cemetery if you have time."

"I'd be honored."

* * *

Back in Richmondville, Donovan was already well into his off-season practice. His body, at the age of thirty-five, felt as strong as ever, his only concession to age being a longer recuperation period between intense workouts. The headaches had reappeared, but only mildly, like some distant thunder, though they nevertheless concerned the Yankee star. He knew not whether the storm on the horizon would eventually move overhead. What he did know was that the nation's top neurologists were wrong. Far from being a residual of the beaning, these were the wages of responsibility denied. The correlation was unmistakable. Each time the legal system seemed about to impose a sanction on him, he found relief. When his counsel was able to throw a monkey wrench into the prosecutorial juggernaut, the pain renewed itself. But the external attempts of society to impose punishment were no match for the internal angel with which Donovan now wrestled. Until Opening Day last, he had lived a life of virtue. Eventually, he would have to come to terms with his deed, if only for the evil intent behind it. The serpentine legal system had a long way to go. As long as it snaked forward, he would follow his lawyer's advice and remain silent. Only the pain between his temples would whisper of it. One day, like the incessant dripping of a leaky faucet, he would find it more maddening than the white noise of a raging river that is soon spent.

The year went by with its characters changing little beyond the pages of their calendars. Kasoff continued representing the People and collaborating with B.D. Weinstein continued with his practice, and his most renowned client kept on hitting .353 with 34 homers, though the Yankees, who finished second, qualifying for the play-offs as the wild card team, lost in the first round.

Greg continued to shine on the local nightly news. He had won the region's version of broadcast media's Triple Crown. Best single feature story, for his report on supermarket pricing errors. Best feature series, for his three-part look at restaurant workers who don't wash their hands. And, the granddaddy of them all, for doing nothing, "most telegenic."

Mary continued her work at the bank and even managed to squeeze in a few more computer programming courses as Melanie helped her out with the baby. Her late husband's grave remained well tended and equally well traversed.

And then one day in early November—gone were the precious days of late October, as McGinniss had labeled autumn's final brilliant sunny weather—Mary received a phone call from Kasoff. "I have some bad news for you. The Court of Appeals has reversed Judge Taft and ruled that Donovan committed no crime, even taking everything we say as true." Mary, who had never shared the prosecutor's conviction that Donovan would ever be held criminally responsible, thanked him, knowing her sister would now point to this development as the time to close the final chapter on Don McGinniss. The thought made her tremble, but of course Kasoff did not understand this when he heard her begin to sob softly.

"It's not the end of the line, though. I plan to ask the State Supreme Court for leave to appeal. Although they generally hear only about two percent of the applications that come before them, I think we stand a better chance on a case this rare. It will be about ninety days before we know whether they will let us in the courthouse door. I'll keep you posted."

"Thanks," she replied, and hung up the phone. She would visit McGinniss once more before telling Melanie the news.

The law, like baseball, is a zero sum game. Even Solomon, in his wisdom, couldn't find a loophole. For every victor, an opponent is tarred with the brush of defeat. If the People are ensnared in the law's seamless web, their target is freed. Weinstein called Donovan with the good news. "Congratulations. The Court of Appeals has ruled in your favor. They've reversed Judge Taft on the ground that the statute which makes murder a crime did not give you fair warning that your conduct on the field could amount to a crime. Hitting a baseball while playing the game of baseball is still legal, no matter where the ball goes."

Donovan's relief was dispelled by puzzlement. "Does this mean that I got away with it because I thought I could get away with it?"

"Well, I wouldn't put it that way. It's all about due process. Prosecuting you would violate your constitutional right to know in advance what conduct is prohibited. You had no notice that your action could make you criminally responsible and, therefore, you can't be held responsible." Due process. The higher court had struck a blow straight at the heart of Taft's blind spot.

"Is this the end of it?"

"For all intents and purposes, yes. The DA may try appealing to the Supreme Court, but I don't think they have a prayer. I'll know within thirty days what they're doing, and within a couple of months after that, assuming they do appeal, I should know whether or not the court has agreed to take the case. But for them, it's the bottom of the ninth, and they're ten runs down. I wouldn't worry about it."

Donovan was looking forward to a sound sleep that night, but a long-neglected corner of his inner self intervened. In the early-morning hours, he dreamed he was in a long room where baseballs were being hurled at him, eight or ten at a time. His only shield against them was his bat. He was swinging furiously to avoid being pelted. At last he saw a door at the far end. He struggled for every inch of ground, flailing away with his weapon, while ducking and weaving away from the hail of bullets in an effort to escape. Finally, he reached the door, still furiously swinging away at the balls that continued to come his way. Throwing his right shoulder into the door as he continued swinging, he forced it open. Somehow, he knew he needed only to complete that final swing to ward off the last of the baseballs and took the most vicious of cuts yet. And made solid contact. But the object of his rage was, to his horror, not the final ball but the pale, though radiant, face of his mother. And the impact was shattering. Donovan jumped up right out of his dream, crying out to dear God for what he had done until the cold sweat brought him shivering into reality. Now that society's external system of imposing behavioral controls had all but surrendered, Donovan's internal mechanism—conscience—was imposing its own brand of justice. Between his temples, his head was screaming for mercy from the searing pain.

The ensuing days and weeks brought little change. The agony was so debilitating that Donovan was rarely able to com-

339

plete his workouts—in spite of his conviction that the crisis was one he would have to work through on his own. He noticed only a hint of relief when he made his annual perfunctory visit to his parents' graves that Christmas. And then, in late January, when the snows were approaching their peak depth at the Donovan farm, he got word that the ninth inning was history. The Supreme Court, as Weinstein had predicted, had refused to hear the case. And that was it for the legal system.

But as the first drippings from the icicles signaled the waning of winter, the game's greatest star couldn't shake the frigid season's devastation. For days at a time, interrupted by only short breaks, Donovan could only lie down, icing his head in an effort to freeze out the voice within. He began to believe that he would be unable to play his beloved game again. Just the thought of flying, with its attendant air pressure changes, magnified his misery. Desperation followed as the days to report dwindled to a precious few. It was time, he decided, to visit once again the grave site of his parents.

A vicious wind triggered by winter's final blast whipped the fallen snow into ever-changing drifts as Donovan approached the tombstones. He stood before that of his father, the man he had so admired, but now drew no comfort. His head persisted in its torment. Now, slowly, he turned toward the marker for his mother. For the first time in more than two decades, he decided he would speak to her. Aloud. Whatever initial awkwardness he felt melted away as the pain suspended its protest. Regret, once expressed, initiates sorrow's purge. He was now so sorry, he told her, that he had not thought of her more often through these years. He apologized for not visiting more often. And he explained, not to excuse, that he could finally acknowledge that he was angry she had left him, angry even when she had to leave the farm for her treatments. He admitted—his voice was louder now—that he had been hurt beyond words, convinced at an early age that life wasn't fair, that mothers could be taken from their children no matter how deeply they were loved and regardless of how much they were needed. And now he thanked her, too, for the loss had rendered him ruthless in his pursuit of excellence in his field. All in an effort to forget the pain of childhood's most vivid emotional earthquake. No one could approach his work ethic, his toughness, his determination to succeed. Or his contempt for the undeserving pretenders who were permitted to play the game at his level in this era of watered-down talent. Like McGinniss, they may have had the raw tools but had no business being in the game at its highest level until that ability had been refined. But now, he wondered, if only for a moment, what would be the reaction of the woman who had given him life had she known what he did to the adversary whose wildness had kept her son from getting into his first Series nearly 18 months ago? Now, his head began to clear at last. He knew what his mother would say. And, finally, he made up his mind that he would watch the entire film she had left him as her epitaph.

The scenes in the aging movie were otherworldly, but the voice of his mother—the voice he had nearly forgotten—rang familiar. Only this time, he heard the word of a loving woman who longed for part of herself—the best part—to remain with her son into adulthood. This was not the mere disconnected voice of a pedantic who had abandoned her child, as he had quickly concluded when, as an adolescent, he had briefly watched a small portion of this film so many years ago. And, at last, the tears absent at her funeral and in all the days since now flowed freely. He had not only missed her; he had missed out on her message. And a man lay in the ground, his family left to grieve a second winter because of his neglect.

Now, this powerful man, this rock of determination and perseverance, surrendered to the emotion so long suppressed. He fell to his knees, and now a son reprised his father's prostrate grief. The moment was life-transforming. Somehow, Donovan would need to find a way to atone. Resolve fused with conscience as an effective palliative for his pain. He would be able to attend spring training after all, though two stops would be necessary first.

In the McGinniss household, baby Don McGinniss was beginning to walk. Like his father, Mary would say, he was too good to be true. Occupied with school and work while her sister helped out with child care, Mary was in no hurry to welcome another man into her life, though she conceded to her sister that the right male influence would soon be important for her Donny.

Kasoff continued at the Prosecutor's Office. The ruling

putting an end to his prosecution had been reported on the inside pages of the papers—unlike Taft's decision to bind Donovan over, which had screamed throughout the Windy City's media for nearly a week. A public opinion poll taken in the metro area after the Court of Appeals ruling still showed nearly two-thirds of Chicagoans supportive of the DA's efforts. Reassured by those numbers, Starstruck congratulated Kasoff on a fine effort.

And once a week, Green would pop his head into Kasoff's office to ask if Mr. Baseball Trivia had come up with the third outfielder on the home and garden team. Kasoff would always reply, "I'm working on it," but, in truth, the detritus of the city kept him too busy to. And each time, Green would celebrate with a pumped fist. For Kasoff, it wasn't the gloating that rankled; it was the losing.

One morning, Kasoff greeted Carol on his way in, only to see her burst into tears. Quietly he signaled to Sharon. "What's wrong with her?"

The secretary explained, "Oh, her seventeen-year-old daughter is six months pregnant with twins, and she doesn't know whether to laugh or cry."

Kasoff quickly saw an opening. "Look at the bright side, Carol. You'll soon be the only living proof that a sexy grandmother need not be an oxymoron!" Carol laughed and cried some more, though now the former predominated.

The People's business leaves no time for dwelling on one's defeats, for the next victim always awaits. Coming weeks after the Supreme Court's order denying Kasoff's application for leave to appeal, the telephone call jarred him out of his preparation for an armed robbery trial. "Hello, Mr. Kasoff."

"Yes?"

"This is Chris Donovan."

"So my secretary said. Is this some sort of joke?"

"No, sir, I assure you. I'm Chris Donovan of the Yankees."

Kasoff's bewilderment gave way to guarded blunt inquiry. "What do you want?"

"I'd like to meet with you?"

"Why?"

"There are some things I'd like to get off my chest."

Why not? thought Kasoff. *The case is over. If Donovan wants to talk, let him talk. He'll get no absolution from me, but what's there to lose?* "So do I," he replied.

"Fair enough. Look, I've got to report to camp Friday. Can I fly in Thursday?"

"I can see you at one P.M. Do you want to meet at a restaurant?" Kasoff thought Donovan might be more forthcoming at a neutral forum.

"Sounds fine."

Kasoff gave him a name and the directions. Donovan offered a respectful thanks in return before hanging up.

Kasoff noticed that Donovan's tone had not suggested any of the confidence he surely enjoyed, secure in the knowledge that he could not be tried again under any circumstances even if he spilled the beans—double jeopardy after all. For his part, Kasoff's voice betrayed no hint of having been humbled in spite of the fact he had recently had his head handed to him by the appellate court. Remarkably, these two conversants, adversaries so long, had spoken as equals. And Kasoff shook his head. He had never shared a table with a target before. And he shuddered to think how McGinniss's widow would feel betrayed if she somehow discovered this representative of the People, the good people, dining convivially with the killer of her husband.

*   *   *

The three days until his meeting passed for Kasoff without any of the excited anticipation he had felt when his prosecution of Donovan was fresh. This, after all, could lead nowhere. It wasn't even a postmortem. It might be nothing more than Donovan's attempt to clear his conscience. On this score, Kasoff resolved, he would not give an inch.

Donovan needed only twenty minutes with him. Enough, the ballplayer hoped, to change a lifetime. Their meeting began auspiciously. "Mr. Kasoff, the people who know me best know that I'm blunt and to the point, so let me get right to it." Here was a man who, like Kasoff, treated conversation like a cold pool on a hot day. Just jump right in. "Yes, it's true I wanted to hit a line shot right at McGinniss's head. Did I actually plan on killing him? Sure, that's all I fantasized about all that preceding winter.

Why else would I check his skull films? And when I stepped into the batters' box that day, I was thinking only of hitting the ball hard. Through the middle? Sure. But I don't think I really believed that it would happen."

"For someone who wasn't expecting it, you sure didn't hesitate to celebrate at first base until you realized you may have been caught on camera. This was more than just a case of hitting well as the best revenge."

"I freely admit that success in fulfilling my fantasy didn't exactly horrify me. But who among us hasn't entertained evil thoughts toward someone who has interfered with our dreams? I don't pretend that's an excuse. Which brings me to why I'm here."

"Don't look to me for forgiveness."

"I know that. And I don't. Look, I know I'm going straight to Hell for what I've done. I've already condemned myself and I'm not asking you to commute the sentence. But I'd like to do something—not to redeem myself, because nothing can make up for this—not even to salve my conscience. Just—"

"What then?"

"I want to do something good, something right for its own sake. I don't pretend that it will balance the scales, but if I can leave this world a little better off than it is right now, well, what's wrong with that? Only God knows which trees were nurtured by the wicked. And I know this, too. I'd want it to involve the victim's family. Now you can understand why I approached you. I could hardly just show up on their doorstep."

"I understand."

Kasoff sat speechless a moment. Donovan indeed had made the one argument he couldn't challenge. If this man was prepared to do good for its own sake, who but the vicious could hinder that? But as long as Donovan's conscience was laid bare, Kasoff's next thought was to prick it. "You know, he left a widow who was pregnant."

"I do. Is the baby OK?"

"Yes. She had a son. Named him Don."

Donovan nodded his head slowly. "Junior," he said, making the most likely assumption. It was the cue Kasoff had waited for.

"No, not Donald. Donovan. After you."

"After—" Kasoff's tone hadn't suggested hostility, but Donovan was now sure that this prosecutor's only intent was to attack him. "I can see that this is not productive," replied Donovan, and he began to get up to leave.

Kasoff quickly placed a hand on the ballplayer's taut wrist. "No, wait. I'm serious. Ms. McGinniss—Mary—named him after you on purpose. She thought that one day you would learn of it. She believed it would appeal to your conscience. Go figure."

Now it was Donovan's turn to be dumbstruck. With the lone exception of a single individual, he had never heard of such a response to injustice. The film he had recently seen immediately brought her to mind. And now he had a chance to honor his mother's memory by doing a deed of which she would have been proud. He could return posthumously her gift to him—he resolved here and now that he would devote the remainder of his life to answering hate with love, just as this grieving widow he had never met had managed to do, when it would have been so much easier to summon hatred in return.

"Now I know what I must do. There's a fatherless child out there who's going to need someone to throw a ball to him, someone to describe every detail of his father's playing of a boy's game. Someone who can not only send him to college but will be available for advice along the way. This, Mr. Kasoff, is what I will do. All I ask of you is an introduction. If Ms. McGinniss named her boy after me, she's no doubt awaiting my visit."

And now Kasoff himself had an epiphany as he shook his head in amazement. Perhaps the world was not all black and white, good and evil, cops and robbers. There were shades of gray and all sorts of colors in between. He had been in too much of a hurry, too convinced of his own rightness, to notice. "Sure," he replied. "I'll be happy to make the arrangements." Then Kasoff recognized that there was one more thing he needed to say and that this might be his only opportunity. "Perhaps, and I never thought I would hear myself speaking these words as I came over here, but perhaps redemption is possible after all. Eventually, I mean."

"Perhaps," Donovan repeated.

Now, both men relaxed just a bit. "You know," began the prosecutor, "I have to admit that in spite of my prosecution of you, I

345

felt just a tinge of empathy for you when that TV reporter shoved a camera in your face and baited you that fall after you were beaned." Donovan nodded, his eyes telling Kasoff they shared a healthy disdain for the cesspool of broadcast infotainment. Kasoff went on to tell Donovan of how his friend in the business, Greg, had started out as a rumor-monger in middle school and had expanded his empire of half-truths from there. Donovan didn't make the connection to the man who had interviewed him in Detroit, and Kasoff was not about to volunteer the information now. They actually shared a laugh, though Kasoff evidenced his residual discomfort by quickly averting his eyes when they met Donovan's.

After a brief silence that was just beginning to get awkward, Kasoff decided to be bold. "There's one thing that I've never been able to figure out."

"Shoot."

"We had experts view tapes of McGinniss for days on end. How'd you manage to figure out how he was tipping his pitches? What was the giveaway, and how did you know where that fast-ball would be coming?"

Donovan's reply sounded flippant, but his eyes told Kasoff he was serious. "I didn't. I studied those same tapes. God, how I did. Nothing. I found nothing. No pattern, no tipping. His mechanics were the same every time. Figuring out where his next pitch was going was as unfathomable to me as it was to anybody."

"Do you mean to say you really were up there just guessing? Playing a hunch?"

"Sure. It was a one-in-a-million shot." Pause. And now Donovan added ruefully, "And so, I'm told, was he."

"On and off the field."

Donovan nodded. With this he could now agree.

Within the week, Kasoff had spoken to Mary and filled her in on Donovan's request. Of course she said she wanted to meet him. "No, I appreciate your offer to accompany me, but I think we need to do this alone. I can handle it. And if I can't, my sister will be close enough to catch me."

"I understand. Good luck, and let me know how it turns out."

Mary, naturally, immediately told Melanie, who, cynical and protective as always, assumed what Kasoff had initially. "How perfectly purgatorial of him. I say let the bastard rot."

"I knew you would, but I need to do this, for myself and for Donny, and for Don, too."

"And I knew you would, too, Mary. I knew you would." And Mary knew her sister understood.

Donovan rang the doorbell, his mouth suddenly gone dry, the moisture having seemingly made a strategic retreat to his palms, a reminder of the moments before he played his first major-league game. He began to relax when Mary greeted him in a voice that spoke softly if not, understandably, with pathos. She put him at ease further by her expression of appreciation for the gesture. She motioned him to sit down, and then he began.

"When I was in high school, I once said something cruel to a female classmate. I brought her to tears in front of everyone. Several years later, when I had grown up a bit, I ran into her in a store in our hometown. She had gone away to school but was in for the holidays. When she recognized me, I immediately saw her face harden like a protective shell, and her curt acknowledgment of my hello told me for certain that she hadn't forgotten. Who ever forgets a slight? Routine courtesy carries no memory. Immediately I told her that I owed her an apology. That I knew that several years was far too long to wait for one, and that it must be meaningless at this late date, but I wanted her to know that I had felt bad throughout that time whenever I thought about what I'd done. That I had no right even to ask for her forgiveness, but I wanted her to know that I, too, had suffered for my cruelty. And as I spoke, I could see the expression on her face soften. And when I finished she smiled, told me she accepted my apology, and gave me a hug. She had to wait four years for an apology, and yet she forgave me in an instant.

"But," and now he sighed. "Those were only words. And though I couldn't take them back, at least they weren't sticks and stones. But I didn't learn my lesson. My mother tried to teach me, but I turned away from her. She dedicated her life to turning the other cheek and, above all, to nonviolence. Thanks to her, I knew better. But I ignored what I knew. Worse, I outright rejected it. I chose the path of fighting fire with fire. Retaliation ten times over. But even that's too charitable. Ten times an accidental beaning is still an accident. What I did was deliberate and out of all proportion to what was done to me. So I can only ask you—please, don't forgive me. I'll be better off if you don't. And I know I can't make it up to you, so I won't insult you by asking you to let me. All I ask is that you allow me to do something positive. I'd like to start by setting up a trust for your boy's college expenses. And I intend to establish a foundation that will give grants to elementary schools to teach kids at an early age the techniques of nonviolent dispute resolution. If I can stop one kid from committing one senseless act of violence, I can at least begin to atone for my conduct. And on a more personal level, I know that one day, your son is going to want to learn how to pitch like his father did. And no one knows better the detailed mechanics of his father's deliveries than me. I can teach him things about the game no one else can. That is, of course, if you see fit to permit me."

For a moment, Mary studied the face she had wondered about for so long, the Sphinx in the courtroom, the one that had stared out at her from every newspaper in town for so long, this face that finally gave voice to what lay within. And now it was her turn.

"Mr. Donovan, you are right. There's no way to make up for what has happened." Now, Mary referred to Donovan's motive, Kasoff having long ago filled her in. "You see, Mr. Donovan, you got it backward. The game is bigger than no one.

"And if I only had myself to worry about, I would not have invited you in. For months, I thought only of myself and my own grief. Replaying that awful day. I saw it happen, you know."

Donovan, who had bowed his head when Mary began, now looked up at her, right into her eyes, and her devastation was brought home to him.

"I was seated in the players' wives' section, in a field box six rows up from the dugout. When I saw he was hit, I began running down the aisle toward the field. I was screaming. An usher caught me just before I jumped the railing. I tried to fight him off, but two more men came over and held me down. It wasn't until Don was wheeled into the dugout that I was allowed to see him. By that time, he was gone. I hated those men for holding me back. It was as though I was just some fan who had no business being on the field. Eventually, I realized they were just trying to protect me from seeing the most horrible sight I would ever see, that it was already too late. But I saw enough. And it will haunt me all the days of my life.

"But, you see, I can no longer think only of myself. I have to put my son first. And I am left with a choice for my child. When he asks me about his father, I can dwell on what I will have missed and how unfair it all is. I can raise him to hate you, and he'll learn to lash out at anyone else who hurts him. And he'll go through life bitter and unhappy and an emotional cripple. But I cannot inflict my sorrow on him, or I would be ruining his life just as surely as his father's was ended far too soon. Raising him that way would be as easy as watching the sweep of a second hand. But for his sake, I must spend the time to do what's much more difficult. After all, the more worthwhile something is in life, the longer and harder it is to achieve." McGinniss was speaking to her now, helping her get through this. "I need to teach my son a better way. His progress—like the movement of the hour hand—may not be immediately discernible, but in the long run, he'll go much further in life. He needs to be bigger than you were, frankly, to be as big as you are now for coming here.

"And when he's seven or eight years old, memorizing every baseball record in the books and pretending he's in the World Series in every game he plays with his friends, I'm sure he'll be thrilled at the chance to be tutored by a Hall of Famer."

Donovan, thoroughly humbled, cast his eyes downward. He knew there were no legal barriers into baseball's shrine—in the eyes of the law, after all, he stood exonerated. But he hardly felt worthy of immortal status at this moment.

"As for your scholarship offer, I can't accept it."

"But—"

"I will leave that up to my son when he is ready for college. If I have been able to instill in him the values I hope to, he will embrace your efforts as well as your offer. If I have failed..." Her voice trailed off, as she did not wish to describe the alternative neither chose to contemplate.

"Follow me," she said. "He's sleeping." Donovan trod softly into the small bedroom off the hallway. And he peered over to gaze at the child. "Come closer; it's OK," she whispered. And he did. The baby stirred, but only for a moment. And when Donovan's eyes welled up, Mary pretended not to notice.

Then, they returned to the living room. "Mr. Donovan, I don't believe that there is a gene for anger. It should not be passed from one generation to the next. Rage must not be recycled, for it consumes all it touches." She paused. "As for loneliness, the thought of longing for the one person whose voice I'll never hear, whose eyes I'll never see, that I have trouble with." And now her own eyes welled up. "And I always will. But my son will not see it. He will not see it. Thank you, Mr. Donovan."

The star caught his breath, nodded, and made this pledge. "I'll make sure you always know where you can reach me, in case you ever need anything. Help of any kind, whether it's financial, medical, legal, emotional. I've got lots of connections I can call on. Thanks again for permitting me this opportunity. Good luck to you, and I hope to see you and your boy again."

Their eyes met once more as he turned back to her before leaving, and then he was gone. And Mary collapsed in a chair, her sobs drowning out the sound of the first three rings of the telephone. "Mary, are you all right?" asked Melanie when Mary finally answered.

"Yes," she managed through the tears.

"I'll be right over."

In just a few moments, Melanie was on Mary's doorstep. The tears had stopped, but the emotional storm hadn't passed. "I don't know, Melanie. I just don't know," Mary shook her head.

"What is it?"

"For over a year, I've fantasized about having the chance to confront Donovan. For much of that time, my plan was to stare him down and demand, 'Why, why, why?' until the words made his head explode. But, gradually, I realized that such ruminating was self-defeating. It only made me angry and he just continued living his storybook life. I knew I would have to find a way to overcome my bitter bile, for my sake as well as Donny's.

"And I thought that, today, when I finally met him, talked to him, I would find some form of closure. But now that my anger has receded—it really has and I'm glad of that—the vacuum has been filled by even more grief than I felt before. Oh God, I just want to see him so bad. And it scares me because I don't know what I'm going to do. I'm always going to feel this way. And it just hurts so bad—" Now, Mary began to sob again, this time the deep wailing that chokes one's breath.

Melanie knew she could not be too indulgent at this moment, for there was a crucial reminder to express. "Mary. Listen to me. You're forgetting the most important thing you ever said to Don and the most important thing he ever said to you." Mary looked up, her expression asking her sister to explain. "You once reminded Don that he only lives once. Now you need to let him return that gift to you. But even more important is what he once told you. Remember when he described for you the story of the time he broke his ankle and he was lying in a hospital bed awaiting surgery and he refused all pain medication?"

"Yeah—" Mary's bewilderment was evident.

"Remember what he later told you about that? That he learned two very important lessons from that experience. As he lay there in pain, he thought to himself that all of the good times he had had in the past, all his enjoyment in life, seemed like nothing as the hurt consumed him. More than that, it was as though those good times had never happened at all, because all he could dwell on was the pain of the present. And he decided that if this was true, the opposite must be true as well. That once he was freed from the pain and could go back to enjoying life, it would be like the pain had never existed. And that's why he knew that loving you forever would be worthwhile. Because even if he only spent the last day of his life with you, the joy of that moment would wipe out all of the past, all of the longing for you, all the days of his life that he missed you, just as though it had never happened. And that's the only thing that would matter."

As Melanie spoke, she could see by the look on Mary's face that she had transported herself back to the past, to their honeymoon when McGinniss had told her that story. Even in what he referred to as the wilderness years, he had never been able to surrender that last shred of hope that he would one day see her again. He had given her one of his big bear hugs when he had finished and then looked at her with tears of joy running down his cheeks, explaining that he would forever be the happiest man on earth and that each time he hugged her, he would squeeze as much of his joy into her as he could.

"Now, Mary, time will eventually heal your pain. You will enjoy your life again. And when you are able to, this will be but an awful memory. It will always matter a great deal to you, but it will lose its ability to wrack you with pain, to stop you from experiencing joy. Your child will help you. Your new career will help you. And maybe one day, you'll fall in love again, and that will help you most of all."

"God, I hope you're right."

"I'm always right." The big sister smiled. But now Melanie realized that she had been wrong to push her sister to move on. It was her turn to atone. "In the meantime, you deal with your grief in whatever way is best for you. If that means reminiscing about the good times, or railing against the unfairness of it all, or having a shoulder to cry on, or just having a companion along when you visit the cemetery, I'll help you through it. But, on the other hand, if you don't see me as part of the picture in the grieving process, then leave me out of it. I'll understand."

"You mean you're going to let your kid sister sink or swim on her own?" Mary smiled.

"You'll float just fine. You're more than capable of keeping your own counsel and managing your own life. I can see that now. So when does Donny—Donovan—wake up from his nap?"

"I'll check up on him in a few minutes. Thanks so much, Sis."

*   *   *

That night, Kasoff came home to a package delivery awaiting. Opening it, he discovered a marvelous painting of a lakeshore at sunrise. The scene looked familiar. This time, he took a good long look at the forested area just beyond the shore. And in the background, upon closer inspection, there it was. A tree stump. With antlers drawn in. There was no need to check the signature, but the note from Lisa and Richard was the topper, explaining that they had finally spotted their quarry and inviting Kasoff for a return visit. Enjoying their sense of humor, expressed in art no less, Kasoff now reconsidered. Perhaps he just might call on them again his next trip east.

Time to check the messages. "Hey, Castoff!" It was Greg. "I made network! I start next month. Moving to LA as correspon-

352

dent to the stars. Gimme a call to congratulate me. Take care."
So what else was new in TV land?

Now, where to hang the artwork? As he looked around, the
obvious choice presented itself. Right there, above the—wait,
that's it! He grabbed the phone and had to dial twice to get the
number right. "Goddammit, Green, it's the Mick! I should've
known, with both of you being from Oklahoma."

"Of course it was Mantle. It's about time. What the hell took
you so long?"

"I guess I was too absorbed in all the things that came so
quickly to me."

"Well, don't lose that. You'll need it in the courtroom."

"Sure, but I may be better off leaving it there."

"Well, I've got to go. I need to come up with a team theme that
will stump you once and for all."

"Well, good luck trying." To himself, Kasoff knew there was a
bit of luck involved. After all, it had taken a stump to lead him to
the answer.

Then, the phone rang. As she had promised, Mary called
Kasoff at home to fill him in on the details of Donovan's visit. As
they concluded their conversation, she was puzzled that he
sounded less gratified than unsettled. She was right. It was easy,
after all, to prosecute and lock up criminals when they were so
clearly the bad guys. There were no ambiguities. They were evil
and he fought for good. There was freedom and there was prison.
There was no place in between and no doubt about who belonged
where. But here was Donovan—one of Kasoff's criminals even if
the judges weren't buying it—offering to do good deeds of which
Kasoff never even thought. Without expecting anything in
return. Not immunity, not a lighter sentence, no reward.

And what about himself, battling for the good guys? Had he
never stepped over the line in pursuit of the greater good? As
much as he strained to deny it, he shuddered at the thought of
that Battson hearing nearly two years before, when he had swatted away the unfavorable jurors like flies—but hadn't he concealed something in that testimony? The memory was vague yet
disturbing. And what about the old home movie made by Donovan's mother? Where was the probable cause to invade this most
private familial communication? What would Madison think of

him now? Could one bend the rules and still be on the side of the angels?

There was an immutable order to the universe, yet here came Donovan, hurtling to earth, knocking Kasoff's worldview right off its axis along with his view of himself. Perhaps it was time to take a fresh look, a closer look, at some old truths.

It had gotten late. Kasoff poured himself a second glass of wine as the midnight movie came on. He dozed awhile and then awoke momentarily to the station's sign-off, the beginning strains of "The Star-Spangled Banner." He fell off again, and as he entered the world of dreams, the national anthem ended, and he was sure he heard an umpire holler, "Play Ball!"